GUARDING POPPY

MEN OF BRAHM HILL, BOOK TWO

CHRISTINE WENRICK

PRINT - ISBN 13: 978-0-9882069-9-1

E-BOOK - ISBN 13: 978-0-9882069-8-4

For information, e-mail Red Tree House Publishing, Seattle, WA at:

christinewenrick@redtreehouse-publishing.com

Cover design by Whitney Maass, Mill Creek, WA

Contact e-mail: Whitneymaass@gmail.com

Editorial by OPA Author Services, Scottsdale, AZ

Contact e-mail: Info@OPAAuthorServices.com

Printed in Unites States of America - Aug of 2014

DEDICATION

For Rachel, Alec's biggest fan,
who championed for a heroine
and a story every bit worthy of
him.
Thank you!

PROLOGUE

Late-September
Brahm Hill, just east of Athabasca River, Alberta Canada

"You shouldn't even be here!" Though the words were spoken under Lucas's breath as harshly as a curse, Alec Lambert understood they were meant purely out of concern for him, so he considered them carefully, just as he considered everything Lucas Rayner said carefully. The man was his most trusted advisor, his number two, and as close to him as any brother would have ever been—if he'd had one. "Reese is obsessed with crossing his family over to the dark side. You are family! So what the hell are you doing out here dangling yourself in front of him like a fucking carrot?"

Alec stared up at the forested mountain they were going to have to climb in the moonlight in order to confront at least a dozen vampire covens now gathering at its crest. The rough terrain would not be easy, but they were prepared for this, especially Alec, who had been anxiously awaiting a second chance to confront the vampire leader he used to call 'Uncle'. "I need to be here," he replied with the vocal resonance of a man who knew he was in charge. "I need to finish this. Reese has caused too much misery to too many."

"Fuck Reese!" Lucas hissed, the hard scowl on his face pulling at the faded scar that ran from his temple through his cheek. "Leave him to me."

"You know I can't do that."

"Are you kidding me? You've an obligation to do *exactly* that!" With a sharp finger, Lucas pointed to the well-trained army of hybrid beings behind them, constructed mostly of Dhampirs (human-vampire hybrids), shifters, and witches. "These men and women who are here, fighting for you now, need a leader. They're counting on you to lead them—which means, you need to be alive to do it! If you go up this mountain, there's a good chance you may not come back down.

That's not serving their interests. It's serving your own need for revenge. It's selfish."

Alec's gaze narrowed on his friend in warning, and his next words were spoken very quietly so as few people as possible around them would hear—which was nearly impossible, since most supernatural hybrids have extra-sensitive hearing. "Careful, brother . . . You know you can speak freely to me and I will always listen. But don't ever accuse me of not considering their interest. I'm here for them. I owe them—more than I'll ever be able to repay."

"Why? Because *Reese's* betrayed them? Reese betrayed all of us. That's not yours to square. He's our past. *You* are The Brethren's future, and every decision you make should reflect to them that you understand that."

There was a long, tense silence between the two men while it seemed not a single sound was being made around them. Alec finally eased the tension when the corner of his lip tugged upward into a half smile and his hand clamped over Lucas's shoulder. "I'll be there to lead them, old friend, because you will have my back . . . just as you always have."

"Of course I do," Lucas agreed, though his expression indicated he had much more to say on the subject.

"Then let's not waste any more time on this bickering. There are more important things for us to use our energies on. Like getting up this mountain."

Without another word, Alec pressed forward, signaling for the group to follow behind him. They moved in silence through the frigid September night and, when they finally broke the ridge to confront the Nightwalkers, Reese Lambert's attention was drawn to his nephew like a magnet. He appeared almost to float over the ground as he parted the group and came towards Alec in the moonlight, weaving a long, ornate silver dagger between his fingers with the fragility and coordination of an object that weighed nothing.

"Still playing with knives, Uncle?" Alec asked him as Lucas stepped in line beside him. Reese's black irises—a tell-tale sign of a new vampire—stared back coldly at his nephew in the surrounding silence. The tensions were so high in that moment, you could hear a pin drop. "I didn't realize Nightwalkers needed weapons these days. Doesn't say much for your fighting skills, now does it?"

Reese suddenly grinned. "Oh, my fighting skills are just fine, nephew. This is a special dagger." He raised the short sword in the moonlight to show it off. The red diamonds elegantly circling its crest sparkled, even in the low light. "Do tell me what you think."

The next few seconds happened all at once.

Reese lunged forward to strike Alec through his heart with the dagger, and at the same moment war broke out on the field Lucas shot a silver-tipped arrow dead center into Reese's chest, just missing his heart by the breadth of the head of a tack. That was unfortunate, because striking a Nightwalker's heart would've stopped the vampire instantly. Instead, Reese was slowed for the blink of an eye, but somehow it was enough time for Lucas to step in front of Alec like a conquering force, blocking Alec's view of the events that followed. Lucas's body was suddenly jerked upward, his feet dangling several inches above the frozen ground while his body seemed to sag forward. "That's it, boy," Reese rasped in a truly dark voice, embedding the blade that, Alec realized, was in Lucas's chest, even deeper. "Just let it come for you . . ."

Reese positioned his fangs over Lucas's throat, one hand holding the weight of his body by the blade struck through him, the other holding him at his shoulder. The Nightwalker stared directly back at Alec as he whispered a single word in Lucas's ear, a word that Alec's human ears couldn't clearly detect with all the chaos of war that had broken out around them. A loud roar then blasted between them. Kane, his Brethren brother, drove Reese violently back from Lucas. That allowed Alec to get his arms around his friend and catch him before he crashed to the ground, the dagger's ornate handle still projecting straight out from his chest.

Alec saw immediately that Lucas was barely breathing and that a disturbingly peaceful expression had settled on his friend's face. He was dying. "No! Stay with me, Lucas," Alec pleaded, an anguished tone in his own voice that he did not recognize. "I can't lead them without you. Do you hear me? I'm supposed to do this *with you.*"

Lucas said nothing in reply, just blinked once.

An almost unbearable grip squeezed Alec's heart as he watched his best friend inhale his last breath. The moment when Lucas slipped away froze Alec's blood in his veins. His former uncle had betrayed him again—this time stealing the one person Alec felt closest to in this world.

He wished he could process all this. He wished he had even a few moments to accept the loss. But the only thought Alec could process was *revenge*. He grabbed a silver-tipped arrow from Lucas's cross bow and rose to his feet, coming around Kane with a blistering curse aimed at Reese just before driving the arrow straight into his uncle's heart, freezing the Nightwalker and sending him crashing back to the ground, stiff as a board.

Alec stood over Reese with more hatred in his heart than he ever remembered feeling for anyone in his life. He pulled a new blade from his fighting belt, fully understanding the consequences of what he was about to do. He would finish this war with his former uncle once and for all, and he wouldn't be sorry for it. He wouldn't regret this. This would *not* be a moment that would haunt him in his dreams from that day forward. That moment of regret would be about Lucas, and living with the knowledge that his best friend had died while forced to protect him—because he wouldn't listen.

CHAPTER ONE

Two Months Later
Somewhere along the granite moorlands of Cornwall, United Kingdom

Poppy Honeywell's entire body stiffened at the sound of the other woman's high-pitched screams attacking her ears. On pure effort and determination alone, she broke free of the two male Dhampir's currently restraining her and sped across the uneven terrain towards the suffering woman who was being pinned flat on her back by supernatural forces. The poor woman was writhing madly to free herself, but her effort was futile.

That did not matter to Poppy. She was confident she would be able to save this woman if she could just reach her. But within seconds of that very thought, Poppy felt her feet pulled out from under her and she went crashing to the ground. Her face slammed against rock and dirt, sending shooting waves of pain through her cheek, while at the same moment her breath seized in her lungs. There was no time even to respond before one of the male Dhampirs she had escaped from pinned her down tight with all his tremendous weight and strength. "You can't stop this!" he shouted, then reached for her left arm at her side.

"Get off me!" Poppy yelled as she fought back, realizing she had only a precious few seconds to escape his clutches before she would have to contend with both male Dhampirs holding her down.

"No! You watch this," he said, trying to force her head up.

Poppy refused to yield. She couldn't allow herself to yield. There was too much at stake! "Let her go! She's done nothing to you. Nothing!" It felt as if the entire meaning of her existence was coming down to this one moment. All those times in her life when she hadn't been strong enough, hadn't been fast enough, meant nothing because, right then, she had to be *both*. "Stop!"

Her attacker responded by snapping her arm back until she felt the bone break clean. She sucked in a harsh breath and swallowed it, her head coming up in natural response. That fraction of a second allowed her attacker to grab her underneath her chin and force her head up to look at the awful sight in front of her. "Watch!" he ordered. "Look at what you've caused."

The woman fighting for her life was mostly blocked from Poppy's view now that her assailant had approached her with full malice. Her screams were even louder. *Oh, God*, Poppy couldn't bear the thought that she was responsible for this moment. She would give anything to change it—anything! Even her own life! The woman's tortured scream rent the air again and the sound was the most agonizing Poppy had ever heard in her life. She had to find a way to stop this. She had to do something!

The Dhampir on top of her must have sensed she was about to try something. He snapped her arm back a second time, breaking it equally as hard below her elbow. Somehow Poppy managed to swallow the sudden, white-hot pain that raced up her entire arm and to use her good arm as leverage to roll over her attacker. Once she was on top of him, she punched her arm back into his ribs, hearing them crack under his grunted breath. She leapt to her feet and was soon within a few yards of reaching the tortured woman. But just before she could reach her, the second male Dhampir tackled her to the ground, twisting the same broken arm behind her back. "Hold her down!" the other Dhampir yelled and then was right there restraining her, as well. She couldn't move an inch, and her breath was frozen as she tried to suck in the tremendous pain lacing through her entire body.

"Please don't!" she yelled. "Please don't hurt her! I'll do whatever you want! But don't hurt her!" Poppy's pleading would do nothing to change what would happen next. As she kicked and squirmed and fought to free herself, her head was once again forced up so that she would have to face what she didn't have the power to stop.

All Poppy could feel in that moment was a lifetime of regret. How she was failing this woman who had needed her to be stronger than she had ever been before. How she should have sensed the dark forces against them were gathering too close. How she should have sought help from the one man who had the power and forces at his disposal to help them— Sovereign Elder of The Brethren, Joseph Davin. The highest leader within the very secret society would have found a way to keep them safe, even if it was just for one day. *One day.* What would it feel like to open your eyes and not fear your own death that day?

Poppy wished she knew.

***

One Month Later
The Oracle, North American Headquarters for The Brethren, Alberta Canada

Alec Lambert was deep in thought. He needed to speak with the Sovereign Elder, Joseph Davin, on a matter of critical importance when he heard someone say, "Elder Lambert . . .?" At mention of his titled name, Alec drew his fingers back from his temple and lifted his gaze to a conference table full of expectant faces. "Wouldn't you agree . . .?" Gideon Janes asked him in his very mannered English accent.

Noticing Gideon's tone and firmly arched brow, Alec suspected he should be agreeing to something. He just had no idea what that was because he hadn't been paying attention for the better part of an hour. His head had been pounding at him all morning, making it difficult, at best, to focus on much more than what was absolutely at the top of the lists, which currently was speaking to Joseph. "I think . . .," Alec replied, choosing his words carefully so as not to betray the fact he didn't know the subject he was talking about, "I shall need more time to give it proper consideration."

The perfect response. Calm, authoritative, appearing as if he were giving thorough consideration to all the details before making a decision.

"You need a more time," Gideon repeated slowly, ". . . to decide whether or not to send Sienna and her team to the Lycan Dead Zone to trap a Lycan?"

Alec blinked towards Gideon. "*Good God*, no! Why would I agree to that?"

Obviously, he should have thought about that response before he just blurted it out.

Gideon cleared his throat uncomfortably and continued, hesitantly, "Well . . . as Sienna was presenting . . . for the express purpose of luring our Lycan killer out into the open?"

"You mean the Wraith?" Alec continued to ask, displaying an inappropriate amount of surprise. The Wraith had been a major thorn in Alec's side for the past couple of months, one he'd be more than happy to remedy. The mysterious, supernatural creature had eluded identity and description because it was just too damn fast for anyone to see. And it was killing off Lycans with the ease of someone killing a butterfly. That was definitely a problem, one he needed to fix, but not by doing something stupid. "That's a terrible idea," he replied bluntly, "and just when-?"

"Why's that a terrible idea?" Sienna Scott challenged him, abruptly, from the opposite end of the table. The current, cold glare the icy blond was lasering him in half with was enough to have Alec bracing his legs under the table in minimal protection of his manly parts. He might be an Elder, but he wasn't stupid. With one sentence he had just managed to piss off the one woman *smart* men did not find themselves pissing off. Sienna had all the assets to make just about any man's blood boil, but on the surface she screamed don't mess with her unless you wanted your balls served up on a platter. She was smart and she was tough, a Dhampir with nothing but attitude.

Sienna lived for the danger and made most men feel inferior in the process. "I believe I just presented *in detail* why this plan is the right course of action—one with results I would think you would readily support. So why is it a terrible idea?"

You weren't supposed to openly challenge an Elder in the manner Sienna was currently displaying, but Alec didn't mind being challenged. He loved a strong woman. He lived with many strong women as leader of The Brethren. If his position was right, he should be able to defend it with logic. That's how his father had raised him. "Don't you think we can handle it?" she continued to press him.

"No," he answered simply. "I think you're in over your head."

Sienna inhaled his answer with a sharp intake of breath similar to absorbing a hard blow. Alec knew the more-than-capable-Dhampir thought he was commenting on the limits of her abilities. He wasn't. Alec wasn't even sure he, with his rather impressive physical strength and thorough training, wanted to engage Sienna in a hand-to-hand fight. He might find himself in the wrong position, horizontal and on the ground. *How in the world had they gotten onto the topic of trapping a Lycan in the first place? They had been harmlessly talking about search zones to the north—last he remembered.*

"I say that not as a reflection of you or your team's abilities. Elder Hawkings would not have sent you here from Munich to assist us unless he believed you capable. But inside the Lycan Dead Zone the advantage is entirely with the Lycans'. Choosing that location to attack is too risky—has too many variables."

"May I remind you, Elder Lambert, that Elder Hawkings sent me, specifically—not for my Dhampir strength—but because of the success I've had infiltrating Lycan Dead Zones with my cloaking gifts. I assure you, they will not see or sense me coming."

"Perhaps not. But they will sense your team coming from miles away. You cannot trap a Lycan on your own, Sienna.

And while you wait for your support to arrive, the Lycans will hunt them with a pack mentality, focusing on the weakest member of your team until they are all destroyed. So . . . no, I'll not give you authorization for a suicide mission."

Her gaze narrowed shrewdly. She wasn't budging an inch, and he hadn't really expected her to—and that, strangely enough, turned him on. "I don't believe, Elder Lambert, you're giving my team enough credit. This is a solid plan. Perhaps we should take a break and return with clearer heads so I may better explain my position."

Oh, yeah, she was definitely pissed.

Why on earth had he not made a move to bed this woman already?

Alec pushed back from the table and rose to his feet. "I'm afraid that further discussion on this matter will have to wait 'til I return from London," he replied. "I'm expected there by nightfall." Without any further delay, Alec left through the private door that went straight into his office. There he would be able to get some space to deal with the pounding pressure in his head in private. For most people, having a headache was rarely seen as anything more than an annoyance, but for Alec it was a problem. Such a common condition was a reminder that he was human. And being human while leading an army of human-hybrid beings—*super beings* that pretty much had the capacity to kick his ass on a daily basis—was hard enough on a good day. Never mind days when he had annoying headaches.

"Elder Lambert, sir?"

Alec dropped his computer tablet on his desk before turning back to face Gideon, who had followed him into his office. "Good grief, Gideon. I've asked you repeatedly to stop calling me sir. I've known you my entire life. In here, call me Alec."

"Yes, sir," he replied, and Alec rolled his eyes, which only made his headache worse. "Are you quite all right today?"

"I'm fine."

"I'm relieved to hear that. You didn't appear to be entirely engaged in that meeting just now," Gideon noted in that quiet, scholarly way he had about him. "I'm also relieved to hear that you don't approve of sending Sienna's team in to try and trap a Lycan inside the Dead Zone."

"Hmm, yes," Alec replied a little absently as he thumbed through different screens on his tablet. "I don't care how good she or her plan is. Trapping a Lycan inside the Dead Zone is too dangerous without sending a Natural Shifter in with her. That's the only way they'll even get close."

"I suppose we could let her borrow a Natural Shifter?" Gideon suggested. "We do happen to have a very good one."

Alec snorted but didn't lift his head from his tablet. "Yeah, and speaking of '*pains in my ass,*' is Kane back from his . . . God, I can barely say the word . . . *honeymoon* and *Kane* should not be uttered in the same sentence. It's like an affront to all the other . . ." Alec seemed to pause in his thoughts as if searching for the right word.

". . . Promiscuous men?" Gideon offered.

"Even lumping Kane into that category is an affront to the rest of our gender."

Gideon lips curled into a smile. "Apparently, he's due back any day now."

"I'll believe that when I see it," Alec murmured. "He's avoiding me. I can feel it. And that means—as usual—he's up to something. Has anyone even seen this new wife of his since he brought her back? I'm starting to wonder if she's a blow-up doll. That's more his speed."

Gideon chuckled softly. "I assure you, I've personally seen Miss Matthews, and she's quite real and quite lovely. Well suited for him, actually."

Alec absently reached his hand to his temple and the headache that refused to relent.

"Are you quite sure you're up for this trip?" Gideon asked him. "Late December is not an ideal time to be dashing over the Atlantic and back. I'm surprised Joseph would ask it of you the day after Christmas."

"It must be important, then," Alec replied evenly as Sampson, his chief guard in charge of his security, entered his office.

"Sir," Sampson seemed to begin a bit uncomfortably, ". . . Miss Scott is here to see you. She claims you were scheduled to meet with her before you left for the jet. I don't seem to have that on my schedule. Shall I send her in?" But Sienna was already pushing in behind him in her no-nonsense way and with a 'you'd better go along with this' gleam to her eye.

"Oh, yes," Alec drawled with a smile back toward the woman, "our meeting. Of course, how could I forget?" Then nodding over to Sampson, "It's OK, Sampson."

Gideon cleared his throat. "I will see you when you return from London, sir. Give my regards to our Sovereign Elder." The Englishman winked at him just before leaving his office.

Alec glared at the door long after he'd left. This 'sir' crap was really getting out of hand.

"You're stalling me on the Lycan, aren't you?" Sienna blurted, cutting off his thoughts. "You know this is a good plan. Why are you being so stubborn?"

Actually, he didn't know a damn thing about the plan. It had already been established that he hadn't been paying attention. But Alec lifted a brow at her with all the arrogance he been raised to display, then let her mull that simple gesture over a bit as he turned his attention to the tablet computer in his hand and scrolled through some more items. After he felt enough time had passed to get her to sufficiently rethink her position, he turned and leaned back against the bowed front of his desk and crossed his arms over his chest. "Now, what would I have to gain by stalling you?"

"I don't know!" she expressed with flailing hands. "I would guess you're underestimating me—just like most men do."

Underestimating her? Not likely. "You're taking this too personally. I've already said my decision has nothing to do with your abilities as a Dhampir—or as a woman. You and I both know you can best many of my men in a fight."

She snorted. "I can best all of them and *you* in a fight, and that's without even using my cloaking abilities." Sienna then erased the distance between them in a blink as she braced her hands on each of Alec's hips. "Let me do this," she said with a sudden softness to her voice that caught him off guard.

Damn Dhampirs. They moved too fast!

Sienna was playing him, of course, and doing a fine job. It was a wonder that he hadn't slept with her already. She was completely his type. Confident, feisty, with a side of sass. But there was something about sleeping with Sienna Scott that just wasn't right—like he'd be sleeping with his sister or something. It was strange. Any red-blooded man would have to be crazy not to make a move on her, yet he hadn't.

"I've heard rumors about you," she began coyly, her hands moving to rest on his shoulders as she stepped forward and up on her toes to bring her face within a breath of his lips. "Certain things you like . . ."

Alec simply smiled at her, refusing to move, knowing this was all an act on her part and curious to see how far she was going to take it to get what she wanted. "I hope they're the good ones," he replied, dropping his arms to his sides, which allowed her to lean forward and rest her slight weight more evenly over his chest. She felt good. She smelled good. Maybe he just needed to sleep with her to get over this thing he had about not being interested in sleeping with her.

Sienna then proceeded to unhook several of the top buttons on his pricy, white-collared shirt and pushed the edges toward his shoulders. Running a small finger over the line of his collarbone, she smiled, a glint of satisfaction showing in her eyes at seeing the scarred proof that the rumors were true. Fucking him was not what Sienna Scott had in mind just then—and quite frankly, neither did he. "So, then the rumors are true."

Alec's breath was detectably slower as he answered. "It's true." And *oh*, how he wanted this right now. He decided it would be the perfect remedy for his headache. Sienna's eyes turned a sultrier shade of brown as she leaned her head deliberately onto his shoulder. Just the thought of what she was about to do—the pain that was about to follow—had his blood racing with excitement in his veins. He braced his hands on her hips. "Just to be fair," he murmured quietly at her ear. "The answer will still be no on the Lycan."

She laughed against the pounding artery in his throat. "We'll see," she said as she ran her fingers through his short, spiky blond hair and yanked his head back. Opening her mouth wide, she sank her Dhampir fangs into his throat like a hard staple punch. The instant jolt of pain had his body snapping to attention against hers as he stared up at the ceiling, groaning at the sizzling, sharp pleasure of her bite. The feel of his blood going from normal to pulsing inferno in seconds was so intoxicating, so seductive. Right now he didn't have to be making decisions or issuing orders. He could simply submit to the pleasure being offered by a beautiful woman. His enjoyment of it outweighed just about everything else—almost everything else. He wasn't twisted enough yet that he preferred it over a good fuck. But it was surprisingly close.

"Damn, Sienna . . .," he breathed, his vision blurring slightly as he started to feel a little dizzy. She wasn't gentle, taking his blood almost too fast, but it only made him want more. His fingers dug deeper into her skin as he dragged her higher on his hips until they were locked against each other. He couldn't afford for it to be known that Alec Lambert could be softened by a little supernatural kink. But, man, Sienna Scott sucked him perfectly.

"Slow down," he murmured. "I want to enjoy this while I can. After all, I still have a plane to catch."

CHAPTER TWO

"Sir, Alec Lambert is here to see you."

Sovereign Elder Joseph Davin smiled as he glanced up from his desk "Yes, send him in, send him in." Alec entered Joseph's private study, which was full of seasonal warmth. There was a glow from the fire, some orchestral holiday music playing in the background, and sparkling lights from the fully decorated Christmas tree. No presents were under the tree now, but Alec imagined just the night before there would have been quite a few for Joseph and his large family. "Alec! So good to see you," Joseph greeted as he rose from his chair. "I appreciate you making the long trip on such short notice. Forgive me for asking it of you just after the holiday. It certainly is poor form on my part."

Alec nodded politely at The Elder. He didn't really mind making the trip to The Hallow site in London. He like the vibrant city very much, and it wasn't like Alec had a big Christmas planned with any family. His father had been lost in his youth, his mother not long after, and the closest person he had to family, his Uncle Reese . . . well, he was just gone. "I know you wouldn't have asked unless it was important."

"It is. Come . . . have a seat," Joseph replied, motioning toward the lounge chairs in front of the fire while he went to the elegantly displayed liquor cabinet. "Would you care for some fine English brandy, along with my apologies for the miserably cold English weather? I swear sometimes it makes us frightful hosts."

Alec laughed quietly. "It's not any warmer in Alberta right now. And yes, brandy would be nice." Alec had to think back for a moment about whether he'd ever even tried brandy. The slow-burning spirit was the preferred drink of many of the

Elders, but Alec, being much younger than most of them, was much more an ice-cold beer-with-lime sort of guy. Still, he accepted the large snifter and sipped at it slowly as Joseph sat across from him.

"How are thing progressing with your Wraith problem there in the Territories?"

Alec savored the brandy's warmth as it burned its way down his throat. The combination of the warm drink, the heat of the fire, and the company of a man he greatly respected relaxed him. "We haven't been able to track him for weeks. I'm sure you're already aware Nathanial sent Sienna Scott and her team to assist us."

"I am. Nathanial felt her cloaking abilities would be of good use for infiltrating the Dead Zone."

Alec nodded, feeling a twinge of guilt about kyboshing her plan so quickly—a plan he hadn't really even heard. "We're currently reviewing a few possible tactical strategies on how to proceed. I'm not entirely comfortable sending her team in there, even with her cloaking abilities. Cloaking only protects her, not the rest of the team."

"Yes, you're right to be concerned. But an Unidentified capable of killing a Lycan with such ease is very worrisome. We need to determine whether or not we're dealing with a new supernatural being here."

"Agreed," Alec replied, and then he took another sip of his brandy. As he did, he noticed Joseph's gaze fixed on the collar of his shirt. Concerned with what the Sovereign Elder might have noticed, he instinctively reached for his collar to close over the bite mark left by Sienna, and quickly realized it was already closed.

"You know, that's dangerous."

There must have been blood drops that had stained through from the inside of Alec's shirt. Normally he was very careful about that sort of thing, but he had been in such a rush to leave The Oracle after letting Sienna drink from him longer than he had planned. "I'm careful, Joseph. I get my shots to counter the

Dhampir's bite. Would you like me to clean up before we continue?"

Joseph shook his head with a smile. "Don't be ridiculous. I'm not so old that I don't remember the appeal of an occasional Dhampir bite. My concern is for you. You seem to be taking a lot of risks since ascending to Elder—like putting yourself on the front line against Reese at Brahm Hill. Lucas Rayner was right to challenge you on your judgment that night."

Alec's gaze flashed up at The Elder with surprise. He had debriefed Joseph about the generals of what happened at Brahm Hill, but Alec had said nothing of his disagreement with Lucas. "I read Gideon's report," Joseph offered, by way of explanation. "The man really is quite thorough in his reports."

Yes, and Alec decided that was something he was going to have to talk to Gideon about . . . except, of course, when he was reporting to *him*.

"I understand that you were raised at The Oracle and trained as a Guardian," Joseph continued. "Protecting someone in your charge is how you've been programmed to think. But you need to start realizing that your responsibilities now extend beyond a single life you're entrusted with."

Alec laughed ruefully. "Funny, Lucas said almost the same thing to me just before Reese killed him."

Joseph was quiet for a long while, an unnatural pause in their conversation. "I do have someone here you could speak with in confidence, if you would like."

"That's not necessary, Joseph. I'm fine," Alec replied evenly. "Death is a part of what we do."

"Yes, I'm afraid it is." Alec was relieved The Elder was not going to press the subject of his speaking with a shrink. He himself had a lot of power as an Elder, but as Sovereign Elder, Joseph had more. If he wanted to force Alec to talk to someone about Brahm Hill, it was within his power to do so.

"Yes, well, I'm sure you didn't bring me across the Atlantic to ask for a status report or to suggest I speak with someone. Joseph, why am I here?"

Joseph stared at the brandy he swirled in his snifter, and even though Alec knew Joseph would eventually tell him what was on his mind, he seemed to be taking his time about it, which was unlike him. "I have a package, of sorts, that I need you to take back with you to Alberta. A rather important package."

Alec raised a brow at that. "OK, you have me curious. I assume we're not talking a Christmas present. You could have just shipped that express."

Joseph smiled thoughtfully. "No, not a present . . . but I'm sure Elizabeth has one of those for you, as well. I've been hiding a woman here at The Hallow for the past few weeks. Someone very important to me—a Dhampir."

Alec stared at Joseph with genuine surprise. "Why would you have to hide a Dhampir? We built these sites to give a home to Dhampirs. You're not about to confess you're a bigamist with a second family, are you?"

"No, nothing like that," Joseph replied, his smile fading, "though there was a time, before she was born, when I believed Poppy could be my daughter." Alec fully blinked back. He had been joking, of course, because in all the years he'd known Joseph there had never been any question he was fully committed to his family. "I was with Poppy's mother, Mary, just before I met my Elizabeth," Joseph continued. "Mary was one of the most amazingly beautiful Dhampirs I had ever seen. And her heart was equally as beautiful. After Poppy was born, I learned the identity of her true father, a man named Charles Honeywell III."

"As in the giant financing family Honeywells?"

"One and the same. And instead of training to take over the family empire as his father wished, Charles became engrossed with learning about his mother's rather secret practice of witchcraft."

"Witchcraft? Not surprising," Alec replied. "It's a powerfully seductive gift."

"Agreed," Joseph replied. "Charles was a good man, though, and he loved Mary the way she deserved to be loved. But his drive to master the craft—to become as powerful as he could, as fast as he could—had him connected to the wrong people, and in the end it cost him his life. He was killed by a vengeful warlock not long after Mary became pregnant with Poppy."

Alec settled back in his seat and inhaled a deeper breath. Just hearing the word 'warlock' had him on high alert. Warlocks were powerful, evil witches who destroyed their own humanity by killing and stealing the power of good witches. Through ritual and incantation, warlocks could absorb most, but not all, of a good witch's essence as they were dying. They had no conscience, no remorse, and with each kill they'd become stronger, making some nearly impossible to destroy.

"The same warlock that killed Charles is now hunting Poppy."

Alec swirled his brandy inside his glass. "Then she's going to need our help."

"Yes, she is . . . though I'm not entirely sure she realizes that," Joseph replied somberly. "I can see that Poppy fully understands the threat this warlock poses to her, but she believes she can handle the situation on her own."

Alec frowned. "If she really believed that, she wouldn't have come to you in the first place. She's having second thoughts—trying to protect those closest to her . . . like you for instance?"

Joseph smiled ruefully, "Absurd, isn't it? I have an entire army of supernatural beings at my disposal, ready to fight at a moment's notice, and she believes she needs to protect me."

"I find when women are protecting those they care about, they often don't make sense," Alec admitted, still swirling his brandy.

Joseph laughed lightly, "I think they would say the same of our gender."

"True," he conceded in return. "But tell me . . . why is this warlock so determined to capture Poppy? He completed his revenge on her father. Is it just about gaining his daughter's power?"

Joseph shook his head in response. "Poppy does not even practice the craft—nor has she trained to strengthen her Dhampir side. It's like she wants to deny the fact that either part of herself exists."

Alec was surprised by this. Never had he met any Dhampirs, male or female, who weren't excited by their strength, speed, and agility—especially the women. In the supernatural world, being a female Dhampir was the great equalizer between the sexes. Most women were eager to learn how to tap into the strength and sensory gifts that were unique to every Dhampir. It made them special, and it was illogical to him that she would see it any other way. "That doesn't make sense. Why would he care about an un-practicing witch who has little power to steal?"

"It makes sense when you stop thinking of the warlock as a 'he'. *He* didn't get revenge on her father—*she* did, because Charles chose to be with Mary over her."

"She?" Alec echoed. "The warlock is a woman? That's rare."

"Irina Danchev. She was a Bulgarian exchange student who studied at Oxford and fell head-over-heels in love with Charles nearly thirty years ago. She was taken in by his world, his education and wealth, and, of course, his love of witchcraft, which she already shared. Irina believed she'd found the perfect partner in Charles. But when Mary entered the picture Irina learned the truth of where Charles's heart truly lay."

"That couldn't have been good."

"No, it wasn't. When Charles left Irina, she called upon the forces of dark witchcraft to exact her revenge on him. The Brethren has been tracking her for a while, and we know she's killed many good witches to gain her power. But in a remarkably short time frame Irina has become the most powerful warlock of her kind, and we have no idea how she managing to do it. She would have to be killing witches at an exponential rate to gain this kind of power."

"What kind of power are we talking about?"

"Extreme mental telepathy. The kind that can cause terrible physical pain in a victim, crush cars, generate force fields, not to mention all the gifts she picked up from others she's killed."

Alec blinked back. "I've never encountered a warlock with that much power. If she poses such a threat, why have The Brethren not gone after her before now?"

"She's been underground for years. We'd lost track of her until recently." Joseph's expression became very still before he took a long sip of brandy and returned his gaze to Alec. "Irina resurfaced about a month ago in Cornwall—the night she killed Mary."

"I'm so sorry, Joseph," Alec offered sincerely.

Joseph nodded as if to indicate a quiet thank you. "Mary fought hard, but Irina's revenge on her that night was exceptionally brutal and cruel. I can't bear to think about how she suffered. I will have to find a way to live with the fact I was not there to help her."

"There are a lot of people who need our help every day," Alec offered by way of consolation, "and a lot of people we save. You can't blame yourself for this."

"I could have done more," Joseph replied, bitter disappointment apparent in his voice. "Irina has been hunting Mary since Charles's death, but she had no idea of Poppy's existence or that she was Charles daughter until the night she killed Mary. Since then, Irina has been relentless in her pursuit of Poppy, but somehow Poppy managed to find her way safely here to me. And I have thanked God every day since that she was not with Mary when Irina found her, or she surely would have been killed, too."

Alec leaned forward, his expression sincere as he rested his elbows on his knees while still holding his snifter. "Tell me how I can help."

Joseph paused, appearing to shake off emotions that perhaps came too close to the surface. "All that matters now is keeping Poppy safe."

"You want me to take her back to The Oracle," Alec said as a statement instead of a question.

Joseph nodded. "She's innocent in all of this."

"Agreed," Alec replied without hesitation.

"I can see the toll Mary's death has taken on Poppy. She has her mother's strength, but she's also not the same young woman I saw twelve months ago. Something has frightened her terribly."

"I imagine having a warlock constantly hunting you could do that."

"I suppose so," The Elder conceded. "There are moments, which she does not think I notice, that she's terribly withdrawn. I wish I knew what she was thinking in those moments. If I did, then maybe I could truly help her."

"She may just need time."

Joseph nodded in agreement. "Irina may not have known about Poppy—but Poppy has known about Irina her entire life. Mary tried to prepare Poppy from a very young age for the danger. Sometimes I wonder if that was a mistake." Joseph stood up and turned to set his empty glass on the bar before going to stand in front of the fire. "Poppy does not let people in. She can be gregarious, even amusing at times, but . . . she doesn't trust anyone."

Alec took a last sip of his own drink and set his glass on the end table beside him. "I think I understand."

"She has been on the run so long . . . I'm hoping The Oracle can offer her some much needed peace—a safe place for her to settle for a little while."

"Of course I'll take her back with me. And you can be assured she will be safe there. But just so we're clear," Alec's voice edged upward into a lighter tone, "are you asking me to use my single-focus *Guardian* skills to protect her—the very same skills you were taking issue with only minutes ago."

Joseph's lips curved into a smile. "Yes, point taken. But what I'm asking you to do doesn't require you to stand in front of an army of supernatural beings like a bulls-eye. There's a big difference, and you know it."

"I suppose I do," he replied easily. "But you know sacred ground won't keep her hidden from Irina forever. It will block her for a while, but eventually, if a warlock is looking for her hard enough, they'll become visible to her."

"Yes," Joseph agreed. "But taking Poppy with you will get her out of the country. Irina will eventually figure out I've moved her, and she'll suspect to one of our sites, but she'll have no idea to which one. That will give me some added time to come up with a more permanent solution to destroying her."

Alec's gaze narrowed. "You need to be careful here, Joseph. Killing a warlock as powerful as Irina is never—"

His next words were cut off by the doors to Joseph's study bursting open just before one very pissed-off woman with hair the color of summer cherries charged inside the room, a surprising amount of thump in her step. "You're sending me away?!" she charged at Joseph. But before Joseph could even answer the question, the ruffled redhead caught the tip of her very pointed high-heeled shoe on the edge of the area rug between the two sofas and proceeded to flail forward through the air with her arms straight out in front of her—right into Alec's chest.

With no warning, her full weight plowed directly into Alec with all the docility of a tank. The woman might not be large but she definitely had strength. She nearly blew the breath right out of his lungs when her hands slammed against his chest, pinning him square against the back of the sofa. The sofa itself wobbled from the force, and the brandy snifter he'd set on the end table beside the sofa crashed to the floor. Alec's hands grabbed her arms to steady her, but also to steady them both from tumbling, with the sofa, back to the floor.

Alec was just trying to catch up to the moment when the thought struck him that there were very few things he knew one hundred percent for sure about women, but one thing he did know—*female Dhampir's were not clumsy!* They were born, in–part, from vampires. Vampires were fast and graceful, practically floating around a room on their light feet without making a sound. It was all so effortless.

It wasn't *this*.

Both of them were breathing surprisingly hard when Alec noticed how huge her eyes appeared on her face. They were almost a burnished gold color and disproportionately large compared to her delicate cheekbones and chin. They locked on him and seemed to pop from her face. Dhampirs were also uncommonly beautiful, and as Alec continued to stare at those eyes surrounded by all those long waves of cherry hair, he decided this Dhampir had no issues with the beauty part.

She was just a mess in all other categories.

"Poppy Honeywell, I take it," he said tightly. Poppy squirmed around on his lap to try and get herself free. Alec's hands for some reason refused to let go of their hold on her arms, and he was still having trouble inhaling a solid breath. Of course, that could have something to do with the fact she'd *blown* the air right out of him when she crashed-landed into his chest. She appeared confused as a tiny wrinkle formed between her brows, but it was gone just as quickly, replaced with a quirky expression, as though she was expecting some sort of explanation as to why *he* was sprawled beneath *her*.

"Excuse me," she offered casually, as if she had just accidently brushed him while passing him on the street. But this was no innocent brush, *this was more like a full-on mauling!* As she tried to push herself off his chest, her hands slipped and her knee fell forward between his legs, pinching him right in the balls. Alec suddenly let out a very unmanly sound at having his man-parts squashed like a giant grape under her knee. His whole expression grimaced as he sucked in a hard breath and his eyes slammed closed. A second huge groan escaped him and he swore he heard holiday bells go off in his head on cue.

"Oh, for Pete's sake, Poppy!" Joseph exclaimed, clearly as startled by the fast-moving chain of events as he was. "Let me help you."

Joseph Davin's attempt to wedge Poppy off of Alec didn't go much better. After deciding he might still be able to have children someday (definitely not that day, however), Alec took a private moment to gnash his teeth and shove his face into a sofa pillow. He was *damn* sure he would be suffering from a case of blue, red and purple balls the entire jet ride home if he didn't get this woman off of him soon.

When she was finally set back on to her feet, Joseph straightened her up a bit and said, "This is no way to introduce yourself to the man who's going to be protecting you for the next few weeks."

"So it's true then?! You're sending me away." Alec couldn't help but glance up at her after hearing the hurt in her voice, though he was perfectly content to just sit there trying to regain enough timbre so he didn't sound like a woman himself when he spoke. "Did it ever occur to you that I can protect *myself*? I've been doing it for years. I don't need the first Brethren meathead you drag in here to volunteer for the job."

"Meathead," Alec objected.

"Poppy!" Joseph said with a gasp. "Alec Lambert is an Elder, and as such will be treated with the proper respect. Do you understand?"

Poppy turned her head, keeping her gaze averted from him and Joseph, and Alec realized it was because she didn't want anyone to see her face at that moment. He couldn't be sure if it was because she was embarrassed about tripping into him, or angry that Joseph had corrected her so harshly on his behalf. But she surprised him when she replied, "I didn't mean offense to him. I just don't want to leave The Hallow. I like being someplace familiar."

Damn. Hearing the emotion in her voice got to Alec. He hadn't expected that after Joseph had warned him that she didn't let people in. But he reminded himself that he was basically intruding on a very private conversation between her and Joseph, someone she did trust. Alec could only imagine what that emotion was doing to Joseph. That was the problem with women. Men hated to hear vulnerability in a woman's voice when they were trying so hard not to show it. At least he did.

Joseph stepped forward to embrace Poppy. "You're not safe here, little flower." Now Alec really felt like he was intruding on a private conversation. "I must protect you the best way I know how. I promised your mother." He then motioned back to Alec. "I trust Alec. He's a former Guardian—and a very good one. You yourself said that you can feel Irina getting closer. Let Alec take you someplace where he can protect you and you can know what it feels like to be safe. In the meantime, I will find a way to deal with Irina."

Poppy dropped her head quietly, and for a moment it seemed she wasn't going to answer him. "I feel safer here with you than I will with a stranger."

"He's right," Alec finally said as he came slowly to his feet, realizing he needed to do something to gain this woman's trust—though he could hardly blame her for being guarded after spending a lifetime on the run. "I may be a stranger to you, but I *can* protect you. And more importantly, I can give you all the tools at my disposal so you can protect yourself. If you have a sense for recognizing the warlock who's threatening you, your Dhampir instincts are telling you that you're in danger. You need to start trusting those instincts."

Those huge gold eyes of hers locked on him fully with a look of utter determination as she walked right up to him—thankfully, straight this time. He had to admit, he flinched just a bit with the possibility she might trip again. "I don't want any part of witchcraft, Dhampirs or vampires. That's not who I am."

"Yes, it is," he challenged her without hesitation. "That's exactly who you are."

Her eyes narrowed as if she were preparing to blast him with a thousand different reasons why that was not true, but instead she replied, "I will agree to go with you on two conditions." Alec simply crossed his arms in front of his chest. What was it about women and their conditions? Why couldn't they just agree? "One, you'll agree to never disagree with me again." Alec's brows arched high at that rather impossible request. "And two, I will only go with you if it doesn't require us crossing an ocean in an air-"

Poppy's words were cut off by her small squeal when Alec caught sight of Joseph sticking a needle into her arm. Her eyes widened in shock and she tried to turn to Joseph, but her limbs gave out from under her almost immediately. Alec reached out and caught Poppy when she would have otherwise collapsed to the floor. "What in the world did you do that for?"

"No worries," Joseph assured him. "It's just a little something to help her relax for the trip."

Alec blinked at him. "Relax? She doesn't like flying?"

Joseph shook his head. "Terrified of it, actually. Unfortunately, Poppy lacks an appreciation for the severity of her current situation. We need to get her out of London tonight—hence, something to relax her. But once she's someplace safe she'll be no trouble at all."

Alec's gaze narrowed shrewdly. By what he had already witnessed in the few scant minutes he had been in this woman's presence, she was the very definition of the term *high maintenance*.

So he doubted that very much.

CHAPTER THREE

Poppy awakened to a steady, vibrating hum against her cheek, and then several small bumps that had her stomach leaping in response. *Heavens*, but she was groggy. Her Dhampir body felt weighted down by sandbags, and it took far more energy than what should be required just to open her eyes. Lying there for a moment, she tried to remember where she was. Her shoes were missing from her feet, but her toes wiggled under the warmth of the blanket covering her. Then the sound of an engine accelerating and some more shaking attached itself to the hum at her cheek and she knew instantly. *A plane.*

She hated planes!

Her heart flew into an utter panic! She swung up from the soft leather cushion she had been sprawled over, her arm whipping out to connect sharply with—not the tall glass of water that had been placed on the end table beside her, no she couldn't be that fortunate . . . but the whole pitcher of water behind it. The carafe and all its contents were launched into the air with the precision of a ninety-eight mile an hour fastball, crashing into a man seated in a chair perpendicular to her and causing him to grunt loudly in response. "What the . . .?" the man started as water soaked the front of his shirt. He came to his feet with a curse and more muscle than any one man should reasonably have. Then he issued a second curse when he bumped his head against the low ceiling of the plane's cabin.

Poppy knew she should apologize to the man for pelting him with a pitcher that had practically become a deadly weapon, but she was just trying to get a grip on the overwhelming sense of panic coming over her at the thought of being on a plane thousands of feet above the ground—or worse, *the ocean!*

She sat up straight in her seat, staring at the man she had just assaulted with glassware, recognizing him as one of the guards of The Elder who had been visiting Joseph. *Great.* The guard didn't seem too pleased as he scowled down at his soaked shirt clinging to his skin and then pointedly back at her. He was about to say something—and she suspected it wasn't going to be nice—when he was abruptly halted by his Elder's silent command, a simple lift of his hand. "It's all right, Sampson."

Alec Lambert, the Elder Joseph trusted with her life, was sitting across from her inside the luxurious jet interior. He balanced a tablet in his lap as he dropped his left hand and nodded for Sampson to return to his seat. Not surprisingly, the giant wall of muscle known as Sampson picked up his weapon, a dart gun with silver-tipped darts to compliment the sheathed knife and holstered side arm, and moved to a different seat at the other end of the cabin, where three other guards were already sitting.

What? Was he just going to let himself air dry?

"Why am I on a plane?!" she turned and demanded from The Elder just as the plane's cabin bumped around some more. Her heart lurched inside her chest at the unnerving jostle and then began to pound loudly like a drum.

"Are you going to panic on me?" he asked her calmly in return.

Panic—yeah, she kind of felt like panicking. She felt hot, her head ached and they were thousands of feet off the ground in nothing more than a large tube! Of course, the headache could just be from the little relaxer Joseph had shot her with before they left The Hallow. She was going to give him an earful about that one. "If I were, would you land this plane any faster?!"

Alec's brows pulled together, yet it was unclear if he was concerned or confused. He glanced out his window into the night sky. "Tough to do when we're flying over a rather large lake at the moment."

Poppy brought her hands to her temples and started to shake her head back and forth. *"Oh, God, oh, God, oh, God . . ."*

"I've another one of these if it would make you more comfortable," he offered as he held up a small, capped needle. "But I didn't agree with this being used on you the first time, so I would prefer not to use this one." For some reason, Poppy noticed his light brown eyes just then as he focused on her intently. They were sincere, warm, and rich like a deep colored whisky. It was strange how she was able to maintain her focus on them in the middle of all the chaos in her head. "So I'll ask you again . . . Are you going to panic on me?"

"Why. Am. I. On. A. Plane?" she emphasized each word as her hands gripped at the luxurious sofa arm beside her. But the modern jet seemed determined to bounce all of them out of their seats as the cabin continued to jostle about angrily. They were definitely in the middle of some mean turbulence, which was to be expected of anyone fool enough to be flying in a small plane in winter conditions.

"Because it's the most efficient way to get someone across an ocean," Alec answered. "We still have about an hour or so before we land. So you're going to have to let me know if you're going to panic on me."

Her gaze narrowed on him angrily as she pushed her next breath through her nostrils. "Can I just hit you instead and we'll call it even?!"

His brow lifted as if he found that comment interesting.

Poppy leapt to her feet inside the small cabin and she noticed Alec braced his hands against his chair arm as if to steady himself. Surely he didn't think she was really going to hit him? "You're not going to trip again, are you?" he asked her.

Poppy glared at him and then down at herself. She was looking for any reasonable explanation to defend the innate clumsiness he'd gotten to experience firsthand within the first minute of meeting her in Joseph's study. "These are very challenging heels!"

Yep. That was the best she could come up with.

The Elder smiled. *No, it was definitely more of a smirk.* "I'm sure they are," he replied. "Now, will you please sit down before you get bounced off your feet? The turbulence may get worse before it gets better."

"*Worse?*" Poppy squeaked. She might very well end up back in his lap if this turbulence got any worse. She didn't like to think of herself as a coward, but when it came to flying she definitely was, even more so than her irrational fear of spiders. They just had too many legs. "Look—you need to understand. I don't fly! Ever . . .! You need to find a way to land this plane, right now!"

"I can't do that. As I explained, we're over a lake."

"Well get un-over the lake!"

The Elder didn't say anything in response, just seemed to contemplate that. He removed the reading glasses that were a dead giveaway that he was human, though, he looked fit enough to give even one of his Dhampir guards a run for their money. He'd certainly felt fit enough when she had crash-landed into his chest in Joseph's study . . . which had been utterly embarrassing. One moment, she'd been fully prepared to burst in and make her case to Joseph about why she needed to stay at The Hallow, and the next, the tip of her shoe had caught on the carpet and she was flying forward straight into a complete stranger.

There had certainly been no shortage of embarrassingly clumsy moments like this in her life. With her, they just seemed to happen. But this one had been particularly noteworthy because in a single moment she had become painfully aware of every detail of this one man. It was weird.

He'd caught and held her in a firm grip while she had stared down at the poster-child for the American California surfer. His blond hair was purposely styled very short on the sides and layered and messy on the top, kind of like someone had just shook their fingers through it. His skin was just slightly golden, so he was obviously no stranger to the sun, and there was just something about his eyes. . . They weren't a particularly unusual color, being that they were light brown, but there was a warmth and intelligence about them all the same. He was definitely not the 'meathead' she had accused him of being. That would have to be true for him to reach the position of Elder at such a young age. She guessed Alec Lambert was no more than four or five years older than herself, which would put him in his early to mid-thirties, and therein lay the contradiction. Surfers weren't associated with such responsibility at that age, and they didn't wear thousand dollar clothing consisting of tailored slacks, a super-soft looking zip-up knit sweater, and fine leather loafers. If she wasn't still panicked from the turbulence, she would want to be seated next to him while finding a way to just touch his spectacular clothing.

"In an effort to have us all on the ground safely as soon as possible, I do not recommend suddenly veering off course to get '*un-over*' a lake. We will be starting our descent shortly."

"Oh God, descent . . .," she mumbled to herself as she rubbed her hands over her face. "This is not good. This is not good."

"It will be all—"

"Where are we landing . . . Elder Lambert?" she added awkwardly, realizing they had not actually exchanged first names.

He returned his glasses to the bridge of his nose and went back to looking at his tablet. "You may call me Alec. I much prefer it to Elder Lambert. We'll be landing in Alberta at The Oracle, The Brethren site I'm in charge of. After discussing it, Joseph and I felt this would be the best place for you to stay."

"Well, isn't that nice," she answered him flippantly. "You discussed it. By any chance—in any of this heavy dialogue— did anyone consider asking *me* if I wanted to go to Canada?"

Alec just sighed in that *'you're going to cause me a lot of trouble, aren't you'* sort of way and set his tablet down on the seat next to him and removed his glasses. The very deliberately calm response infuriated Poppy, but what she found even more infuriating was the fact a woman would have to be blind not to see how handsome this man was. His easy presence and authority drew you in, and he had the intelligence and arrogance to match his title. But there was also a remoteness about him, as though he was purposely keeping himself at a distance. Not that she wanted him any closer. She just noticed it. "It's not my intention to keep you at The Oracle against your will, if that's what you're asking me?"

"Good to know. Let's turn the plane around, then." The plane dipped sharply in response to her words, and then the engine revved. Poppy grabbed onto anything within her reach, which happened to be the back of a nearby chair. As soon as the plane straightened out again she bolted for a private corner seat, buckled her seatbelt and closed the shade of the window next to her, even though it was pitch black outside and she couldn't really see much anyway. She had to shut away the reminders that she was flying over water with no way to land any time soon.

After a couple minutes of quietly chanting to herself, Poppy sensed someone next to her. She opened her eyes to see Alec standing beside her, handing her a glass of water. When she didn't reach to take it, he set the glass down on the tray beside her and then moved to the seat across from her. "Why did you agree to this?" she finally asked him. "Why would you agree to take me somewhere without my permission?"

Alec pulled a folded piece of paper out of his pocket and lifted it towards her. She stared at it blankly but didn't reach for the paper. "Joseph asked me to give you this," he said gently. Poppy finally took the paper from his hands.

My Dearest Poppy,

I'm sorry I felt it necessary to take matters into my own hands without discussing them with you first, and most especially for not being able to say goodbye. I know how difficult this journey will be for you, and if there were another means at my disposal to get you to The Oracle quickly and safely I would take it.

You will be safe there with Alec. I trust him. And know, nothing means more to me than seeing you finally safe and free. Take comfort in the fact that by the time you read this letter you will be on solid ground again. And remember, my sweet flower, when you find yourself in trouble:

Take three deep breaths.
Each deeper than the last.
Let them remind you that the demons of this world
that haunt you will soon be put to past.

Love always, Joseph

Poppy slumped into the seat and clutched the piece of paper to her chest. She closed her eyes, inhaling a steadying breath and repeated the phrase from the note several times. When she opened her eyes again she was surprised to see Alec now seated in the chair right beside her. "What were you saying just now?" he asked her, the prominent cleft in his chin pulling a bit with his interest.

"Nothing," she replied. "Just something my mother used to say to me."

He sat back in his chair. "Joseph told me about your mother. I'm very sorry."

Poppy inched forward just a bit. She saw something there in his eyes—perhaps recognition, like he truly did understand how it felt for her to lose her mother. But then it was gone just as quickly, replaced by that remoteness he seemed to slip into as easily as many would a smile. "How soon did you say it would be before we land?"

"Less than an hour. Despite the weather, we've made good time."

Poppy closed her eyes and tried to focus on the even rhythm of her breathing while she continued to repeat the phrase in her head. Then she heard Alec say, "I can't do anything about the way this trip was forced on you. Nor can I promise you that The Oracle will feel like home, but I think you will like it there if you give it a chance. And you'll be safe."

No, he couldn't promise her The Oracle would feel like home. Poppy had never known what it felt like to be home. She and her mother were never in one place long enough. But once they had stayed in this quaint little summer house for nearly six months. Everything around them had been peacefully sleepy, and being able to watch the sun set every night over the ocean from the exact same place was one of the safest feelings she had ever known. "No one can know I'm there," she replied to him. "You must keep me separated from the others—separate floor, separate room—whatever it takes. I can get my food at night after the kitchen is closed. That's how I did it at The Hallow."

Alec blinked back at her as if what she was saying were crazy. "Why would I do that?"

"Because I can hurt them. I am cursed."

CHAPTER FOUR

"Excuse me?" Alec asked, positive he hadn't heard this woman right. Clearly, Poppy Honeywell had to be one of the oddest women he had ever met. He could understand her fear of flying. He hadn't been a fan himself of small planes until he was forced to do it regularly as an Elder. But then there was the clumsiness, the refusal to even want to acknowledge her supernatural gifts, and now her newest claim. "You're cursed?"

She nodded at him quickly, looking as confused as he was. "Didn't Joseph tell you?"

"That you're *cursed*? No, he forgot to mention that."

Her gaze roamed the floor of the plane as if she were somehow hoping to find answers there. "Well, he cares for me, so he refuses to believe it. But it's true. Irina cursed me while I was still in my mother's womb."

Alec's gaze narrowed on her questioningly. Joseph had told him that Irina didn't discover that Poppy even existed until a month ago, so how could she curse Poppy when she didn't know about her? He also believed—and he bet he could get Gideon to confirm it about thirty seconds after they landed—in the supernatural world curses on a true innocent—by definition, a life that has not yet had a chance to sin, like a baby—were nearly impossible, even for a powerful warlock.

The real question was, why did Poppy believe this?

"I see," he replied carefully. "So what exactly happens to all of these unfortunate souls who fall victim to this curse?"

Her eyes widened and the gold color sparked with a bit of blue, a sign her Dhampir side was pushing forward. "You're making fun of me? I wouldn't be so glib if I were you considering you're sitting right next to me and my curse could rub off on you."

He smiled at that, pleased to see her focused more on their conversation than the shaky plane. "I hate to break it to you, but curses don't *rub off* on people."

She straightened herself in her seat. "And what would you know of it? You're not a witch."

"Neither are you, apparently."

The plane, unfortunately, didn't cooperate with Alec's diversion tactics, hitting another patch of turbulence just then and banking to the right. Really only long enough to shake the cabin for a couple of seconds, but from the sudden pale cast of Poppy's face it was clear she thought the plane was in a vertical nose-dive. She closed her eyes and started whispering that little poem to herself again, and it was in times like these that Alec really hated the fact he was only human. If he were Dhampir, or even a pain-in-the-ass shifter like Kane, he would be able to hear what she was chanting to herself. For some reason, it just seemed important for him to know.

The captain's voice erupted from the intercom asking everyone to buckle up because they would be starting their decent early to avoid further turbulence. Poppy paled even more at the news. Maybe he was going to have to give her the shot after all, but he really didn't want to. He hadn't liked the reason for the first shot, despite Joseph's good intentions.

Alec knew he needed to try and keep her calm before she ripped apart the arms of her chair. As a Dhampir, whether she acknowledged that side of herself or not, she easily had the strength to do it. "Have you ever considered that maybe you're not cursed?"

She kept her eyes closed and shook her head. "No. I'm cursed."

"So, then, you've hurt people?"

She nodded, which actually surprised him. He wasn't expecting that answer. "It started when I was thirteen and my first boyfriend kissed me. He left the apartment where we were staying on his bicycle and was struck by a car."

Alec was stunned. Not by what she was telling him, but that she could possibly believe such a random incidence was her fault. "Poppy, that was an accident," he replied. "Things like that happen to people all the time. It's unfortunate, but that doesn't mean it has anything to do with you being cursed. Perhaps, instead of separating yourself from everyone, you should try to interact just a bit more. That'll allow you to prove to yourself that you're not cursed."

She blinked back at him. "And what if I hurt someone?"

"I'm sitting next to you right now and nothing's happening to me." The jet picked that moment to begin its decent, and Poppy appeared to take it as a sign that she had already tempted fate too far. She started to breathe faster, despite repeating the little poem to herself. Alec decided he wasn't doing a very good job of calming her down and needed to come up with something fast before she started to hyperventilate. "Poppy, look at me."

She stubbornly kept her eyes closed and shook her head, all that wavy mass of dark cherry hair spilling around her shoulders. He reached his hand out to touch her cheek and turned her head to face him. "Please look at me."

Her hands scrunched into little fists, as if she were debating whether or not she should, but in the end she still refused to open her eyes, so he did the only thing he could think of to do.

He kissed her.

Alec leaned in and sealed his lips over hers, feeling her jerk with a small squeal of surprise as she realized what was happening. And really, why wouldn't she? He hadn't exactly planned this either, but he'd be damned if he would regret it now. The feel of her lips was soft beneath his. Her skin, her hair, everything about her was soft as he strummed his thumb and fingers through the long strands. She wasn't resisting him, but neither was she completely relaxing into his kiss, though it wasn't exactly relaxing him, either. It was charging his blood!

A light, floral fragrance with a hint of peppermint seemed to wrap around him like a comforting blanket. It was at that moment Alec decided this woman's name fit her perfectly—Poppy. Like the sweetest, most perfectly opened flower, yet with enough fire inside her to keep things interesting. He liked it. And, *by damn*, if he was going to do this, then he was going to do this *right*.

Alec curled one hand at the base of her neck, dragging her forward and tilting her head so his lips could move over hers exactly in the way he wanted them to. She responded to it, letting her body mold to his as his other arm snaked around her back to pull her close. He just had to have her closer. Soon, any resistance she might have had initially began to fade as her body pressed against his. She fit nicely against him, and he drank in her kiss with a true hunger for a woman he hadn't felt in a very long time.

He forced her to open her kiss, caressing his tongue with hers, making him feel like a king as he took both hands to her cheeks and held her steady. The blood in his veins continued to pump and burn out of control, like he'd never truly experienced the full pleasure a woman's kiss until that moment, which was ridiculous because he had, *many times*.

Just not like *this*.

When that realization hit him like a bucket of cold water, he pushed back from her, breathing hard as he stared into her gaze, which appeared as alive as he felt at that moment. She looked happy, and he couldn't think of a time when a woman looked any more beautiful. "There," he smiled. "That ought to do it."

The words slipped out before Alec had a chance to think better of how they sounded. *He wanted* to help her relax for landing, but the words came out all wrong, like he was bragging or something. The kiss had been pretty damn fantastic, if he did say so himself, but it was possible the idea had sounded better in his head when he conceived it.

Poppy's smile faded almost immediately as she once again straightened in her seat, covering her hand over her kiss-swollen lips before glancing around her to see where Alec's guards were. His guards would show no signs of noticing anything, even though Alec knew they were aware of every detail happening with him at every moment. It was just something he had gotten used to as part of his protection. But Poppy wasn't used to it, and he could immediately see the regret in her eyes—and he hated it.

How had he managed to screw up a well-intentioned kiss so badly?

CHAPTER FIVE

Poppy had not said a single word to Alec the entire ride back from the jet, choosing instead to stare out the SUV window at the wondrous mountain landscape around them. And while it was true she was just grateful to feel her feet on solid ground again, it was snowy ground. As in a foot of snow! All the reflectivity of the landscape brightened the night sky so she could see the outline of jagged, snowcapped peaks that surrounded the lake in front of them. They appeared so close, she was sure she could reach out and touch them with her fingertips. That was the one positive thing about running your entire life. You got to see many beautiful places along the way—but she wasn't sure if she'd ever seen anything this beautiful. The whole area looked unflawed, almost untouched, as if she had traveled back in time to see nature at its finest hour, before man had invaded.

"Those are part of the Canadian Rockies," Alec pointed out, sitting beside her and obviously noting her admiration for them. "The lake was carved out by glaciers. Pretty incredible, isn't it? I never get tired of looking at them." Poppy just scowled at him and stiffened her shoulders, but she could hear the sincere admiration in his voice for the nature around them, and she had to admit that she liked that about him. He was an Elder with great power, yet he took time to appreciate the things like the natural beauty that surrounded him where he lived. But that still wasn't a good enough reason to look at him. "Not talking to me, huh?"

"Not when you refuse to take my warnings seriously."

"And how am I not taking them seriously?" he asked her.

She stared back at him, amazed that he even had to ask. "You," she then suddenly lowered her voice as quietly as she could, ". . . kissed me! After I told you I was cursed."

"Yeah, I guess that kiss could be a problem if you are, in fact, cursed." Alec had answered in a normal voice, completely unconcerned about the others hearing their conversation, and he didn't stop there. "What do you think, Sampson? Are you worried that I may now be cursed?"

"Terrified, sir," he replied blandly from the front passenger seat, as if he were completely bored. Alec laughed lightly at hearing his guard's obvious lack of concern.

Poppy decided she only had herself to blame for this latest embarrassment. She wasn't sure what had gotten into her, telling Alec about her curse and then letting him kiss her so thoroughly on that plane she was dizzy before they even started to land. You would think a man had never kissed her before, which was ridiculous. *Plenty* of men had kissed her. Hell, she had even done a lot more than that a few times, and all it had gotten her were some harsh words of warning from her mother (the one true confidant she'd had in her life because they moved around so often) about taking too much for granted with regard to Irina's curse.

Of course, Poppy couldn't have remained a virgin forever. It had been bad enough when she waited 'till she was twenty-two. After her mother realized that Poppy had become sexually active, she warned Poppy that her curse could bring death to those who touched her. Poppy argued fiercely with her mother over the subject. She didn't think it was fair she was expected to live the life of a nun because of one curse. But then even more bad things happened to the people around her. So Poppy eventually stopped, with only a slip here or there, and now, six years later, she basically thought she had conquered any desire left inside her—until that kiss.

Alec's kiss was like feeling everything at once. She buzzed, she tingled, and she floated. Then, while a ridiculous avalanche of romantic notions were still floating about her head, he had said those five little words that absolutely snapped her right back into reality. "*That ought to do it.*" Those words evoked an emotional equivalent to a man satisfied at how he had just fixed a faucet in a woman's kitchen sink. They deflated her faster than she could blink—down to the point where she'd lost any tingles he might have awakened inside her.

"Have you even heard of the term *humility*?" she asked him.

His brows lifted at that. "Most women find confidence an attractive quality in a man."

"There's a difference between confidence and arrogance. You are *arrogant!*"

"I didn't hear any complaints while I was kissing you."

Poppy gasped and turned her head away from him for good, staring fiercely out the window. Reasoning with him wasn't working, at least not while they were riding in a car full of guards overhearing their whole conversation. Better to not say anything at all.

"Sampson," Alec sighed once it became apparent she wasn't going to be engaged in any further conversation, "call ahead and have Gideon meet us out front."

"*Out front?*" Poppy questioned loudly as she swung back around to see they were coming towards a huge chalet-style building that sat atop a rolling bluff just above the water's edge. The Oracle was spectacular, especially with the lake and peaks as a backdrop and the colorful holiday lights all along its exterior. You couldn't get much more 'out in the open' with all that light. "Don't you have a back entrance?" she asked. "You must. Joseph has about three of them."

Alec simply leaned toward her in his seat, quickly erasing any distance she had managed to put between them, and Poppy wondered if he was going to try and kiss her again. She responded by pulling her head back, thumping it against the cold glass behind her. It wasn't a hard thump, but it definitely smarted. "I'm not bringing you through a back entrance, Poppy," he said. "I don't believe for one second that you're cursed with anything more than a little clumsiness, and I'm going to prove it to you."

She stared back at him with her mouth agape. "You would risk the safety of your own people just because you think you're right?"

"I am right," he replied with so much arrogance that she just wanted to smack him.

"And what if you're *not* right and I do hurt someone? For all we know, it could be you."

"Fine," he said blandly. "I won't kiss you again."

"What?" she questioned.

"You heard me. I promise you right now in front of my guards—and out of fear for my own wellbeing and safety—that I will never kiss you again. Better?" She was so stunned and embarrassed that he didn't seem to care that his guards were listening that she didn't know what to say. "Well, actually," he continued, pausing for effect, ". . . never is a long time. Better to put a more reasonable timetable on these things. How about thirty days? That certainly sounds reasonable."

"But you just said-"

"Too much?" he interrupted. "Fine, then we'll compromise and call it a week. That really makes the most sense anyway, considering your clumsiness and all. Why, you could trip and fall into my lap again and then I'd have to do something about it."

She scowled at him. "Are you ill in the head?"

"No, I'm fine." The vehicle rolled to a timely stop. "And I'm not wrong."

"You *are* wrong," she informed him, lifting her nose into the air.

He smiled at her. "As an Elder I've learned to trust my instincts, and my instincts are telling me that you've been taught to believe certain things about yourself so you will accept them. Why, I don't know. But I'm going to find out."

"You can't be serious?"

His hand lifted towards The Oracle's front entry to offer proof of his point, then smiled at her as he opened his door. "Here's where your life changes, little flower."

Poppy just sat still in her seat, breathing roughly as she processed the fact that Alec had just used Joseph's endearment for her. What was she going to do? Joseph had assigned an arrogant, crazy person to watch over her. A crazy Elder, no less!

As Alec stepped out of the vehicle his guards flocked around him while several more men began to unload the luggage from the back. An older man, who she could only assume was Gideon, the man he called ahead for, came to greet Alec warmly, and they exchanged familiar pleasantries. "Did you have a good trip, sir?"

"Gideon, we've talked about this. I'm in no mood for the *sir* crap."

"Yes, and as I mentioned, *sir* is a sign of respect for your position." Alec just proceeded to frown at him, unconvinced. "Very well. What can I do for you, then?"

Alec came back to the SUV. As he swung opened the door, a rush of freezing cold air whipped against Poppy and right through her thin clothes she left London with. As a Dhampir, she was more tolerant of the cold, but that didn't mean she had to like it. Alec reached for her hand and at the same time nodded to one of the guards, who immediately brought over a thick men's coat. He wrapped it around her as she exited the vehicle, taking the biting chill out of the air and making her feel instantly warmer. "Gideon, I would like to introduce you to Miss Poppy Honeywell."

"Alec!" she blurted, angry that he was making no effort whatsoever to conceal her identity, but also suddenly aware that she shouldn't refer to an Elder with such familiarity in front of his men. "I mean, Elder Lambert."

"*Good God*, not you, too? You are our guest and definitely can't call me Elder Lambert. It's worse than *sir*. You may only call me by my given name. Alec."

"Fine, *Alec*," she snapped irritably. "This isn't going to work for me. I demand that you bring me around to the back."

Alec simply smiled at her, with challenge in his eyes, before disregarding what she had said completely and turning back to Gideon. "Joseph has asked me to look after Poppy for a while, so she'll be our special guest here at The Oracle."

Gideon nodded once with approval. "I hope you enjoy your time here, Miss Honeywell. If there is anything you need, please do not hesitate to ask."

"Yes, well there are a few things," Alec continued, to Poppy's surprise. "I'd like her set up in one of our finest rooms so she can get a good night's sleep. It has been a rather long day for all of us."

"Shall I set her up in one of the Elder guest suites on the top floor, then?" Gideon asked. "She will have plenty of room and plenty of privacy."

Alec glanced over his shoulder at her and gave her a truly wicked smile. "Oh, no. I want to make sure she feels right in the thick of things. You know what they say about idle hands and boredom."

"We . . . do?" Gideon questioned, looking completely confused.

"You wouldn't dare?!" Poppy challenged him.

"I'm thinking the eighth floor. I believe the suite next to Maya is available."

Gideon raised a brow, realizing that Alec surely was up to something, but just not something he had the slightest clue about. "Yes. It's a good sized room and has its own bathroom, so she won't have to use the common one on the floor."

"*What?*" she screeched. "Alec, are you crazy?"

"What? He just said you get your own bathroom. You won't even have to share," he replied—with way too much amusement in his voice. "Oh, and Gideon, we're going to need something for Poppy to do to occupy her time. You know, help out and make herself useful. Any good ideas?"

Gideon now looked thoroughly confused. "Yes. The idle hands concern." ". . . Well, Mrs. Stippich and the staff have been working on preparations for our New Year's celebration in five days. I'm sure they could use an extra hand."

"Perfect." When both men turned back to Poppy she must have looked truly stricken.

"Matthias?" Alec called to another guard who had come to stand beside Sampson. He wasn't as big as Sampson, very lean actually, with long, dark hair and an elongated nose. "Please escort Miss Honeywell to her room and see that she's settled." Alec then turned to Poppy and winked—*yes, winked at her.* "Good night, Poppy Honeywell."

With that, he turned and marched inside The Oracle double doors, leaving her standing there in the snow—for the moment, utterly speechless. She let the feeling stun her only for a moment, however. She was not going to let this arrogant Elder get the best of her, even if he was a friend of Joseph's.

"You want to play games, Alec Lambert?" she said under her breath. "You just picked the wrong woman to challenge."

CHAPTER SIX

Having trouble getting any restful kind of sleep, Poppy woke a few hours later in her mini-suite—complete with a fireplace, a Juliet balcony, and, as promised, a decent sized bathroom. She kept coming awake, hearing what she thought were a woman's tearful, muted cries. When she would try to go back to sleep, she'd just end up tossing and turning while her internal clock reminded her that it should be dinner time at The Hallow. So instead, she just lay there thinking up ways in which she could torment Alec Lambert.

In just one long day, the man had become the bane of her existence. *And arrogant!* How could he not take seriously her warnings that she was cursed? She didn't want to be responsible for hurting anyone. She genuinely liked people, though, and she hated having to constantly explain her innate clumsiness, so she had stopped trying. Despite what Alec thought, Poppy was going to remain in this room. There was absolutely no way she—

A knock at her door stopped Poppy mid-thought.

Her natural Dhampir senses kicked in right away and she could tell her visitor was not male, which meant it definitely wasn't Matthias coming to give her another request from Alec. The knock came again, and, not entirely sure how she should handle introducing herself to the people at The Oracle without having her curse rub off on them, she slowly eased her way towards the door. "I can hear you in there," a soft female voice said from the other side. "Are you going to answer your door?"

"Yes," Poppy answered but still made no move to do so. That was when she realized she was being ridiculous. It's not like she hadn't ever had to interact with people before. But she and her mother had always tried to interact as little as possible, keeping mostly to themselves when they went for supplies or mixed with people as they held down odd jobs for money.

"Are you sure about that?" the woman questioned from the other side. Poppy opened the door slowly, just enough to peek through to see a striking brunette with straight cut bangs and the most brilliant blue eyes Poppy had ever seen. Her eyes literally leapt off her face, like whitecaps on the sea on a bright, sunny day, thanks to her ink black hair. "Hello," the woman said, smiling broadly, "my name is Maya, Maya Brunetti. I'm in the room next door."

"Hello," Poppy replied. "So . . . Alec didn't send you?"

The woman blinked her long, lovely lashes and replied, "No. Should he have sent me?"

"No, I supposed not."

After another long, awkward pause, Maya clasped her hands together and added, "I heard you come in this morning, and I just wanted to introduce myself. We have the two suites at the far end of the hall. We're very lucky. The other rooms on this floor are pretty small—and they have to share a bathroom."

"Yes, I was told of our good fortunate with regard to the in-suite bathroom."

Maya nodded. "This place used to be an old hotel before they converted it. There are a few inconveniences, but still, they did a very nice job. Everything feels pretty new." Maya smiled again, and Poppy noted that it was hard not to immediately like the woman, given that smile and her obvious ease with small talk. "It's been a while since I had a neighbor. I was starting to wonder if Alec and Kane were doing that on purpose."

"Who's Kane?" Poppy asked.

"Oh, of course. If you just arrived you wouldn't have met Kane yet. He's on his honeymoon. But when you do, you'll know. The man is," she paused to smile again, the kind of smile that said she had a secret, "well, noticeable," she finished.

Poppy opened the door a little wider. "Why would they want to keep this room empty? It's a very nice room."

Maya stared at her questioningly. "Does that mean I can come in?"

Poppy shook her head. "No. We better keep things to the hallway."

"Right," Maya replied, with exaggerated slowness, and Poppy realized she must sound like a moron to this woman.

"You don't understand," Poppy further explained. "I'm dangerous. It's completely dangerous to be around me."

Maya laughed quietly. "We're all dangerous. That's what's so great about this place. We can help each other understand our gifts, learn how to control them."

Poppy looked at her sincerely. "Then you have a dangerous gift, too?"

"Not at the moment," Maya replied with a frown. "My Dhampir gifts are a bit on the fritz."

"I didn't know they could go . . . *on the fritz.* Is that why you think Alec has kept this room empty?"

Maya sighed and nodded. "He's been worried about me. I think he believes he's helping by giving me plenty of space. That is, when he's not smothering me with his concern."

"Oh, so are you and Alec . . .?"

"*God, no!* Don't get me wrong, he's like, well, you know," she gestured grandly with her hands, ". . . hot and all, in that overbearing brother sort of way but . . . but he's like *a brother.*"

"Yes, brother. Got it." Poppy was surprised at how relieved she felt by Maya's answer. The notion was completely silly to her that she would feel jealous of any woman over Alec after one stupid kiss, but she did. And who wouldn't be intimidated after meeting Maya? Her whole face seemed to light up with her enthusiasm, but it wasn't a little girl's face; she definitely had a woman's face with wide-set eyes, defined cheekbones, and sultry lips.

"So, does this Kane feel like your brother as well?"

Maya blinked at Poppy as if she had just asked a most ridiculous question. "I don't think any woman thinks of Kane as a brother. I've heard other Dhampirs say the man is trouble with a capital 'T'. And you know how women love trouble."

"Well, I don't," Poppy answered emphatically. "Love trouble, that is. So I'll be sure to steer clear of him."

Maya's brows lifted as though to say, OK, but then she seemed to let it go. "The problem is, Alec and Kane are way too similar—even though they refuse to admit it—and way too overprotective."

"That sounds like a lot of 'way too's."

Maya snorted at that. "Definitely!" She then glanced down the hallway as if to observe who might be around, and Poppy realized how silly it was that she still was making Maya have this conversation while standing in the hall. But she didn't want to take any unnecessary chances, especially because she was starting to really like this charming woman. Once she was satisfied that everything was all clear, she turned back to Poppy. "It's not entirely their fault, though. You see, I lost someone, and he was close friends with Alec and Kane and another man we lost that night. Ever since then they've made it their mission to—she put her finger up in quote marks—'watch over me'. But they're so overprotective sometimes; it makes me want to pull my hair out. I'm sure Phinneas would say . . ." Maya's voice faded as her words trailed off. It was obvious she found this man difficult to discuss, which was why Poppy was surprised that Maya was sharing it with her, a complete stranger. But she sensed Maya just really needed someone to listen to her. Poppy could do that without her curse rubbing off, she thought. "Well, I guess he would say a lot of things, not that any of them matter now."

"I see," Poppy began carefully. "Maya, I don't mean to pry, but I thought I heard a woman crying last night? By any chance was that . . .?" Poppy paused, waiting.

Maya's eyes widened. "No," she replied, and Poppy knew instinctively that Maya was lying. She couldn't really blame her. Poppy had asked her a very personal question without any warning, but it had made sense that Maya had been the one she heard after Maya confessed that she had lost this person recently, a person who was obviously very important to her.

"Hey, baby!" Poppy leaned forward and turned her head through the door to see an attractive young man with wavy blond hair coming down the hall. He was dressed casually in jeans and a tee shirt, and as he approached he smiled warmly, wrapped his arms around Maya's small waist, and pulled her in for a kiss, obviously not caring that he was doing it in front of a total stranger. "I was just coming up to grab you for lunch."

Maya's cheeks flushed a bit as she glanced back at Poppy, which didn't really surprise her, given the conversation they were just having about another man. "I was getting to know my new neighbor."

Poppy could see it was dawning on Maya just then that Poppy had not given her name. While on the run with her mother, she had been taught to give as little information about herself as possible, but Alec certainly had no intention of keeping her identity a secret, so she didn't see any point in trying and conceal it. "It's Poppy," she finally replied.

"Poppy. I love that name!" Maya said cheerfully. "It fits you, with your long red hair. This is my, uh, friend, Simon Kendrick."

As Poppy smiled at Simon, she could see he was a little discomfited being referred to as a 'friend'. It was obvious he held great affection for Maya, and from everything Poppy could see, Maya was fond of him, as well, but that certainly didn't explain the tears she heard, did it?

"Nice to meet you, Poppy," he said, holding his empty hand towards her before fisting it closed and reopening with a perfect red poppy sitting in his palm, which he offered to her.

"How did you do that?" Poppy asked with a smile as she reached through the door for the flower, careful not to make contact with his hand.

"He's very sweet like that," Maya said proudly. "Part-time magician and a very gifted fulltime witch."

"You're a witch?" Poppy echoed, the smiling fading slowly from her lips. She knew she couldn't go around acting as though witches were bad. Warlocks like Irina, who stole their power from good witches, were bad. There was a big difference. But Poppy still couldn't help but be extra cautious when she met a new witch.

"Is something wrong?" Maya asked her.

"No. I should just get back," Poppy wasn't quite sure what she was in such a rush to get back to, ". . . to unpacking?"

Maya appeared disappointed. "Well, OK. If you aren't able to join us for lunch, would you like to meet me downstairs in a couple hours? A few of us are putting together some decorations for the New Year's party."

"I'm not sure that's such a good idea." Poppy was surprised how her heart was tugging at her to go. She really liked Maya, and now she had spent time in the presence of a few people here and nothing bad had happened. When she kept contact to a minimum, as she had in the past while waitressing or working other odd jobs for money, she didn't seem to have any problems. It was when she was growing close with someone that everything went sideways.

"Oh, come on, pleeeaase," Maya pleaded. "It'll be fun!"

Simon smiled, amused by Maya's plea.

Poppy sighed. "All right. But just for an hour or so."

"Yay!" Maya cheered. "See you downstairs—third floor dining hall."

Closing the door behind her, Poppy fell back against it. "What am I doing?"

***

Alec was sitting at his desk, rubbing his hands over his tired eyes as he tried for about the sixth time to read the message in his inbox. The dull ache in his head that had plagued him for the past few weeks had returned. He decided he needed more sleep, but there had been too much to do after his return from London, including a debrief with the team that had been tracking a newly discovered coven of rare Daywalkers (vampires who could tolerate some daylight), a satellite call with two other Elders to discuss the allocation of Brethren resources between their locations, and a not unexpected phone call from Joseph, who wanted to make sure that he and Poppy had arrived safely at The Oracle. Alec hadn't even had a chance yet to go down and check on Poppy since he'd left her standing at a loss for words earlier that morning.

He smiled to himself. Her stifled temper had been a fun amusement for him. Alec had enjoyed pushing her buttons when he informed her that she would be staying down on an occupied floor. The look on her face had been priceless. Those gold eyes of hers had rounded with such surprise as her mouth dropped open—and, *Lord, help him*, she had *such* a pretty mouth. All morning long he had images of that mouth. What it had felt like to kiss her, taste her. She was sweet, with perfectly bowed lips that tasted of cherries. Alec swore the Almighty was doing a solid favor for the male gender when he created Poppy Honeywell.

He then sighed roughly. Why was he still thinking about Poppy when he had so much work to do? He had to admit he'd been fairly distracted by her all morning and that wasn't like him. He always had a capacity to separate his duties from the after-hours fun stuff. Poppy was no different . . . except that she was. She was like a daughter to Joseph, which spelled hands off for him. Clearly, he needed a distraction from what had been distracting him all morning. Perhaps even another female distraction. "Sampson?" he called over the communication link on his desk. "Has Sienna Scott returned-?"

Alec didn't get a chance to finish his sentence because the door to his office burst open and in waltzed the biggest pain in his ass (who was unfortunately also a friend), Kane, with a cocky, fresh-from-his-honeymoon sort of grin and Sampson right on his heels. "My apologies, sir," Sampson began, "but you did say you wanted to see him as soon as he returned."

Alec rolled his eyes as Kane lifted his arms high and proclaimed, "I'm back! Did you miss me?"

"It's all right, Sampson," Alec replied, rubbing his hand one last time over his forehead for good measure. "Expecting Kane to *knock* before he enters my office is like asking the world to stop spinning."

Sampson frowned. He had been very loyal to Alec since Lucas's death and hated to let The Elder down even on the smallest level. Alec was very lucky to have him. "Would you still like me to find Sienna Scott, sir?"

"Sienna, huh," Kane smiled as he plopped into one of the chairs in front of his desk. Alec had hoped that little request would slide by as he quickly shook his head, silently dismissing Sampson. Of course, nothing that had to do with a woman ever slipped by Kane. "I have to say I'm a bit surprised. She's not your type."

Alec scowled back at him. "I don't have a *type*, you asshole."

Kane snorted loudly. "Oh, yes, you do. Redheads."

Redheads? Poppy was a redhead. At least Alec thought she'd be considered a redhead. Her hair was very clearly red in the light, but at other times it appeared more brown. It was fascinating how it changed color, actually. Then suddenly Alec felt irritated with himself for allowing Kane to sidetrack him like this. "Kane, does this conversation have any point?"

Kane gave a slight shoulder shrug. "Not really. This is your meeting. I'm just here."

"And how is it *my* meeting when *you're* the one barging into my office?" There was no doubt Alec was being short tempered from a lack of sleep, but it was just Kane. He and the Shifter had an understanding. They liked each other, would fight to the death for one another, but never verbally admitted to liking each other.

"Dude, you really need to get laid," Kane replied. "Or better yet, *sucked*. And I'm not talking your Johnson."

"Kane!"

Kane threw his hands up in defeat. "All right, all right. You go ahead and pretend a Dhampir's bite is not your thing, even though I know damn well it is. Actually, I do have something important to discuss with you."

"Well it can just wait," Alec suddenly replied as he stood to his feet behind his desk, "because I've been waiting an eternity for an explanation as to *why the hell* I still don't have a report from you regarding the Wraith." Alec then pointed his finger sharply at Kane. "And I don't want to hear any more excuses. New wife or not—and believe me, I give her all the credit in the world for agreeing to marry you—I need to know what we're dealing with here."

Kane just stared dully back at him. "When have I ever given you a written report? You know I'm not a paperwork kind of guy. I leave that to Gideon. You also seemed to be forgetting that you and I have already had this conversation about twelve times."

"I'm not forgetting. I just don't buy the bullshit story you're telling me—even for the twelfth time."

"Well, then I guess I'll repeat it again—slowly. The Wraith never showed up once I returned to Wood Buffalo National Park, and I haven't seen him since I left Yellowknife. Neither has Lucky or his team. So I can only assume the Wraith is gone. Or one of the Lycan's got him."

Alec just stared back at Kane with a hard scowl. He didn't buy this flimsy explanation for a second, but he also couldn't understand what Kane would possibly have to gain by keeping the information from him. *They were on the same side, weren't they?*

"Well?" Kane added as he lifted his hands. "Do you know something different?"

Alec came around his desk and leaned back, with his arms crossed, right in front of Kane's chair. "You know what, Kane?

As usual, I think you're full of shit. I don't buy any of that crap. You're hiding something from me and I'm going to find out what it is. And when I do, you're going to receive no mercy from me. I don't care how long we've known each other."

Kane just returned a perfect, pearly-white smile. "Do I look worried, oh, Elder one?"

Alec breathed out roughly, putting his fingers to his temple. "How do I get you to understand that this is serious? Sienna wants me to authorize her team to go into the Dead Zone so they can trap a Lycan to try and draw out this Wraith."

"That's a terrible idea!" Kane snapped as he shot to his feet. "Don't tell me you're even considering it. What is with all these women throwing themselves in the middle of a hot mess? Is Stippich putting something in the food?"

"Well, since Nathanial sent her to us specifically because of her cloaking abilities and past success with fighting Lycans, I need to have a good reason to say no or come up with a better plan . . . which I can't do without that damn report!"

"Good point."

"Great! Does that mean I can expect a report anytime soon?"

"Yeah, I'll get working on that," Kane replied with absolutely zero sincerity in his voice as he turned and started pacing Alec's office. "Now let's discuss the real reason I came in here."

Alec smiled back at him with the same lack of sincerity. "Of course . . . I'm all ears."

"What're you doing about that little asshole, Simon Kendrick? He's sniffin' around Maya like a fox in heat. I don't trust him. He's way too goddamn cocky for her."

Alec raised a brow at that. "*You* think Simon is cocky?"

Kane hitched his hands at his hips. "Yeah, don't *you*?"

"Kane, I'm a little busy here. What exactly would you like me to do? If Maya feels like enough time has passed and she's ready to move on with someone, then we can hardly stop her."

Kane snorted loudly and threw back at him, "Of course we can! We've been meddling in her life for months now. That was kind of the point of promising Phin you'd take care of her."

"I promised him I'd take care of her—not forbid her from seeing any men she might be interested in."

Kane tossed a dismissive hand in the air. "I can tell you right now, Phin wouldn't approve of that little punk—not for Maya."

"You don't approve of anyone for her who isn't Phin."

Kane shrugged his shoulders. "Duh."

"Phin is dead."

Kane focused his gaze directly at Alec. "You know I don't believe that. And even if you do, I'm not buying the idea that you think Simon's good for Maya. He's a frickin' witch, for Christ's sake. Witches are a boatload of trouble—always chanting spells and making shit appear out of nowhere. It's not natural, man."

"*This*, coming from a shifter." Kane just continued to stare at him as if he had no clue to his point. Alec rubbed his head one more time. "Oh, all right," he sighed, a tight grimace coming over his face as he turned from Kane and rapped his knuckles on his polished mahogany desk. "If I say I agree with you—and let's make it clear, I rarely ever want to agree with you—it has to do with the fact that she's just not ready. Not that Simon is a witch. Witches are on our side, remember? And Simon has proven himself to be a very good witch. We need him."

"Whatever," Kane replied. "You're still admitting you agree with me."

"Only because I know she's still crying herself to sleep."

"Really?" Kane questioned with an arched brow. "And how, exactly, do you know that?"

Alec stared back at him dumbly. "Obviously, I have a Dhampir listening nearby."

"As in '*the room next door*' nearby?" Kane grinned. "You know, maybe I don't give you enough credit for knowing what you're doing."

Alec gave him a hard scowl, and the same moment Sampson returned inside the room. "Sorry to interrupt, sir, but Matthias needs you downstairs right away."

Alec stared back at him, remembering he'd sent Matthias to check on Poppy a while ago. "Is there a problem?"

"Oh, yeah. There's a problem."

CHAPTER SEVEN

"What the hell happened?" Alec blinked repeatedly as he stood with Kane at the entry of the industrial-size kitchen, scanning several hundred bone-white plates that were shattered into thousands of bits and pieces all across the red-tiled floor. Despite its age and high-volume use, this room never appeared in disarray, or even less than meticulous, for that matter. That was because its head mistress, Mrs. Wanda Stippich, would never stand for a plate out of place. She was as fierce as she was organized and didn't take nonsense from anyone, human or hybrid. But at this moment Wanda Stippich looked as if she might be sick as she screeched something in high-pitched German to Matthias, who was desperately trying to calm her down.

"Mrs. Stippich—English, please," Alec said to her.

"That woman is what happened!" she immediately replied, her arms failing in the air in apt description. "Look at what she's done to my kitchen!" She went on and on, barely taking a breath, and when she appeared to run out of words in English she once again started rattling them off in German.

"What woman?" Alec demanded, and the instant he asked the question his face grimaced as he realized he already suspected the answer. He knew only one woman, *one Dhampir*, who could trip over her own two heels. No, he had to be wrong.

"The redhead!" she charged, and Alec shook his head. Nope, he wasn't wrong.

"Redhead?" Kane asked with definite curiosity. "Well look who's been keeping secrets."

"Shut up, Kane," Alec replied in a quieter voice.

"I'm just stating my utter admiration, that's all. I mean, one woman created this entire mess? She would have to been really pissed off to do this kind of damage. Trust me, I've had a few close calls with women and plates—in this kitchen, in fact."

"*You!*" Stippich accused with a second sharp finger pointed at Kane. "You're not allowed in my kitchen either!"

Kane threw his hands up in innocent defense. "Hey, I'm a married now. There'll be no more playing around on the butcher block." As the older woman's expression dropped at the man's arrogance, he added—flashing a wicked smile, "Well . . . unless it's with my new wife."

Stippich looked about ready to explode, so Alec stepped in to save Kane's butt yet again. "Enough! Both of you. Where's Poppy now?" he turned and asked Matthias.

"Who's Poppy?" Kane asked dumbly, and Alec felt as if he wanted to punch something—preferably Kane, since he more than likely deserved it for something, but he couldn't explain what had sparked this fierce reaction in him.

"She ran out of here," Matthias answered. "I was going to follow her, but Mrs. Stippich has been a little . . . upset."

"It was an accident," Maya chimed in, and they all swung around to face her. "I didn't see what happened, but I know Poppy didn't mean to do it. She'd been helping me set up for the party and came in to grab some linen for the tables, when all of the sudden there was a huge crash. When we came in she was standing in the middle of a big pile of broken dishes."

Maya's crystal blue eyes appeared wider than the lake in front of The Oracle itself as she glanced up to where neatly folded linens were still sitting atop their high shelf. Several rows of shelves that had been stacked below with hundreds of glass pitchers, bowls and plates below were now gone, crumbled under the weight of one falling on top of another. From there it was easy to put two and two together and come up with a Dhampir who seemed to have a knack for freakish accidents like he'd never seen. "I tried to follow her, but she warned me to stay back."

Alec suspected he already knew why. Poppy feared that her curse would rub off on Maya, so she wanted her to stay away.

Poppy herself was probably already locked up in her room by now. *Damn* this blasted curse nonsense. "It has nothing to do with you," he said to Maya.

"She didn't want to leave her room," Maya added. "But I convinced her to come down here and help with the party."

Alec went to Maya and brushed a gentle hand along her arm. "You did the right thing. And thank you for befriending her. She can use a friend. I don't think she's had the luxury of very many in her life."

Maya nodded in understanding just as Simon Kendrick rushed inside the room. "Baby, are you all right?"

Kane stepped in front of him, preventing him from going to Maya. "She's fine," he growled, and there was a *real* growl behind it, courtesy of Kane's shape-shifting jaguar half.

"Kane," Alec responded. "Not now." Kane shot him an ugly look that was rare for a man who, looks-wise, had nothing ugly about him. He saw Maya's surprised expression and backed off, even though it was obvious he didn't like it one bit.

Simon continued to Maya and pulled her into a tight hug. "I'm fine," she told him.

"Mrs. Stippich," Alec began calmly, "I will make sure you have ample help to get this area cleaned up and the funds necessary to replace all of these items."

"What about dinner tonight?" she demanded more than asked.

Alec frowned at her. "I realize you have a difficult task seeing to the needs of hundreds of hungry people, but I'm sure we'll all survive eating off of paper plates for one evening." Alec started to leave the kitchen. He wanted to go upstairs and check on Poppy, make sure she was all right, but he turned back to the head kitchen mistress as a thought struck him. "And let me be clear. I agree with Maya that this was an accident. Miss Honeywell is a guest here and, as such, will continue to be treated with every respect. So I don't want to hear any nonsense about her being banned from the kitchen. Is that understood?"

"Did you say Honeywell?" Kane asked, his voice tinged with genuine surprise. "*Poppy* Honeywell?"

"Yes." Alec answered guardedly because when Kane recognized a woman's name with that 'per chance' look, it was almost never good. There was usually some sordid story behind it, and that *really* didn't sit well with him, for some reason. "Are you about to tell me the close call with the woman with plates is her cousin or something?"

An amused smile curled over Kane's lips. "No. I just thought I remembered a friend mentioning her name before."

Alec's gaze narrowed on the Shifter. He knew something Alec didn't, and it was pissing Alec off—again! Instead of trying to get the information from him, which he knew darn well he wasn't going to get if Kane hadn't told him anything to this point, he turned without saying another word and headed for the stairs. Alec decided he needed to walk off some tension before he checked on Poppy. He wasn't quite sure why he was so tense. Normally he was very calm and deliberate about his reaction to news or situations, but something was off today. Some healthy exertion would be good for him. So he took the stairs two at a time. As he reached the eighth floor landing he could feel his breaths were harder in his chest, which wasn't the case at all with his hybrid Dhampir guards who were right in step behind him.

Damn, sometimes it sucked being human.

When he reached Poppy's room he knocked lightly on her door. "Poppy, its Alec. May I come in?"

When she didn't reply he looked to Matthias for conformation. "She's in there."

"Poppy?" He knocked a little louder. ". . . Please, I would like to speak with you."

Still nothing.

Suddenly he felt irritated because he suspected she was hiding herself in her room because of this damn curse nonsense. "OK, let me be more clear. Open the damn door now or I'll break it in." His voice was very calm, but you could definitely hear the deep, determined undertones, so he fully expected to hear the latch turn any second.

Instead, he couldn't believe when he heard, "Go away, Alec."

He blinked back at the door. "That wasn't one of the options."

"Well, you only gave me two. Neither of them I liked. So go away!"

His hands hitched at his hips as he scowled at the door. This woman was starting to make him look silly in front of his own guards. Was he an Elder who was in charge of this place or not? "You want another option?" he replied with clear sarcasm in his voice. "How about I stand out here and pester you to death until you open the door." She was silent on the other side, and Alec wondered how long she was actually going to debate the three unfavorable options in her head. *Man,* the woman could be stubborn. Joseph hadn't warned him that she could be so stubborn. "One . . . Two . . ."

The lockset finally clicked. "Wait outside but stay right here," he instructed Sampson and Matthias before finally entering her room. Poppy was standing there, at the ready for him, her posture straight as a board with her arms at her sides and her lips pinched into a tight line.

"What!" she said to him, suddenly and animatedly flailing one of her hands through the air, but she kept her other arm strangely stiff at her side. "Yes, I broke a bunch dishes. I'll pay to have them replaced."

"I'm not worried about a few dishes," he replied as he walked right up to her.

"*A few?*" she questioned. "You did go into the kitchen, right? Saw the big pile . . .?"

He smiled a gentle smile. Her self-deprecating humor lightened his mood almost immediately. "Yes, I saw the pile. Pretty impressive, considering you were down there all of what, an hour?"

There went that hand flailing through the air again. "This isn't funny, Alec. This curse on me is very real. Why do you refuse to take it seriously? I could've hurt someone."

He nodded toward the other arm remaining pinned at her side. "It seems the only person you managed to hurt is yourself. Let me see."

Poppy appeared to have been ready for any rebuttal he may have given her—except that one. "It'll be fine," she replied quietly. "I just cut myself a little. I've already wrapped it. It'll heal quickly."

Alec was shaking his head as he slowly pulled her arm away from her side. She had torn one of her pillowcases into strips and wrapped the wound tightly, but he could see there was so much flowing blood underneath that the cloth was already soaked through. "I'm taking you to see Dr. Li."

"That's not necessary. You know as well as I do that this will heal within the hour."

He stared at her for a long moment. "Yes, I know that. I'm just surprised to hear you admit it, since you seem to want nothing to do with your Dhampir side. Look, I'm glad you're going to be all right, but I still want you to be checked out by Dr. Li."

"I'm staying here."

Alec raked his hand through his messy hair. "Don't tell me your stubborn refusal to get medical attention has something to do with this curse nonsense."

"It's *not nonsense!* And if anything, what happened downstairs should prove that to you."

He frowned at her. *How did this woman rile him up so fast?* He was in charge of hundreds of people on a daily basis, dealing with some of the biggest supernatural bad-asses this world had to offer. So why did this *one* woman spark his response like no other? "What happened downstairs doesn't prove a damn thing. It was an accident."

"It was not an accident! Why do you refuse to believe me?"

"Because I'm sane!" Once again the words came out of his mouth before he'd taken time to reconsider them. The injured look in Poppy's eyes had him regretting the words the instant he had said them. He never once considered her insane. He was just frustrated that this smart, intelligent woman was so ready to believe she was cursed. "I'm sorry," he said in a calmer voice before following her to where she had walked away from him to stand in front of her balcony windows. The gray light cast soft shadows on her face, and he swore to himself that sometimes this woman was the most beautiful female he'd ever seen.

Even though he knew logically other Dhampirs at The Oracle could be pointed to as being more beautiful, there was just something about her. He'd definitely known women who were more coordinated. *Hell*, every other woman at The Oracle was more coordinated! But sometimes, like when that pitcher of water went crashing into his biggest guard Sampson's chest on that plane, her clumsiness made him smile. He hadn't laughed or smiled very much in the past year. He used to laugh a lot. He used to be a lot more fun. Before he became Elder. Before Phin had been bitten by the Lycan. Before Lucas had been killed by his uncle. "That wasn't how I meant that to come out," he continued. "What I meant to say was that I can't believe someone as intelligent as you can truly believe you're cursed."

She turned her head back to him, her cherry hair falling behind her shoulder, and it happened so gracefully and naturally that it struck him how strange a fact it was that this was the same woman who tripped over her own pointed heels. "So, you're saying you don't believe in curses, then. Seems a little odd for someone who spends his days battling against supernatural creatures that most people would not believe exist unless they could see them for themselves."

"I believe in the supernatural world it is possible to be cursed," he clarified. "I don't believe *you* are cursed." She looked like she wanted to say something in reply, but she remained silent. As he stared at her in the quiet room, Alec found himself wanting to kiss her again. *No*, he wanted desperately to kiss her—to feel her responding to his kiss as she had on the plane. *What the hell had he been thinking to promise her he wouldn't kiss her for a week? Of course*, he was going to kiss her. In fact, he was going to stop thinking about it and kiss her right then. But as he tried to move closer her breath inhaled sharply and her eyes widened with intuitive awareness and she suddenly took a small step back, away from him.

Or, maybe he wasn't going to kiss her. "How did you cut your arm?" he asked instead.

"The broken edge of a plate did it as I tried to stop one of the shelves from collapsing," she replied. "It all happened so fast and I was embarrassed. I just ran out."

She paused for a long moment and then sighed, "I wish things could be different. That I wasn't . . ." she glanced back up at him but didn't finish her sentence. She didn't need to finish it because he already knew the answer—cursed. She wished she wasn't cursed.

He took a step towards her and erased the distance she had put between them. "Poppy, please tell me you can see this was just an accident. That it had nothing to do with a curse."

When she didn't answer, he tipped her chin up with his knuckle. "I know this day didn't end as you wanted it to, but I'm glad to see you tried to interact with the people here. And I hope this won't stop you from trying again tomorrow."

Poppy stared up at him, her gaze searching his. "I can't interact with them. I will hurt them."

She said the words with such sadness. Slowly he reached out until his fingers were stroking along the edges of her face as his thumb traced the rise of her cheekbone. "It's not in you to hurt anyone. I can see that."

"You don't know me!" she said in a sudden, loud outburst. "You don't know what I'm capable of!"

"Maybe not. But I trust my instincts. They have saved my hide countless times. You need to start trusting yours—and yourself. It's time to stop running, Poppy."

Her gaze drifted away for a moment and then came back to him. "Running is easier. It's what I've known."

Alec looked at her for a long while, appreciating her honesty. He could definitely understand a person wanting to revert to want they've known when they feel pushed or threatened. He lifted her arm and examined it one more time. He was pleased that she didn't try to stop him. "I'll tell you what," he began. "If you allow me to keep Matthias outside your door for the night, I won't make you go see Dr. Li." A smile pulled at her cheeks, and its effect sank into him surprisingly quick and deep. "If," he added with a raised finger, "you also promise to let him know if it's not healed over the next few hours as it should. Deal?"

"Deal," she replied, practically lifting up on her toes as she said it.

After leaving her room and giving Matthias his instructions, Alec walked back towards the elevator that would take him to his floor. He decided he could give Poppy this one thing because he was going to ask a lot more of her in the coming days. He would see this woman come out of her self-imposed asylum and, with a little help from Maya, she would realize all of this nonsense stuff about a curse was just that—nonsense. Poppy was the daughter of a witch and a Dhampir, and underneath all this clumsiness she was gifted and powerful.

He truly believed that.

CHAPTER EIGHT

Three days later, and much to her surprise, Poppy found herself laughing as she sat with Maya in the dining hall. She was doing something as simple as checking for burned out bulbs in string after string of twinkling lights, but her enjoyment of the task was made easy by Maya's warm and gregarious presence. Granted, they were seated in a far corner of the hall, somewhat isolated from everyone else participating in the holiday decorating, but she had at least felt involved the past few days, which was nice. She had been exceedingly careful, though, to make sure that her *tendency* for unfortunate accidents hadn't led to any more minor disasters like the one in the kitchen.

"You're being ridiculous. Of course, no one can be *that* clumsy—especially not a Dhampir," Maya would assure her. And then, after Poppy would trip and crush several unfortunate bulbs under her shoes, Maya would then say, "But you are lacking a bit in the agility department."

"That's a very nice way of putting it," Poppy acknowledged.

Maya frowned gently. "Have you been this way your whole life?"

"Pretty much. You just get used to it."

"I think I'm already used to it. Especially after having to come up with a story to Mrs. Stippich to explain that we somehow managed to lose three sets of lights."

Poppy laughed. "She knows they're in a crushed pile somewhere. Why do you think she refused my offer to help restack the new plates?"

"I gotta be honest with you, Poppy. I don't think I'd let you restack the plates either, if I were in her position." They both laughed hard until Maya finally added, reassuringly, "I'm just glad you didn't let it stop you from coming down here and participating. This can be such a wonderful time of year. These festive traditions remind us of the human side of ourselves. After dealing with so many supernatural life-and-death situations, it's good to be reminded of simpler things once in a while."

Poppy nodded in agreement. She could definitely relate to wanting to be reminded of simpler traditions. That's why, after Alec had left her room the other night, she had decided to participate in the New Year's event. There had been many hours of mental deliberation to get her to that point, included a pros and cons list, which was one of her mother's favorite things to do. But the result was Poppy promising herself that she wouldn't let what had happened in the kitchen keep her locked in her room. And so far, she hadn't. Her arm had healed just fine, and the next morning she was right there at Maya's door asking if she could go downstairs with her to help with the decorating. Maya was gleeful about it, of course.

Just then, Poppy heard a familiar voice at the entry to the hall. Alec appeared just outside the dining hall doors, talking casually with several other men, but as always, he seemed to stand out from everyone. Once again dressed in some of the finest clothes she had ever seen, he was more casual than she'd seen him in previous days. Dark denim and a pale crewneck sweater, which appeared touchably thick and soft from across the room, fit him exceedingly well. His broad shoulders were relaxed and he, in general, appeared more at ease. She decided that Alec Lambert was a very handsome man when he appeared at ease.

"He's checking up on you again," Maya said at exactly the same moment Alec's eyes found Poppy's in the room. He nodded towards her as if to exchange a private hello to her across the distance.

When Poppy finally realized that Maya was implying something, she pulled her attention from Alec back to her new friend. "What do you mean?"

"I mean, if you knew him better, you would know that since he became an Elder it's not normal for him to find reasons to come down here five and six times a day. In truth, he's barely left his office in the last three months."

"I'm a guest here—placed in his charge by Joseph. He's doing his duty by checking on me, nothing more."

Maya shook her head. "I think he's interested," she said as she smiled in that shy way she had about herself and squirmed in her seat. "We should do something about that. Maybe find you something extra sexy to wear for the party?"

"You're a trouble maker."

"Alec doesn't need to check on you. He's had Matthias over there"—Maya nodded over to the tall man who had been Poppy's shadow for the past three days, which seemed to make the Dhampir, who could no doubt hear their conversation, uncomfortable—"following you around like a puppy. If he needed to know if you had an eyelash out of place, he would just ask his guard."

"I don't think we should be discussing this here. Matthias can hear us."

"Matthias can hear everything. It's practically his job to filter out all but the important stuff—stuff with regard to Alec's protection. And Alec's human, so he can't hear what we're saying now across the room."

Feeling as though this was a ridiculous subject that she wasn't quite sure how they'd gotten onto, Poppy was going to let the matter drop, but then she found herself just having to add, "Alec hasn't spoken to me since the day of the accident in the kitchen."

"And that bothers you?" Maya asked.

"Not really bothers, more . . . just . . . I'm not sure what he expects of me."

"You shouldn't worry about that. Alec's one of the most truthful people I know. Even when he must sometimes put the best face on things completely out of his control, you always have faith he will find the answer. He's just one of those people."

"That's a lot of pressure for one man."

"Yes, and also why there are only twelve Elders with The Brethren. Men like Joseph and Alec are rare, even among the Elders."

Poppy smiled. "I suppose you're right. Is that why he spends so much time in his office? I mean, surely there must be other activities he enjoys doing with his free time."

Maya seemed to give her answer considerable thought before she spoke. "The Oracle is his free time. That, and . . . he loves to train. He works hard to present himself as this indestructible leader we all need, but . . ." her voice trailed off.

"But?" Poppy pressed.

"But he's been . . . sad, though I don't know if you'd ever get him to admit it. Brahm Hill has been hard," Maya continued. "The night we lost Phinneas and Lucas was hard on all of us, but for Alec it was more than that. His uncle—former Elder Reese Lambert—was directly responsible for their deaths."

Poppy sighed. "I didn't know."

Maya nodded. "I think he carries that with him every day. You have to understand . . . he lost so much that night. He had just barely ascended to his position as Elder when two of the men he trusted most—who had been part of his team—were just gone. Since then, he keeps people at a distance—a very polite distance. You know what I mean?"

"I do." Poppy said as she glanced back at Alec. Her breath caught for a moment when she realized he was already watching her. He smiled at her, the dimple in his chin stretching as he nodded, then returned to his conversation with the other men. She felt a strange tug on her heart and its beatings picked up its pace. There had been a few times since she had met Alec when she could definitely feel the walls he had carefully constructed around him. Then there were times, like now—like on the plane when he'd kissed her—when it all disappeared, but it was always temporary.

"I'm sorry about Phin," Poppy said sincerely, as she focused back on her tasks of unwinding the chain of lights. She referred him to him as Phin instead of Phinneas because it seemed everyone at The Oracle referred to him as Phin. Only Maya seemed to use his full name, which Poppy thought was kind of endearing. "How did he die?"

Maya's lips formed a sad smile as she inhaled a little deeper. "I don't know if he is dead. He was bitten by a Lycan that night. I'm sure you must know a Lycan's bite is poisonous to us, just as it is to a vampire."

Poppy was surprised that Maya seemed to be lumping her into the same category as herself and Phin, because Poppy didn't think of herself as a Dhampir. Her father was a witch and her mother was half Dhampir, which meant she had a little of both in her blood, she supposed. But she had never really tested her abilities, even though her mother was always attempting to persuade her to. Poppy just believed that all these supernatural gifts were the reason her life had been put into such chaos in the first place—a life constantly on the run.

"If he survived the initial bite," Maya continued, "and somehow the hunting Lycans gathered around the perimeter, the poison would've continued to work through his blood until he turned into a Lycan on the next full moon. Selfishly, I'd like to think he survived the bite, even though I know he would hate that life. But there's just some part of me that's stronger believing he's still here with us in some way. Even if he's not the same man I fell in love with." She shook her head and reached for the next chain of lights. "I know that probably makes no sense. It's just that if I admit he's dead, then I'm admitting a part of me is dead, too."

"It makes perfect sense, Maya. You obviously cared about him very deeply."

"I loved him," she replied without any hesitation in those wide blue eyes of hers. "I loved him with every part of myself I had to give. I loved him in that way you just know will never happen again in your lifetime. And I never questioned that he loved me the same way in return. In many ways, even though it was only for a short period of time, I am luckier than most people for getting to just experience it. I know that."

"And what of Simon? It's obvious he cares for you, too."

Maya looked around, always careful of who could be listening. "I care about Simon deeply. He's been wonderful to me, even when I've been at my darkest. He's told me he loves me, and he wants to"—she rolled her hand out in front of her— "you know."

It took Poppy a moment to figure out that Maya was referring to sex. "*Oh!* Oh, that."

"Yes, that," Maya replied with an impressive flush to her cheeks—considering she was part vampire. "I had saved myself for Phinneas because I thought we were going to be together forever. Pretty dumb, huh?"

"That's not dumb. That's romantic."

"Yeah, well, it seems like a dumb reason to wait now because we never got the chance before." Her expression grimaced miserably. "I know I should just say yes to Simon and get it over with. Lord knows, it can't be nearly as big of a deal as I've made it out to be. And I do care for him—very much. But I just can't seem to get myself to do it."

Now it made more sense to Poppy why she had heard Maya crying in her room only hours before she put on a perfectly happy face for Simon. She was forcing herself to move on, even if she wasn't ready to. Probably in an effort to feel anything but the pain that had drowned her after Phin was gone. "Well, I can't say I know how it feels to lose a great love like that, but I do know how it feels to lose someone you're close to."

"Have you . . .?"

"Oh, God yes," Poppy said quickly in return. "Years ago." Poppy then glanced around, just to make sure Alec was still out of earshot. "The first man I was with I cared for, but it had been more about being tired of waiting. You see, my mother and I traveled a lot. When you never stay in one place for very long, at some point it becomes important to just feel really connected to somebody . . . even if it's just for a little while."

"And sex made you feel really connected?" Maya asked, her wondrous curiosity showing through.

Poppy shook her head. "Not in the way I was hoping," Poppy replied honestly. "I mean, the sex was good. It felt good. He was very careful with me, so it didn't really hurt too much. Would I do it differently now? Maybe. I knew I didn't love him—and certainly not anything near what you felt for Phin, but I think I was ready for the experience."

"Have you ever been in love?" Maya asked.

Poppy shook her head. "In fact, my physical experience with men really isn't much more than your own. And I'm envious of what you had with Phin. It seems pretty rare. Maybe you should consider giving yourself more time to accept what's happened before you jump into anything too serious with Simon."

Maybe," she sighed. "I guess I was hoping if I made that connection with Simon, someone I do care about, it would help me move on and just accept that Phinneas isn't coming back."

"Well, my guess is if Phin loved you half as much as you seemed to have loved him, then he would just want you to be happy, whatever it is that makes you happy." Poppy set down the string of lights, stretched and rose to her feet, feeling a little stiff from sitting in one position for so long. "It's going to be dinnertime soon. I should probably go back upstairs."

"How about you stay down here for dinner?" Maya suggested. "Tonight, that would make me happy." Poppy returned a small but sincere smile. "Nothing bad has happened to anyone, Poppy."

"Trust me, Maya, it will, and I've learned that the hard way. I've already pushed the boundaries more than I should. It's just that it's nice to be out and about. Alec suggested that I explore the grounds a bit. Maybe that's what I should do later and get some exercise at the same time."

"That sounds like a wonderful idea. Would you like me to go with you? Knowing Alec, he would probably want one of us to stay with you outside The Oracle."

"You already have dinner plans with Simon, and I'm sure my shadow, Matthias there, won't let me out of his sight." Both women laughed as they immediately looked for confirmation from Matthias standing there in the corner, who quickly averted his head as though pretending he hadn't heard a word of their conversation. Their laughter stopped, however, when Poppy came heard an immediate crunch beneath her shoe. She looked down to see several crushed bulbs just before the chain of lights she had just finished flickered out for good. "Oh no, not again."

Maya just laughed. "There are some extra bulbs in that blue box over there."

"I know," Poppy muttered. "I had to fix two sets yesterday."

That caused Maya to laugh even harder. "Well, sit back down and get comfortable. We still have a little time before dinner, so we can discuss what you're going to wear for the New Year's party."

Poppy snorted rather ungracefully. "Don't be silly. I can't go to the party. Knowing my luck, I'd probably find a way to bring *all* the lights down."

"That would be impressive," she teased. "Of course, you're going to the party. So don't argue with me."

"But—"

"Doonn't," Maya warned.

Poppy frowned. She really didn't see what the point would be to risking the endangerment of so many people . . . for what? A passing glance from Alec Lambert? But she had a feeling she wasn't going to win this battle with a very determined Maya.

***

Alec's attention was drawn to the sound of Poppy's laughter all the way across the hall. He liked her laugh. The sound was tuneful, effortless and genuine. He should have returned to his office at least twenty minutes ago, but he found himself still down here talking with people, watching her, listening to her laugh. It was unlike him, especially considering the mound of tasks that awaited him upstairs.

Poppy laughed again, and the sound was so lovely it made him want to cross the room to engage her in conversation with him right then—but that was a bad idea. Alec had been intentionally keeping his distance from Poppy for the past three days. He wanted to think the reason was because he feared she might trip into him, mash his nut-sack again with her knee, and thus finish the job of ensuring he would never be able to have children. But that wasn't even close to the truth. The truth was, Alec found himself way too distracted by this oddly distracting woman and, in the process, forgetting why she was here in the first place. He was to protect her, ensure that nothing would happen to her on his watch, as he had promised Joseph. And that's exactly what he was going to do.

"Excuse me, gentlemen," he said when he could no longer pretend to be engaged in conversation regarding security during the New Year's party. He knew they already had that all mapped out. His people just liked to 'double cross their tees' so to speak

She was still laughing.

Yep. He was going to have to go over there.

"Alec," Sampson called just as he took his first step forward. His guard spoke low in his ear. "You have a call on the sat line."

A direct call on the satellite line meant it was another Elder, and that always required his immediate attention. He glanced one more time at Poppy to assure himself that she was fine before making his way upstairs to the private conference room adjacent to his office. Sampson entered the private code to let him inside, and he was surprised to see that not one but all of the Elders were on screens around the room—all except for Joseph, that is. "Will Joseph be joining us shortly?" Alec asked as he took his seat in the large room.

"I'm afraid we have some disturbing news on that front, Alec," Nathanial Hawkings, the second highest seated Elder on The Council, began. "Joseph is very ill."

"What?" Alec questioned hard. "I just saw him in London a few days ago. He was fine."

"Actually, that confirms something for us," Nathanial continued in a thick English that flecked with his native German accent. "You were the last one of us to see Joseph, which means you probably left there with a woman named Poppy Honeywell."

"I did," Alec confirmed without hesitation, even though he didn't like where this conversation was going. He always believed in telling the truth and facing whatever consequences came from that truth. That was how his father had taught him from a very young age to conduct himself. After his father, Gerard, had died, it was important to Alec to hold onto the thing that made his father the most proud of him. "He asked me to get her out of London and protect her here at The Oracle."

"Is she with you now?"

"Yes," Alec offered, not hesitating but speaking more slowly, "but what does that have to do with Joseph being ill?"

"We will get into that, but right now we need you to return this woman to The Hallow as soon as possible."

"I'm not doing anything until someone starts explaining some things here." Alec growled, frustrated that no one was answering his questions. There were times when the other Elders definitely made him feel like the youngest Elder, even though his family seat was third highest among The Brethren. That's why he respected Joseph so much. The Sovereign Elder never made him feel less than the others. "I'm not one of your servants here, Nathanial. And I'm not going to simply disregard what Joseph instructed me to do without first discussing it with him."

"I'm afraid that's not possible," Nathanial replied. "Irina Danchev infiltrated The Hallow two days ago. She has put Joseph under some sort of hypnotic spell."

"And I'm just hearing about this now!" Alec nearly yelled.

"We thought we had the situation handled, but The Hallow's most gifted witches have been unable to break the spell up to this point. It seems Irina's using some sort of black arts spell, one that only she can release him from. Right now, he's barely alive and she refuses to reverse the spell until we bring the woman to her."

"Absolutely not," Alec replied firmly, feeling how deeply he was digging in his heels. There was no way he was letting Irina within fifty miles of Poppy. "I made a promise to Joseph. And spell or no spell, he wanted her kept safe from this warlock at all costs. That is what I'm going to do."

"That cost does not include our Sovereign Elder's life. This is not your decision to make, Elder Lambert, and I suggest you remember your place among this Council," Elder Jacob Hofmann warned him. "I'm sure you don't need to be reminded that as Sovereign Elder, Joseph's life comes before hers—before any of ours."

Warning heard. Alec was outnumbered here, so he would have to handle the situation carefully if he was going to protect Poppy. As a group, the Elder's Council had the power to get what they wanted, but that didn't mean Alec was going to simply roll over. "I understand we need to do everything within our power to save Joseph. I want that, too. But you do not have all the information here. Trusting Irina Danchev to keep her word after handing a defenseless woman over to her is not the solution. She butchered Poppy's mother only weeks ago, and she will do the same to Poppy the minute Irina has her. I will *not* allow that to happen."

"Perhaps Joseph is not the only person this woman is important to," Nathanial offered in a not-so-subtle suggestion.

"Quite frankly, Alec, I'm surprised we're meeting this kind of resistance from you. You certainly know that as a Council we vote on everything. Right now, aside from you, it is unanimous that we do whatever is necessary to save Joseph. As Elders, none of us can base our decisions on those closest to us. It is our sworn duty—and, I will remind you, Joseph's as well—to put the good of The Brethren first."

"I don't need to be reminded of that," Alec replied with a carefully tempered voice. "I am merely suggesting we come up with a better plan instead of bowing to what this warlock wants, or we will end up costing both Joseph and Poppy their lives."

"Alec makes a good point," Owen Maberey began. Owen, though a few years older than Alec, had ascended to Elder the same time as Alec after his father, Callum Maberey, conspired with Reese to create an army of hybrid super soldiers that had so far led to the death of ten Guardians at The Oracle. Alec and Owen had been connected by a shared shame over their families' actions, and Alec was glad to see he had some support from him now. "We've no reason to trust Irina will keep her word after we give her the woman. We then will have lost our only leverage to saving him."

"Give me a better option then, gentlemen," Nathanial pressed. "We've already exhausted several to get us to this point. And while Joseph grows sicker, Irina seems to be one step ahead of us."

"Do you think she has someone on the inside?" Owen asked. "Within The Hallow, perhaps?"

"I don't believe so," Nathanial replied. "At least, no one who has correct information, or she would already be at Alec's doorstep. I still maintain that Joseph's life is not worth sacrificing for some personal vendetta Irina has with this woman. But I agree, we need to deal with her from a position of strength, not weakness."

Alec was relieved to hear that Nathanial was at least being more open to discussion on the matter. Unlike him or Owen,

Nathanial had a lot of influence with the rest of The Council because of his high seat and tenure. "Joseph will go after Irina with the full force of The Brethren five minutes after he discovers she's killed Poppy," Alec informed them. "Irina knows that, too. There is no way she will return Joseph to us alive."

"He won't do that," Nathanial insisted, "because his personal matter is not in the best interests of The Brethren."

"With all due respect, Nathanial, you're wrong," Alec replied. "When I was at The Hallow Joseph told me that in a very short amount of time Irina has managed to become the most powerful warlock out there. And she's not going to stop just because she gets her revenge on Poppy. The Brethren cannot afford to stand by idle while she only gets more powerful. So, yes, it is in The Brethren's best interest to do something about it now."

"Did Joseph say how she's been able to gain all of this power so fast?" Nathanial asked, and Alec felt he was truly listening now. "We know a warlock can take in the essence of a good witch as they are dying, but the power they gain is limited."

"That's the troubling part. He had no idea. But to gain power as fast as Irina has, she would have to be killing good witches at an exponential level."

"What about the Black Arts you mentioned, Nathanial?" Owen suggested. "She must being using that somehow."

"I agree," Nathanial replied, distracted by his current internal thoughts. "And the problem is that the witches at The Hallow cannot use Black Arts without crossing that line into darkness. I'm not sure what the hell we should do, but the more I hear the more I agree with Alec that Irina is not going to simply release her spell from Joseph once she gets what she wants. Her attack on The Hallow was too precise. Absolute. She had been planning it for some time."

"What if we had another option," Alec proposed. "Nathanial, you know I have Sienna Scott and her team here helping me with our Wraith problem. What if we use her team to lead Irina into a trap?"

"Look, I believe Sienna is about the best there is, and without meaning to sound crass, this certainly sounds right up her alley for a good time on a Saturday night. She would volunteer for the assignment in a heartbeat. But Irina's not going to fall for Sienna being Poppy."

"No, not Sienna," Alec replied. "Kane."

"Your Natural Shifter?" Owen questioned. "That just might work."

It would work. As insane as Kane drove Alec sometimes, the man definitely had his uses. As a Natural Shape-shifter, Kane could shift into any form, as long as that form was of reasonably similar size or something he could project larger, like a bear. So shifting into a fly was out of the question, but taking the form of a woman was definitely possible.

"Since Poppy is already here at The Oracle, Kane can get close enough to her to take in her form. He'll then be able to shift long enough to convince Irina we're giving her Poppy. That's when we'll trap her. Sienna and her team can back Kane up, and I can also send Simon Kendrick. He's young, but he's already proven to be our most powerful witch. It's worth a shot if we can save both Joseph and Poppy, isn't it?"

Nathanial seemed to consider Alec's proposal while the other Elders waited for his measured response. "I agree with you, it's worth a shot. But if you're wrong . . . if Irina doesn't fall for it . . . it could mean Joseph's life."

"I'm not wrong," Alec replied. "Kane can do this. I've seen him do it. It's just a matter of whether you trust Sienna and her team to pull off the rest."

"I do, especially with her rare ability to cloak herself. Irina won't even sense she's there until it's too late," Nathanial replied without hesitation. "Very well. Have the team assembled to leave for London within the hour. We'll have a full debrief when they arrive."

Alec nodded. "I'll contact you after they're in the air." He disconnected the SAT and took a deep breath, praying he was right, because both Poppy and Joseph's lives depended on it. He then activated the conference room communication link. "Sampson, find Kane—now!"

***

Poppy had finished up with the last of the lights and decided to venture out for her walk of The Oracle grounds while everyone else was at dinner. She was about to leave through the Lobby doors when she passed a man leaning confidently against the wall, his arms folded in front of him. He was outrageously handsome, with black hair and very unique silver eyes. The kind of handsome women tended to notice after they finished blinking. And given the way he leaned there with a naughty smile on his lips, he definitely knew that was the response his good looks caused.

"Venturing outside?" he asked her.

Poppy would have preferred not to stop, still cautious about her contact with other people at The Oracle, but he kind of pushed from the wall to block her path. "That was the plan. Now if you'll pardon me . . ."

"A bit nippy, don't you think?"

Poppy swung back on him, positive she had not heard him right. "Excuse me?"

"Outside," he clarified. "It's a bit nippy outside."

Poppy furrowed her brow at him, not sure by the sarcastic tone of his voice if he purposely intended that comment to sound so naughty, or not. If the smile he was currently giving her was any indication, it was definitely intended—as in *'I've already pictured every inch of you naked while you were standing here'* kind of intended.

"I'll take that under advisement," she returned, trying to sound unaffected, but she was more than puzzled. There was no denying that this man was a 'stop traffic' sort of good

looking, but he was also strangely odd. Then it dawned on her .
. . "Your name wouldn't happen to be Kane, would it?"

"Heard of me already, have you?" he replied as he slowly
circled around her, his gaze staring her up and down as he did.

"More like warned," Poppy replied dryly.

"*Warned?*   No need for warnings here, darlin'. I'm a
married man now."

"How fortunate for your wife."

He laughed. "Yes, it is. You must be Poppy Honeywell.
Our guest from across the pond. I must say, Alec did not do
you justice in his description of you." That comment certainly
did not make Poppy feel very charitable towards The Elder in
that moment. *What?* Could he not remember how to describe
the women he's kissed thoroughly enough to feel her tonsils?
"Perhaps in another life . . . or an alternate universe . . . you
and I could've had some fun."

Poppy scowled at him. Maya had been right in that Kane
was *'noticeable'* but Poppy didn't remember her mentioning
that he was *noticeably odd.* "Alternate universe? I don't believe
in alternate universes, and you and I getting together is
definitely *not* happening in this one."

"Size six, right?" he continued as he walked around her
again, and now Poppy was so flabbergasted she wasn't quite
sure what to say.

"Seven and a half shoes . . . thirty-eight, twenty-"

"Excuse me?" Poppy cut him off and found herself saying
again for the second time in one conversation, "What is wrong
with you? Do you act this way around all guests who come to
The Oracle? I will mention this to Alec—I mean, Elder
Lambert."

"Damn," he replied quietly, and she thought she heard a
slight animal growl in his voice. "Redhead, even. The man is
done for."

"Who are you talking about?" Poppy asked with frustration
as she gave him her most baleful stare, which evidently wasn't

all that baleful because he was still smiling at her with that same naughty grin.

"Oh, no one," he sighed as he turned without warning to walk away. The man's walk was just as sexy as the rest of him. "Enjoy your evening stroll, Miss Honeywell," he said lightly over his shoulder, and then he added, "Stay on her, Matthias, or you're going to be one sorry Dhampir."

CHAPTER NINE

"You can't be serious!" Poppy exclaimed while standing in front of Maya's mirror the next night, her lengthy five-foot-nine-inch frame barely covered in a tight silver sequined, spaghetti-strap dress that felt like it was about four or five inches too high on her thighs. "I can't go to the party dressed in this. I feel half naked."

"Well, look at it this way," Maya began delicately. "Alec would definitely notice you. And you want him to notice you, don't you?"

"*Alec?* The entire party would notice me in this thing! And I never said I wanted Alec to notice me."

"You're going to the party, aren't you?"

"Yes, because you practically bullied me into it."

"I would do no such thing," Maya defended with her shy smile.

Poppy cocked her hands on her hips. "Well, have you ever worn such a revealing dress to a party?"

"It's in my closet, isn't it?"

"The tag's still on it, Maya." Maya giggled, and Poppy pulled the dress down on her thighs as much as it would allow without ripping the fabric. "And you're at least four inches shorter than me."

"Well, OK, maybe I haven't worn it before. I bought it last year and was hoping to get the courage to wear it for Phinneas when I decided the time was right to . . . you know."

"Maya, you can say '*have sex*'."

"Not around here you can't. There's always someone listening."

Poppy leaned in and whispered quietly. "I'm pretty sure those people are having sex, too."

Maya stared up at Poppy with those huge blue eyes of hers. "I never thought of it that way."

After a moment of silence, both women laughed and Poppy gave her an imploring smile. "Look, I get it. Alec would probably like this dress because he's a man, and this thing leaves very little to the imagination. In fact, I'm pretty sure every man there would like this dress . . . but it's just not me."

Maya sighed. "I know. It was never me, either."

"That would explain why the tags are still on it," Poppy replied. "Let's face it, Maya, we're not the kind of women who do 'in-your-face' sexy. Ours is a more subtle approach. If I admit to you that I wouldn't mind if Alec noticed me—"

"I knew it!" Maya suddenly squealed.

"If I admit it," Poppy restarted, ". . . then I want *Alec* to notice me. Not every man at the party. There is a difference. Understand?"

"I do, and I might have just the thing," she replied with enthusiasm racing through her eyes. "Wait right here." Maya ran to her closet and thumbed through several hangers before pulling out a white zip up garment bag near the back. She set aside two dresses before holding one up in front of her. "I bought this a few months ago and haven't worn it. I loved the color 'cause I thought it worked well with my eyes, but it didn't quite fit me right. I always meant to return it, but never got around to it."

The dress was beautiful. Simple, yet elegant. It was one of those tailored, shirt-styled dresses with a wide collar and delicate cap sleeves, but dressy and sleek, with lavish silver-blue silk that would forgive nothing where it formed on a woman's figure. *Heavens*, Poppy hoped she didn't have anything to forgive. Small, crystal buttons lined the front and sparkled in the light. As she held it up to herself, the length showed just the right amount of leg to entice. "It's perfect, Maya!"

Maya clapped her hands together excitedly. "Well, let's get you ready then. The party starts in just a couple of hours."

***

A little more than two hours later, Poppy inhaled a deep breath before stepping under the sparkling lights of the transformed dining hall, glittering with garlands, immaculate table settings and loads of food and drink. *Why in the world did she agree to come here?* Standing just outside an enormous hall full of hundreds of people seemed like the most foolish thing in the world to her. She should be safely ensconced up in her room remembering what her mother had sacrificed for her this past year. Yes, she should be remembering that she did not have a normal life. That a powerful warlock wanted her dead for circumstances she had no hand in, and none of that was going to change because she decided it was all right for her to come to this party.

"Are you nervous?" Maya asked, breaking into her thoughts.

Poppy nodded. "Is it that obvious? I haven't been around this many people since . . . well, since ever." She shouldn't be nervous, though, because she was pretty sure no one would recognize her. Maya had done her make-up smoky around her eyes and searched high and wide for some silver, jeweled pumps to wear which made her feel really tall. For jewelry, she simply borrowed a set of silver bracelets that clinked a little on her wrists as she moved. She very much liked the sound.

"You look perfect," Maya said, showing a hint of pride that was also somewhat aimed at herself. "Fashion consultant and make-up artist should be my next career if I never get my Empath gift back."

"It's still there, Maya. I know it is. You're one of the most feeling, empathetic people I've ever met. You can't lose something that's a part of you."

"I hope you're right," she smiled. "I miss it."

"Well, I'm just sorry you've to settle for me as your escort tonight. Simon must have been terribly disappointed he was called away on New Year's Eve."

"He was, but he said his mission was important. He couldn't give me any details, of course. Super-secret stuff," she whispered with a finger over her lips.

"It would have to be for him to miss being with you tonight," Poppy replied as she scanned the large crowd gathered in the huge room. Everyone seemed to be in the holiday spirit, laughing and dancing, but Alec was nowhere to be found. She supposed she shouldn't be too surprised. He had been incredibly busy the past few days with all of his responsibilities as Elder, and she was sure he had a hand in the mission Simon was called away on.

"You going to do fine," Maya murmured to her. "Think of all the time you spent around people the last few days and nothing bad has happened. Just be confident and smile when a man asks-"

A male voice cut off her conversation. "Maya, would you like to dance?"

Poppy turned to see Maya's cheeks flush a bit as a young man extended his hand to her. "OK," she replied with her sweetest smile, and then she winked back at Poppy. "Are you going to be all right here by yourself?"

"I'll be fine. I'm going to get something to drink."

A little while later, Poppy sipped slowly from her second glass of champagne, which tickled her nose even more than the first glass. And despite Alec's continued absence from the party, she was in the mood to celebrate. She was at a party, surrounded by a room full of complete strangers for over an hour, and not a single bad thing had happened. She had even had a couple of invitations to dance, although she turned them down as gracefully as she could because she didn't want to press what little luck she had. Still, she couldn't help but think . . . had Alec been right? Had Irina led her mother to believe she was cursed when she really wasn't?

The last of the champagne bubbles tickled her nose as she finished her glass, suddenly becoming aware that she felt quite light on her feet. "May I have another?" she smiled at the rather attractive man serving drinks behind the bar. He smiled back at her and even engaged her in a little bit of conversation. Poppy decided she must be a little buzzed from the champagne because she couldn't seem to stop laughing. She laughed at everything, and suddenly she realized she was happy. Tonight she didn't feel hunted. She was a woman enjoying a holiday party. It all felt so normal.

"Poppy!" Maya called just then, and when Poppy turned around to find her friend she ran smack into another woman who was passing by, knocking both of their glasses out of their hands and directly down the right side of Poppy's dress. The woman appeared completely startled, as if she had never witnessed someone spilling a drink before—and she probably hadn't. Poppy sensed immediately that the other woman was a Dhampir. Only apparently, *she*, like every other Dhampir on the planet, had some agility and grace.

After both women exchanged apologies, Poppy stared down at her dress and sighed. Unfortunately for her, champagne did not come out of silk. So much for looking pretty, she now looked ridiculous, and her human side was starting to feel a very real chill from her wet dress. "What happened?" Maya asked her.

"Oh, I spilled champagne all down the front of your dress. I think I better go upstairs and change into something less . . . wet."

Maya giggled. "Do you want me to come with you?"

"No, you should stay here at the party. If it's all right with you I'll just slip into your blue dress and come back down."

"Hey, there always the silver, strappy number," Maya teased.

"Yeah. No."

Maya laughed. "Come find me later."

Poppy headed off through the lively crowd, trying to avoid brushing past people as she exited. She nearly made it to the entry doors when she stopped to make room for a couple to past her and felt a large hand come over her low back.

Swinging around, her breath caught for a moment as she faced Alec standing there with a very quiet expression on his face. "Going somewhere?" he asked, and Poppy realized she had turned herself in his arms, with his hand remaining at her low back. "It's still early, and I haven't had a chance to hear how The Oracle's honored guests has fared over the past few days."

Her hands came up quite naturally to his arms, feeling his firm muscles under her palms. They stood, interlinked with each other, like a couple about to dance. "I've fared well . . . No major mishaps, which I'm sure my shadow Matthias has reported to you." Alec gave her a smile that said he knew exactly what she was talking about. "And I enjoyed helping with the party."

"I'm glad to hear that. No more hiding in your room."

Poppy wasn't quite sure why, but she squeezed her hands over his shirted arms, a gesture that seemed to warm and brighten the color of his eyes to more of a heated whiskey color under the lights. That, combined with his fine clothing and short, tossed hair, made it hard to notice anything else in the room. "I was on my way upstairs to change."

"I really wish you wouldn't do that," he replied, his fingers stretching over her back, pressing her closer to him with his wide palm that skimmed over the silk. "I like the dress."

Poppy smiled. She couldn't help it. She could hear in his voice that his compliment was very sincere. "Well, thank you, but I spilled champagne all over the front of it."

"I know," he laughed in return. "I saw." She realized that they were slowly swaying to the music and she liked the feeling. She wasn't about to go anywhere. "I think you truly scared Serena there."

"The Dhampir . . . Has she never had someone spill a drink on her before?"

Alec laughed harder. "No, probably not." Poppy frowned with a partial smile, having to live down the embarrassment of the fact that she was just plain clumsy. "I can only stay a little while to enjoy the festivities. I'd really like you to stay, if you're not too cold?"

"I'm sure I'll survive," she smiled at him in return, feeling strangely giddy inside about the notion that he didn't mind dancing with a woman in a wet dress. He then removed his dress coat and wrapped it around her. The coat was a very fine double-button cut, lined in something super soft that made her just want to sigh. He pulled her close against him and she felt the tremendous heat radiating from his body. That was something she loved about human men. How their bodies always felt so warm compared to hybrids.

"Better?" he asked.

She nodded and tipped her head against his shoulder as they continued to sway in each other's arms. "I wasn't sure you were coming down tonight."

"Were you looking for me, Poppy?"

"I . . . ," she began and then restarted herself, realizing in that moment she was perhaps getting a little too carried away by a sense of familiarity between them. She reminded herself that she and Alec still knew very little about each other, despite her heart sometimes wanting to tell her differently. "I was just curious about whether you join everyone for celebrations like this, what with you being Elder and all."

"What? And miss all these wonderful lights you managed not to crush under your shoe?" He laughed again, a very quiet laugh that felt as if it were just between them.

"Very funny. I'll have you know I didn't-" Poppy was about to say 'didn't break any', but Alec was arching his blond brow as though he knew that she was about to lie. ". . . I only broke a few sets."

"That sounds about right," he replied. "I wanted to come down to the party sooner, but I have a couple of things I'm juggling tonight."

"Hopefully nothing too serious. I heard about Simon being called away."

"Nothing I can't handle," he replied as their feet began to move with the swaying and Poppy realized he was now leading her to one side of the hall. "I'm afraid I still have some things to wrap up later, though."

"Ah, I know that line well."

Alec lifted his brows curiously. "I do have things to finish."

"No, I didn't mean it like that. I've just heard that often from Joseph. Its code for you have a team in place and ready to move and you need to be there to monitor the situation."

He laughed again and she decided she loved the sound of Alec Lambert's laugh. "Something like that." The slow pace of the music ended just then, replaced with a much faster beat that didn't seem to fit the moment between them. Poppy let Alec lead her outside the hall to a quieter, more private corner of the lobby where one of the three Christmas trees for The Oracle were decorated. This one wasn't quite so ginormous, only about fifteen feet high, but it was actually her favorite tree, trimmed in reds and golds. And though they had escaped to a more private area, they definitely had company.

"Are you ever alone?" she asked him sincerely as she nodded towards Sampson and Matthias who stepped into place in front of them with their backs to them.

A momentary glint passed through his eyes, something between sadness and surprise. "You should know the answer to that as well, from observing Joseph."

"I guess, I do," she replied with a sigh. "And it makes me sad for the both of you. This isn't like some four-year Presidential term. It will be this way for you for the rest of your life."

"Yes," he confirmed without hesitation.

The music and conversations of the hall seemed to disappear just then as Alec leaned forward 'til she felt his breath on her lips and a wall pressing at her back. "I know I promised I wasn't going to kiss you," he murmured, "but I should give you fair warning that I'm going to break that promise tonight."

Poppy shook her head as she stared up at him. "You must keep your promise to me." For a moment he looked as if he wasn't quite sure what to say until she slid her hand behind his neck and pulled him to her lips with a smile. "But I never promised you anything."

What followed was a kiss that, even though she had been the one to initiate it, had completely caught her off-guard. That was because kissing Alec Lambert required no effort, no thought, just the ability to feel. Once she made contact he took over, his lips teasing with spine-tingling efficiency, his tongue reaching for hers as he tipped her head back. A hot shiver ran through her entire body when his hand slid under his jacket around her and the heat of his body jumped into hers. No longer was she wet from the champagne because with one kiss he had steamed her dry from the inside out. No longer did she care that they had two guards standing right behind them who could hear exactly how heated their exchange was becoming. All she cared about was feeling more.

Soon she heard Alec's open palm slam against the wall behind her before he turned his head and deepened their kiss. His other hand, previously preoccupied with feeling along the curves of her body under his coat around her, curled on the outside of her thigh and lifted it from the floor, forcing Poppy to grab around him for balance as he pressed her against the wall. She felt breathless, boneless, and utterly desirable when it came to this man. How had all of this happened so fast? Absolutely, she shouldn't be doing this. She knew what she was risking with the threat of Irina's curse, but he tasted like champagne and berries, and it brought a smile to her lips knowing he was with her at a party, relaxing with the people around him, not feeling the pressure of all those he was responsible to for just a little while.

Her hands fell and slid across his low back. Alec responded immediately, his hips jerking forward with a growl. "Touch me, Poppy," he whispered in a voice so rough it was almost unrecognizable, dragging his lips over her jaw and then down to her throat.

Oh, please, never let this end.

"Sir?"

At the word, Poppy blinked her eyes open to see Alec pull back from her with swollen lips, a heaving chest and a glassy gaze—a gaze that went sharp with awareness in two blinks before turning to their intruder. "Gideon, I have repeatedly asked you not to call me sir."

"Yes, but I thought you might like to know Nathanial Hawking and Jacob Hofmann have just arrived."

The happy and relaxed sound in Alec's voice died in an instant, replaced with one that was cold with authority. "They're here? At The Oracle?"

"Yes. Just. They are waiting for you in your office, but I think you should know, they have two guards currently mingling throughout the party." Gideon nodded around the corner to one of the men searching through the hall. He hadn't spotted them yet because they were outside the hall, but it was only a matter of time.

Alec swung back around to Poppy and she could see a wall had gone up within him just that quickly. Any trace of the gentle, open man underneath was pushed behind the focused leader that was now at the forefront. He shoved her not-so-gently toward Gideon, keeping her out of sight of the guard. "Take her out the back, and stay out of sight until I call you," he said in the lowest possible whisper. "Don't tell me where you're taking her. Understand?"

"Alec, what's going on?" Poppy asked him, completely confused. "I want to stay here at the party."

He leaned in close and spoke low at her ear. "Go with Gideon, Poppy."

"Why?" she demanded, though there was clear worry within her voice. "Has something happened with Irina? Has she found me?"

Alec's eyes flashed as if it just occurred to him that he might be scaring her. "No! I promise you she has not found you." At her hesitant expression he shook her gently. "Trust yourself. What're your Dhampir instincts telling you? Can you feel Irina near?"

Poppy took a couple of deep breaths. "No. No, I don't sense her. But then why—?"

Alec didn't wait for her to finish, motioning her to put her arms through his coat she was wearing. When she was wrapped up he said to Gideon, "Go. Now!"

"But Alec—"

It was too late. Alec had rushed off towards the hall, immediately shifting the searching guard's attention towards him. Before she knew what was happening, Gideon had pulled her all the way down the back corridor and out the exit door into the cold night, having no idea where he was taking her or why.

CHAPTER TEN

Alec was cursing himself the entire way back up to his office. Sampson and Matthias were right behind him, while two guards that had come with Nathanial and Jacob remained downstairs searching through the party. Alec knew the guards were searching for Poppy. He was just damn lucky Gideon had warned him in time so he could get Poppy out of there before Nathanial's men had spotted her.

Alec burst into his office to find the two Elders seated in lounge chairs, already availing themselves of his liquor cabinet. He wished he could demand, *"What the fuck are you doing here?"* but Alec had to keep his temper in check, play his hand carefully if he was going to protect Poppy. "Gentlemen, I'm surprised to see you here. I thought the plan was for you to be in London when our operation goes into motion tonight. If you'd given me notice you were coming, I would have sent a team to meet you."

Nathanial, an extremely tall man with a disproportionately large nose and silvering hair, arose from his chair. "The plan has been altered," he began, in rough English. "The Council thought it best we observe the operation from here."

"For what reason?" Alec suspected he already knew the reason, but he wanted to hear it confirmed by their currently highest ruling leader.

"On the chance our mission does not succeed tonight, which we are all hoping is not the case."

"We are in agreement on that," Alec replied, trying to stall for some time to figure out how to get Poppy out of the middle of this mess.

Nathanial poured himself another glass of brandy, swirled the snifter in his hand, then added, "Elder Maberey is handling the operations in London. But should the mission fail tonight, we will, unfortunately, have to avail ourselves to the only other course of action left to save Joseph."

"You mean sacrificing Poppy to Irina."

"You know I do. The woman will return with us to London tonight. Whether you want to admit it or not, there's a chance this mission will fail. If that happens . . . well, let's just say it's an option I'm not willing to let go of."

Alec ground his teeth against his jaw. "I see. So you come to my facility with your guards—on a night my people are celebrating—to take custody of a woman who has no idea she is about to be a sacrificial pawn to the woman who has hunted her her entire life?" Alec was now right in Nathanial's face. "After I've said I won't allow that. Is that about right?"

"I think you will remember your place, Elder Lambert," Nathanial replied evenly. "And what's at stake here."

Alec crossed his arms in front of him. "I know what's at stake—and I know the promise I made to Joseph. I'll not go back on my word to him—that I would protect her. And if that means protecting her from my own Council, then so be it."

Nathanial's brows slashed at him in warning. "I expected resistance from you, but not defiance. You are walking a very thin line here." Alec stood tall, refusing to back down even an inch. Poppy's life was a stake here. As an untrained Dhampir she would have no chance once she was turned over to Irina. "Tell me, Alec . . . Have you informed this woman what has happened to Joseph?" Alec didn't respond because he knew exactly where Nathanial was going—and he didn't like it one bit. "My guess is, no," Nathanial continued, "even though it would be your duty to inform her regarding something that directly affects both her life and Joseph's. The two guards who knew Joseph had been hiding her at The Hallow agreed, she loved him like a father. If she knew his life was at stake because of her—"

Alec launched forward, getting right in the Nathanial's face. "You'll not put what's happening to Joseph on her! What

Irina's doing is of her own volition—her own making." The display of unfettered anger was a critical mistake on Alec's part. Both Elders would see that as weakness and use it to their advantage. Mentally, he believed himself to be smarter than the emotions tearing away at him. "She's innocent in all of this— merely another way for Irina to sate her appetite for revenge that will never be satisfied. Yet you expect her to sacrifice herself without thinking twice about it."

"Yes, I do," Nathanial replied. "And I'm willing to bet, so will she. Once she's told the truth about what has happened to Joseph. That's really what's bothering you, isn't it? That you know I'm right."

"What's bothering me," Alec growled with irritation, "is that once again this organization—which claims to be good and righteous—is putting itself before the life of an innocent. They're all innocents until it goes against serving our purpose. Then they are just expendable." Alec meant every word he said, but he also had little doubt that Poppy would sacrifice herself to save Joseph. She might do it even if their trap for Irina worked, because she would see it as sparing anyone else she cared about from Irina's wrath.

"Save your speeches for Council. See how far they get you. Right now they are of no use to me. This woman will return with us tonight one way or another."

Just then, Sampson entered the room. You could literally cut the tension among all of them with a knife. "Sir, the SAT feed is ready in the conference room and Kane is on standby."

Alec stared back at both Elders with a calm hatred he wasn't quite sure he'd ever felt with his peers in such a heated moment. "At least we can agree, Gentlemen, if we do our jobs tonight there will be no need for Poppy to go anywhere. So let's focus on that, shall we?"

Without a reply, Nathanial and Jacob left for the conference room, while Alec followed behind and tried to bite back his anger and anxiousness for the possibility that he could fail Poppy this night. Fail her because he could do no more than watch everything unfold in front of him—which was a position he hated.

When someone's life was at stake he wanted to be on the front lines. He wanted to be the one who directly controlled the outcome of a fight. It's what made him a Guardian in his soul, but he was destined to be a leader. On days like this he felt like the world somehow had his role backwards.

So, he would be damned if this mission would fail tonight. He would save Poppy Honeywell and see her live to have a normal and happy life, as Joseph wanted. But he wouldn't allow himself to get any closer to her. He wanted her to live, and those around Alec—around The Brethren—mostly died.

CHAPTER ELEVEN

"You're bringing me to a chapel?!" Poppy questioned Gideon as they rushed up to the entry of the small stone building near the edge of Oracle property at the base of the mountains. The quaint but unassuming building was tucked beneath an endless cluster of trees, making it easy to miss if you weren't looking for it. Gideon pulled her through the chapel's doors, then turned and searched the dark path behind them for anyone who might be following, which was sort of laughable when you considered he was an aging human man with deteriorated hearing and sight and Poppy was a Dhampir.

"Right now, this is the safest place to bring you," he answered her. "Can you hear anyone behind us?"

Poppy pulled Gideon fully inside. "We need to keep moving. They picked up our trail and are not far behind." She took a look at the small, modest chapel interior, noting its wooden pews and candlelit interior. "Although, I have no idea where you expect to hide in here."

"This way," he said, pulling her towards the front. "There's a door up there to the left. Go through there and down the stairs. Hurry."

Poppy did as he instructed, but after making her way down the stairs she asked, "Why are we running from the Elders' guards? I don't understand any of this." She had recognized immediately the names of the two Elder's that Gideon had told Alec about.

Gideon Janes now wore an even more perplexed expression than when he'd informed Alec about the guards . . . and that was not comforting. "The Elders are here to take you back with them to London."

Poppy's whole expression brightened as she reached the bottom of the stairs and swung back to face him. "Has Joseph asked for me to be sent back?" she asked, but then frowned as she realized that didn't make any sense. "Wait. Why wouldn't he contact me himself?"

Gideon touched her arm gently and continued to press her along what looked to be a newly constructed underground passageway. "Miss Honeywell, Alec doesn't want you to leave with these Elders. But Nathanial, being of a higher family rank, has the power to override him. So he's counting on me to get you to someplace where their Dhampir guards cannot detect you. I'm imploring you as courteously as I can to keep moving."

Poppy wasn't sure what to believe, but right now she trusted only two people in this world, Joseph and Alec, and she wasn't even sure when she had come to trust Alec so much. She hadn't known him for long, but from the first moment she awoke on the plane she had seen in his actions that he was concerned for her wellbeing. He brushed aside any risk he was taking on to himself by protecting her. She felt safe with him.

Her Dhampir sensitivity having kicked in when she realized the gravity of the situation, Poppy heard footsteps coming from upstairs just inside the front doors of the chapel. She turned to Gideon and placed a finger over her lips as she pointed to the floor above them, signaling to him that they were no longer alone. A few more steps and they reached a giant, metal door that looked nearly impossible for even a Dhampir to break through. Gideon stepped forward and entered a fifteen digit code . . . at least Poppy was pretty sure she counted fifteen.

"Down here!" one of Nathanial's guards called at the top of the stairs.

"Gideon, hurry," Poppy implored as the enormous door began to swing open on its own, because it was too big and too thick for anyone to move it. They squeezed through as soon as the opening was big enough but then had to wait anxiously for the door to open fully and begin to close back up behind them.

"Hurry," One of the guards called. "It's closing!"

Poppy grabbed onto to Gideon's shirt and recalled the memories of what it felt like to be constantly on the run. Even in the few days she had been here she had grown comfortable with not having to look over her shoulder every minute. That was a luxury she could not afford if she wanted to stay alive, and moments like this reminded her of that.

One of the guard's arms came into view through the door opening. The guard tried to use his weight and strength to hold the door from closing fully, but nothing was going to stop this door that looked like it was out of a futuristic Sci-Fi movie. The guard was forced to snatch his hand back just as the giant mass of metal slammed closed.

Poppy fell back against the door, closed her eyes for a moment while she collected her thoughts, and then looked back to Gideon. "Why doesn't Alec want me to go back to The Hallow?"

"We need to keep moving," he responded, avoiding her question by turning and moving them down a corridor. As they entered the long hall, lights flickered on above them until she could see an entire row of glass-fronted medical labs. Everything was high-tech and state-of-the-art, in complete contrast to the rustic, old chapel built above them.

"Gideon, what is this place?"

"These are Oracle labs that have recently been renovated into a medical facility for treating Hybrids. We need to stop in here and pick up something before we move on, but we must be quick about it."

Poppy didn't really understand the need to be quick. Where, exactly, was there for them to go? "Wait," she said, grabbing Gideon's arm. "The guards are speaking into some sort of comm. link." Poppy listened to the voices coming through the device at the other end. The first one she didn't recognize, but the second she definitely did. Elder Nathanial Hawking, whom Poppy had met through Joseph, was ordering Alec to give him the code to the door. At first, Alec didn't respond, and she realized he was taking a great risk to protect her by defying the other Elder, and she didn't understand why he was doing it. Joseph would never expect that from him. Which begged the question in her mind: why was Joseph allowing any of this to happen in the first place?

There was a long pause before she heard Alec say, "The first five digits are . . ."

Poppy jerked her head up to Gideon. "Alec's giving them the code to the door."

Gideon nodded quickly. "He would have no choice. He's just trying to stall for time."

"Stall? We're trapped in here, Gideon. It's not going to matter once they have that code."

Gideon pulled her into an office at the end of the hall and went to a locked cabinet. After he entered the code for the lock, he pulled out a box about the size of a small shoebox. "I have a way to get us off the property, but first we're going to need this," he said pulling out a black velvet box and opening it to show a beautiful, heart-shaped ruby necklace.

Poppy reverently touched the truly stunning jewel with the tip of one index finger. "It's beautiful, but a jeweled necklace is hardly going to help our situation here. And Irina can track me off the property, can't she?"

Gideon nodded. "But we're going to change that. Put this on." Poppy placed the jewel around her neck, noticing that the incredible stone appeared partially hollow inside—with some sort of dirt moving through the center of it. "The jewel contains sacred ground," Gideon explained. "Once we leave the property, this will help blur you to other supernatural beings in the outside world, including Irina. For a little while, at least."

Poppy's head turned back towards the lab's entrance. "They've almost got the combination. Thirteen . . . fourteen . . . fifteen," she said as she mentally counted the number of clicks they entered onto the keypad. "They got the combination!"

Poppy was standing there, breathing hard, pretty sure she was about to burn a hole right through the wall back towards the front of the lab, when she heard one of the guards say over the comm., "It won't open! He gave us the wrong code."

"What's happening?" Gideon asked.

"The door won't open. Alec must have given them the wrong code."

A hard frown pulled over Gideon's brow as he stared at her for a long while. "He wouldn't give them the wrong code. He wouldn't lie."

"Well, he just did. How else do you explain it?"

"Actually, I'm beginning to suspect something altogether different." Gideon pulled her back into the hall. "This way," he said. "Let's get you out of here."

***

"I don't have time for games, Alec," Nathanial began sternly. "Give my men the correct code."

Alec met Nathanial's hard gaze straight on. "That was the correct code. Perhaps your guards didn't enter it right." Alec grabbed a pen and piece of paper, scratched down the code he had just verbally recited and shoved it at Nathanial. "There's the code. Spend your time punching in codes if you like, but we have an operation to focus on—and Joseph's life is at stake. Kane and Sienna *will* succeed. And when they do, will you really want to explain to Joseph how you spent your energy attacking the one person he wanted most protected through all of this?"

Nathanial was glaring at Alec when Sampson interjected, "Sienna Scott is calling in."

Without ever removing his gaze from Alec, Nathanial hit the communications link to his guards. "Stand down for now, but remain outside that door. Poppy Honeywell is not to leave those labs. Understood?"

"Yes, sir," came the reply.

Nathanial then nodded to Sampson to bring up the visual satellite feed that was linked to their communications link at the ground. He was able to zoom in from space above the open, rough grassland of Bodmin Moor in Cornwall, England where the meeting with Irina was set to take place. Alec and the others would all be able to monitor what was happening from the conference room. "We will discuss your actions with regard to Miss Honeywell after this mission is complete," Nathanial added to Alec, but kept his head facing the screen.

"I look forward to the discussion," Alec replied easily, revealing an unobserved, tiny smile.

"Are we going to do this thing, or what?" Kane questioned the Elders on the other end just before he grunted out his next breath.

Sienna appeared beside him out of thin air and dropped the elbow with which she had just wedged Kane with to her side. "Focus, Kane," she said, flashing one of those tight, little smiles of hers.

"I hate when you just show up out of nowhere like that," he grumbled in reply.

"Well, get over it. Irina's just beyond that hill to the west of us. She came alone. I don't sense anyone else nearby, human or hybrid."

"Did she sense *you*?" Kane asked her, as if to point out the more important question.

Sienna scowled at him. "What do you think this is, amateur hour. Of course she didn't."

"It's surprising she would come with no backup," Simon remarked, "especially since she had to be expecting The Brethren would send a team."

"No, its not," Kane replied quietly. "That's how the most dangerous beings warn you. They show you they have no fear. You'd do well to remember that."

"I'll keep that in mind," Simon replied, the tension between the two men easily readable.

"Let's stay focused," Alec reminded them over the comm.

"She's waiting for us," Sienna added. "She knows we're here." Using hand signals, she motioned her team to spread out wide to each side of them into a flanking position, then looked to Kane and Simon. "Are you ready?"

Kane removed his clothes and dropped his head forward, his fit, muscled body starting to shake as he transitioned into a startlingly accurate rendition of Poppy right in front of them. Even Alec had to admit he would be fooled, and that the naked female body Kane was now mimicking was exactly how Alec had imagined Poppy's toned body to look underneath her clothes.

Beautiful.

Sienna handed Kane a dress from one of her men's packs. "How long can you hold her form?"

"For hours, as long as I'm not exerting too much energy. I can't mimic her voice, though. It's not going to take Irina long to figure out something's up if I don't speak."

"All we need is thirty minutes," Sienna answered confidently as she cloaked herself again and disappeared from view of everyone.

Kane nodded to Simon. "You ready?"

Simon nodded in return. "Let's do this."

Alec checked his watch. It was 10:45 p.m., which meant it was 5:45 a.m. their time. Sienna and the team needed to move quickly, for as the sun rose the Dhampirs would lose their superior night vision, the one critical advantage they had over Irina right now.

"Proceed, Sienna," Nathanial ordered. "Keep everything to exactly as we discussed.

"You got it," she replied, and it was obvious from the apparent direction her voice came from, her cloaked form was already way out ahead of everyone as the team climbed over the hill. As Alec watched, Kane walk forward, he had to remind himself that it wasn't Poppy; that she was here and tucked away safely by now with Gideon.

The team approached the lone woman who was now standing at the top of the bluff. Irina Danchev looked nothing like the person Alec had imagined. She was an older woman who still displayed striking features that made it easy to see why Charles Honeywell III would have found her so attractive in her youth. Long, black hair that should be showing numerous signs of gray was, instead, flawless in its solid color. Shapely red lips, the color of blood, jumped out on her pale face. And her equally pale green eyes had almost a lighted glow about her as she stood there in the hour before the break of dawn.

Several dozen swords, lances and arrows were spread all around her feet at the ground. The display of such heavy weaponry was meant to intimidate their team. Alec knew his team was well trained on how to handle these kinds of situation, but it still gave him pause. "Simon," Alec said into the comm., quietly. "That's a lot of weaponry for one woman to get out there by herself. Be prepared for anything."

Simon blinked his eyes once, slowly, communicating to everyone in the room that he understood, while Alec suddenly had a bad feeling Irina was even more dangerous than any of them had realized.

Irina's gaze focused immediately on Kane, or rather, Kane as Poppy. "It's been too long, Poppy. The last time we were together you showed commendable effort in fighting me. Too bad it wasn't enough to save your whore of a mother."

What. The. Hell.

Alec sat there in his chair with his hands clenching the edge of the table. Joseph had told him Poppy was not there the night Irina had killed her mother. The revelation that not only had she been there but also had witnessed her mother being brutally tortured suddenly made sense and explained the introverted behavior Joseph had mentioned, and he himself had witnessed a few times since she had been at The Oracle.

Kane responded to the new information better than Alec had. He attempted to yank himself away from Simon's firm grip, as if he were conflicted by emotions of fear and fight. That brought a smile of satisfaction to Irina's lips. "Oh, all is not lost, dear. But I am pleasantly surprised at how willing The

Brethren is to trade your life. They've no reason to trust that I will keep my word and awaken Joseph from his dreams."

"You *will* keep your word," Simon warned her as he yanked Kane back towards him for dramatic affect.

"Don't overplay it, Simon," Alec whispered to himself.

"You'll not get ten feet closer to Poppy without having the full force of The Brethren bearing down on you. You're smart enough to know—despite your power—that's not something you want."

Irina simply raised a brow at Simon. "Such arrogance for one so young. Are you so certain I fear the full force of The Brethren?" Irina then lifted her open palms out to each side of her and whispered a few words under her breath. A dozen or so weapons on the ground elevated to the level of her hands right before she whipped her palms forward. As she did, the weapons blasted towards Simon and the rest of the team like exploding projectiles. Several of them dove to the ground just out of the weapons path, while one team member was struck just shy of his heart, sending him crashing, and severely wounded, to the ground.

Simon and Kane regained their feet, now shielded from taking any more direct hits by an invisible energy shield that suddenly surrounded them. Simon lifted his hands and turned them in front of him as he controlled the energy that was molding around them, protecting them from further harm. He began to chant a spell in a language Alec did not recognize and enlarge a part of the shield with his other hand to literally jump through the air and cover the rest of the team.

"Your witch has impressive power," Jacob Hoffman commented as they continued to watch the events unfold on the screen.

"Why do you think I sent him," Alec replied evenly, but even he had to admit he was impressed with the power Simon was currently displaying against Irina. Her expression morphed into rage as she spouted off another spell in what he guessed was Bulgarian. A circle of fire was drawn along the grassy moor until it closed up around Kane. The fire grew higher around Simon's shield and eventually burned through it, drawing hot flames closer to Kane. Simon, under significant stress and strain to himself, continued to keep the shields around Kane and the team.

"Bring her to me!" Irina yelled. "She owes me. She carries her father's blood—her father's gifts. And now it's time for her to repay me."

"Repay you how?!" Sienna demanded as she cloaked back into view right behind the Bulgarian woman, catching Irina off-guard and pulling the warlocks hands tight behind her back. "By killing her and stealing her essence? She's an un-practicing witch. She has no power to steal."

Irina turned her head slowly over her shoulder, as if unconcerned by the fact that Sienna had just surprised and bested her. "That is a neat trick, young one. Something I could use . . ."

Alec came to his feet and walked toward the screens that were revealing the battle scene. His instincts were pricking at him that something was wrong.

"You think this is simply about killing a witch?" Irina laughed, wickedly, her eyes reflecting the orange of the flames around Kane. *"Omnia mors aequat!"*

"Latin," Sienna replied, tugging harder at Irina's arms as she spoke in her ear. "Death makes all things equal."

"Very good. What I covet is infinitely higher than death. A force beyond the boundaries of the supernatural world. And she's the key."

"Simon, drop the shields," Alec ordered firmly. "Hold Irina here and get Sienna away from her. Do not let her leave Bodmin Moor."

"Alec, what are you doing?" Nathanial questioned. "The plan was—"

"Something's wrong," Alec insisted. "We're missing something."

Kane remained completely calm within the circle of fire that trapped him, even though the extreme heat had to be making it more difficult for him to hold Poppy's form. Simon responded by nodding once towards Sienna's team and then dropped the protective shield from around two of the Dhampirs. They made a well-timed move towards Sienna and Irina, but Irina was able to hold the circle of fire around Kane with the focused energy of her mind while simultaneously launching another round of weapons at them. She appeared completely unafraid of being outnumbered and for all intensive purposes, also being strapped down by Sienna.

"Simon, now!" Sienna called.

Upon hearing his name, Simon once again recited a spell in a language no one recognized. The ring of fire around Kane began to harden until it was nothing more than a frozen ring of ice. He then used his foot to kick at the ice, shattering it into thousands of pieces that dropped harmlessly to the ground.

"You think you can challenge me, young witch?" Irina hissed, and the rage inside her radiated as truly ugly as she glared at Simon. "I'll show you what real power is about." With another chant, Sienna's body was suddenly jolted into the air and then slammed back down against the rocky ground, flat on her back. Sienna tried to engage her cloaking ability, but a shield of energy instantly came around both her and Irina. "Oh, no you don't," Irina challenged her. "You're not going anywhere with that neat little trick."

Sienna suddenly cried out, which shocked everyone back at The Oracle because they knew how strong Sienna was. She never cried out in pain. But a line of blood had begun to draw down along her chest underneath her shirt and Alec realize Sienna's chest was being flayed open right in front of them.

"Stop!" Simon yelled with a rough voice. "Do you want to make the exchange or leave here empty handed?!"

Irina then took a step forward within the circle of energy she created, giving pause to the tremendous pain Sienna was under. The fight remained in Sienna's eyes, but she couldn't move a muscle as she lay there pinned against the ground under Irina's control. "So Poppy's life is not worth this girl's life and that of your Sovereign Elder. You are all such fools."

"Why?" Simon challenged her. "Why should The Brethren not hesitate to trade this witch, who means nothing to us, for their Sovereign leader?"

Simon was going off script and had apparently hit a bulls-eye with his question because Irina simply ignored it and slid her gaze to Kane. "Shall we find out—together? Bring her forward."

Simon nodded for Kane to take several steps forward. When Kane reached the halfway point and stopped, Irina closed her eyes and began chanting once again. A few moments later, Nathanial received a phone call from Joseph's guards confirming that he was awake, groggy but awake. The room cheered, except for Alec. "Have the witches secure him inside a protection spell," Nathanial ordered. "Your plan worked, Alec!"

In a low, quiet voice Alec replied, "I don't think so."

"It is done," Irina declared as she surrounded Kane with another shield. "Come, come, dear. Time to go." Kane began to walk forward, and Irina's victorious smile fell into an uneasy one as she watched his stride slow into a lazy stalk. All those watching in the conference room could see it in her face. In that moment she realized she was tricked, even before Kane's form changed. "I ain't going anywhere, darlin'."

"Nooo!" Irina shouted, just before a thunderous boom popped through the dawning sky like a crack of thunder, followed by a white ball of light exploding all around them. It was so bright that everyone watching from the conference room had to turn away or else be blinded by the sheer brightness of it.

"Kane, what's happening?!" Alec shouted.

CHAPTER TWELVE

"What is this place?" Poppy asked, nearly tripping off her feet as she crossed the threshold of the quaint, one-room cabin. Luckily, she managed to catch herself just before she did a rather ungraceful face-plant right into the rustic wood floor. But Gideon had definitely noticed and appeared concerned, showing an extremely scrunched expression across his brow.

"This is the old Headmaster's quarters that came as part of the deed to the property," Gideon answered. "No one's lived here for thirty years, but it's used periodically by the staff. I doubt Nathanial even knows it's here." Gideon then walked over to Poppy and placed a gentle hand under her arm to support her. "You're tired."

Poppy nodded, hating to admit such an embarrassing thing. She was supposed to be a strong and powerful Dhampir, but after racing across the cold property in a wet dress and high-heeled shoes she definitely felt a little out of sorts. "I'll be fine. I'm just clumsy."

"Dhampirs are not clumsy," Gideon stated in a matter-of-fact tone of voice, as if the very notion was illogical. "It is simply not in their nature. Dhampirs are born in part from vampires, who are gifted with exceptional strength, balance and agility."

"Well, evidently my body didn't get the memo because I've been clumsy all of my life. My mother . . ." Poppy paused for a moment, unsure about whether she wanted to discuss her recently departed mother but deciding there was no harm to finishing her thought, ". . . My mother could have told you some stories that would've had you flat on your back, laughing."

Gideon pulled out a stool and took a seat in front of her, his manner quiet, non-threatening, and very concerned. "You're not clumsy, Miss Honeywell. What you're experiencing right now is fatigue. Not physical fatigue, but more like mental exhaustion." Poppy stared back at him, completely confused as to what he was suggesting. "Do you understand what happened with the door tonight, back there in the lab?"

"Yes," she frowned at him. "Alec bought us more time by giving the guards the wrong code."

Gideon shook his head. "Alec didn't give them the wrong code. He couldn't. If he had the punishment from The Council would've been swift and severe, and he knew that."

"Well then how else do you explain a two-ton door not opening?"

"That's simple. *You* kept the door from opening."

Poppy laughed lightly in response. "Gideon, you're not making any sense. I was standing next to you. I could hardly be there and keeping the door closed at the same time."

"You could with your mind." Poppy was literally speechless, doing nothing more than blinking back at him several times. "Has no one ever explained this to you before? Perhaps your mother?"

"Explained what?"

"You are exuding quite prominent signs of psychokinesis," he answered. "In the human world, it's the ability to affect inanimate objects through mental focus. There have been some published accounts of people with telekinetic abilities, but in the supernatural world it is a much more dynamic and powerful mental gift. One reserved mostly for those with the most power—warlocks."

"I'm not a warlock, Gideon. I'm not even a practicing witch."

"No, you're not a warlock. But I'm familiar enough with the symptoms of psychokinetic exhaustion to recognize it when I see it. You were fine when we entered the lab, but when the guards were trying to come through the door you worried about the door remaining closed—so you focused all your mental energy on that very thought. In doing so, you made your objective happen, blocking the door from being physically opened, once the code had been entered correctly, simply with the power of your mind. But you also expended a great amount of mental energy, which is why you feel so drained and fatigued now."

"Do you know how crazy that sounds? I've never been able to do anything by just thinking about it."

"Actually, I think you have. You just didn't recognize it. After you arrived at The Oracle, Alec asked my opinion regarding one of your episodes of-"

"Clumsiness?" she finished for him. "My clumsiness was bothering him enough that he felt compelled to discuss it with you?"

"Yes. Well, you caught him off guard a bit. He's never seen that characteristic in a Dhampir before, and frankly, neither had I. Alec suspected something else was going on, and Elder Lambert's instincts on such matters are extremely sharp. And after what I witnessed tonight I am quite confident he was right."

"So what's wrong with me?"

Gideon smiled gently. "Nothing is wrong with you. In fact, I believe you may be quite special. You're not a practicing witch, yet somehow your power is strong enough to will things to be done with no incantations or spells—merely your thoughts. That indicates a truly powerful supernatural force at work. The most powerful warlocks, like Irina, have the ability to do this, as well, but they've obtained that power by stealing it from many good witches—in essence, compounding its strength. But for an un-practicing witch to have such power is, well . . . rather remarkable."

Poppy rubbed her forehead, feeling the beginnings of a headache coming on. "I think you've taken a simple incident with a stuck door and misinterpreted it into something that just not possible. I am a klutz—a disaster. Not some mind-powerful witch."

"It's not one incident. You're just misinterpreting what occurs."

Poppy stared up at Gideon intently, truly curious if there could possibly be another explanation for all her unfortunate clumsiness other than bad luck of the draw. "What do you mean?"

"Well, there are many prevailing theories on the basics of witchcraft. But many believe, regardless if a witch's intentions are good, their actions or spells can cause *harm* as well as good. In your case, if you think about something hard enough, you will make it happen—good or bad. Conversely, if you think about something *not happening* hard enough, you may still end up with the same result. Like reaching for some linen tablecloths on the top shelf and focusing really hard on not collapsing the shelves beneath it. For you, it's about where you're expending your mental energy—your focus."

Poppy looked away for a moment, trying just to process what Gideon was saying. "You mean like praying someone won't get into a car accident as they drive away from you?"

Gideon nodded at her with an expression of empathy. "Yes," he replied.

"But I don't want to hurt anyone."

"You don't have to be afraid of this. Now that you understand why these things are happening, you can learn how to control it. We can teach you how to target your mental focus towards the results you want. And when you do that, it's very likely your clumsiness will disappear in time, as well."

Poppy stood up and walked forward towards the only small window in the cabin, which looked out over the lake. She pulled the suit jacket Alec had given her to wear tight around her as a realization started to hit her. "Gideon, are you saying that Alec was right? That I'm not cursed? That Irina lied to my mother??"

"I think that's a far more likely explanation than successfully cursing a true innocent in the womb. As far as I know, that cannot be done, not even by the most powerful warlock in in the supernatural world"

Poppy was trying to control the conflicting emotions swirling around her head. All this time she thought she had been truly, miserably cursed. But Alec had been right. And he'd seen it right from the start. He could see a truth that she couldn't see. "Why?" Poppy asked with frustration. "Why would Irina make me believe this?"

"I'm afraid I don't have the answer for that. But what's important right now is keeping you safe while we teach you how to control your gift. Then we can work on those answers and, hopefully, give you the normal life you deserve . . . or at least normal for the daughter of a Dhampir and a witch."

Poppy was quiet for a long while. She squeezed her hand over the ruby necklace that was keeping her blurred to the outside world. Just the thought of a normal life was more than she ever dared to hope for. "Shouldn't we have heard from Alec by now? I still don't understand why these Elders want me to return to London with them? And why Joseph did not summon me him—" She cut herself off, realizing that, after everything Joseph had done to try and help her, there would be only one reason he wouldn't tell her of his plans himself. He couldn't. She stared back at Gideon. "*Oh, God,* I've been so stupid. Something's happened to him, hasn't it? *Damn it, damn it, damn it,*" she cursed under her breath. "Is it Irina? Did she do something to him?"

Gideon remained silent, as if carefully considering what to say next. To Poppy it seemed he didn't want to tell her or he wasn't sure. And both of those answers terrified her.

"Please don't tell me he's dead," she said with a quiet plea.

"He's not dead," Gideon assured her quickly. "But he's not well. Irina has placed him under some sort of Black Arts spell. She's demanding the Elders deliver you to her in London in exchange for releasing Joseph."

Poppy jumped to her feet and tapped her chest just under her necklace before throwing her arms out wide. "No problem. I'll go with them. Now take me back to The Oracle."

"Alec will never agree."

"I don't care what Alec agrees with! Why's he trying to stop this in the first place? I'll not let Irina hurt anyone else I care about. I can fight her! I understand now that I have a gift that I can use against her."

Gideon walked over to her, his expression sincere and troubled. "You cannot fight her alone. Knowing you have a gift and understanding how to use it are two remarkably different things. It's not like flipping on a switch. You could endanger yourself more by not understanding."

She stared up at him, pleading. "I have to go back. I have to help Joseph. *Please!* He has already sacrificed so much for me. I'll not let him sacrifice his life. And I cannot allow Alec to draw the wrath of the Elders because he's trying to protect me. It wasn't fair of Joseph to ask him to take on so much risk in the first place."

"Let me assure you, Alec can handle himself with the other Elders. He's an Elder by birthright, but he's a leader—exceeding those equal to his station—because he rises to the challenge when things are most difficult. He's doing this to protect you, but also because he knows if you were traded to Irina there would be no reason for her to keep Joseph alive. She would kill you both."

"That might happen," Poppy reasoned. "It might not. But if you don't turn me over to Irina, then Joseph *will* die. I understand Alec wants to keep his promise to Joseph, but I release him from it."

Gideon smiled gently. "I know him pretty well. I don't believe he's doing this just to keep a promise to Joseph."

Poppy fisted her hands at her sides. "Well, then I release him from whatever stubborn reason he thinks he's doing it for! Now, are you going to take me back to The Oracle or do I have to tie you down to that chair and find my own way back?"

Gideon's brows lifted as if he found that idea completely unnecessary. "Truly, Miss Honeywell, I ask that you reconsider this. You're going to have him very upset with me."

"Well, that makes two of us if you don't," she replied as she grabbed his hand and dragged him towards the cabin door.

CHAPTER THIRTEEN

Poppy was standing just outside the Elder's private Library, knowing she was about to do the right thing but still somehow feeling a little anxious. Somewhere on The Oracle grounds, between here and the cabin they just came from, an out-of-breath Gideon was valiantly trying to catch up after Poppy had seen The Oracle come into view and had doubled her sprint speed. In addition, all the way down the long hallway between the elevator and the Library, Matthias had been explaining to Poppy, rather emphatically, that Elder Lambert was not to be disturbed—but she didn't care. She was going to do what was right. And obviously, Matthias and the other guards were not going to resort to force to stop Alec's guest.

"Alec?!" she called loudly as she burst into the plush, gentlemen's-club-type room, which was decorated for the holidays with a roaring fire, festive lights, and even some champagne chilling. What she hadn't expected was to burst into an eerily silent room. She had prepared herself for plenty of disagreeing and yelling, perhaps a curse word or two, but meeting a bunch of stoic, male faces the moment she entered the room caught her off guard.

Alec had been turned towards a large bay window, away from the other two men in the room, when he swung toward her on his heels after hearing her practically torpedo into their presence. The expression on his face was not *at all* happy. Still dressed in his formalwear, (minus the jacket, which Poppy still had wrapped around her—and which one of the Elders seemed to take notice of) Alec's hands were shoved into his pockets and his broad shoulders were being held stiff, obviously clear signs of tension. His hair was even messier than it had been earlier, which told her he had been pulling his hand through it all night long. He walked towards her with a scowl. "What're you doing here?"

Nope, she definitely wouldn't be receiving any more kisses from him anytime soon

Poppy reached her hand out to squeeze his arm before she could think to stop herself. "I came to help."

"Poppy," he warned her in a whispered breath. "I told you to stay with Gideon." Rational or irrational, she found herself irritated that he so refused to let her help. She proceeded to march right past him. Unfortunately, that was also when she proceeded to trip on the carpet and launch herself right into one of the Elders, her palms smacking against his chest so hard he groaned with an audible exhale on impact.

She definitely had a feeling of déjà-vu in that moment.

Removing her hands as quickly as she could, she decided Gideon was right. Knowing about your gift and knowing how to control it *were* two different things. "I'm Poppy Honeywell," she began. "And I want to return with you to London as soon as possible."

"No, you don't," Alec growled, suddenly right behind her and pulling her back toward him.

She whipped around and gave him an ugly expression. "Yes, I do!" It seemed to catch Alec off guard, and then he was even more caught off guard when she swatted him across his shoulder and quietly said to him, "And you should've told me what was happening with Joseph."

"You hate flying!" he countered, ridiculously, as if it were the only thing he could come up with to try and stop her in that moment.

"I'll get over it," she replied as she tried to turn back toward the Elders but Alec wouldn't let her.

"Excuse us," he said, just before he yanked her across the room, well away from Nathanial and Jacob. "Where the hell is Gideon?"

"I imagine by now he's made it back to the building."

Alec sighed and pulled her in close, and the scent of him—
something like the sun mixed with sand and sea—sent her
stomach whirling as he leaned in and whispered, "Joseph's all
right. He's being examined by his doctors now." Poppy felt her
shoulders collapse into him with relief. Since her father had
died before she was born, Joseph was the closest thing to a
father Poppy had ever known. She couldn't bear the thought
that anything would happen to him because of her.

Poppy stared up at Alec, feeling what seemed like dozens
of converging emotions hitting her all at once. "Please, I need
to see him."

Alec frowned hard. "No. I can't let you do this. It's still too
dangerous for you to return to England at this time."

She blinked and shook her head. "What do you mean, *no*?
Alec, I need to see him. I need to see for myself that he's all
right"

"No," he repeated firmly. "Joseph would want you to stay
here."

Poppy was not only about to swat him again, but she was
getting ready to drive a fist into his gut when one of the Elders
behind her said, "She's made her choice to return with us,
Alec. Guards, escort Miss Honeywell down to the vehicles and
see that she's made comfortable before we leave."

"What the hell!" Alec said fiercely as he pulled her behind
him, using himself as a shield between her and the approaching
guards. "You're not taking her. Joseph is fine!"

"We don't know that he's fine," Nathanial replied. "We
don't know if Irina has the power to put him back under that
spell now that she realizes she's been tricked."

"Tricked . . .?" Poppy questioned.

"Yes, Alec had a good plan tonight that worked in getting
Joseph back, but we suffered some casualties."

"Casualties?" Poppy echoed in a more worried voice as she
tugged at Alec's shirt. "The mission tonight with Simon . . .
that was for Joseph . . . because of me? *Oh, God*, are they all
right?"

Alec didn't get a chance to answer her question. "Miss Honeywell, Joseph may still need you," Nathanial added.

"Of course," she said as she tried to come around Alec, but he wasn't letting her go anywhere.

"No!" Alec barked. "Joseph's going to be fine. He or his guards will be calling us any moment to confirm as much. They know this," he added, nodding back to Nathanial and Jacob. "But they want you to leave with them before he has a chance to make that call."

Poppy hesitated for a moment, starting to process the fact that maybe she should wait to hear from Joseph before she went flying back across the Atlantic. "Can I talk to him when he calls?"

"Yes," Alec replied, but then Nathanial's guards grabbed hold of Poppy and pulled her away from Alec. Alec threw the first punch in trying to reach out to her as more guards held him back and Poppy found herself suddenly being dragged out of the Library.

***

"Nathanial, you son of a bitch!" Alec yelled. "Wait for that phone call. Joseph wants her here!" At hearing their leader's angry voice, Sampson and Matthias stormed into the Library and went immediately to Alec, warning Jacob's guards to let him go that second or be dealing with them. They did, but, unfortunately, Poppy had already been rushed out of the room.

"Alec," Nathanial warned. "You know this is what needs to happen. If we bring her to London and Joseph decides to return her to The Oracle, then so be it. But right now my priority and concern is for our Sovereign Elder."

"You could get her killed taking her back to London! Irina will sense you're bringing Poppy right to her!"

"I'm done discussing this with you. If you don't stand down, I will call The Council to an immediate session to discipline your actions here today. Then you'll have zero power to help anyone."

"Don't threaten me," Alec nearly hissed. "You can't have me removed from my seat unless I do something that is considered treasonous to The Brethren."

"And what do you think putting this woman's welfare above that of our Sovereign Elder is?"

"She's an innocent!" Alec roared. "And Joseph will support me on this one hundred percent if you just give him five *goddamn* minutes to call us back!"

Nathanial waved his hand in dismissal as he and Jacob headed for the door. "This discussion's over. We're returning with the woman to London. For all you know, he may want her to be there with him now."

The guards nearly slammed the door to the Library as they followed The Elders out. Alec could feel his heart thundering against his chest and the blood boiling in his veins as he turned to his two most trusted guards. "Matthias, get us a SAT comm. link. We're going to need it. Sampson, I need you to get on that phone and do whatever's necessary to get Joseph on the line and patch him through before that plane leaves the ground. I mean it! I don't care what you have to do."

"Yes, sir," Sampson replied as Alec and Matthias raced out of the Library.

***

Poppy was being hauled down the Elder's private elevator, out one of the back entrances of The Oracle, and into the waiting SUV. The Elder's guards were not hurting her, but they definitely meant business as they moved her towards the vehicle. There was nothing Poppy wouldn't do to help Joseph, especially if he was in danger because of her, but she was starting to ask herself the nagging question *'Am I really doing the right thing?'* And once again, Alec was the reason. He had been so insistent that she should not go with these men, and she did trust him. She just couldn't afford for him to be wrong about Joseph.

"Call ahead. Have the plane fueled and ready," Nathanial announced as he and Jacob met them at the vehicles. "We'll be leaving straight from the tarmac."

"Yes, sir," one of his guards answered.

"Good," he replied and moved to the other side of the vehicle, glancing back at Poppy momentarily as the guard opened the back door to move her in. "You're doing the right thing, Miss Honeywell."

She nodded uneasily and then felt a tug at her side as she turned to see Alec pulling the guard's hand from her arm and inserting himself between them. He gave the guard a lethal stare. "You're riding in front," he commanded as he gently rubbed his thumb along her arm where the guard had been holding her and then eased her into the back seat. "You're not going anywhere," he whispered in her ear before taking a seat beside her.

He looked angry.

No. He looked furious.

But he held her hand so comfortingly in his own that she understood most of that anger was not directed at her. And what was clearly directed at her was his concern, not his anger. At that moment she was really grateful for his presence because she was starting to get nervous. She looked up at Alec with an anxious smile. "I hate to fly," she said quietly.

He squeezed his hand over hers and replied, "I know."

There was just something so familiar about how he said those words. Like he already knew her better than anyone else in the world.

"What are you doing?" Nathanial grumbled at Alec from the other side of Poppy.

"Escorting you back to the plane and seeing that you get off OK," he replied, but there was no kindness in his voice. The vehicle started to move, and Alec glanced back to see Matthias jumping in the back of Jacob's vehicle.

"Come now, Alec. You're trying to throw a wrench into our plans. It's not like you to lie."

Poppy could see Alec's eyes swirling with challenge at The Elder as he replied, "I never said I was seeing Poppy off."

The long, tense ride in the few miles to the landing strip seemed to Poppy to take forever. As they pulled in front of the jet that looked as if it were all gased and ready to go, Poppy could feel her hands tightening in Alec's as her breathing became a little shallower. Nathanial exited the vehicle along, with his guards, and she found herself not wanting to move from her seat.

God, she hated flying.

She stared up at Alec, who was already watching her closely. "Do you have that extra shot Joseph gave you? I think I could use it right about now."

He pulled her close and kissed the top of her head. "No, little flower, I don't. But you're not going to need it."

"I have to go with them, Alec. It's the right thing to do for Joseph."

Alec answered her by stroking his hands along both sides of her face and then holding her head up to face him. "Joseph is fine. And he is strong. He doesn't need you to do this for him."

Poppy felt herself being pulled out the door of the vehicle as one of Nathanial's guards said, "Let's go." She glanced back to see Matthias there, with Alec, at the other side door, shaking his head as a deep frown appeared on Alec's face. Whatever he had planned, it was not happening.

"Come on, Sampson," Alec murmured under his breath.

Poppy stared up at the jet and took a deep breath, knowing she was going to have to suck it up for the next seven to eight hours on a small jet. *Couldn't someone just punch her and knock her out?* Poppy reluctantly walked up the stairs, her stomach starting to twist into more than a few knots. She hadn't even had a moment to say goodbye to Alec, who was being kept at a safe distance by the guards, as Jacob and Nathanial said a final few words to him and then followed behind her. She was just about to cross the threshold onto the plane when she slammed her hand up against the outside of the door and her feet refused to move any farther.

"What's the problem?" Jacob questioned, his voice hard with frustration.

Poppy turned slightly but didn't lift her head, not wanting to see Alec's disappointment at what a coward she was about flying. "I've a fear of flying," she murmured quietly.

"Mist!" Nathanial remarked while shaking his head and covering his eyes. Poppy suspected that he was not talking about the English word for haze, but rather the German word for something not very nice. It was nearly four in the morning by now, and he didn't seem in the mood for this. "How did Alec get you over here in the first place?"

"I was knocked out for most of the trip." She continued to brace herself against the opening, refusing to let herself cross inside. "And I think I'm going to need to be knocked out again before I get on this plane."

"Fine," he growled in reply then nodded to the guard behind her. "There's a tact-kit inside. Grab-"

"Oh, Nathanial?" Alec interrupted from below with a surprising lift to his voice, which Poppy thought strange considering the situation. "You've a phone call. It's Joseph, and he wants to speak with you right away."

Nathanial came back down the steps and grabbed the satellite phone from Alec, who simply crossed his arms over his chest and smiled. "What're you up to?" she heard the Elder hiss at him before he held the phone up to his ear.

Poppy turned around more fully to see Alec watching her as her Dhampir hearing picked up the conversation between Joseph and Nathanial. "I'm going to say this only once, Nathanial, so listen carefully," Joseph began, and Poppy dropped her head in her hands in relief at hearing him sound so strong. "Poppy is *not* to set one foot on that plane. She's to remain there with Alec. *Period.* I'll see you when you arrive here in London."

The connection was terminated and Nathanial, without saying a word in response, simply cleared his throat and looked up at her. "Miss Honeywell, there's been a change in plans."

CHAPTER FOURTEEN

"What were you thinking?!" Alec barked, the tension tight in his shoulders as he swung around on Poppy once they had returned to the Elder's Library at The Oracle. "I told you to stay with Gideon. But noooo, you had to come charging in here and offer yourself up to Nathanial like some sacrificial lamb— *volunteering* to go back to London, where you know Irina is just waiting for you." Alec had been holding his frustration all the way back from the jet, and once he'd gotten past the immediate problem of ensuring that Poppy wasn't going to be unceremoniously carted back to England he evidently was ready to let it fly. "If Joseph had not contacted us in time, there would've been nothing I could've done to stop Nathanial from putting you on that plane."

"I was *thinking* . . .," Poppy started in return, sarcasm dripping from her voice, "I wanted to save the life of a man who's been like a father to me!" She recognized that Alec needed a way to release the exceptional stress she could see he'd been under all night, but now that she had time to breathe, she was feeling a little ticked-off herself. Why had he not told her at the party the reason The Elders were there? And that the mission he had to oversee tonight was tied to her? Her frustration then seemed to extrapolate itself into wild gestures with her hands as she paced back and forth in front of him. "I should've never gone to The Hallow to ask for Joseph's help. Irina must have tracked me there. I brought this danger to his door."

"That's ridiculous, Poppy," Alec answered, trying to keep his voice reasonable. "Of course you should've gone to Joseph. He's the only one with the resources *to* help you with someone as dangerous as Irina. You can't take her on by yourself. You have no training."

In her growing anger, Poppy suddenly decided she was through with the suit jacket that she had been wearing all evening—Alec's jacket. She removed it roughly and tossed it at him before pointing a finger at him. "I can handle her just fine. And *you* telling me *no*—that I couldn't go see Joseph—just didn't cut it."

"From where I'm standing, *no* cut it just fine!" Alec replied before tossing his jacket onto a nearby chair. Apparently, he didn't want the coat any more than she did. "Did you ever stop to think that this is exactly what Irina wanted? For you to feel responsible for Joseph and race right back to London? Then she doesn't have to expend any energy in finding you! She can just sit there and wait for you to come right to her! She played Nathanial, and she played you, perfectly. And she nearly got what she wanted."

Poppy could only manage to press her lips into a tight line as she stared back at him. *Of course*, that would be what Irina wanted all along. And when Poppy went silent on him with no snappy comeback, he knew he had her. "When I promised Joseph I would protect you from Irina, it wasn't a, '*Sure, I'll protect Poppy until your life is put in danger*' sort of promise. It was a '*I'll protect Poppy even when she's doing dumb-shit things like trying to fly straight back to London!*' sort of promise."

There went his hand through his hair again. No wonder it had been nearly standing up straight when she had returned. He had to have been raking through his roots all night long. "I mean, you're terrified of flying, Poppy! What were you thinking?"

Poppy just continued to stare at him wordlessly as she watched him walk over to the console table behind the sofa and pull a bottle of opened champagne from the ice bucket and proceed to pour himself a glass. He took a good-sized drink before setting the glass down again, not so gently. "You don't understand the risks you're taking here. And why are you so willing to shoulder the responsibility for what Irina's doing? You didn't ask for any of this." He was undoubtedly angry with her, but there was also clear worry in his voice. She had seen it in his face when Matthias had silently communicated with him at the jet that he'd not heard from Sampson. She could see it now in how he stood with his hands gripping the edge of the console table.

"I do understand the risks," she said, softening her tone as she moved toward him. "It's *my* life, and I've faced death at the hands of Irina almost every day of it. You can't expect me to just stand by and watch while she's threatening all the people around me."

"What I expect is for you to trust me," he replied, his calmer voice conveying a surprising amount of conviction. "Trust that I know what I'm doing when it comes to your protection."

"I don't know you," Poppy replied honestly. "I mean no offense, but the only people I have ever trusted have been Joseph and my mo-" She was going to say 'mother' but she stopped herself before she finished. Sometimes it was still so hard for her to believe that her mother was gone. If she had lost Joseph, too, she wasn't sure her heart would have been able to take it. Strangely, when she looked back up at Alec he wore an expression on his face that said he'd known exactly what she'd been about to say. "You should've told me what was happening instead of trying to manage me."

"Yes, you're right, that's exactly what I should have done," he said to her, a barely detectable growl of irritation in his voice. "I should've told you everything so you would have your excuse to start running again. Finding some random place to haul yourself up in—never coming out except for the occasional clumsy stumble into a pizza delivery boy?"

That stung. Thanks to her conversation with Gideon at the cabin, Poppy had a better understanding of what was behind her clumsiness, but Alec didn't realize that yet. Still, he had to know how sensitive she would be about her lack of grace, especially after the episode with the dishes in the kitchen. She didn't understand why he would try to hurt her that way. And she certainly wasn't going to let him continue. Walking up to him, she pushed up on her bare tippy toes so she could get nose to nose with him, her strappy shoes having been long since discarded once the two of them had reentered the Library. "I've got four words for you. Not. Your. Problem. Anymore."

Alec didn't even flinch. "Right now, sweetheart, I'm your biggest problem."

"Not anymore. You're fired!"

He stood to his full height just then. "You can't fire me."

"Just did," she informed him as she turned to march towards the doors, feeling utterly victorious in her decision to put this arrogant man in his place, and she wasn't going to look back. But she didn't even make it one full step before he whirled her around and she suddenly found herself caged between him and the console table behind her. Poppy looked up at him with startled surprise and she definitely felt the pent up energy in him in the short moment before his lips came down on hers, locking them in a kiss that fused her to him instantly and just about knocked her knees out from under her.

How did he keep doing this to her? She was supposed to be angry at him, but just like downstairs at the party when he kissed her, she felt instantly hot against him. She wanted to crawl up on his body, weaving herself into his strong arms, but he made that impossible as he pinned her hips against the table. His mouth was warm and his lips were demanding, which she really had no problem with at the moment—aside from the fact that he was leaving her absolutely breathless.

Although this kiss had caught her completely off guard, she understood that things were happening way too fast and that she needed to slow them down, but she couldn't seem to get her mind or body to get on board with the concept. Alec Lambert was a really good kisser! He kissed much in the same way he led the people of The Oracle, calmly but with unchallenged authority. But there was that damn arrogance factor again! He never considered that she might object when his rough hands seduced her further by roaming possessively over her thin, silk dress. Never considered as he felt his way along every curve on her body that he shouldn't. And as much as Poppy hated to admit it, she loved that confidence about him. She dragged her mouth away from his kiss, exhaling hard over his shoulder and gasping twice when his hands caressed her breasts.

He then lowered his hands and bunched her silk hemline in his fists, slowly pulling the fabric up on her thighs. "Alec," she whispered with the split second of breath he allowed her, but that was all he gave her. She squealed as she felt his hands scoop under her legs and haul her onto the console table as if she was weightless. There was nothing angry or rough in the way he was handling her, but he was definitely just as out of breath as she was. He balanced her on the narrow end of the table while his fingers began dexterously pulling at the delicate buttons on her dress. Her heart was beating like crazy in her chest, but never once did she consider stopping him. He pulled the dress down from her shoulders to her waist and dropped his head over her chest. She was holding onto him for dear life when she felt him nip and lick at the edges of her bra, then his hands left her hips and his fingers found the straps and slip them down along her arms until one of the creamy white mounds of her breasts was fully exposed to him. "Alec . . .," she said, breathily, a second time.

"Just relax," he murmured and then nipped at her ear. That nip caused her hips to roll up into him, and she could feel his hardness against her inner thigh. Her breath now heaved out of control as she felt the heat from his body somehow transfer to a place deep inside her. Her hands started to grab at his clothing, but he pushed them away, then picked up the glass of champagne he'd been drinking from, tipped it up, and he took in a large mouthful. Then, putting the glass back down on the console, he lifted one of her breast in his hand and brought his lips to the hard nipple. Poppy squealed as she felt the cold, carbonated bubbles and the heat of his mouth surround that sensitive nipple. His tongue swirled over the tip and a streak of white-hot pleasure shot straight through her body, a feeling that was sharper and more exciting than anything she had ever experienced in her life. The room felt as if it was spinning out of control as her head dropped back and her breast was taken even more deeply into his mouth. "Alec," she gasped again— because she couldn't think of any other word to say.

He took another swig of champagne and moved to her other breast. His hands scraped up her thighs, continuing to draw the dress upward until it puddled around her hips. Then he pulled her forward to the very edge of the console table. His fingers began to massage over her panties and she wanted to scream. "White lace," he murmured as she grabbed onto him for balance. "Very nice."

Next thing Poppy knew, his fingers were slipping inside the decorative fabric and then inside her. He was greeted with warmth and undeniable proof of her willingness and acceptance of what was happening between them. He started to stroke her with two fingers, causing her to moan. Poppy dropped her head back and bit at her lip as she balanced herself on the table, her nails digging into his shoulders. She was now surrendering to him completely as she opened her legs wider.

Poppy didn't understand what was wrong with her. She was supposed to have banished her need for a man years ago. She was supposed to have her desires well under control, but there was nothing controlled about what was happening between them!

His fingers moved expertly within her until he'd pulled every last sensitive nerve tight inside her own traitorous body. Her inner muscles began to coil and tighten around his fingers, the heat inside her becoming an inferno that was in sharp contrast to the cold tongue that currently flicked back and forth over her nipple. She felt her entire body release in a silent scream as wave after wave of pleasure blasted through her, blurring her vision for several long moments before she felt his fingers pull from her flesh. But his thumb continued to roll in small circles over her clit.

Poppy sensed him moving above her, sensed him pulling her lace panties from her legs, but she was so dazed she couldn't focus. "Let me have you," he said roughly, and she could hear the tension in his voice as he fumbled through a drawer in the console table.

She managed to get her head to stop rolling on her shoulders long enough to stare up at him dazedly. He appeared hungrier than any man she had even seen, and she hoped she was more than just a meal to appease his current appetite. She nodded in wordless agreement, and within seconds Alec had his slacks open and she could feel the wonderfully full pressure of him pushing the head of his cock just inside her. She suddenly stopped him. "Condom?" she asked, inhaling a deep breath.

"Taken care of," he replied.

Just where the hell had he pulled a condom from?

Her heart began to beat wildly in her chest as she anticipated what it would feel like to have this man buried fully inside her. She didn't have to wait long. He aligned himself with her body and began pushing forward as he uttered a long, drawn-out groan. Her breath caught with her pleasure. "*Oh, damn*, you're tight," he said, feeling the pressure, too, as he pulled back long enough to let her catch her breath before pressing forward again. This time more slowly. He groaned each time he withdrew nearly to his tip and then thrust forward again, returning deeper with each thrust until he was finally fully inside her.

He felt amazing. *They* felt amazing together. They fit. Barely.

Poppy had a feeling of pure contentment come over her, something that she'd never felt before. She opened her eyes and stared at him as he arched his back, pushing himself to the very deepest parts of her, his body stretching out as though pure pleasure was licking up his spine. But his eyes were staring blindly at the box ceiling above them. Not at her.

"Lock your legs," he said to her, and when she complied he started to thrust inside her, hard. Poppy allowed herself to give into the sensations fully. He was not being gentle as he took her there on the top of the console table. And quite frankly, she didn't want him to be gentle. She was a Dhampir. Her body could handle the strength of a vampire. So, as a human, Alec couldn't physically hurt her. He seemed to be quite aware of that, thrusting faster and moving so powerfully inside her that she no longer seemed able to breathe.

Alec cursed as his hands dug at her hips and the console table continued to rock beneath them. The ice bucket and its open bottle of champagne, along with his now empty glass crashed to the floor at their feet. The noise and mess of it should have given him pause, but he didn't even slow down. Alec was working himself towards his own release, but he still wasn't looking at her. That's when Poppy realized what was happening between them, as wonderful as it felt at that moment, was simply fucking. Mindless, casual fucking between two people who had a lot of pent-up energy from one dramatic night. Nothing more.

Poppy wished she could tell herself that the emotion behind the act was more important at that moment. Or that she didn't need the physical response he was stirring up inside her body. But she couldn't. In a lot of ways, her body felt starved for this kind of hungry attention. And this time when she released, her scream was not silent, but exhaustive, as her second orgasm rolled through her with the momentum of a speeding freight train. The feeling was so powerful she was about to squeal the merits of simply fucking a man to the entire world.

But once her orgasm finished—and she had felt Alec shudder with his own release—she inhaled a few slower breaths. Felt the complete stillness of the room. And then she felt strange. One heartbeat. Two heartbeats. Three. All of a sudden, Poppy had been given too much time to think about how she could have lost such control.

Alec pulled from her body, discarded his condom in the trash and zipped himself up as if very familiar with the procedure. "Are you OK?" he asked her, perfectly polite, and yet perfectly distant.

"I'm good," she replied, because she wasn't really sure what else to say.

"You're . . . good?" he questioned with a frown.

"Yep, good," she confirmed as she tried to hop from the table to her feet, but he caught her in mid-hop and swung her around until her bare feet missed all of the glass that was broken beneath him.

"Careful," he said. "You've no shoes on." She stood there staring at him while he returned the straps of her bra and worked on the buttons of her dress. She couldn't believe she had just said '*I'm good*', like he had just flagged a cab for her or de-iced her windshield.

"I've got this," she said as she moved her hands to quickly finish the last of the buttons, straightening herself as best she could, considering.

She could feel he was watching her closely as she turned to leave. "You can stay for a little while," he said after her retreating form, ". . . have some more champagne, if you'd like?"

Her whole expression faltered. His offer had been almost painful to hear. It sounded as if he was offering her use of the room to enjoy some champagne on her own. "No, it's late and I'm tired. I'll see you tomorrow." Then she remembered the whole one-night stand awkwardness and turned back to him. "I mean, I won't see you tomorrow."

One of his brows arched as he looked at her strangely. "You won't?"

She shrugged her shoulders. "No, I have stuff to do."

"I see," he said. "I didn't realize after five days your time here was already so committed."

"That's right, it is. You're not the only one who has important things to attend to."

He crossed his arms over his chest as he looked back at her. "I never claimed that I was."

Feeling sure that she'd adequately extinguished any possible misconception that she had *any desire* for something like this to happen again, she swung around to leave. Only she swung the wrong direction and smacked her forehead straight on with the corner of the wall.

Nope. Still clumsy.

Poppy heard his empathetic hiss behind her as her hand went to the soon-to-be new bump on her forehead. Before Alec even had a chance to respond, she waved her hand casually and said, "I'm good."

"After a short pause, he repeated, quietly, "Still good."

She then rushed out of there before the embarrassment of the moment caught up with her. When she was safely behind the door to her own room, she closed her eyes and sighed. "Poppy, what were you thinking?!"

CHAPTER FIFTEEN

Two days later, as darkness was falling, Alec was sitting alone in his office replaying in his head the events at Bodmin Moor. He wondered if he could have handled the situation differently. Should he have foreseen what was going to happen that night? And could the outcome have been better if he'd only trusted to his instincts sooner.

It was not like him to question himself. When so many people were counting on you to lead them, to make the right decision, there was no room for indecision. But that's exactly what he seemed to be falling prey to ever since another night he wanted to banish from his memory—Brahm Hill. He didn't want to remember the mistakes he had made that night. He didn't want to remember the friend he lost because of those mistakes. And he was starting to question whether or not he could be the leader the people of The Oracle needed him to be as long as he had so many ugly memories chasing him.

One memory he didn't mind, however, was his encounter with Poppy in the Elder's Library. His blood pressure shot up just thinking about what it had been like to touch her, and he ached to touch her again. The same ache he'd had about forty-five times over the last two days. Her skin had been soft and just a little fleshy in his grip as he drove his body into hers on that console table. She felt perfect. She smelled perfect. Like peppermint and some sort of sweet flower. A scent he swore had somehow been branded to his brain and triggered as easily as if someone were walking around spraying perfume over his head.

Maybe his distraction with how this woman smelled would explain why he had behaved like such a Neanderthal the other night. Taking her with an urgency that blinded him from any common decency or manners he'd been raised with was not something he was particularly proud of. He'd treated Poppy as if they had been lovers for months and were intimately familiar with each other's bodies, instead of exploring the wondrousness of their first time. But *son-of-a-bitch*, the sex had been good! She had been unbelievably tight for not being a virgin, and the way her body gripped him . . . reached for him . . . had him groaning just thinking about it now. At one point during the quickly escalating encounter he had nearly forgotten where he was, he was so lost in the orgasm that nearly shook his legs right out from under him.

She had been so unexpected.

Alec had been pumped full of adrenaline by the events of that night, and at one point he became just plain scared for this woman when he realized the truth that she'd been there the night Irina had killed her mother. What had she seen? He feared the worst after what he'd witnessed himself with the team's mission. All that energy and concern for her just seemed to coil into one giant ball, until the next thing he knew he had her bent back and was fucking her like he was starved and she might be the last great sex he would have in his life.

And it was great sex!

But Alec was also very realistic about these things. At thirty-two, he'd been around the block enough to know that great sex always faded. Though Alec had enjoyed his encounter with Poppy, as evident by how much he kept thinking about it, he recognized he had too many responsibilities and not enough time for a committed relationship. He enjoyed sex with different women, and he certainly wasn't going to get tangled up in a long-term affair with a woman Joseph thought of as a daughter. He'd already screwed up on that front by sleeping with her in the first place. Joseph would castrate him if he had any idea how rough he'd been with Poppy the other night. He'd probably castrate him if he heard Alec had been with her at all!

Still, he'd been walking around The Oracle with a condom in his pocket for the past two days, like some devirginized-highschooler, just hoping there was a chance for another steamy encounter with her. Problem was, he had to find her first.

The woman had to be hiding from him in rooms he didn't even know existed inside The Oracle. Sampson had assured him that her guard, Matthias, was on her like glue, but wherever that was, it was the opposite of where he was at the moment. And he suspected that was very much on purpose. That certainly didn't bide well for *her* enjoyment of *his* performance the other night. Although, she had screamed out loud with her second orgasm. He'd definitely heard that scream. His guards would've heard that passionate scream throughout the floor! Who knew such a fireball of sexual energy was hidden inside such a clumsy woman?

He did.

Alec knew it that very first time, when she fell on his lap in London and all that bright cherry hair of hers spilled over her shoulders. *God*, he could feel his blood heating now at just the thought of her. Pushing back from his desk, he marched over to his office door and swung it open. "Sampson!" Sampson was already standing on the other side of the door, waiting for him as if he'd been waiting since before Alec even thought about getting out of his chair. "Where's Matthias?"

Alec was surprised when the normally emotionless Sampson looked as if he were trying to contain a smile. "I believe he's currently keeping tabs on Miss Honeywell . . . as you requested."

"Well, good. Then maybe he can tell me where the devil she's been hiding for the past two days. How the hell are we supposed to protect her if we can't find her?"

Sampson didn't dare answer that question because he was smart enough to know there was no right answer. Yet, he wasn't smart enough to completely hold his tongue. "You seem a bit . . . agitated this morning, sir. Is something wrong?"

"Just find Matthias. I need our elusive guest up here in an hour," he growled before slamming the door behind him.

Nearly an hour later, Sampson still hadn't returned with any news of Matthias or Poppy, but Gideon was knocking quietly at his door, and he was carrying a somber expression on his face. Alec sighed and got up from his chair, walking over to the window with his shoulders held tight as he peered out at the magnificent view, knowing the words Gideon was about to say next. "You wanted me to inform you when the team returned with her body."

Alec simply nodded. His thoughts of Poppy had been a needed distraction from being reminded that they'd lost one of their own at Bodmin Moor. Sienna Scott. They had been able to save Joseph without sacrificing Poppy, but it had required another sacrifice in exchange. He'd taken that knowledge with him in his sleep for the past two nights, in dreams that kept coming at him like darts. This was the life they all faced—had all chosen—but any death was still unacceptable for him, especially the brutality with which Sienna had died. "Has Kane returned?" Alec asked.

"He has . . . and I remember that you asked how he was doing. I've spoken with him, and I suspect, in time, he'll be fine. He's angry, of course, and disturbed by what he witnessed, as I'm sure you all were." Alec didn't say anything in reply, even though it was obvious Gideon was baiting him, just continued to stare out the window. "Don't you think it's time we discuss what you witnessed?"

"There are no words, Gideon," Alec replied quietly. "Sheer brutality, I guess. Once Irina realized she had been tricked, she cut open Sienna's chest inside that energy field and pulled her heart out into her hands." Gideon's expression drew grim as Alec continued. "Then she just ate it, right there in front of everyone. And there wasn't a damn thing anyone could do. It was simply the sickest, most brutal thing I've ever seen. I've never seen such enjoyment of killing someone. Not even from a Lycan."

"She ate Sienna's heart?" Gideon questioned, though, he asked with less surprise than Alec had been expecting. Alec nodded as he turned back to face Gideon. "That gives us our answer as to how Irina has managed to gain her power so fast."

Alec paused for a moment. "I'm not following,"

"There are stories in old texts that suggest the heart as being the center to the power in many supernatural beings. If Irina is using some form of black magic to bind her victims' powers to them as they're dying—but then consumes their heart before that death is complete—she, in essence, is gaining all of their power, not just a portion that comes out with their essence."

"Whatever it is, it's sick. Irina has gone off the deep edge."

"Yes, and it makes her obsession with coming after Miss Honeywell all the more alarming."

Alec stared grimly at Gideon. "I think Poppy knows exactly what Irina is capable of. At Bodmin Moor, Irina told the team that Poppy had been there the night her mother, Mary, was killed. I think Poppy watched Irina do the same thing to her mother."

"Oh, dear . . . The shock of seeing such brutality on a loved one like that would be especially difficult."

"I don't think you or I can imagine it," Alec replied quietly. "Mary was the only constant in Poppy's life. *Damnit*, Irina isn't getting anywhere near Poppy—not while I'm breathing!" Gideon just looked at Alec as if he hadn't expected him to say anything less in response. "But if I'm right about this, how do I help her?"

Gideon smiled at him, understanding and empathizing. "You can't push her. To talk about such an event means re-living it. That may not be something she is ready for."

"That's good advice," Alec replied quietly as he patted Gideon lightly on his arm and walked back towards his desk. "I will try to not push her, even though I want her to trust me enough to tell me she was there that night. She hasn't even told Joseph the truth."

"I think, if you are patient with Miss Honeywell, she will come around. I believe she already trusts you more than you realize."

"Let's hope so," Alec replied somberly.

"And what of you?" Gideon continued. "I know you take losses like Sienna's very hard."

Alec knew Gideon was only asking out of concern, but he didn't seem to have the patience for it today. Regardless of how Sienna's loss affected him, he could never appear distracted or weak to those who were counting on him. "I'm fine. Now, if that's all, I'm expecting—" Right on cue, Matthias stepped into his office, with a sourfaced Poppy following behind him. The second Alec laid eyes on her he again felt a wild tug-of-war in his heart, at one end of which was the conversation he and Gideon just finished, and at the other was a tightening in his muscles that told him he was starved for this woman.

She was dressed warmly in dark leggings, ankle boots, and a long sweater that didn't do nearly enough to conceal the sumptuous figure underneath. Her hair was pulled loosely back, a handful of strands falling about her face. She was gorgeous. Out of everyone's view, he squeezed his hand at his side just before he motioned for her to come forward into the room. "Matthias, will you wait outside, please?"

"He doesn't have to leave," Poppy spoke up with a bit of unease that Alec found discomforting. He wondered if she was uncomfortable being alone with him now. If she was, he would rectify the situation with her right away. He never wanted her to be uncomfortable with him, though, he could certainly understand it after how he'd behaved the other night.

Matthias never questioned Alec's order and retreated into the hall.

"Yes, well, that is all I had," Gideon said with a clearing of his throat, "so I'll be on my way, sir."

Alec scowled at the man. "Gideon, if you don't stop calling me sir I'm going to ship you back to England." Gideon said nothing and closed the door behind him. Alec then focused his attention on the woman who had been driving his mind to complete distraction for two straight days. She stood perfectly erect, but her gold eyes held a fire inside them that plainly said she was irritated with him. "You bellowed, sir," she replied with sarcasm.

***

Poppy was irritated by the fact she found herself once again alone with Alec Lambert in his office, even after she promised herself she would avoid all private contact with him— indefinitely. Meaning, someone else needed to be there in the room with them so that this out-of-control lust thing she had going on didn't burst into flames at the very sight of him.

He certainly wasn't helping today, standing there so calm and confident, in grey slacks and an elegant contrasting shirt, leaning back against his desk with his arms crossed in front of him. All of the sudden she flashed on a memory of what it was like to hold onto those strong arms and her cheeks began to warm. "Where the devil have you been?" he asked her.

So much for calm.

Poppy inhaled a steady breath, trying not to let her *frustration,* she would call it, get the best of her. "I didn't realize I was supposed to report my whereabouts to you every hour of the day."

"Every hour? No. Every couple of days? Yes. Especially considering that I am supposed to be guarding you."

"I thought Matthias was guarding me."

That comment really seemed to ruffle him, which she found confusing, since it was obvious he had assigned Matthias to follow her around The Oracle like a puppy. "*I'm* guarding you," he said with a surprising amount of bite to his words.

"Fine," she answered, perhaps a bit too agreeably, which immediately drew his suspicion. "In answer to your question, I've been busy helping the staff with table set-ups in the banquet rooms for the young students' training."

Alec scowled back at her. "Have you broken anything yet?" Poppy harrumphed at the comment, and he immediately waved his hands in apology. "No, that isn't what I meant. I meant to remind you that you're a guest here, not an employee. You shouldn't be doing chores."

"I like helping out," she answered. "I like helping the children. Most of them have no family here. And I'm also trying to mend fences with Mrs. Stippich for all the broken plates."

"I already replaced all of the plates," Alec replied, as if he couldn't believe this was still an issue. "Has Mrs. Stippich said anything to you to indicate the matter is not closed?"

"Not at all. But this is about more than just a monetary replacement of some dishes."

Alec scrubbed his hand through his hair, still seeming to be completely confused. "Poppy, you should be concentrating more on learning how to develop and control your abilities. Not setting plates. Gideon has updated me on what you discussed at the cabin. This is important news. I think you should train while you're here at The Oracle."

She raised her chin to him a bit. "Are you offering to train me?"

"Yes. I've been thinking about this quite a lot, actually. I really think learning how to use your gifts can help you. We can work together in the mornings, if you don't mind starting early."

"No, thank you," she replied with a light voice that caused Alec to do an involuntary double-take. "What do you mean— no, thank you?"

"I mean no, thank you," she answered simply.

"Care to give me any more reason than that?" he asked, still scowling at her.

"No."

Poppy was not stupid. Training in the mornings with the man she had just had lustful, emotionless sex with on a console table with was the very definition of a bad idea. How could she stamp down her libido if she was rolling around the floor touching, holding and sweating with the man she was continuing to have suggestive thoughts about on a lot of comfortable mats beneath them? Of course, maybe that had been why he'd suggested the idea in the first place. Or maybe the thought of having sex with her again hadn't even occurred to him. But it certainly had occurred to her. Her traitorous body still craved him, and that was no good.

For his part, Alec looked stunned. When he finally appeared about to say something, Sampson knocked at his door. "Sir, everything is set up for you in the conference room, per your request."

"Is everything secure?"

"Secure," Sampson confirmed.

Alec stepped forward and reached for Poppy's hand, pulling her with him as he led them towards the conference room. "We'll discuss this more later—because I happen to be right about your training, and I *am* the best person to teach you."

"Of course you are," she said in bland return.

"Right now," he continued, "I've something I'd like to show you."

Poppy tugged her hand with some energy, trying to wrench it from his, but Alec didn't let go. "What if I don't want to be shown anything?"

Alec just continued to pull her through the conference room door, which Sampson closed behind them, locking the two of them inside. "Are you trying to be disagreeable today?"

"Maybe." Poppy was a little uneasy to find herself locked in a private conference room with the man, but she quickly realized they were not alone. On the large screen at the front of the room was Joseph, his whole face lighting up in a smile when he saw her. "Joseph!" she cheered as Alec let her hand go and she rushed to the front of the room to stand right there in front of the enormous screen. "Are you all right? And don't give me some, 'I'm just fine' answer. I really need to know you're OK."

Joseph laughed. "My doctors have checked me out and declared than I am one hundred percent. Really . . . I am just glad to see you looking so well. How has Alec and The Oracle been treating you?"

"Fine," she replied quickly, perhaps a little too quickly, which caused Joseph to raise a questioning eyebrow. "Everyone has been very kind," she added. "But I worry about Irina trying to come after you again while I'm here. I think I should come back—"

"Not an option, little flower," Joseph interjected quickly. "I've been moved to another secure location, so you don't have to worry about me. And I can assure you that Alec and I have plans in place to handle Irina. But in the meantime, just to be safe, I've asked Alec to heighten security around The Oracle and to have you moved to the secured floor."

"This floor . . .?" An entire floor with only her, Alec and his guards was the very opposite of avoiding private contact. "That really isn't necessary, Joseph. I'm just fine on—"

Alec cleared his throat and she swung around to see a smile tug at the edges of his lips. "Your things are being moved up to the guest suite off the Library as we speak." *Oh*, he was enjoying this way too much. How was she supposed to avoid him when she was on the same locked off floor as him?

"Thank you for handling my request so quickly, Alec," Joseph replied. "I'll feel better if Poppy is as secure as possible until we've found Irina." He then turned his attention back to Poppy. "But I'm afraid we must keep this conversation short. I didn't even want to risk this much contact over the SAT line, but Alec convinced me that you really needed to see for yourself that I was doing just fine."

"I did," she said with such emotion in her voice that it caught her off guard.

"Very good, then. I want you to continue to do as Alec instructs. He's obviously been doing a good job keeping you safe. I will speak with you again soon. Love you, little flower."

"I love you, too, Joseph," she replied as the screen faded to black, a little teary in spite of herself, though they were happy tears. There was a long silence in the room as Poppy continued to stare at the blank screen. She had been so focused on it that she hadn't realized Alec had walked up right behind her.

"Is something wrong?" he asked her.

Poppy wasn't sure what had come over her just then, but she swung around and threw her arms around him, hugging him tight as she spoke over his shoulder. "Thank you," she whispered. "Thank you for letting me see and know that he was all right."

Alec's hand reached up and stroked through the loosely-tied back of her hair, and she swore his touch tingled all the way through to her scalp. That was when she became more aware of his body. Of how they were embracing each other fully in that moment. Of how the lines of his lean muscle, the heat of his body, and the sunny-salty smell of his skin seemed to sink into her senses. The night they had been together they had touched . . . *boy* had they touched! But he had also kept his distance from her in a very definitive way—by not looking at her.

Now he *was* looking at her, and there seemed to be nothing in the world between them. Their bodies molded into each other as she felt her own breathing growing deeper, and suddenly she realized what a huge mistake she was making. Poppy tried to pull away from Alec, but his hands slid over her back to keep her pinned to him. *Oh, God,* he had that same hungry look in his eyes he had the other night in the Elder's Library—like he could devour her whole. The tension between them became so thick that it felt as if it could be cut with a knife.

She knew this was it. *This* was that moment she would always remember for the rest of her life. The moment that would be defined as her strongest moment, the moment in which she had protected her heart at all cost and refused to give in to her body's desire—or her dumbest moment, where she would fall flat on her face and always ask 'what in the world was she was thinking'. "Alec . . .," she began.

***

Later that night, the darkness outside The Oracle was hauntingly bathed in the glowing cast of a full moon. As Maya lay in bed, staring out at all of the night's unsettling beauty, she pulled the covers all the way up to her chin and let her tears fall silently down her cheeks. By now, crying in this bed was something Maya was very familiar with. She had cried over Phinneas's death nearly every night, it had seemed, since she lost him at Brahm Hill. But crying in this bed after just giving a man her virginity . . . That was something entirely new.

Maya wasn't really clear why she was crying or where all of this unforeseen emotion had welled up from. Earlier that night she had just been so grateful that Simon had returned from his mission safely. Ever since word had reached her that his mission at Bodmin Moor had taken a dangerous turn and that the team had lost one of her own, Maya had been a ball of nerves. She couldn't lose another man she cared about—not so soon.

Thankfully, Simon had come straight to her room upon his return, to show her he was safe. In her relief, she grabbed onto him and refused to let him go. Maya held him in her arms and told him she didn't want to waste any more time; that she wanted him to stay with her that night. Maya then took Simon into her bed freely, and he had been as gentle with her as he could, considering how excited he was about the fact she had finally said 'yes' to him. But Maya had not expected to feel so strange afterwards. It wasn't like she thought her first time was going to rock her world or anything. She just thought, as much as she cared for Simon, she would feel something . . . more.

Now, as she lay there beside him she felt as utterly exposed as she was naked, while he slept peacefully, one of his arms still wrapped around her. She wondered if Poppy had been right. Maybe she wasn't quite ready for this so soon after Phinneas. The whole situation was ironic, really. Maya had waited so long to be with Phinneas, the one person she had truly wanted to give her virginity to, because she thought they *had* time. And then she chose to give her virginity to Simon because she feared they wouldn't have enough time.

Maya felt alone in that realization, even though Simon was sleeping right beside her. She buried her face in her hands as the tears continued to come. If it hadn't been for a piercing howl that had cut through the night and echoed off the mountain peaks nearby, the tears might not have stopped for some time. But the sound she heard in the distance was disturbing and yet familiar. Maya recognized the howl as the cry of a Lycan, and it was disturbing because they almost never heard a Lycan's howl this far south.

For humans, the howl of a Lycan sounded like that of a very large wolf, but Maya could always tell the difference. There was a pain underneath, something that reverberated in the sound that was human, not animal.

The howl sounded again, only this time it was stronger, angrier . . . closer.

Slowly, Maya moved Simon's arm from around her and slipped from his grasp beneath the covers. She pulled a robe around herself, went to the sliding glass door of her small balcony, and stepped outside. Some of The Oracle's trackers were quickly preparing down below to go after the Lycan. They would hunt the Lycan mercilessly until it was either dead or injured and pushed back into Lycan territory. But at that point, the creature might as well be dead. Lycans wouldn't hesitate to attack and cannibalize the weakest among them. It was a brutal and raw world they lived in, where only the strongest survived—to ensure their species as a whole would survive. And as she had every day since Brahm Hill, Maya found herself rooting for that loner Lycan. In fact, every Lycan she saw or heard now caused her to wonder whether, somehow, it could be Phinneas—just trying to survive.

The next howl cut through the night with an intensity that relayed how upset this creature was becoming. Was it because of hunger? Or was it pain? The humanness she could feel underneath this one was so strong that for a moment it felt like she might have gained her Empathic gift back. She fought to hold onto to every second of the experience, hearing the creature's heartbeat in her own head as the evening wind blew against her cheeks. Th—thump. Th—thump. The steady sound of it was calming . . . and familiar. "Phinneas?" she whispered into the night air.

The sliding door to her balcony suddenly opened behind her and she felt Simon's arms wrap around her from behind. Maya had been so focused on the Lycan's cries that her Dhampir senses had not detected that Simon had risen from bed. "Baby, what are you doing out here? The snow's too cold for you to be out here in bare feet and a robe." He kissed the top of her head and squeezed her gently. "Come back inside and let me warm you up."

"The Dhampirs are getting ready to go after a Lycan," she replied before discreetly wiping the last of her tears from her eyes and turning to him to see that he was standing there completely naked. "I can't be the only one who is cold," she remarked. Simon was a handsome man in the moonlight. His light blond hair glistened, his body was firm, toned, and he was obviously very comfortable with his nakedness.

"There's a Lycan this far south? That's certainly unusual. Maybe I should go down and offer to help. I've gotten pretty good with my Lycan tracking spell."

"No!" Maya answered quickly. "I mean, you just got back. Stay here with me." She then looked back out into the night, hearing the Lycan's howl once more. Only now, the sound was fading into the distance, and secretly she hoped the creature would keep running. "You can hunt Lycans another day."

He seemed to pause to consider that for a moment. "For you, baby, anything."

***

Poppy rushed into her new room on the twelfth floor, slammed the door shut behind her and slumped back against it, releasing a groan as she realized her shirt hadn't even been buttoned correctly when she had past several guards between here and the conference room. "Poppy, what were you thinking?" she murmured to herself as she slapped her hand against her forehead. She was dangling her shoes from her hand, and she was pretty sure her hastily reconnected bra was about to snap open in the back. "How could you let this happen again?" she said miserably. "Have you *zero* self-control?"

Her body answered with a deep, satisfied trembling of her inner muscles, a sweet exhaustion that seemed to hum through her from head to toe. Unfortunately, she didn't have a chance either to immerse herself in the sweet feeling or hate herself for it because . . .

Bang! Bang! Bang! The sound of knuckles on wood came from right behind her head, startling her straight onto her feet. She knew it was Alec banging at her door. She could smell his unique, sunny scent all the way through the thick wood. Poppy inhaled a fortifying breath and opened the door to meet him and his perturbed expression. He marched right past her into the room and swung on his heels. "What the hell was that?!"

The question confused Poppy. She thought it was abundantly clear what had just happened. Another rushed, uncontrolled, steamy (and still unconnected on his part) round of sex on a table—a conference table this time—because evidently he very much liked hauling her onto tables. "I believe that's what they call a quick fuck," she replied smartly. "And you seemed to have enjoyed it, so why are you here barking at me now?"

"No, I know that," he started in a sort of flustered agitation, ". . . I mean, yes I did enjoy it. I'm talking about why you ran out of there without so much as an *'I'm good'* this time—as you seem to be so fond of saying."

"Well," she began, flailing her hands through the air, ". . . I thought it was perfectly clear that I was good. No need to go into some big, long discussion about it."

Alec sighed and stepped forward toward her. With nothing more than a purely protective instinct to try and save her heart from being crushed any further, Poppy answered him with her own step back, keeping some important distance between them—but it seemed to catch Alec totally off guard. He swallowed thickly. "Poppy, did I hurt you tonight?"

She stared up at him and was instantly moved to see that his expression appeared sincere. Her heart was hurting; she was starting to care about this man who had kept himself at such distance from her until this very moment. For just a brief second it seemed he was letting his guard down and letting her in. "Of course you didn't hurt me. I'm a Dhampir."

"I think you know . . . I wasn't asking if I hurt you physically."

Poppy rubbed her fingers over her temples; she hadn't been prepared to have this conversation with him while standing there with her clothes unbuttoned and messy from their second steamy encounter. "What do you want me to say, Alec?"

"I want you to tell me the truth. I always want you to tell me the truth."

The truth? The truth was, in the conference room, even though she had tried to slow things down by saying his name, he reached forward and kissed her. Then he really kissed her. And then she really kissed him. Before she knew it she was lying flat on her back on the conference table, taking him into her body, willingly, as he thrust inside her so deeply she gasped, panted and screamed her way to an even more powerful orgasm than the first time around in the Elder's Library. Just the memory of it already had her skin flushing several shades of pink.

Afterward, however, with their bodies still intertwined and their clothes still disheveled, they both lay there in sweaty silence on the table until he broke that silence by nuzzling against her neck and murmuring, "Drink from me. Please . . ."

Drinking from his throat was something Alec needed from her, but Poppy couldn't oblige him. She knew as a Dhampir that drinking from a human would be more intimate for her because she would be taking his blood into her system; in some ways it would connect him to her. For Poppy, drinking was like the next serious step in a relationship—*which they didn't have.* They didn't even have a first step—a simple date or shared a meal together. They had gone straight to hot sex on tables, and now that he knew she would put out for him he was all over her. And why shouldn't he be? She had allowed it to go this far. That's when she knew that she had to get out of there— fast.

"Do you know," she began, slowly and a bit hesitantly, ". . . we've now had sex twice and I haven't even seen you outside your shirt? I have no idea whether you're smooth or rough with hair over your chest. I haven't searched your body with kisses to find that one special spot that gets you the most excited. I don't even know how you like to be touched." It surprised Poppy when she saw Alec's physical response to her words. He swallowed hard, his eyes a little less focused and more dilated, and his breathing became noticeably shallower. "Those things are nice, too—sometimes," she continued. "But with us it's all so intense—and then it's over."

"Do you want to know how I like to be touched?" he asked her breathily as he took another step forward, his hand reaching for hers.

She nodded. "I want to feel connected to you in some way. But you don't look at me," she declared painfully before pulling her hand back. "We fuck on a table and it feels great . . . but it's empty. You don't see me."

Alec stared back at her just then, either in disbelief or surprise—she really couldn't tell. "What are you talking about?

I see you. I think you're one of the most beautiful women I have *ever* seen, Poppy. And it feels damn near perfect to be lost inside you."

"What feels perfect to you, then?" she asked him, reaching up to pull his collar back on his shoulder and exposing the many scars from where previous Dhampirs had drunk from him. "Is it *this*!?" she hissed, her fingers tracing over his scarred flesh. There was such ugliness and pain in those scars on an otherwise beautiful man. "The perfect moment, when you to experience pain and pleasure yet remain disconnected from the Dhampir who's giving it to you?"

Alec blinked back at her, then removed her hand from his collar. *There it is,* she thought, *that dullness in his eyes that says he is pushing me away once again.*

"You don't know what you're talking about. I've known you less than two weeks, Poppy. I like you. We've slept together a couple of times and I've enjoyed it—a lot. But I'm not going to stand here and listen to you describe me as if you know me well. You don't. I'm sorry if I hurt you. I truly didn't mean-"

"You're right," Poppy stopped him, not sure how much more of this *truth* she could take. "I don't know you. I appreciate what you've done to help me at Joseph's request, but I think it's time for me to return to The Hallow."

"No," he practically growled at her. "You can be mad or hurt by me all you want, but you'll stay here and let me and my men protect you until the danger from Irina is over. End of discussion."

Poppy snapped her hands to both her hips. "*Excuse me!?* . . . End of discussion? What the hell? If this is about some macho thing with you not wanting to break your promise to Joseph, let me assure you I will speak with him myself. He'll be fine with me returning."

Alec stepped forward until his breath was right there over her lips. "If you *did* know me better you would understand that I may be an Elder by birthright, but I'm a Guardian in my soul.

And I don't just give up a charge because things get difficult. You'll stay here at The Oracle . . . and you will stop running. And I swear on my life I will protect you."

"I can protect myself," she defended.

"Not yet, you can't," obviously referring once again to her lack of training. He didn't wait for her to respond to that and released her from his hold. Then he turned to leave her room, but not before he whirled back and said to her, "I won't touch you again."

Poppy's breathing halted from the impact of his words. Alec said them as if he were physically recoiling from the idea of touching her again. Instead of showing him how much his words hurt her, she simply yelled back at him, "Is that a promise?"

He slammed her door behind him.

CHAPTER SIXTEEN

Somehow Alec knew it was going to be one of *those* days as soon as he opened his eyes and rolled over in his insanely large bed that morning. He wasn't quite sure how he knew, but he knew. He dragged the silk sheets from his nude body and tried to rub the sleep from his eyes. It was still dark outside as he lurched from the bed toward the dresser, feeling as though he could sleep for at least another hour, and grabbed a pair of shorts and a clean tee shirt before heading off to the private gym that was just down the hall from his suite.

As he came through the gym door, looking forward to sweating the tiredness right out of him, he came face to face with Poppy. He hadn't seen her since the night when they had argued, nearly a week earlier, and if he thought that having some distance from his woman was going to be the solution to his problems—well, he was sorely mistaken. All it took for him to get the hard-on from hell was a two-second flash of her in form-fitting yoga pants and a bright crop shirt darkened with a little sweat. The hard-on wasn't his immediate problem, however. His immediate problem was the fact that she was pinned to the mat, flat on her back, with Matthias holding her down!

Obviously, Matthias was going through some training exercises with her, *but Alec didn't care!* He didn't want Matthias touching her. Matthias seemed to read his mind and jumped to his feet, helping Poppy up from the mat. "I'm sorry, sir. I wasn't paying enough attention to the time."

"Yes, I can see that," Alec replied, a slight morning growl showing up unbidden in his voice. "So, you've been training Miss Honeywell?"

Matthias nodded quickly. "For the past week. She's a fast learner and has good strength for a partial Dhampir, but I've been trying to work with her on defending her blind side."

Alec raised a questioning brow at the man, one of his most trusted guards, while Poppy ignored both of them and walked over to where she had left a water bottle and a towel on a bench. Taking a long sip of the still-cold water, she placed a hand on her hip, drawing out the natural curves of her body as her cherry hair swung loosely in a ponytail. Alec swore he felt his own tongue go dry with thirst for a second. This was the first time he'd seen her in such form-fitting clothes—an outfit that left nothing to the imagination. She was toned and shapely, and it was killing him that he'd slept with her twice and never seen her like this. Matthias had seen her in these skimpy clothes for an entire week! "Where's her blind side?" Alec asked, choosing to ignore the caveman jealousy shouting in his head.

"Her right shoulder. She pulls it forward, turning her away from that side and leaving her more vulnerable to attack."

Alec motioned for Poppy to come to him at the center of the floor, but she wordlessly shook her head at him and took another sip of water. He rolled his eyes because he half expected as much from her. Obviously, the week of physical distance had not done a whole lot to improve her mood towards him. "Do you want to learn?" he challenged her.

There were immediate sparks of challenge in those gold eyes as she snapped her head back around. "You heard Matthias," she replied. "We've been working on it. It's fine."

Alec smiled. For some reason he liked that she was being snappy with him this morning. Her irritation woke him up. "Then this should go quickly, shouldn't it?" Poppy appeared to be debating in her own head for a moment or two, but she eventually returned her towel and water bottle to the bench and walked over to meet him on the mat. Alec moved to stand behind her. "Tell me why you pull this shoulder forward?"

"I don't know. I just do."

"That's not a very good answer," Alec replied as he brought his hands up and pulled both her shoulders back until they were straight.

"Well, it's the only answer I have."

Alec slowly passed his hand across her back as he watched her for a response. She stayed still, but he could see she was tensing her shoulders, as if preparing for the worst. "When we've developed bad habits," he continued, "weaknesses that an enemy can spot and take advantage of, it's important to understand where those habits came from in order to truly break them." Alec then proceeded to move his hand far out to the left, then back to the right, without touching her. She couldn't see his hand behind her but, being Dhampir, could sense the movement. Alec looked to Matthias, who was standing off to the side in front of Poppy. The guard nodded to Alec to indicate that she was tracking the movement of his hand behind her with her senses. Alec was pleased with her concentration, but in the next moment he noticed her right shoulder beginning to pull forward. It was pulling forward because she was turning her head, ever so slightly, to pay extra attention to her *left* side.

His hands went to her shoulders again, pulling them back straight and forcing her to straighten her head. Then he slid his hands down to each side of her hips. "Keep your hips straight with your shoulders. Relax, Poppy." There *was* an actual point to what he was trying to show her but he couldn't help noticing how the curve of her hips felt perfect in his palms. *Man, he had been an idiot.* In their two encounters together, although passionate and certainly fiery, he hadn't taken any time to explore her beautiful body. In fact, he had done barely more than get his pants down far enough, he was so desperate to get inside her.

What the hell had been wrong with him?

Her right shoulder popped forward again. "You're trying to protect your left side. Why?"

Poppy remained silent, and he suddenly suspected that she knew exactly why she was doing it; she just didn't trust him enough to tell him. Alec came around her so he was directly perpendicular to her at her right side, the side opposite from the one she was protecting. He straightened her shoulders again. "Keep your eyes and head forward," he instructed her. "Matthias, will you go stand behind her on the other side."

As he suspected, Alec could hear Poppy's breathing change almost immediately as her eyes tried to follow Matthias. She was becoming uncomfortable—fast. Alec could see the tension ratcheting up in her.

"A little more to the left," he instructed Matthias, wanting to see how much more the situation stressed her—not to be cruel, but to gage her response. He knew it was important. A Dhampir was only as strong as her biggest weakness, and right now Poppy had a giant one that would make her vulnerable to attack. "A little more, Matthias. Good. Now take a step closer."

Poppy's breathing was becoming so labored it started to show as her chest and shoulders lifted.

"OK, one more step," Alec said behind her neck, and Poppy couldn't take it anymore. She swung around, not caring that she was leaving herself open to attack from Alec, who was on her right side. She cared only about the would-be attacker on her left. Poppy was surprised to see, however, that Matthias was nowhere near her. Alec's hand had been extended, directing the guard to stay back, a good distance away from her, actually. She swung back around to Alec, prepared to defend herself from him, but he was still just standing there, staring at her curiously. "You weren't using your senses to track where he was in the room. You became fixated on the point I was leading you to. And instead of sensing that I was deceiving you, you left yourself open to attack."

Her lips tightened further with the realization that he was right.

"Poppy, tell me why you are favoring your left side."

Poppy continued to appear agitated and tried to push away from him. He reached for her left arm again, which he really should have reconsidered. A nasty little smile crept onto her lips just before she snapped her arm away, swung around on him, and brought her knee up sharply between his legs. Alec was able to twist somewhat out of the way, but he wasn't fast enough. She caught him partially in the balls, and he hissed out a blistering reply as he dropped to his knees, while Poppy rushed to grab her things and dart out of the room.

Matthias was trying to help Alec up, but he waved the guard off, staring at Poppy's backside as the door slammed after her.

Yep. This was, indeed, the beginning of a very bad day.

***

"Sir, you have a visitor," Sampson announced. It was exactly two o'clock. "She's not on the schedule but has asked to see you."

Alec looked up at his guard, his thoughts still on the incident with Poppy that morning. She was clearly favoring that left side, more than likely because of some sort of trauma she had experienced at some point that compelled her to protect herself. He wished he could get her to trust him just a little bit. He knew he could help her. As long as she allowed her fear to control her, she was a sitting duck if attacked by another Dhampir, let alone a powerful warlock like Irina. "Not today, Sampson," he answered, rubbing at his pounding head, taking note that it had actually been a while since he'd had a headache.

"Sir, it's Judith Lambert . . . Would you prefer me to schedule her for another day?"

Alec's gaze swung back up from his paperwork. "My Aunt is here?" he questioned, coming to his feet and contemplating the large distance she would have come to see him. "Send her in."

Judith Lambert was a small woman, still attractive in her twilight years. She had been married to his uncle Reese for forty years and was full of more love than any woman Alec had ever met, even after being betrayed, like the rest of them, by his ass-of-an-uncle, Reese. She greeted him with a warm smile as she gave him a loving embrace. "Hello, there, you handsome boy. I swear, you've become the mirror image of your father at this age. He would be so proud to see you now, God rest his soul."

"Aunt Judy, why didn't you tell me you were coming? I would've come down and greeted you when you arrived."

She waved a hand dismissively. "I made the decision rather last minute to come—on the off chance you'd be available to see me. We missed you for the holidays. The girls would've loved to have seen you at Christmas."

"Forgive me . . .," he replied. "I actually had important business to attend to in London. But I would've loved to have seen Antonia and Veronica. Perhaps I can come down to visit them in the spring."

"Don't try to fool an old woman, Alec Lambert. I swear, this position of Elder keeps you even busier than it did your uncle."

Alec did not respond. He simply preferred to avoid in engaging in conversation about Reese these days. There was no one who could really even get him to discuss his uncle . . . except maybe Judy. "Can I get you anything to drink?"

Judy shook her head as Alec led her to the soft seating in his office, a set of four wingback chairs in an obnoxiously large mauve and gold print fabric with bright gold, nail-head trim. His Aunt scrunched her nose in displeasure as she took a seat in one of them. "I've always hated the design of this office. Reese had truly horrid taste when it came to furniture. I'm surprised you've not changed it."

"It's on the list of things to do," Alec acknowledged, and it was . . . just not very high up on the list when compared to other life-threatening matters that needed his attention. "Really, how are the girls?"

"Wonderful," she smiled with pride. "Veronica's starting Yale in the fall. It's her dream, and she's so excited I cannot get her to stop talking about it. And Antonia and her new husband have recently moved to Connecticut."

"Wow, she's moved already?"

"Yes, pretty soon I would've had that big house all to myself. That's actually part of the reason I came here today. I wanted to let you know that I've decided to sell the house. I think we've already found a buyer and the sale should close in a month or two. I'll be moving closer to both of the girls."

"I'm happy for all of you, but I will hate having my family even farther away," Alec replied.

His Aunt reached over to him and cupped his cheek in her hand. "Such a sweet boy. How is it you've managed to escape finding that right woman?"

"Just lucky, I guess," Alec teased her, but Judy frowned at him as if she didn't find it very funny.

"Seriously, I've been worried about you. I've seen firsthand the toll this position can take on a man. You need balance in your life, given your new responsibilities. Things you enjoy." She then smiled coyly. "Perhaps even that right woman?"

"Ah, so you've come on a fact-finding mission today, have you?"

Her brows lifted at that. "Well, an old woman can't wait forever to see her favorite nephew find a bit of happiness in his life. Not to mention, it's time for you to start thinking about producing some little ones of your own."

Alec thought carefully about how he wanted to respond. He loved his Aunt dearly and knew she wanted only the best for him, but he could hardly tell her that the closest thing he'd experienced to love these days were two really great nights fucking a particularly pretty Dhampir's brains out. And considering the fact said Dhampir wasn't currently speaking to him, he decided he wasn't even doing that very well. "First of all, I'm your only nephew, so of course I'm your favorite. And secondly, when I have something to report on the female front, I'll be sure to let you know."

"You'd better," she smiled, reaching for his hand in the chair beside her and putting her hand over his. She was then quiet for a long moment, during which Alec realized that something else was obviously on her mind. There would have to be something that compelled her to travel all this way to see him, unannounced.

"What is it, Judy?"

Judith pulled a small, bound journal out of her purse, set it on her lap, and inhaled a deep breath. The journal drew Alec's attention immediately because it flickered in the back of his head that Reese used to have a journal, just like this one, that he kept regularly through the time he was at The Oracle.

"When I married Reese, I knew he was a deeply flawed man. But I loved him despite those flaws. And sometimes, between two people, that's enough."

Alec remained silent. He found it difficult to believe his aunt could speak of Reese in kind terms after the man had planned to cross her—and their children—over to the Immortal dark side with him. He had always been a selfish husband and father in every way.

"And sometimes," she continued, "you discover, even if your partner made you mostly happy, that they did not honor that love in the same way you did." She lifted the book from her lap. "This is a journal Reese kept soon after we were married. It's one of a whole stack of journals that I had forgotten about until I finally had to go through the things in his study."

"I remember," Alec finally replied. "I thought you had gotten rid of all those things."

"I did. Most of them, anyway. He used to write in these journals every night after dinner, and they seemed such an important `part of the man I married that I wanted to hold onto them. I didn't read them for the longest time, but one day, when my anger towards him had finally lessoned, I found myself hoping that they could give me some answers about why he did the things he did."

Alec sighed deeply. "I'm sorry for the pain he's caused you and the girls. But I don't think the answers you're looking for are in those journals. I'm not even sure Reese knew why he did the things he did. I just know he was thinking only of himself."

"You're right. But you might be surprised what he did write about. This journal, in particular, affects you."

"I don't need to know," Alec replied. "I don't need him affecting my life any more than he already has."

Judy nodded her head. "I can certainly understand that. But also, please realize, it was difficult for me to come here today. It's hard for me to bring this journal to you. It's hard for any wife to admit that she's lived with a man for forty years and never really knew him."

"He's hurt so many people," Alec answered. "I hate that he's continuing to hurt you, even in death. I think you should burn these. Put him in your past. I have. And nothing in that journal will change that."

"See, that's just it, dear boy. I'm not sure you have put him in your past. I see how you've changed . . . You keep us all at such a polite distance. And that's in part because of him— because of how cruelly he betrayed the trust you had in him."

Alec was becoming increasingly uncomfortable with this conversation, mostly because it reminded him of the argument he'd been through with Poppy just a week ago. He had accused her of not knowing him, but did she really see him much more clearly than he realized? He squeezed his aunt's hand, released it, then rose to his feet, walking to the window, his hands fisted in his pockets as he looked out towards the lake. "If I've changed, it's *all* because of him."

"Perhaps. And perhaps you're just still grieving. I've held onto this journal now for a few weeks, trying to decide when the right time was to tell you . . ."

Alec turned back to her. "Tell me what?"

She lowered her chin as a sad cast came into her eyes. "Reese was unfaithful to me at the beginning of our marriage. He offered no explanation for it in the journals other than he believed he was settling into his permanent life. This journal talks about the affair with the woman and the child that was conceived from that affair."

Alec hissed out a curse just then. "He has another child? Why does that not surprise me? Don't tell me he abandoned the child . . . because it will take my opinion of him to new lows I didn't think existed."

"He did, a son. But he didn't abandon the child, Alec. He kept him close to him, though, the child didn't know it."

Alec watched her carefully as a sinking feeling started to crawl in his gut. "What're you saying? Who was the child?"

"Alec," she replied carefully, with such empathy to her voice. ". . . It was Lucas."

Alec was speechless, suddenly feeling as if the room was spinning out of control. Lucas! The boy Alec grew up with from childhood, the kid who believed himself to be an orphan his entire life. Lucas! The man he came to love like a brother and whose features were so similar to his own. The man who fought devotedly and died by his side, killed by Reese's hand . . . He was Reese's son!

"Knowing how much Lucas meant to you, I felt you needed to know the truth," his aunt continued, but Alec was long past hearing it. In an instant, he was jerked back to that night at Brahm Hill, the last night he had seen both Reese and Lucas alive. When Reese had stabbed Lucas in the chest with the Red Diamond Dagger, ending his life, Alec had assumed that his friend Lucas had stepped in front of the blade that was meant for him. Everyone had thought the blade was meant for him. Reese had made it clear he wanted to turn his family to the dark side with him, and in his crazy, demented mind he believed that the lethal dagger would somehow help him accomplish that. Now Alec was forced to wonder if he had completely misunderstood the significance of the events of that night.

Then, in a flash of vivid memory, Alec was taken back to the moment when Reese whispered something in Lucas's ear as he held him off the ground with the blade firmly embedded in his chest. Reese was watching him die, and he whispered one word, one single word that, at the time, Alec couldn't hear. But now, as he replayed the moment in his head, he recognized the single word that had passed from his uncle's lips.

Son.

Reese had said, "Just let it come for you, *Son*."

CHAPTER SEVENTEEN

Alec somehow managed to keep his cool just long enough to see his aunt off and to return to his office. Then the rage building inside him exploded in front of his guards. "You son of a bitch!" he cursed as he flung one of the hideous side chairs at his desk across the room, smashing it in half against another chair. Then he did the same thing with an end table, this time smashing it against his desk. A desk lamp crashed noisily against the wall. And so on, and so on, until Alec managed to break or completely destroy every item in his office. A tornado might have caused less chaos. Alec wanted no physical item that could ever remind him again of the uncle, whom he now hated more than ever, with every fiber of his being.

Reese Lambert never acknowledged the son who was a fighter by spirit and more trustworthy and loyal than any other man Alec had ever known. There seemed to be no reasonable explanation for Reese's coldness other than that his uncle simply didn't know how to love. In Alec's opinion, Reese never deserved Lucas's faithful service to him for all those years while having no idea he was serving his own father.

It made Alec sick. "Why?" he shouted. "Why??"

Lucas Rayner grew up believing both of his parents died shortly after his birth. He had no brothers or sisters and thought himself alone in this world except for his close friendship with Alec and Alec's father, Gerard.

Alec roared out even more loudly as he tipped the huge desk over onto its back and then began smashing it with what was left of one of the chairs. Had his own father, Gerard, known that Lucas was Reese's son? Was that why there had always been a special kinship between them? Would his father have kept something like that from Alec when he knew how much the truth meant to him? Alec didn't want to believe it, and yet the doubt that was ringing in his head made him even angrier.

Even the pleated drapes on his office windows were not spared Alec's fury. He was yanking the fabric down, inadvertently dragging every picture and painting with it, until they all shattered on the floor at his feet. A blurry haze of fury seemed to own the Elder's very being, and Sampson and Matthias could only stand and watch all the destruction. The noises of that destruction and the roar of Alec's shouting were so loud and penetrating that the two primary guards were soon joined by about a half dozen others. Soon Sampson ordered all his men to do nothing to interfere. Their job at that point was just to make sure Alec didn't hurt himself in the process of destroying his office.

When finally there was nothing left to being broken, crushed, ripped or shattered, Alec dropped to his knees in the middle of the room, huffing with very real human sweat and drained to a state of complete exhaustion. After a few moments, he slowly raised his head and saw all of the guards positioned around him, collectively as silent as he had ever known them to be. Behind them all, in the hallway, stood Poppy. She looked at him with such quiet sadness that he hated seeing it, because it seemed too damn close to pity. He never wanted pity from her. He didn't know what he wanted from her, but it was never pity. "Leave me," he instructed all his guards, then looked straight at her and repeated the word, "Leave."

Poppy eyes widened as if she were surprised that Alec had singled her out so clearly. She recovered her expression, turned quietly on her heels and headed straight for the elevator.

"Matthias . . .," Alec called with tiredness in his voice. "Stay with her."

"Yes, sir," his guard responded and immediately headed for the stairs, leaving the door open. Alec knew that all of his guards were still waiting just outside his office, barely out of view. They would never dare leave him, as he had ordered. And that was his life as an Elder. You weren't allowed to have moments when you could lose your shit in peace. There was always someone there.

Alec wasn't sure how much time had passed while he sat there in the middle of the pile of office rubble when a familiar voice spoke to him from the door. "Well. Decided to do a little redecorating, I see." Alec glanced through the window and noticed that it was getting dark outside as Kane closed the door to the office behind him and turned on the overhead lights. "Personally, I think it's about time. It made no sense why you had the ugliest room in the building. This look you got going on now, though . . . is a bit organic."

"Kane, I'm in no mood," Alec paused, then sighed, then replied with clear warning in his voice, " . . . so just turn your ass around and march right back out that door."

Kane completely ignored him and plopped himself on the floor in front of Alec, since there was no piece of furniture left in any condition to sit in. "No can do, Oh, Elder One. I need to savor this moment. The moment when Alec Lambert finally loses his shit."

Alec just rolled his eyes at the fact Kane had used the same description he'd been thinking in his own head for his little meltdown. "You *will* do it, or I'll give Stippich permission to ban you permanently from the dining hall."

Kane waved his hand dismissively. "Ahh, me and Stip are good. *You*, however, do not look so good. And I just have to point out that I saw this coming."

Alec raised his eyes to Kane once again. "You saw *what* coming . . . exactly?"

"Dude, for months now you've been wound tighter than bacon wrapped around cheese-stuffed chili peppers. It was only a matter of time."

Alec pressed his fingertips over his temples to quell his growing headache. "Let me guess . . . We're back to the Spanish honeymoon? Why do you torture me so?"

"Just think of me as the yin to your yang. Batman to your Superman. The epic to your fail."

Alec scowled at him. "Why do you get to be Batman?"

"Really? You're going to complain about being Superman? He's, like, the most powerful being in all the world—and he can fly."

"Batman has all the cool toys."

"True . . . But that's why the analogy works so well for me," Kane said, with a wag of his brows, and then shoved away what was left of Alec's bookcase with his boot. "So, you want to tell me what all this destruction is about?"

"Not really."

"All right, then, how' bout I take a guess. I saw Judy downstairs before she left. Classy woman. I walked her to her car, and we had a nice little chat while it seems you were busy going to war with your furniture. So—and I'm going to go out on a limb here—I guess your mood has something to do with your dearly departed uncle."

Alec slowly stood up, his shoulders held stiff. "I hate him," he answered in a quiet voice. "The man is dead—and I hate him as though he were still alive and breathing."

"You aren't going to hear me criticize you for that. The man was a first-class ass. So, since we all agree on this, why are you letting him bother you from the grave?"

Alec gave Kane a level stare. "Judy found one of Reese's journals. He had a son with another woman when they were first married."

"Well, isn't that a shocker. He had been such the pinnacle of moral character up to that point."

"It was Lucas, smart ass."

Not even so much as a blink of surprise flashed through Kane's eyes. "That certainly does explain why the two of you looked so much alike." Kane then returned to his feet and leveled a stare at Alec. "And?"

"And what? Isn't that enough? Lucas was his son—the *eldest born* son in the Lambert line. That means *he* should've been Elder of The Oracle—not me."

Kane stood there, scowling. "Lucas never would've wanted to be Elder. You know that."

"No, I don't know that!" Alec snapped. "His birthright to rule was stolen from him by that no-good bastard of a father." Alec then threw his hands up. "Christ, I helped take it from him! And *I* sent him up that hill that night to fight—practically dared him. Now he's dead because he tried to protect *me* from his own father."

"Ahh . . . And now we're really getting to the point, aren't we?"

"What point?"

Kane paused a moment for effect. "That you still refuse to admit you're grieving. All this bullshit about what *could* or *should* have been is pointless! This is about how you still feel responsible for Lucas's death. You lost someone who was closer to you than a brother. And instead of dealing with it, you've been walking around here like a goddamn robot for weeks!"

Alec blinked back. "I've been doing my job. Nothing has slipped through the cracks."

"That's just my point. You're operating like a machine. What the hell happened to the cocky Guardian who took calculated risks based on instinct—who wasn't afraid of the truth?"

"I'm not afraid of the truth!"

"Good. Then we're in agreement that nothing you learned today about Lucas changes a damn thing. You're still Elder! The people here still believe in you—and they want *you* to be their leader. *Lucas* wanted *you* to be their leader. And I'll bet you a thousand times over, if he'd known the truth about Reese, it wouldn't have changed anything."

Alec turned away from Kane, emotions roiling through him. He wasn't sure he agreed that Lucas would not have changed anything. And, thanks to Reese, he would never know.

"You can destroy your office as many times as you want, Alec . . . but it won't change the fact that it's still yours. All of this belongs to you. It always has." Alec then sensed that Kane was right behind him. "I think the real question is: do you still want to be Elder?"

"You know I don't have that choice. I'm the last one left of the Lambert line. Until I have a son there's no one else to do it."

"And if there was?"

Alec was silent for a long while. What would he choose if given the option to step down as Elder? This life at The Oracle was all he had ever known—all he'd ever been prepared for. There never had been any other choice, so he always believed it was what he wanted, but now he wasn't sure. He felt lost in a way he hadn't at any other time in his life, not even when his father died. And he didn't dare voice that to anyone, not even Kane. The people there deserved more than to hear that the leader they were counting on had doubts. "There isn't a choice, so there's really no point in discussing it."

"If that's truly how you feel, then let me give you a piece of advice," Kane offered. "Find someone to smooth out the rough days . . . perhaps get you started on creating that son. And then be the best damn Elder you can be. Because these people who are loyal to you deserve it."

Alec turned to watch Kane head towards the door and was amazed that for someone who irritated the hell out of him most of the time he made an awful lot of sense. "Kane?" Kane stopped and turned back to him. "Thank you."

Kane nodded. "You're a good man, Alec. Better than most of us will ever be. You've just gotten sidetracked for a little while."

***

Poppy found herself walking the grounds of The Oracle for just the second time since she had arrived there. The scenic, snowy landscape and vistas all around the former hotel made it such a majestic and peaceful place, she couldn't help but feel a little awe struck by it—and cold. She had not put on any extra layers of clothing, or even a coat, before rushing outside. She just *really* needed to escape. When Alec had ordered her to leave, it had hurt. Despite her anger at him, she had been worried when she had heard him tearing apart his office like that. She was curious about what would drive him to such destruction and rage. She wished he would have at least wanted her to stay, even if he didn't want to talk with her. Instead, he'd ordered her to leave as simply as he ordered his guards.

She sensed Matthias's presence close by, and he had probably been silently watching every move she had made since she left Alec's office. Her sense of him seemed to blip in and out, however. Being on sacred ground interfered with a Dhampir's senses. Things just were not as clear as they were in the outside world. Lately, she had found herself wondering if Irina was actually closer to her than she realized because she couldn't sense things clearly if they originated outside The Oracle itself. But in that moment, she was almost positive she could feel someone watching her from beyond sacred ground. It didn't compute; she shouldn't be able to sense much of anything beyond the line of sacred ground, but she did. She had also felt someone watching her briefly when she was with Gideon at the Headmasters quarters.

Poppy needed to be sure it wasn't Irina she was detecting. If the warlock *was* close, she would have to make a run for it. Alec and his guards had done an admirable job of protecting her to this point, even from their own Brethren. She really had felt safe here and actually found her training empowering, but there was no way she would allow anymore sacrifices from these people she had grown to care about—as there had been at

Bodmin Moor—fighting Irina on her behalf. Not when she had seen, firsthand, how powerful and sickeningly cruel Irina's vengeance could be.

Realizing what she needed to do, Poppy quickly scanned the hillside behind her before making her way down the rolling bluff towards the lake. Matthias was somehow managing to stay out of sight, but he was there, still close. He wasn't going to give her much time to do what she needed to do, so she would have to be quick.

Sacred ground ran along the lake's embankment on both sides of her for hundreds of yards. Matthias probably felt pretty comfortable she wouldn't go off of the protected land. There was one way off, however, but it was going to be very cold.

She turned towards the lake's moonlit edge and dove head first under the water. The icy pool froze her innards instantly, making the pressure on her lungs painful and her limbs feeling like they had just been slammed against a glacier. But using those few, precious seconds, she focused on keeping herself beneath the water, relaxing so she could let her senses take in the energy around her. There was definitely something there, but it was not moving any closer. It . . . or he . . . or she just seemed to be observing her. And though her body physically hurt from the freezing water and trying to hold the air in her lungs for as long as she could, she felt herself sag with relief when at once she realized the energy she was feeling was not Irina.

But it *was* someone.

In the very next moment, a loud splash whacked the water above her, and there was no delay before Matthias hooked his arm around her waist and hauled her to the surface, causing her to spit and sputter out some water she had inhaled after getting yanked so hard. The Dhampir had her back on sacred ground so fast she literally only had seconds. "Are you crazy?!" he snapped as he continued to drag her up the hillside and straight back towards The Oracle. "Alec will chew my ass, *but good*, for this. What did you think you were doing?"

"I thought I sensed something," she defended through chattering teeth.

"Christ," Matthias cursed. *"I'm dead."*

CHAPTER EIGHTEEN

"What the hell were you thinking?!" Alec barked at Matthias as both the guard and Poppy stood before him, soaked to the bone and dripping all over his office carpet. Poppy knew Alec was going to be mad about the whole diving-in-the-lake incident, but she didn't think he was going to be *this* mad. "Not *only* did you let her wander to the very edge of the property line, you actually watched her leave sacred ground?!"

"To be fair," Poppy interjected, "I dove off sacred ground."

"I'm not asking you," he growled.

For his part, Matthias looked as if he wanted to crawl under a rock. "I'm sorry, sir. I never thought she would dive into the water in these temperatures."

"Yeah, well, we're kind of figuring out that she is *crazy!*"

"Hey," Poppy squeaked through chattering teeth as, at the same moment, Sampson rushed into the room with a warm blanket and wrapped it around her shoulders. "I'm standing right here. Besides, this wasn't Matthias's fault. I thought—"

"You weren't thinking! That's the point," he answered back with a sharply pointed index finger, obviously in no mood to debate the issue with her. "You know that if you step off this land, Irina has the power to get a clear fix on you. I can't even comprehend why on earth you would do such a thing. You've spent your entire life running from this woman. *And what*— have you decided you're bored because she's not been around to terrorize you lately? You thought you'd help her out by jumping into a freezing lake??"

Poppy's mouth dropped. Referring to her as '*bored*' made her sound like a spoiled brat, not to mention that he basically was calling her stupid. "Of course that's not why I did it. If you would just calm down and listen, I'd explain."

"I don't have to calm down," Alec shouted back, then jammed his hand through his hair. "This was an incredibly dumb thing you did, Poppy—well deserving of my temper. In fact, I should bend you over my knee and spank you like a little girl!"

Poppy sucked in her breath on a gasp. "You wouldn't dare!"

"Try me!"

No one had ever threatened to spank Poppy before as if she were some sort of child. Suddenly, the reasonable explanation Poppy had been about to offer him flew out the window and was replaced by her own growing temper. "You ordered me to leave, so I left!" she yelled back at him, getting right under his chin, feeling as she did so some the wetness transferring from her clothes to his.

"So you dive into a lake? That's logical!"

"Hey, if you're not happy with where I *left to* then that's your problem."

Alec didn't move an inch from where he was standing but placed his hands at his hips, causing his shoulders to widen in front of her. "You know I didn't mean for you to leave sacred ground and expose yourself to Irina. Come on! You're not that stupid!"

Two seconds later . . . "Ow!" Alec ground out.

Poppy had kicked him. The kick was just in the shin but it was a good shot, and he deserved it for acting completely irrationally. Her stepping off sacred ground (OK, *diving* off sacred ground) for a few seconds was not the end of the world. *What the heck was wrong with him today?* First he was tearing apart his office and then he was completely overblowing a small incident. At least, in her mind it was small.

Alec's glare shot to Sampson and Matthias. Neither had spoken so much as a syllable for the last two minutes. "You two—wait outside!" As soon as the door closed, Alec was on her again. "What was that for?!"

"You're being unreasonable!"

"I tend to get that way when women do stupid things. I mean, look at you. You're a live Popsicle!"

That really pissed Poppy off. "And destroying your office wasn't a stupid thing? Look at this place," she said, slapping her hands against her thighs, which was actually rather painful because they were still so cold they felt frozen even in the warmth of the office.

Alec's lips tightened into a thin line. "You don't know what you're talking about."

"Oh, and you do . . .? You've been so busy being upset you haven't even giving me a chance to explain."

"Fine," he said throwing his hands up before crossing them in front of him, putting some distance between them. "Explain what possible reason you had for diving into a freezing lake and exposing yourself to a warlock."

"I thought I sensed something." Poppy replied as Alec's eyes widened to the size of saucers at her answer. She guessed that hadn't been the right thing to say. "Now before you go all alpha on me," she defended, "and point out that I shouldn't be able to sense someone off of sacred ground when I'm on it—I know that. If you'd rather I call it woman's intuition, then— fine. But I know what I felt, and someone definitely was watching me tonight. I was trying to determine if it was Irina."

"And was it?" he asked with and exasperated breath.

"I don't think so."

"So let me get this straight," he began in a dangerously low voice, and Poppy was starting to reconsider how she should've presented the whole thing. "You're off wandering the grounds alone and you sense someone is watching you. And the logical reaction you come to is *not* to tell me or Matthias but to go off the land that is blurring you to them and into a freezing lake so they can then clearly sense you—essentially making yourself bait?"

Well, when he put it like that it didn't sound so smart.

"Never mind," she said, deciding she needed to quit while she was behind as she turned and started for the door.

Alec stopped her, swinging her back around to face him. "Poppy, we're not finished! You're not leaving this office without telling me everything you know."

She yanked her arm away from him, her eyes narrowing in anger at his tone. "You're right. As Joseph so accurately pointed out to me the day I met you, I should give you all the proper respect you deserve as an Elder." Poppy then raised her chin defiantly, whipped her hand out in mocking salute and presented her back to him, slamming his door loudly on her way out of the room for emphasis.

***

Later that night, when Poppy was much calmer *and warmer* because she was out of her drenched clothes and soaking under the bubbles of a hot bath inside the largest tub she had ever seen, she decided that being up on the top floor did have some perks, despite her having to put up with Alec's foul mood that day. She still wasn't sure how they had ended up arguing so fiercely. In her opinion, Alec had definitely over-reacted to her little dive into the lake. But then again, she hadn't exactly taken the high road once she realized how upset he was about her actions.

Once Poppy decided she was done dwelling on what she couldn't change, she exited the tub and luxuriated in some quiet time, rubbing on her favorite floral scented lotion, which had just a hint of peppermint she really liked. She then slipped on a comfortable set of lounging clothes that were super soft and in a fun lime and dark blue color combination that reminded her of summer even though it was still freezing and then some outside. Later, she would crawl under the thick covers of her huge king-sized bed and let this awful day sink into the past.

That was until she heard the knock at her door.

Poppy sensed it right away; it was Alec at the door, and she dropped her head into her hands in defeat. She really didn't want to argue with him again. As she opened the door and he came into view, she was pleasantly surprised to see he appeared calm . . . relaxed . . . handsome . . . and her stomach flipped. "Easy, little flower," he teased her with a half-smile. "I'm not here to pick another fight with you."

He had changed into some casual jeans and a soft blue tee shirt that, with his messy, blond hair, made him appear younger and more at ease than she'd ever seen him. She imagined this was how people at The Oracle knew him before he became Elder—casual, supremely fit, and just as confident as he appeared in his expensive designer clothes. "May I come in?" Poppy hadn't realized she'd been blocking him from entering. She stood at the door appearing tense and on guard but instead feeling soft as putty inside her stomach.

Damnit.

Simply turning her back on him, she walked deeper into her room, leaving the door open for him if he chose to enter. And, *oh,* could she tell the moment he'd walked into the room, because the scent of ocean and sunshine hit her like a torturous feather.

"So, I'm getting the silent treatment," he stated as he watched her take a stiff seat in front of the fireplace at the end of a very large ottoman that was practically the girth of a dining table. He confidently joined her but left a comfortable distance between them while leaning his elbows forward on his knees. Once in this pensive position he turned his head back towards her, his eyes conveying a sincere expression. "I can't say that I would blame you after how I behaved today. I'm sorry, Poppy. I shouldn't have yelled at you in my office like that. But I was dealing with a lot, and you're little dive into the lake didn't help," he said as a quiet, rumbling chuckle began to develop in his throat. The sound was conciliatory and soothing, and she could tell he was trying not to push her.

His apology surprised her, and Poppy couldn't help but be drawn to Alec in that moment as she scooted back towards him just the smallest little bit. He sat up with straighter shoulders, turning to her and giving her a small smile, his dimple digging deep into his chin. There was something much more open about him just then, and it was a nice change from how closed off he'd been with her that day. "Why were you so angry?" she asked him.

He dropped his head again and sighed. "When you don't place the highest importance on your own safety—like tonight, by diving into the lake—I get scared for you because I know what Irina is capable of."

"I told you it was not Irina I sensed. That is good news. And whoever it was that I did sense made no effort to come closer to me. I probably just over-reacted to sensing someone," Poppy offered reasonably. "That tends to happen when you've spent your life running."

"But in doing so, you put yourself at risk. We may not even fully know the ramifications of that just yet. That makes me crazy, because I think you know exactly how dangerous Irina is. I think you've seen what she capable of."

Poppy blinked at him slowly as he offered her his hand, silently asking for her to take it. When she did, all that human heat in his skin seemed to warm her instantly before he pulled her close to him. Just like that, she was right beneath his chin, pressed against him, with his arm held firm around her back as he stared down at her with those beautiful, light eyes. "I know what Irina is capable of," she replied quietly. "That's why I had to jump into the lake. I had to know if she'd found me."

Alec pulled back from her a bit as a small frown creased his expression. "And if she had? Would you have told me? Or would you have just run?"

She stared up at him, feeling a tear well up in each eye. That had caught her off-guard. "That's just it. I had to know if it was her because I know I'm running out of places to run." Alec stared at her in silence for a long moment, then threaded his fingers through her hair, pulling her to his lips for a gentle kiss. There was nothing hurried or hard about this kiss. It was caring and sweet and left her stomach squeezing in response. He kissed her again and then traced his fingers over her temple

and through the loose strands of hair that were falling from the
pins she had set before her bath.

"Then stop running," he murmured. "Trust me to protect
you—trust me to teach you how to protect yourself. I can . . . if
you'll only trust me." His hand lifted her face to meet his gaze
just then. "Stop running."

Poppy lifted his other hand and held it in her two smaller
ones. "Will you tell me what happened today?" she asked
quietly. "In your office earlier. That wasn't about the lake."

"That had nothing to do with this."

A slight frown marred her brow. "You want me to trust
you, but you won't tell me what had upset you so much." He
lowered his head and shook it, as if trying to shake out a bad
memory, and Poppy could see the pain in his expression.

"I lost someone," he replied, so honestly it squeezed at her
heart. "A good friend. No—a brother. He was more loyal to me
than any person in my life. I still miss him. And I'm not
handling it very well."

"I understand," she nodded. "I still miss my mother every
day."

"Of course," he said somberly. "Of course, you would
understand."

"It's OK to miss him, Alec," she continued. "He was your
friend."

Alec was already shaking his head at her. "No, it's not. I've
people counting on me to be sharp, focused. *You* are counting
on me. But instead, I've been angry and distracted."

"Being Elder doesn't mean you're perfect. Your people
don't expect you to be perfect. They just need to see you're
doing what you can to lead them . . . as best you can."

Alec smiled ruefully. "I wasn't supposed to lead them
without Lucas."

"So you've been sad." She said this as a statement, not a
question. Alec didn't say anything in reply but Poppy could see
it was the truth. Now she understood why he'd had such a wall
up around him. Why he'd been so distant. He was grieving for

his friend . . . but he wasn't giving himself permission to grieve. He just kept pushing forward.

Poppy ran her hands up his chest, feeling the hard planes of muscle under his soft tee shirt before brushing over the scarred bite marks on his neck. The marks left by other Dhampirs were clearly visible, and Poppy suspected they were the reason she had never seen Alec in a tee shirt before now. "So much pain," she murmured. "Do you like the pain?"

"Yes," he replied simply.

She gazed at him for a long while and then asked, "Why?"

For a moment it didn't seem he was going to answer her, but then he finally said, "Because I can feel it."

Poppy felt her breath inhale sharply with the realization of the absolute truthfulness of his answer. Alec Lambert had felt so little since his friend's death that he needed things to be sharp, driving and powerful in order to break through the numbness. Like the slash of a Dhampir's fangs cutting into his throat. Or rough and urgent sex on a console table. "Can you feel tenderness?" She asked the question in barely more than a whisper because she wasn't sure she wanted to hear his answer.

"I've felt it with you."

She looked at him skeptically. "That hasn't been tenderness. That has been sex."

He stared down at her. "I wasn't talking about when we had sex."

Poppy couldn't help but smile. He was being sincere with her. He was open. She ran her hands up his chest again, only this time she pulled the tee shirt he was wearing with her. His heart began to beat faster and more strongly inside his chest as she pulled the soft fabric up over his head. Her eyes took in their fill of his broad shoulders, his defined chest. Alec Lambert was, indeed, a beautiful man. He was smooth and formed, with hard planes of muscle and bronzed skin and a light dusting of blond hair over his chest. She drew her hands down his sides until they rested at his hips and then leaned in, kissing him several times over the scars on his neck. Alec hissed in a breath as his hands jerked up to hold her there to him. "Drink from me, Poppy. Please . . . I need this. Let me feel those sharp little fangs of yours."

She pulled back and ran her hand over the side of his face as she shook her head. "Not tonight," she responded. "Tonight, I want you to feel something . . . more . . . more than pain."

Alec nuzzled against her neck and responded with a playful growl in his voice. "I will feel something if you drink from me," he pointed out, his hands going to the edge of her lime-colored nightshirt to begin exploring the soft skin underneath, sliding upwards towards her breasts. There was no way she would be able to concentrate on what she now knew she needed to do while he was caressing her like that. So she pulled his hands away from her skin and pushed them back down to the ottoman. "Only I get to touch this time."

"I don't think so," he replied with a laughing smile. Then he pushed his hands right back up to her breasts where they had left off, and it was amazing how much of her skin those big hands of his covered. Poppy gasped at how electric his caresses felt. She wasn't quite sure she'd ever felt such a sweet charge in her life. "I need to touch you," he whispered. "I need you to drink from me. Then I need to be inside you, driving into you until you scream for me again. I loved hearing you scream as you came on that console table."

It took a wholly concerted effort to pull back from Alec just then. The man was *way* too sexy for his own good . . . and *way* to playful when he knew he was about to get lucky. Poppy quickly stood to her feet in front of him, staring back at him with a troublesome frown. He wasn't going to be able to feel what she wanted him to feel if lust was revving his body up so fast he was thrusting into her before she could stop him—*or herself*. She knew what she had to do, and it was a big gamble. But the reward might just be that he would view her—and view sex with her—as something more than having just another woman to cover his pain by giving him pain.

"Well, then . . .," she said. "We need to change that."

"What?" he replied blankly, as if he thought she were quite possibly, crazy.

***

Dear God, where does that woman think she's going? Alec was hard as an iron stake while Poppy rushed around the suite going from drawer to drawer in that lime-colored pajama top she was wearing that literally made his tongue want to lick her up and down like a Popsicle. She probably had no idea where anything was, since they had just moved her up here, but he was enjoying watching her skitter around. Well, almost enjoying . . . he'd prefer to be kissing her again. "Poppy, can we get back to what we were doing?"

"In a second," she called in reply after disappearing into the bedroom.

A second might just kill him, he decided. Alec had a chance to be with Poppy again, and he didn't intend to waste any of them. If she wanted to slow things down, explore each other's bodies, feel more tenderness, then she was about to get a boatload of it! He may not be able to feel much anymore, but that didn't mean he couldn't give tenderness to her. Alec wanted her to feel cherished and cared for while they were together. He wanted her to be breathless with her own happiness.

As for him, his enjoyment was easy. He just needed to be inside her, lost in her.

Poppy returned from her bedroom holding one black silk scarf and one blue wool one. Alec's brows lifted curiously as he watched her run her hand over them. "Are those for you?" he asked with a smile that pulled at the dimple in his chin, ". . . 'cause, I'm all in for that."

"Not quite," she replied, lifting the large blue scarf in front of him and nodding for him to lift his hands.

"Uh, yeah? That's not really going to work for me. I need to be able to touch you," he said squeezing his hands as if to accentuate his point.

"Listen," she replied. "My way, you get lucky tonight. Your way, you don't. It's your choice."

Alec's smile dropped. *'Not getting lucky' was* not an option as far as he was concerned. "All right," he replied slowly, "we'll play it your way for a little while."

Poppy immediately began to tie his hands together in front of him with the blue scarf. "Sorry, I didn't have two silk scarves," she commented, then pushed him down flat on his back on the ottoman.

Alec grunted in response. "Careful now," he began playfully. "Soon, it's going to be your turn. And I plan to dish out double what I get."

Poppy ignored his warning and hopped up from him, went around to the other side of the ottoman, where she reached for his now tied arms and stretched them tight over his head. She then tied the ends of the scarf to the heavy wooden ball foot of the sofa behind him. A curious frown crossed Alec's lips because he was starting to feel like a trussed up turkey the way he was stretched out over the ottoman. He liked it, but he was wondering how far she was really going to take this. When she started to cover his eyes with the black silk scarf, he saw where this was going. "You don't need to cover my eyes," he said, roughly, his breathing definitely more excited. "I *very much* want to watch you do . . . whatever it is you're about to do."

"Remember the not getting lucky part?" she replied sweetly, then proceeded to cover his eyes with the scarf.

Once he was securely blindfolded, her fingers lightly brushed over his bare chest. Her touch was just the lightest sensation that made Alec groan out loud in want to get to the harder sensations. "Poppy, you're killing me here."

She laughed, and since he couldn't see her, only hear the sound, it was one of the most engaging and sweet laughs he could remember hearing from a woman. "I'm afraid things are about to get a little more torturous for you." Alec tried to blink his eyes under the scarf but that didn't quite work. "There'll be no '*being inside me*' tonight, as you put it. Not unless you're walking around with another condom in your pocket."

The smile died on Alec's lips just before he cursed under his breath. He was trussed up to a sofa leg like a goddamn turkey with his hands tied and his eyes blindfolded. And no damn condom! "You've no condoms here?"

"Nope. Didn't exactly get a chance to pack them when I left London, did I?"

Alec was cursing again under his breath as he suddenly heard Poppy running about the room again. *This whole situation was not working for him.* "Well, I've got some in my room. Untie me and I'll be back in two minutes."

"Got it," she said, appearing to completely ignore what he'd been saying while rushing back across the room. "Oops," she added with a bit of a thump, then, *"Ouch!"* Oh, God! Now was not the time for her to trip and jam him in the nuts again with her knee. This time he wouldn't even see it coming and he just might have to kiss the idea of having children and a male heir goodbye forever.

"Uh, Poppy, maybe we should discuss this before-," his words were cut off with his own sharply inhaled breath. Poppy's cool hands had returned to his chest and were sliding down low on his stomach. Then one hand moved lower to palm over the hard bulge that had formed in his jeans. She began to rub him back and forth, back and forth. Alec's breath grew deep and rough at her touch—fast! He had to find a way to untie himself and get a goddamn condom!

"What would you like to discuss?" she asked him as she slipped his wide leather belt strap through the metal catch and then pulled the belt free from the loops of his jeans. For his part, Alec had practically stopped breathing altogether

"I have no idea."

"Good," she replied.

Even though Poppy had a Dhampir's strength, her touch was incredibly gentle. She was in control, and she undressed him slowly, which was a stark contrast from the hurried beast he'd been with her the first two times, only allowing enough time to get his pants down before he entered her hard. Alec hadn't been that way with other women in the past. So why had he been that way with Poppy? Someone he seemed to care about more each day he knew her.

Poppy slipped off his leather loafers, then tugged down the last of his clothing. His erection had long sprung free and stretched high, seeming to be looking for his navel. "Do you trust me?" she asked him in just a whisper.

"Trust is a relative thing, here," he replied breathily. "I do hope we can avoid any unfortunate . . . accidents, since I would not have the good fortune this time of seeing anything coming."

She laughed again, another wonderful, effervescent laugh that made the whole of his body hard with need. "Afraid of me, are you? Well, thanks to Gideon, I think I might be learning how to get my clumsiness under control."

"Can we please not bring Gideon's name up when you're about to ravage me? It will kill the moment."

Alec then heard some rustling of clothes falling to the floor before he felt her weight on the ottoman next to him. She lay beside him, and at contact with her skin he was instantly reminded how soft she was compared to him. He swallowed thickly at the image building in his head of her form lying there, completely naked, next to him. It was so unfair! They were slowing things down, had all of their clothes off this time, and he still had never seen her body naked. He'd promised himself that the next time he would explore her, take her in painfully slow increments. That was hard to do when you were tied up.

Alec felt something soft and pleasingly fragrant brushing over his collarbone. The scent was a flower, though, he had no idea what type. He smiled. Although he appreciated her efforts to seduce him, he really didn't need any seducing. His body was tight, hard, and raring to go. Absolutely no seduction required.

All the same, the petals tickled on his skin and he found himself squirming just a bit before he felt her lips come down over his in a sweet, ripe kiss. She tasted good, and he tried to return her kiss ten times over as he inhaled her breath and locked her lips in a kiss he wasn't about to release. She moaned a little, her soft body moving over him, and he was yanking at the damn scarf to get his hands free. "Be good," she warned him, her hands reaching up for his as she continued to kiss him and squeeze his wrists.

"I don't want to be good," he complained. "At all." She pulled back from him and kissed a line down to his shoulder, then across his collarbone to the other shoulder. Each kiss was tender and slow, teasing him with just the right amount of tongue. His brain could not process any other thought than what it would feel like to be inside her tight body right that second. "Poppy, seriously, we need to get a condom."

Next, the sound of rattling in a glass. Alec was trying to clear his lust fogged brain when he suddenly felt a sharp, cold prick against his nipple. His breath caught in his throat. *Damn*—it was ice! Visceral and biting on his fired skin, the frosty cube circled around until wet trails of liquid rolled from his heaving chest down to his stomach. It was almost like she was playing a game, trying to hit a hole-in-one as the cold liquid drops got closer and closer to dripping into his bellybutton. Her tongue followed behind, teasing him, licking up the wetness. Alec hissed in a sharp breath and his hips jerked as she concentrated her efforts around the little hole in his stomach. Those luscious lips of hers were so close to the aforementioned 'iron rod' that he couldn't get the thought of her taking him into her mouth out of his head.

His hands were pulling fiercely against the scarf. He was stretched tight and nearly panting, cursing himself in his own head for not bringing a condom. But he hadn't come here for that. He'd sincerely come to apologize. "*Damn, Poppy!*" After today he was going to walk around with a damn condom in his pocket for the rest of his life! He needed to be inside her. He needed to feel her warmth, her sweetness, her pleasure.

Then, almost as if she had stolen the very thoughts from his head, she shifted lower and he felt her hand take hold of him at the base of his cock. Her tongue, cold from the ice cubes, licked over the head just before she took him fully into her mouth.

Oh. My. God.

His breath rushed in harshly, all the blood surging to his head in an instant. He was being hit by a dozen sensations that melded into something he couldn't describe. None of them were painful, but they all added up to something euphoric. She sucked him and he could hear by her moans that it was exciting her, too. Then she would pull back, squeezing him at his base with her hand and then begin to suck him all over again. She would build him up to a sharp edge where he believed he would break, then she would pull back until his breaths calmed back down.

He wasn't going to survive this.

While that thought was stuck in his head, she drew him into her mouth again. There, she held him and sucked him with an enjoyment similar to the Popsicle he had given so much thought to earlier, and now his body began shiver. He couldn't put into words what it felt like to want this woman so much, yet she was the one with all the control. Poppy Honeywell was sucking him with a mind-blowing mix of adventurous excitement, genuine curiosity, and a self-awakening that was in sync with the tightness he felt every time he slid himself inside her body. She hadn't been a virgin when he had her that first time, but he guessed she wasn't far from it, and that thought made him crazy possessive to keep her all to himself.

He was groaning as his thighs bunched and he pulled harder at the scarf that bound him. As if punishing him for trying to get free, she dug her nails into his hips, and the sensation was so sharp he growled. *God in heaven*, if he didn't know any better he would swear she was a devil's servant made to torture him—to tempt him from the numbness with which he'd been living his life for months now. *"Poppy,"* he begged, desperate for her to hear him because he wasn't sure how much longer he could hold himself back before he exploded in her mouth. He was not sure she was ready for that. "I'm close." Instead of pulling back she took him deeper, and Alec lost all words except for the curses blaring in his head at knowing he had rushed the first two experiences with this woman. What the hell had been wrong with him? Now all he wanted to do was take his time with her. With his hands untied.

Alec was about to rip the damn scarf in half when he heard her moan just before she slipped her mouth from him. The pain of her absence had him gasping and about to beg for her to finish him when the blindfold was suddenly pulled from his eyes. He blinked them several times to see her right there above him. She was beautiful. She was perfect. Breathing hard, the nipples on her handful-sized breasts were rosy and tight as he watched her irises tinge with a brilliant blue and her mouth open to reveal her small Dhampir fangs. Poppy was as turned on as he was, and that explained why she had stopped so suddenly. The Dhampir part of her had grown so excited by the taste of him in her mouth that it had drawn out her fangs. That primal part of a female Dhampir was the one thing he loved above all else. A man could visibly see the heights he was taking her to, because she lost the ability to control the vampire side of herself. The thought that she found so much pleasure from giving him pleasure made him feel more powerful than any supernatural being on earth at that moment.

Unfortunately, he also thought he might die from implosion if she didn't finish him soon. "Poppy, please . . ."

Her eyes never left his as she wrapped her hand around his aching shaft and began to stroke him firmly, quickening her pace until his hips locked and his eyes blinked hard. When his release surged forward from the back of his spine, he was quite sure he'd never felt anything so powerful in his life.

He'd felt it.

He'd felt every moment of it.

Tears fell over his temples as he just lay there, staring at the ceiling in a lost haze. What the hell had just happened? It was like he had suddenly come awake. Poppy continued to stroke him until the last of his semen was spilled onto his stomach. For the next several minutes, Alec wondered if he were having an out-of-body experience as his limbs shook with exhaustion and he felt the warm cloth wipe over his stomach. Poppy kissed him several more times along his body before finally releasing his bound and now raw hands from the wool scarf. Naked and warm, she curled up beside him on the ottoman and closed her eyes. He found himself holding onto her tightly, understanding that the exhaustion he was currently experiencing had just as much to do with an emotional release as it did a physical one.

"Were you able to feel something?" she asked him, quietly, and he could hear the sleepiness in her voice. "Something stronger than pain?"

She had done this all for him without expecting any physical pleasure in return for herself, and her generosity staggered him. He pulled her close and kissed her ear. "I felt everything, Poppy. Everything."

CHAPTER NINETEEN

Before dawn the next morning Poppy was lying in bed fully awake, a smile tugging at her lips as she realized that the man she had fallen fast and hard for the past few weeks held onto her in his sleep. Alec had stayed with her on the ottoman after she'd fallen asleep, and sometime during the night he moved both of them to the bedroom. And he hadn't left. Instead, he had curled up under the covers with her and she had felt his strong arms around her all night as they slept. The feeling of closeness to this man who had previously kept such a distance from her was remarkable, and she feared she was already used to it.

Things had changed between them last night. She could feel the change like a physical presence there with them. Alec had been with her, open and connected to her in every way, when he found a powerful physical and emotional release that seemed to touch something deep within her own soul. In that moment, when he had submitted completely, he had never shown greater strength. Poppy knew then that she had somehow fallen in love with Alec Lambert back on that first day when she stumbled into his lap at The Hallow. And it terrified her, because she knew there was a good chance she was setting her heart up to be broken.

If he did feel something for her—which he had never stated—there was this pesky little problem that a psychotic warlock was still after her. Her life would never be simple. She would always bring danger to those around her. She wasn't free to stay in one place for very long. Wasn't free to fall in love or be connected to anything more than what she could carry in a single bag. That was life on the run. The life she had known since she was a little girl. And suddenly it felt so empty.

Alec stirred in his sleep, squeezing his arms around her as if to confirm she was still there with him before finally waking. She loved that. It seemed such a simple thing, but Poppy had never awakened in the arms of a man she cared about, in a place where she felt absolutely safe. "You're awake," he said in that hoarse, morning voice so many men have when just waking from a deep sleep.

She nodded, stroking the arm he had wrapped around her. "I don't need much sleep."

He laughed in a sort of rough grumble that was incredibly sexy. "So you're to make me feel lazy this morning, is that it? Why didn't you wake me?"

"You were sleeping pretty soundly. It appeared you needed it. Besides, I didn't want you to feel like you had to get up and leave."

"Ah, but I must . . .," he answered as he kissed her right at the edge of her lips. "I work out in the mornings before I meet with Gideon. The old man will start getting fidgety if I make him wait for more than fifteen minutes." Then a small smile, somewhere between joyful contemplation and a slight frown, spread over his lips. "I guess you already know that—after your training sessions with Matthias. Are you meeting him this morning?"

There was definitely a ruffled edge to his question that, for a second, sounded like jealousy. Poppy wanted to laugh because, although the Dhampir guard was—*mysterious* was the right word for it—he was completely not her type. "I don't think Matthias will want anything to do with me again after the way you tore into him yesterday. Really, what happened was my fault, not his."

"It was his job to protect you."

Poppy curled into Alec and kissed him once, gently on the lips. "I thought *you* were protecting me?"

"Touché," he smiled, rolling her onto her back so he could roll over onto her and kiss her properly. His hand curled around her outer thigh and folded her leg around his. Poppy could feel the hard ridge of his morning erection against her inner thigh. "I need a damn condom," he growled. Poppy laughed, but the laugh quieted as she tipped her head to his shoulder. "Did you sleep all right?" he asked her. Poppy nodded her head but remained silent as he continued to hold her closely. "I don't like that you sensed someone watching you yesterday. I had trackers sent out to search the perimeter last night. But I would've heard something from Sampson by now if they'd found anything."

Poppy pulled her head up from his shoulder. "Do your guards know you're here with me now—that you stayed here last night?"

He frowned at her in that playful way that made her wonder whether or not she was asking a serious question. "Of course they do. Sampson and the others *always* know where I am. Does that bother you?"

"I'm not sure," she replied honestly. "Do you think they heard us . . . you know?"

Alec responded with an expectant lift of his brow, as if that had been a dumb question. "They're Dhampirs, Poppy."

"Well," she said, suddenly feeling a little flustered. "Do you think we sounded good together?"

Her question caught Alec by surprise, and his responding, hearty laugh reflected as much. "I think we sounded *very* good together." He then nipped at the fleshy part of her shoulder and growled playfully into her neck, "So, you're going to make me ask, aren't you?"

She turned her head curiously.

"Since Matthias is, no doubt, avoiding you—"

"Which is your fault," she reminded him.

"—will you work out with me this morning?" He tipped his head to hers and squeezed her tighter in his arms. "We could get a bit of training in, maybe even work some more on that blind spot of yours." Poppy dropped her head, lowering her eyes, as well. "Hey, I promise I won't push you more than you're willing to be pushed."

She shook her head. "It's not that. There's something I need to tell you."

***

Alec said nothing, just waited patiently for Poppy to continue; he could visibly see something was bothering her. "I was there," she finally said. "The night Irina killed my mother. I was there."

Alec hadn't forgotten for a second what Irina had said to a Poppy-shifted Kane at Bodmin Moor, "... *you showed great strength in fighting me. Too bad it wasn't enough to save your whore of a mother.*" The thought had terrified him beyond words. Remembering how Sienna died at the hands of Irina the cruel way that she did, Alec hadn't wanted to push Poppy about that night, but he was very hopeful that she might be opening up to him now.

"I told Joseph I wasn't there because I didn't want him to worry. I didn't even know how to explain what I was feeling, what I saw. But he knew something was wrong."

Alec pulled Poppy into a tight embrace, then rolled them both back to their sides on the bed. He couldn't seem to hold Poppy tight enough. "I know this is difficult for you to talk about, but will you tell me what happened?"

Poppy took a deep breath. "I tried to get to my mother. But Irina held her inside some kind of force field. I couldn't break through it. She was lying on the ground, with Irina above her, and she couldn't move. Her screams were terrible. I will never, ever forget those screams as long as I live." Poppy looked as if she were about to crumble into tears as she buried her head into Alec's neck, her voice now cracking as she spoke—and it absolutely ripped at him. "Irina cut into her chest . . . she reached in and pulled out her heart . . . I couldn't think . . . I couldn't speak. I just watched my mother die in the worst way I could possibly imagine—and I could do nothing to stop it. And then . . . and then," Alec felt tears come into his own eyes as Poppy started shake more violently in his arms.

He did the only thing he could think to do and held onto her as tightly as he could because he knew what she was about to say. "She began eating my mother's heart. She consumed it. And she forced me to watch her do it. She wanted me to watch my mother being tortured—to hear her scream. *Oh, God*, I hated her! I just—*hated!* And then I don't know what happened. All that hate I felt . . . just . . . I didn't mean for it to happen."

Alec pulled back from Poppy just then so he could look at her directly. "Wait. You didn't mean for *what* to happen?"

"The Dhampirs. I fought against Irina's Dhampirs and managed to get free from two of them, but a third one surprised me and pinned me down to the ground. He broke my left arm in two places to warn me not to fight him."

"Poppy, I'm sorry," Alec murmured. "I'm so, so, sorry." That was why Poppy had a blind spot. She was protecting her left side—and probably her whole mind—from a memory and a physical pain that were connected.

"The Dhampir released me when Irina came for me. She still had my mother's blood on her hands. She told me my mother died because I wouldn't listen to her warnings about my curse . . . that if I'd just come to her, then maybe she wouldn't have had to die. But now many more people were going to die."

"It's not your fault," Alec reassured her. "None of this has ever been your fault. Irina's a sick, twisted woman who will tell you anything to get you to do what she wants."

At that moment, Alec could hear as well as see Poppy breathing harder. She shivered again. "I felt more hate than I'd ever felt in my life. I cursed all of them to burn in hell and . . . and-"

"And what?" Alec prompted, still holding her tightly.

"They did. The Dhampirs suddenly bursts into flames. Irina was just standing there watching while they were screeching out in pain—as loudly and as frighteningly as my mother had been. For a moment, for the smallest second, Irina looked at me as if she were staring at someone more frightening than she was."

Poppy jerked her head up to face him. "That's how I know I am cursed. *I killed all of them with just the anger in my head!*"

"No!" Alec ordered. "Listen to me! You are not cursed. And you are not evil."

Poppy's breath came out even harder. "I ran," she gasped. "I just ran as far and as fast I as could." Alec could see the absolute terror and devastation in her eyes, and now he understood why she had forsaken all of her abilities and chosen to lock herself away from people. *How had she survived running her entire life like this?* The simple things he took for granted every day, like having the same bed to sleep in, were completely foreign to her.

Alec stroked his hand gently over the distorted contours of her face. "You're not cursed. And I'm going to find a way to prove it to you, sweetheart. I swear I'll prove it to you."

CHAPTER TWENTY

"I can't believe I didn't see it," Joseph said, his voice as quiet as Alec had ever heard it. "She was showing signs of trauma when she first arrived here . . . I just didn't want to see it."

Alec sat up straighter in his chair before leaning forward a bit toward the satellite communications screen in his private conference room. "She didn't want you to see. She's scared by what she watched Irina do to her mother. And confused by a gift she doesn't yet understand."

"When did she tell you all this?"

Alec tapped his fingers against the wood table, remembering what it felt like to hold Poppy closely in bed while she confided everything to him. He couldn't remember the last time he felt so connected to a woman after sex—and just oral sex, at that. He hadn't been able to get that entire night out of his head. "Two days ago. I would have told you sooner, but-"

Joseph raised his hand to stop him. "No need to explain. I've been sequestered since this whole ordeal with Irina began."

Alec nodded and continued to tap his fingers on the table. "You know, Joseph, I need more answers if I'm going to be able to truly protect her."

Joseph stared at Alec with surprise. "I'll give you whatever information you need. But I've told you just about everything I know."

"I hope that's not the case because there are several things here that still just don't add up."

"Such as . . .?"

"Did you know that Poppy believes she was cursed while still in Mary's womb? Mary had apparently told her this. But when I came to you in London you told me Irina didn't even know of Poppy's existence until the night Mary was killed. How could Irina curse a child she never even knew about while that child was still in the womb?"

Joseph rubbed his index finger back and forth along his chin as he appeared to consider Alec's question. "I don't have an answer for that. As far as I know, Irina learned of Poppy's existence on the very night Mary was killed. And that makes even more sense now that we know Poppy was there."

"Yes, it does."

"What I do know," Joseph continued, "is that a warlock cannot curse a true innocent inside the womb. Not even Irina is powerful enough to do that."

Alec nodded. "Gideon already confirmed as much for me. Did you and Mary ever talk about whether she believed her daughter was cursed?"

"Mary did believe that Poppy was cursed by Irina. Of course, she didn't want to believe it at first. Poppy was her child. But there were too many accidents and deaths around Poppy for her to continuing dismissing them as coincidence."

Alec swung up out of his conference chair and turned his back to the screen. Those weren't the answers he wanted to hear. There were so many pieces of the puzzle that still didn't fit. It seemed the only person who had answers was Irina herself, and she was certainly not going to offer any explanations. "How could any mother allow her child to believe she's cursed? Regardless if she thinks it's true or not. I certainly don't believe it! Do you?"

Joseph remained calm as he replied, "No, I don't believe it. But Mary wanted Poppy to be prepared for what she was going to have to face. And as much as you or I may disagree with that decision, that honest preparation may well be the reason she's still alive today."

Alec felt his hands fisting tighter and tighter at his sides. What if he had never met Poppy because Irina had killed her along with Mary that night? "Irina is not going to get anywhere near Poppy," Alec replied fiercely. "Not as long as I'm breathing."

Joseph was silent for a long while, causing Alec to turn back to the screen after a few moments. "You care for her," Joseph said, obviously curious, "more than just as a charge from me." Alec believed in telling the truth, but he debated the wisdom in admitting to Joseph his growing feelings for the woman his Sovereign Elder considered a daughter. He ran his hands roughly through his hair and while Alec was hesitating, Joseph added, "Perhaps it would be best for me to have her move to the French site with Owen Maberey."

Owen Maberey? A sudden streak of white-hot jealousy swept through Alec at the mere suggestion. Owen would not know how to protect her. He was—*French!* He might be only a few years older than Alec, and admittedly he was attractive to women, but he was arrogant, and if he touched Poppy, Alec would kill him. Fellow Elder or not. "That's not necessary. I can protect her best here," Alec finally answered, as calmly as he could. "It's true, I've come to care for Poppy a great deal. I won't pretend otherwise. But it changes nothing. You chose me because you knew I would protect her to my very last breath. And that's what I'm going to do."

Joseph's gaze narrowed as he assessed Alec's words. "Getting personally involved with her changes quite a lot, actually. Your judgment may be compromised. Why do you think I put her in your care instead of keeping her in my own? I'm too close to her."

"My judgment is fine," Alec defended. "That's why I came to you with all of this. I want us both to protect her. She needs us both. Poppy isn't going to trust Owen if you ship her off to him now. To her, that would be no better than always running. She needs consistency . . . and assurance to feel safe . . . in one place. That place is here at The Oracle."

The Sovereign Elder paused for what seemed to Alec to be an eternity, as the two men engaged in a silent standoff. Alec was trying to decide what in the hell he was going to do if

Joseph ordered her sent to France. "I'll let her stay," Joseph finally said, to Alec's immense relief, "only because it's too risky to move her from sacred ground for any length of time right now. But I warn you, Alec. Do not hurt Poppy or abuse her trust in any way, or you and I are going to have serious problems. Are we clear?"

"We're clear," Alec assured him, and he meant it. After the other night, Alec knew he was developing deeper feelings for Poppy. He was just trying to sort out exactly what they were. Until he did, he would give Joseph no reason to take her away from him—especially to France and Owen Maberey.

Just then the door to the conference room opened and Kane, whom Alec had been expecting, was escorted in by Sampson. Respectfully (to Alec's relief) he bowed his head to Joseph on the SAT screen at the front of the room and quietly took a seat across from Alec. Kane was pretty much a wild card most of the time, believing himself to be nothing more than an independent contractor to The Brethren. But when times called for it, and Kane knew the stakes were high, the leader side of him took control. It was like flipping a switch from 'off' to 'on'.

"I have asked Kane to join us, Joseph, because he brought to my attention some additional information regarding the night on Bodmin Moor that I think you will find interesting."

"Really?" Joseph replied, the warning tone in his voice completely gone. "Go ahead."

"When Irina believed I was Poppy," Kane began, "she made a telepathic connection with me."

"Not surprising. Irina has stolen many powerful gifts from good witches," Joseph pointed out. "Stealing a strong telepathic gift might well be one of the strongest powers she could acquire."

Kane nodded in agreement. "What was strange was that she told me not to be afraid—that she had no intention of killing me—yet."

Joseph frowned. "And why didn't you bring this to our attention sooner?"

"Because Irina implied as much herself at Bodmin Moor," Alec interjected.

"Yes," Kane replied, "but there was something I sensed. There was a part of her that was reluctant—possibly even afraid."

Alec turned back toward the screen. "Poppy said something similar to me when she told me about the night her mother died. She said that Irina seemed unsure for a moment when she had witnessed Poppy's power with the Dhampirs . . . but then it was gone."

"That doesn't make a lot of sense," Joseph replied. "Witches are far from the most powerful beings in the supernatural world. To suggest that a witch like Poppy, who has had no training, could cause fear in a warlock like Irina— who has killed hundreds of good witches—is not logical."

"You and Gideon agree on this," Alec replied with a long exhale. "But I still feel there's something we're missing here. I'm sure of it. Have you had someone there tracking Irina's whereabouts since the night she escaped from Bodmin Moor?"

"We have. It appears that Sienna did manage to injure her that night before she died. I think that has been slowing down her plans a bit-"

They were interrupted when Sampson knocked and entered the conference room. "I'm sorry for the interruption, sir."

"What is it, Sampson?"

"We've just had a report that one of Dr. Li's staff, Lily Abbott, was attacked down in the labs. Dr. Li is requesting that you come down there immediately."

"Is she all right?" Alec asked.

"He didn't say."

Alec nodded and stood up again, looking back to Joseph's image on the screen. "Do you mind if we cut this short?"

"Of course not. Sounds like you have a situation to deal with there."

Alec turned back to Sampson. "Tell Dr. Li I'll be right there."

"Who attacked her?" Kane growled at Sampson before he could leave the room.

"It was one of the super soldiers, Zane Merrick."

"*Damnit!*" Kane cursed under his breath.

"Zane Merrick is one of the only men left from those cockamamie vampire blood transfusions Reese conducted, is he not?" Joseph asked.

"He and Aiden Rowan," Alec replied. "We recently noticed some things about Zane that concerned us, so Dr. Li has been keeping a close eye on him. There've been no signs of any problems with Aiden, however. He checks in weekly."

Joseph sat forward in his chair. "He's not being monitored there at The Oracle?"

"He stayed up north to continue tracking and monitoring our Wraith situation. It's been a year since the transfusions, and he's shown no signs of abnormal aggression."

"He's been fine," Kane added firmly, which wasn't a surprise, considering he and Aiden had been best friends for years.

"It doesn't matter," Joseph replied. "And quite frankly, I'm surprised you both don't see that. Those super-soldier experiments Reese conducted were immoral and irresponsible. These men are an unnatural cross between the human and the supernatural world. I empathize with what they are going through, but we can't have one of them running around out there unsupervised, no matter how well he *appears* to be handling things."

"Aiden would never hurt an innocent!" Kane barked at Joseph, his temper slipping out of his control for a moment.

"Kane!" Alec snapped. "I'll see you in my office. He then nodded to Sampson to escort Kane out of the room.

"Perhaps, Alec, you're too close to this," Joseph suggested after they had left the room. "You want these men to be all right because Reese was responsible for what's happening to them. But you know as well as I do that may not be possible."

"Reese was responsible for a lot of things he should've had to live to answer for. Death let him off easy," Alec replied roughly.

"Being mauled and fed upon by a Lycan is hardly an easy death," Joseph pointed out.

"It was an easy death for him. And you're right. I do owe it to Aiden and Zane to do everything in my power to spare them from the same fate as the other Guardians. I'm asking you to trust me to handle this the right way. And if I'm wrong, you can hold me directly responsible for whatever the consequences are."

"If you believe there's a chance to save these men, then you'll have all of The Brethren's resources available to you to make that happen. But Alec, if we do this your way and innocents are hurt, then I *will* hold you responsible for the consequences."

Alec nodded. "In exchange, I'll send a team to retrieve Aiden as soon as possible."

***

Minutes later Alec returned to his office, where a very upset Kane was pacing the room. "What was that all about?" Alec demanded. "You know the quickest way *not* to get what you want is to challenge Joseph like that."

"I'll not stand by and watch Aiden be locked up by The Brethren! The Brethren is responsible for what's happened to him." Alec said nothing in reply, regarding him with an even expression. Kane kicked his foot into the air in frustration because there wasn't a single piece of furniture left in the room to kick. All of the rubble from Alec's little breakdown had been removed, but there was nothing to replace it with yet. "You're sending a team after him, aren't you?"

"I don't have a choice."

"Don't bother. Aiden will be here within a day of hearing what's happened to Lemon. He cares for her a great deal."

"You mean Lily," Alec said back to him.

Kane slapped his hands against the side of his legs. "Yes, that's what I said."

Alec just sighed. The man was strange sometimes. "I need to get down to the labs."

"I'm going with you," Kane growled. "She had better be all right or I'm going to kill Zane myself."

CHAPTER TWENTY-ONE

Poppy landed flat on her back just before the breath was whooshed right from her lungs—*for, like, the third time!* She lay there, staring at the ceiling for a moment, wondering what the heck had gotten her so inspired to train for battle against an all-powerful warlock she had run from her entire life. She rolled onto her stomach and blew a hard breath to move the loose strands of hair that had fallen into her eyes. "Maya, how does such a small woman pack such a powerful punch?"

Maya giggled with a big smile. "I was trained by the very best; Alec, Lucas, and, of course, Phinneas."

Poppy frowned as she rubbed her hand over her hip, triggering the memory of a particularly hard bounce on her bottom while training with Alec the morning before. "Yeah, I was starting to notice Alec's a little intense with his training."

"Is he ever!" Maya declared. "Alec's all about empowering female Dhampirs through proper training—so they can understand their true potential. It's kind of sweet when you think about it. It just doesn't feel sweet when he's actually teaching you"

Poppy couldn't help but laugh at that. Naturally, being of the feminine persuasion, she had played up the hard landing on her ass until he offered several kisses of apology in return . . . which she only felt slightly guilty about because he was such a good kisser.

"You should take it as a compliment," Maya continued. "If he pushes you that hard, it's because he thinks you can handle it. That says a lot about how fast you're learning."

"I hope that's true," she replied, taking Maya's hand to help her back to her feet. "But I sometimes wonder how much is just his concern that I learn as much as I can as fast as I can."

"Personally, I think he likes having a reason to spend time with you. In fact, I'm surprised he let you come down to the third floor today. He seems rather fond of keeping you locked away with him on the twelfth floor."

"He doesn't exactly know I'm down here. He was up way before dawn and locked away in meetings this morning. But I'm sure it's only a matter of time before my shadow tracks me down."

"How did you ever manage to give Matthias the slip?"

"The balcony," Poppy replied flatly.

Maya giggled again. "Poor guy. You constantly have him in trouble with his boss."

"I don't mean to. I never asked for a twenty-four-seven bodyguard. And I missed getting to see you—just getting out."

"Sounds like someone's coming out of her shell. That's good. Have you told Alec that you miss being out and about? I'm sure he would be happy to hear it."

Poppy shook her head. "He seems pretty committed to the idea of Irina never getting a peak at me . . . which is good, but . . ."

Poppy's thoughts seemed to drift away from her just then, and Maya brought her back by touching her arm. "You're worried."

"I just don't want to be locked away anymore. Even if it is to protect me."

"That's the best thing you've said since you arrived here," Maya smiled. "You should talk to him. I know he never wanted you locked away in the first place. I think he's just come to care for you and wants to keep you to himself for a little while."

"That part I don't mind," Poppy smiled. She couldn't help it. Three weeks had passed since Alec had spent that first night with her in her room. And he'd spent every night with her since. He would come to her in the evenings when he was finished for the day. Some days for him were harder than others, but they would usually enjoy a quiet dinner together and he would ask her questions about her life on the run. About the places she had been. About the things she had experienced. It was almost like he wanted to free his mind of the events of his own day, so he never talked about them. That concerned her, but she didn't push him on it.

Once in a while, though, he would open up about the people in his life he had lost, and that was important because Poppy could then understand how those losses had formed the man and leader he'd become. When his father died he had lost his hero. When his Uncle Reese had been turned into a Nightwalker and killed his best friend Lucas Rayner, she could see the terrible scar it had left on his soul.

When he talked about Lucas's death he became very quiet, almost as if the words were still difficult to speak. Poppy wondered if Alec would ever truly trust someone in a meaningful way again after his uncle had betrayed him so deeply. And then she caught herself. Was a woman on the run her whole life really any better at trusting than a man who had lost most of the people close to him? Trust meant planting roots into something. Depending on someone, even when you knew they might occasionally give you reason to doubt. Finding hope when you lose someone, as Alec had lost Lucas. Trust was, in many ways, the most difficult thing for both of them.

But, little by little, Alec was starting to open up to her more often. He seemed to laugh a little more and was much less closed off. Sometimes they would lie in bed sharing stories, and sometimes they would just touch each other to make a connection. Then they would make love all night long until each was too sated to speak and they would end up curled in each other's arms. At least to Poppy, it felt like making love. Alec took her slowly. *Excruciatingly slowly*. He was obviously making up for their first two rushed times. The result was torturous—sometimes. Wonderfully torturous. Even to think back on it now it made her whole body shiver. "He's just so amazing," she said with a slight catch to her voice, "and sweet.

I don't want him to worry that I can't handle myself. He already has enough on his plate to worry about. So, I really appreciate you doing these extra sessions with me."

"Of course," Maya replied. "You really are doing well. Your strength and core balance have improved—your concentration. Keep this up and pretty soon Irina will be the one on the run."

"You think so? I still keep tripping on these stupid mats."

"And what did Gideon say about that?"

Poppy sighed. "He says it's when I focus on trying *not* to do something that I most often will," she answered with a very poor impersonation of a British accent. Maya lifted her brows expectantly as Poppy added, "and that as the daughter of a witch and a Dhampir that I have the power within me to control the energy around me."

"Exactly," Maya said, adding emphasis with a firm nod of her head.

The smile faded from Maya's lips as both women turned towards the training room doors. Simon Kendrick came through them, his sandy blond hair a bit disheveled and his blue eyes appearing a little strained. He seemed surprised to see Poppy there. Walking up to Maya, he bent to kiss her on the cheek. It was the same simple, affectionate gesture he had always done with her, but something had now changed between them. "Hello, Poppy. Do you mind if I speak to Maya alone for a moment?"

"Not at all. I need to be getting back upstairs, anyway, before Matthias gets into any more trouble. Thanks again for your help, Maya." With that, Poppy turned and headed for the door.

"Oh, wait," Simon called back. "I almost forgot. Gideon suggested that I start working with you on your spells and incantations. It's important for you to understand how they are connected to you and how you can draw on some basic ones if you're ever confronted. We could meet down here tomorrow after lunch to work on it."

"That sounds great, but I can't do tomorrow. I can meet you down here on Thursday, though."

"Don't be late," he said with a wink.

As soon as Poppy stepped outside the door she wondered if perhaps she shouldn't have been so quick to say yes to Simon. The current scowl on Matthias's face suggested she might never be allowed off the twelfth floor again. The stalwart guard stood against the opposite wall with his arms crossed over his chest. Perhaps sneaking out her bedroom window wasn't the smartest idea. "Am I in trouble?"

"You want me to put odds on that?" he asked, offering a humorless smile. "Because whatever they are, the odds that *I'm in trouble* will undoubtedly be twice as high."

"Oh, don't be so dramatic, Matthias. I'm sure Alec's been so busy this morning he hasn't even noticed that I'm not up there."

Matthias just stared at her blandly. "He's already asked to see you three times."

"Really?" she smiled, feeling some unexpected heat coming into her cheeks. "That's so sweet." Matthias evidently didn't find it sweet at all. Seeing his irritation, she cleared her throat, straightened up, and started back towards the elevator. "I realize I'm not the easiest person to . . . *guard*," she acknowledged, "but surely you can appreciate my free sense of adventure."

"No," he replied. "No, I really can't."

***

Poppy realized just how serious Matthias had been about Alec asking to see her when she got off the elevator and saw the door to his office wide open. Matthias led her straight inside, and as she followed him through the door she found Alec leaning against his brand new desk with his arms crossed as though he had been expecting them the moment the elevator bell had sounded. Surprisingly, he was dressed very casually, in dark jeans, a gray V-neck sweater with a white tee underneath that fit him nothing short of delicious. She definitely liked the more casual side to him. It made him appear younger and more relaxed.

"Thank you, Matthias," he said. "That'll be all."

Poppy stood there pondering his mood for a moment, considering Matthias had warned her he'd been asking where she was all morning. No barking, no standing with his hands on his hips, no scowl on his face. So she was utterly confused as to what his mood was. "OK, so let me explain," she began, walking towards him. "I did sneak out my window this morning and went down to the third floor, losing the shadow you've assigned me, Matthias, for just a little while. But it was for a good reason. I've been doing double-duty training with Maya, and I have to admit I'm getting rather good at kicking butt."

Alec smiled, and she instantly knew she didn't have to say anything else. "Come here," he said, crooking his finger and a suddenly projecting a naughty gleam from his light brown eyes. When she did, his hand came up to her neck and he pulled her to his lips, stealing a kiss that robbed her of her sense of North and made her feel delightfully weightless on her feet. When he finished and pulled his head back slightly, she realized she was somehow completely leaning against him— and he didn't seem to mind.

"You're not upset?"

"Yes, I'm upset," he replied, yet with a playful tone to his voice that definitely did not match his words. "I'm upset that the entire third floor got to see you running around in those sexy yoga pants this morning but I'm just now getting my first glimpse. I'm upset that I've thought of nothing else all morning except stretching you out over this brand new desk of mine and christening it before lunch."

"Christening it, huh?" Poppy smiled as she ran her fingers over the elegant, dark-stained walnut. This new desk seemed much more suited to Alec's persona; bold, clean lines, with just a few modern touches like brushed stainless pulls. "I do like this desk," she commented.

He then leaned into her neck and nibbled playfully at her ear just before executing the rather graceful move of hauling her off her feet and swinging her around until she found herself lying flat on her back on that very desk. "Wait until you see the new lounge chairs. I expect us to be christening each one of them, too, by the end of the week."

Poppy blinked with a surprising rush to her breath. "Each one? We're going to be busy this week, aren't we?"

He laughed huskily. "Yes we are."

For a long few seconds, Alec just stared at her lying there on the desk. His expression seemed to promise that he would burst into a smile at any moment. "I'm happy, Poppy," he suddenly declared. "You make me happy."

Poppy felt a huge grin come over her own face as she stared back at him. "You're really not upset then that I snuck off this morning?"

"No," he replied. "I'm sorry that you feel like you have to sneak off. I get that it's no fun being kept away up here and having Matthias shadow you twenty-four-seven. Believe me, I get what it's like having guards around the clock. I was just kind of hoping it could be something you could get used to."

Poppy wrapped her legs around him and pulled him down closer to her. "You mean, getting used to dating a man with the responsibilities of an Elder?"

He nodded with one of those smiles that wonderfully pulled at the signature dimple in his chin. "Yeah, something like that. I know this life I've chosen is not easy, but I would do everything in my power to make to easier for you."

Poppy suddenly felt her eyes well up with a burst of loving emotion than swept through her. "I think that is the nicest thing any man has ever said to me."

Alec kissed her, his hands smoothing along her hips. He pulled gently at the colorful waistband of her yoga pants, drawing them down over her hips. "I mean every word of it, as long as you promise not to dive into any more lakes."

"No more lakes," she breathed, and Poppy felt herself getting considerably stirred up. She knew she needed to take advantage of Alec's accommodating mood before she completely lost every thought in her head. "So then, you wouldn't have a problem if I trained on the third floor again on Thursday—with Simon Kendrick."

"I always have a problem with you training with another man," he replied, moving the focus of his kisses to the exposed skin below her waist, then down low on her hips, letting his tongue do all sorts of adventurous things across her increasing nakedness.

"Yes, I can tell,"—she gasped out loud as his tongue slid even lower on her thigh—"you're really, uh, *bothered* by it."

He laughed against her skin. "Terribly. How could you think to let another man train you?"

"It was actually Gideon who suggested it to Simon. He thought Simon could help me with my incantations and spells." Alec's head suddenly popped up, his expression frowning at her. "What is it?"

"Nothing," he replied but he was still frowning. "It's a good idea, actually. Simon has become quite an accomplished witch. I'm just surprised Gideon didn't suggest it to me first."

"Oh, poor Elder," Poppy teased as she pulled him back up to her lips. "Is someone keeping you out of the all-knowing loop?"

"Never!" he charged, nibbling at her neck.

She squealed in response to his little bite and squirmed in his arms. "What in the world has you in such a playful mood today?"

"You mean, beside the fact I'm about to get some on my brand new desk?"

"Yes, besides that fact."

His smile faded into an expression that still showed complete happiness as he strummed his knuckles along her cheek. "I have good news. Kane has been in London, working with a team from The Hallow. They're closing in on Irina. This whole nightmare may be over with for you in a few short days."

Poppy blinked back her surprise. "Really. They're going after Irina as we speak?" Alec nodded his confirmation. Poppy then threw her arms around him. "Thank you! Thank you! Thank you! I can't remember ever feeling this happy."

"You can stop running, little flower," he said sweetly—and then kissed her again. For a moment, Poppy thought she might melt into him completely as he pulled her close and his tongue slipped inside her mouth and wrapped around her own. Their kisses melded into one another and Poppy forgot completely that they were in his office and atop his new desk. His breathing was hard on her skin as she felt her Lycra top lifted over her head and his mouth coming around her left breast. *God*, the man had a mouth on him. He could make her entire body shiver with just his lips and tongue without even trying.

Simultaneously, Alec's hand pressed between her thighs. Her back arched off the desk as she felt his fingers begin to stroke her while his mouth never left her nipple. "Alec." She said his name several times as his dexterous fingers brought her right to the edge of her release and then stilled while she came down again. He was working her into a frenzy—and it wasn't fair. "Alec, it's time for you to finish with the business of getting lucky," she gasped.

"You think so?" he asked, even though she could feel him working frantically at his jeans.

"Yes!" she breathed out hard. "Do you have a condom in this new desk somewhere?"

Alec contorted himself awkwardly as he reached above her to the drawer on the other side of the desk. "Are you kidding?" he said. "I've got a whole box." A handful of condoms rained down on her as his hand swung back from the drawer. She started laughing, but that did not stop Alec from the task at hand. He ripped open the condom package with his teeth and rolled it on faster than Poppy had ever seen a man roll on a condom before. He then lined his body up with hers and entered her with one hard, long thrust that fully seated him inside her.

Poppy moaned long and loudly in response, elated at feel of this man she had fallen head over heels in love with inside her—possessing her body as if he owned her completely. She had never felt this connected to Alec during their previous encounters. Sex with him now was not just fucking. Alec was not staring at the ceiling as he thrust into her. He was staring at her. Never taking his eyes off her. He was fully engaged and connected.

***

Alec couldn't take his eyes off Poppy. She was breathing hard in her passionate excitement, exposing her sharp fangs, while her long cherry hair spilled around her and her gold eyes swirled with blue. She was beautiful to him. Never more beautiful than when she was lost in the mindless pleasure of their fucking. *No*, he thought. This was not fucking to him— not anymore. With her, he didn't see how it ever would be again. He wanted no other woman. Her body was heaven to him. The way her inner muscles responded to having him inside her, the way she moved with him, pulled at him. She felt *right*.

He shifted her slightly on the desk, wanting to find that perfect spot where he could drive into her and rub her clit just-so along the way. One. Two. Three. Bingo. Her nails dug into his back as her legs curled higher around him. "Oh, God, Alec!" Her mouth opened wider as she arched her head back, showcasing those dangerous fangs, and Alec couldn't imagine her being any hotter.

"Ahh, we're really going to have to talk about you drinking from me soon." Alec could feel something big building at the base of his spine that he might have to put into the category of epic. "I want it, Poppy!" He continued to rock her while

Poppy's body spasmed around him and he growled out above her. Her hips lifted, drawing him deep into her body at the highest point of her orgasm. "*Oh, shit,*" Alec gasped, his hips canting forward and jerking several times, exploding inside her.

When he was spent he fell against her on the desk, and the only sound they could hear was each other's breathing, back and forth, which was falling into rhythm as their passion subsided. As soon as Alec could gain enough strength to move, he slid his body from hers and disposed the condom in the trash. Poppy looked confused by his rush to leave her in the glorious aftermath to dispose of a condom. Alec came back to her, nestled himself back in her arms, his voice calm as he said, "The condom broke."

"Wh—What?" Poppy stuttered. "Alec, I'm not on any birth control." Alec hated seeing the worry on her face as she nibbled at her bottom lip. He didn't want her to worry. "It just wasn't something I had regular access to being on the run so much. And I didn't really need it—until I met you, that is."

Alec couldn't help but have an 'inner caveman' gleam in his eye. He suspected Poppy had not been with very many men, but he liked hearing it confirmed. He wanted her all for himself, which was definitely unusual for him, considering he'd known her for only a little over a month. "Hey," he replied, kissing her on her cheek. "We've been careful. Chances are there's nothing to worry about, so I don't want you to worry. *If* you have reason for concern later, then you'll get tested. And we'll deal with the results together, whatever they are." She was still nibbling at her lip. "I mean it, Poppy. You're not alone in this."

She continued to stare up at him with those wide, gold eyes that so fascinated him. "Alec, have you really thought about whether you're ready to be a father?"

He sighed. "That's not really a fair question to ask me. I've always known it's my duty to produce a son to continue the Lambert seat on The Council. I've never questioned that I would be a father—someday. I don't know if I'm exactly ready today . . . but I'm not afraid of it. And I would want *any child* conceived between you and me."

Poppy sat up on the desk, drawing Alec with her as she pulled her workout top over her to cover her nudity. Alec leaned in beside her, strumming his fingers playfully on her leg. "I haven't thought about being a mother . . . about having a family. It isn't that . . ." She stopped for a moment. "I just never imagined my life stopping long enough to let that happen. I've been this clumsy woman with a vengeful warlock practically on my heels for as long as I can remember. *What have I been thinking?* This isn't a game. My life could mean death for any man or child connected to me."

She tried to continue dressing but Alec stopped her with a question. "If you didn't have to worry about Irina. If you had a normal life, would you want those things?" Alec asked, finding himself surprised at how he was anxious to hear her answer.

Poppy stared up at him, her eyes slightly watery, and it killed him to see her struggle with something that should be a basic right for all women. "But I *do* have to worry about Irina."

"*Not* for much longer."

"I hope your right. But if not, I've seen firsthand what she'll do to the people I love. I've been living this fairy tale with you, locked away up here, playing house, for the past few weeks . . . but I fear it won't last. She'll find me again. And when she does, your life will be at stake; anyone connected to me here will be in danger. So my answer right now would have to be 'no'. I don't want those things."

CHAPTER TWENTY-TWO

"Let's start off by making sure you understand the difference between a spell and an incantation," Simon began as Poppy set down the things she had brought with her to the third-floor training room. It was early evening outside, but already dark in the gym when she met Simon for their scheduled training appointment. She was actually kind of excited about better understanding the witch side of herself.

Poppy had never known her father, Charles Honeywell III, since he died before she was born, but her mother spoke of him often and told her repeatedly how much he loved and respected the craft. Poppy resented the craft for a long time because she believed it was the reason she never had a chance to meet her father, but now she was starting to entertain the thought that if she understood witchcraft better, the very thing he loved so much, she might be able to understand her father a little better, as well.

"All right," Poppy replied, walking over toward Simon. His hair seemed blonder than she remembered when she first met him—really blond and really shiny. He was definitely attractive, in that sort of polished, educated way, but he also seemed somehow kind of guarded or stiff. "I know that a spell is a set of words, said aloud, that bring about a magical action."

"Very good," Simon replied. "Spells are a specific series of words or phrases that are typically written down and must be said in a certain order. They must be recited by a witch with supernatural gifts, someone who believes *completely* in the craft—or else the spell may fail. Now, an incantation is more of an intention you are putting out into the world. Incantational words can be created in a moment and repeated in a certain order to bring about a specific result that you want. If it's a more ceremonially-based incantation it could require the presence or use of items such as magical herbs, potions or amulets—also designed to bring about a specific result."

"That makes sense, I guess."

Simon thought for a moment as he rubbed his hand at his chin. "Now, from what Gideon has explained to me, you've also been exhibiting signs of having the power of telekinesis, which is much more rare. I would actually like to start there today. A strong mental gift, in combination with an incantation, can be very powerful. But in order for it to work, you must *channel all of your energy and focus on the one result you most want*. Let's try a small exercise. Then I can assess where we can best to go from there."

"What would you like me to do?"

Simon looked about the room as if he were searching for something. He stopped and fixed on a single light in the ceiling. Pointing up at it, he said, "There. A witch who exhibits signs of telekinesis can focus energy on one particular object or thought, willing that desire to happen. Now, it takes quite a bit of practice, so I don't want you to expect too much of yourself the first time. But try to focus on that single light and turn it off."

Poppy frowned at him. "That one light? But there are, like, twenty lights in here. How can my mind flip off one specific light when they're all on a single switch that's clear across the room?"

"Don't think of it as flipping a switch. Try to think of it as harnessing and controlling the energy around that particular light—go inside the light. Once you have a firm hold on that energy, you can bend it to your will." She frowned at him again but turned towards the light, anyway. She couldn't imagine the act of turning off a light in her head, but she was willing to try. "You need to be completely relaxed," Simon continued. "I want you to inhale several times—deep breaths. Focus solely on this one thing that you really want. Turn off that light . . . just that one light."

Poppy more sighed than breathed, then closed her eyes, thinking only about the light she wanted to turn off.

"Count with me, Poppy. One . . . Two . . ." On the count of two, she suddenly heard Simon say "Oh, shit!" and then heard a giant *pop*. As she opened her eyes she realized that the entire room had gone dark. Poppy gasped as she looked outside and realized there was no light anywhere. The whole building had gone to blackness.

She whipped her head back around to find Simon in the darkness. Her Dhampir eyes, just as exceptional at seeing in the dark as they were at night, could clearly see his startled expression. No, he looked worried—worried or constipated, she wasn't quite sure which. But she guessed she had just done something she wasn't supposed to be able to do. "Oh, shit," Poppy echoed quietly under her breath.

***

Alec had barely seen Poppy for three days. It seemed she was avoiding him a bit since the mishap with the condom. She told him she didn't want children or a family, and he'd found himself thinking about that a lot the past few days. He wondered whether, if Poppy were free to want those things without the threat of Irina hanging over her head, she would choose differently. He'd like to think she would. Alec was starting to envision Poppy as part of his future, and that included children, especially a little girl running around with long cherry hair just like her mother's.

Smiling to himself, Alec found it ironic how only six week ago he felt lost and detached from life. Now all he was thinking about were attachments, *permanent attachments*. He was thinking about his future, about children and one beautiful (and if he were honest himself, still a bit clumsy) woman who had somehow swept into his life and became his constant, his North Star. He had been with a lot of women in his thirty-two years. Even one he believed was *'the right one'* for him, Gemma May Walker, a sweet but sharp-tongued Dhampir he had fancied himself in love with for three '*sewing his oats*' kind of months in Seattle just before becoming an Elder two years earlier. But looking back on it now, Alec realized he still had a lot of growing up to do at the time. He needed to better understand the man he would become as a result of his role as Elder and what he truly needed in a woman he would consider sharing his life with. Aside from the obvious stuff like shared passion, laughter and love, he needed a woman who understood the responsibilities and time demands his role as Elder required. He needed a woman who could accept his chosen life and not resent it even though it would most certainly always be his shared mistress.

He believed Poppy could be that woman.

But he had to get her to stop avoiding him first.

"You seem a bit distracted this evening," Gideon said, bringing Alec out of his thoughts. "I called your name just now as I came in, but, I dare say, you didn't hear me."

Alec stared across the room at Gideon from his comfortable seat in one of the new lounge chairs that had just been delivered to his office. He rather liked them. They were straight-line styled, comfortable and oversized, and he couldn't wait to christen them with Poppy. *No, he wasn't distracted.* "First of all, I'm quite certain you didn't call my name but used that *sir* crap. And secondly, with as much as we're juggling right now, I'm entitled to be lost in thought every once in a while, old man."

Gideon laughed quietly. "I suppose you are. I've good news to report, though, with regard to Irina. Kane and the team have found where she's been staying, an old abandoned ancestral castle near the Irish coastline. She was not there, but the team found her spell book and supplies. The fireplace was still burning, so she had recently been there. They will stay back and wait for her return. It should be just a matter of time."

"That is good news," Alec said, his expression revealing considerable relief. He wanted more than anything to tell Poppy she would never have to think about running again.

"According to Kane, Joseph is now overseeing the operations from London and providing additional backup in case it is needed."

"Good," Alec replied. "I will contact Joseph and follow the operation from here."

Gideon nodded. "If there is nothing else, sir, I will leave you to your thoughts."

Gideon started to exit the office when Alec stopped him. "By the way, Gideon, I've been meaning to express my gratitude for your suggestion that Simon work with Poppy on her spells and incantations. I think it will be good for her to better understand that part of her gift."

Gideon stared back at Alec curiously for a moment. "Well, I certainly can't take credit for that. It was Simon who came to me and suggested he work with Miss. Honeywell. Of course, I supported the idea because I agree it is what she needs to gain a better handle on her gift—and her rather unfortunate predisposition for, umm, clumsiness."

"Simon suggested it . . .?" Alec questioned.

"Is that a problem?"

"No, no. I just heard it was the other way around. I must have misunderstood."

"I can think of no one better to teach her. Simon has become a remarkably accomplished witch since his arrival here a few month ago. And it sounds like if not for his actions, more would have been lost at Bodmin Moor."

"No, you're right about-" Alec's sentence was cut off by the power suddenly going out and thrusting the two of them into total darkness. He blinked in his surprise because he couldn't remember the last time the power had gone out at The Oracle.

"The power's out? That certainly doesn't happen very often," Gideon commented.

"Probably just the freezing temperatures outside," Alec replied, more to give a reasonable explanation to himself than to Gideon. "The emergency generators will kick in soon." But strangely, the emergency generators didn't kick in, and Alec was starting to have a very uncomfortable feeling.

Sampson charged into his office, a lighted flashlight in his hand, which he immediately passed to Alec. "Sir, I've just been informed the power's out."

Alec raised a brow at the guard. He knew the Dhampir would still see his expression just fine in the dark. "Yes, Sampson, I can see that. Why have the backup generators not come on?"

"The maintenance staff is down there now. Evidently, the backup generators are off-line as well."

Alec became very concerned that something was not right. "Gideon, follow us. Sampson, let them know we're on our way down to them. I need to know why even the generators have been knocked out." Alec then threw over his shoulder at the same time Sampson was passing along the message on his comm. link, "Where did the power spike initiate from?"

Sampson exchanged more conversation with the people at the other end of the line before replying, "According to reports from the staff, it started on the third floor."

Alec swung around on his heels. "Third floor? Poppy's on the third floor tonight."

***

Now she'd done it. Poppy groaned, half in misery, half in annoyance, as she looked back at Simon. "*Oops*," she said. "I swear, I was just trying to focus on the one light."

Simon rushed to the window and peered out into the pitch blackness. "It looks like the power is out as far as I can see for miles."

"Well, let me try to focus on bringing it back on," she offered, getting nervous someone might come for her for cutting the power for miles.

But Simon shook his head. "No. I want to keep working on this. This is truly remarkable, Poppy. An untrained witch like you should not be able to knock the power out of a whole building, let alone an entire power grid. If you don't mind, I'd like to try some other tests, but I think we should be a safe distance away from everyone here at The Oracle."

"I'm not really supposed to leave the building," Poppy told him, although she wouldn't mind leaving the building because she was having a hard time avoiding Alec these days. Having the condom break on them the other day had snapped Poppy back into reality. She couldn't afford to get pregnant. She couldn't afford to think of children or a family. Those were things that kept you rooted in one place, and Poppy didn't have that luxury in her life, no matter the fairytale she had been living for the past month with Alec. Eventually, she knew, she would need to leave The Oracle, so she needed to detach herself from Alec now before she no longer could.

Simon stared back at her, confused. "I think in this case, Elder Lambert's not going to object to having you a safe distance away."

As though on cue, the doors to the training room flew open and Alec appeared with Sampson, Gideon and several other guards, all of them holding flashlights. "He came right up to Poppy, placing his hands gently on her arms and then, as an expression of deep concern, stroked along them, up and down. "Are you all right?"

She nodded, a bit puzzled. "Yes, I'm fine. It was a spell I was learning. I sort of overshot while focusing on this one light. I'm sorry. Simon and I were going to continue our work outside so something else didn't happen."

Alec suddenly adopted a very cool, quiet look that showed in his eyes as he turned to Simon. "She's to remain here," he said, calmly but authoritatively. "Thank you for working with her, but training is done for today."

Simon got the message, loud and clear. "Of course, Elder Lambert." He picked up his items and quickly exited the training room.

Alec turned to Sampson. "Everyone wait outside for a moment. I would like a word with Poppy—alone. Have

Matthias meet us to escort her back to her room after we've finished."

"Yes, sir," Sampson replied as he motioned for all of the guards to follow him out of the training room.

Once Poppy and Alec were alone, and they were shut back into total darkness except for the beam of Alec's flashlight, he turned to her, the dimple on his chin very prominent as he quietly said, "You've been avoiding me." Poppy was caught off guard by the direct statement, and once again she was reminded how much Alec Lambert valued the truth. She would at least give him that much, even if she could give him nothing else.

"Yes. What happened the other day, with the condom reminded me that I have been letting myself get too comfortable with this situation."

"Situation?" Alec questioned. "I hardly think you and me being in a relationship is a situation."

Poppy sighed as he continued to rub her arms reassuringly. "You know what I mean. I can't pretend that I can stay here forever. Or even for another month. What we've shared has been . . . really wonderful. But we both have to accept the reality of the situation."

Alec's hands squeezed her arms reassuringly, just above her elbow. "Sweetheart, I understand that you react this way because this is how your life has been up to this point—that you believe you can't stay in one place for very long. But I'm telling you now, things are different this time. I just need you to have a little faith in that."

He kissed her and, even in the dark she had created, Poppy felt like she could melt from just one kiss. He was tender and loving, and sometimes when he kissed her—the way he would almost pause, as if he were totally absorbing in the moment— he made her believe he could love her. She had missed kissing him for the past three days. How in the world was she going to get used to not kissing him after she left?

"Have dinner with me tonight in my suite. We'll get dressed up. Just enjoy some time with each other, OK?" He could see she was contemplating whether or not that was a good idea. "Seven o'clock? I have some news that I think you need to hear. Please say you'll be there."

After another long moment, she finally nodded her head. "All right."

CHAPTER TWENTY-THREE

The significance of asking Poppy to meet him for dinner in his penthouse suite was not lost on Alec. Over the course of the last three weeks he had made love to her in the Elder's Library, in his conference room, on his office desk, in the training room and, almost every night, in her room. But he had never once brought her to *his* room—his home. He wasn't quite sure why, now that he thought about it. He didn't mind where they were together, just as long as they were together. But tonight was different for him. For the past week Alec saw Poppy Honeywell very differently. He saw her as the other half of him. He didn't know how the heck it happened so fast, but it had happened.

For the first time in his life, Alec's world felt complete, and he wanted to show Poppy his amorous appreciation by giving her the perfect dinner. Although to him, it wouldn't matter if the mango salad was just OK, or if the double cut lamb chops he ordered special from Mrs. Stippich were dry, or even if Poppy did one of her unfortunate preatfalls into the small dining table he'd prepared and crashed all the dinnerware to the floor. All that mattered was that she was there with him— because when they were in the same room together it just worked.

When Alec heard the knock at his door, he answered in confident fashion, dressed in his tuxedo trousers, dress shirt and vest, but he was immediately left standing there with his mouth agape, staring at the vision in front of him. Poppy was stunning dressed in one of those body-hugging little dresses that clipped her gorgeous legs just right above her knee. The bronzy color worked well with her gold eyes and red hair that flowed in waves to a spot below her shouldersand gold eyes.

So much so, he felt as though his body temperature just skyrocketed about ten degrees. "I don't think I even want my guards seeing you in that dress," he said with a proud smile.

"Is it too much?" she asked, smoothing her hands over the intricate lacy design.

"Oh, no," he answered, while his eyes appeared about to light her on fire. "I like it. I definitely like it. But I hope this is only for me."

Poppy smiled back at him, all that dark, cherry hair flowing in waves to a spot below her shoulders. "Only for you," she agreed, and it just made his hands itch in his desire to pull her to him and kiss her, which he did. She tasted of cherries and peppermint, and Alec knew he needed to get her inside his room right away so he could have her all to himself.

He instructed his guards to stand a little farther down the hall, and he made it clear that they should not be interrupted unless the world was coming to an end. That statement was met with some curious lifts of the brows, but Alec didn't care. "Make yourself at home," he said as he closed the door behind him and watched Poppy curiously move throughout his home. True, for the most part it was a large hotel suite, but it was home to him—and he wanted her to like it.

She dropped the brown, beaded wrap she had about her shoulders on a chair and let her gaze settle for a few moments on the dining table he had accented with a giant bouquet of freshly-cut red poppies. A soft expression settled on her face as she walked over and smelled their fragrant scent. "They're beautiful."

"Just like the woman," he said in sincere reply.

Poppy smiled at him and continued to walk around. Alec was surprised at how much he enjoyed watching her explore his home. He wanted to share this private side of himself that very few people within The Oracle ever saw, except maybe for Gideon—and Lucas, when he was alive. Two sliding panel doors were fully opened so she could see into his bedroom suite. She stepped inside for a few moments and glanced around before moving on, and Alec couldn't help but smile. He very much liked his bedroom. He couldn't take any credit for the design—featuring an enormous canopy bed draped with deep gray velvets at the corners and dressed in white silk sheets that made one just want to sink into its heavenly softness. That was done by the architects for The Elders at the time of the remodel of the twelfth floor. But seeing Poppy standing within it was definitely giving him some ideas. His whole body seemed to suddenly jump to attention at the thought of her naked body lying next to him in all that silk.

"So this is home," she said, breaking into his wicked thoughts.

"Mmm hmm," he replied, intentionally softly. "I know it's not large, like a house, but it's a good size. There's a kitchen through there, and two more bedrooms."

She turned to him. "It's beautiful. It feels like . . . a home." Silence slipped comfortably between them and he watched her continue to look at pictures and touch items he had lying about, including an open set of leather-bound supernatural textbooks on witches and witchcraft that Gideon had loaned him.

"Have you ever had a home, Poppy? Or at least, someplace you thought of as home?"

She shook her head. "Not really. When I was fourteen we had a place in Christchurch, New Zealand, for about six months. It felt like we were living at the end of the world—the last place on earth. For a while I believed it would be impossible for Irina to finds us there." Poppy moved back to the fireplace and touched some photos above the hearth. Alec found himself right behind her, as if he were drawn to her by an invisible cord. "I was wrong," she finished and touched yet another photo of a man and woman with a very young boy. "Is this your mother?"

"Yes," Alec replied, still speaking very softly.

"I don't believe I've ever heard you talk about her."

"Not a lot to tell, I guess. She separated from my father for a time when I was still a young boy and moved to Alabama to be closer to her sister."

"She didn't take you with her?"

Alec shrugged his broad shoulders almost imperceptibly. "She was not allowed to take me with her, since I was the first son and direct descendant to The Council. After my father died she wanted me to come to live with her in the South. She never wanted this life of an Elder for me . . . But I chose to stay here with Reese and my Aunt Judy."

"That's curious," Poppy began. "She must have had some idea what life she was getting into when she married your father—what it would mean being the wife of an Elder."

"My father told me he had discussed it with her. But I think it's hard to grasp it fully until you live it, you know. That's why it would be important to me to find a woman to share my life with who understands this world, this commitment I have made to The Brethren." Alec was pretty sure his not-so-subtle message to Poppy was clear enough. She smiled at him and continued looking through the pictures on the hearth.

"So you wanted this life, even then?"

"Yeah, I did. I wanted to be like my father—like my uncle, at least back then."

"And what about now?" She turned to him and their gazes locked.

Alec reached out to grasp her hand, and he swore an arrow could fly between their noses that moment and he wouldn't notice. "I still want this life. I'm not sure I would have said that a few weeks ago, but now I see things differently. I see them differently because of you. You've changed me." He lifted her hand and placed a gentle kiss on her palm before clutching it close to his heart. "I'm in love with you, Poppy Honeywell." Her eyes rounded with surprise as she inhaled quietly but deeply. "I don't know how this happened in the middle of everything seeming so bleak, but there it is. I love you."

"Alec." She said nothing else for what seemed like an eternity and the only sound he heard was the powerful beating of his own heart. He hadn't actually planned on telling her that he loved her that night, but now that it was out there it seemed vitally important to him that she love him in return.

"Do you love me?" he asked with a bit less breath than usual.

"It's not a matter of loving you, Alec. You are an easy person to love. I think I knew I loved you when you danced with me in that wet dress at the New Year's party. You were somehow bigger than all the bad stuff that brought me here. But just because we love each other does not change our situation. I'm not free of Irina. And I can't—no, won't—risk her finding out how important you are to me."

Alec pulled her to him, his lips so close that they were just a breath away from hers. "When we take care of Irina—and *we will* take care of her. I'm waiting to hear word any moment that she's in Brethren custody—you'll be free to stay wherever you want, for as long as you want. I just need to know if you want to stay here with me. Do you want to build a life with me, Poppy?"

Shiny tears welled in her eyes. "It's hard for me to accept that after all these years I won't have to run anymore. But if it's true, then there's no place I'd rather stay than here with you, Alec Lambert. I do love you. I love you with everything I have to give."

His answer to that . . . he kissed her. The kiss of a man who had no choice in the matter because the pull of his heart was in complete control over his body and mind. With one kiss, one taste, he began to relax in the sure knowledge she was his as the faint scent of peppermint began to infuse every fiber of his being and told him he was right where he should be—in her arms. Alec had stopped trying to figure out how this woman had become as vital to him as the air he breathed. He just accepted that she was. For all of his insistence that he had no time for a committed relationship since becoming Elder, Alec had never felt as committed to any woman in his heart as he did this woman.

With Poppy, things were much more elemental, like a statement of truth or fact that couldn't be challenged. He liked that. And he liked the fervor with which she kissed him back. The way her arms held onto him tightly, as if to steady herself. The way she sighed breathily when he kissed along her jaw. Alec was already dangerously close to a point at which he would have to have her or cease to breathe, and that wasn't a part of his plan for this evening—yet. He was supposed to have dinner with her first. "Sweetheart, we need to slow down here," he breathed roughly as he pulled from her lips.

She stared back at him with a dazed look. "Is something wrong?"

"No, nothing's wrong. I just wanted to discuss something with you before things get to that point." That certainly didn't ease her concern as he led her to the L-shaped sectional sofa. He sat to one side and drew her down beside him. A little crease formed between her brows. He wrapped an arm behind her while he traced her collarbone with his index finger. "Now that we've both said how we feel, I want us to talk about taking the next step. I want us to make love tonight without a condom. I want to experience what it feels like to love you with nothing between us." Poppy's smile faded, which wasn't exactly the response he had been hoping for, just before she tipped her forehead to his. "Do you not want to?" he breathed roughly.

She shook her head. "It's not that I don't want to. I would love to be with you that way. It's that I'm not protected."

He cupped his face in her hands, tipping her chin up to face him. "If you don't want to do this because you need more time, or are not ready for the possibility of children, then we will end this discussion right now until you are. But if you are ready, I want you to know I am committing myself to you now. I'm saying I want a life with you, Poppy Honeywell, and I want there to be no question that you belong to me."

"What exactly are you saying?"

"I want you to connect us," he affirmed in a voice that was absolutely clear. Poppy's whole expression blinked and Alec could easily read her concern. He was asking her to mate them by exchanging their blood, a commitment in the supernatural world that was even more binding than human marriage (which he also had every intention of proposing) because once a mating was complete, it could not be undone. They would be tied to each other for the rests of their lives.

"Alec, I don't know. Are you sure?" Poppy appeared stunned, but her watery eyes also brimmed with hope. He could see that she wanted to reach out and grab everything he was offering her, but she was holding herself back—and Alec really couldn't blame her. He was asking a lot from a woman who had never known the security of having a normal life, a constant home, or a rooted family. He wanted to give her all of those things, but that would require a heavy dose of trust on her part. "What about Irina?" she asked, more worried now than ever. "Alec, I know you say they are close to capturing her, but until they do I am not free to commit to something permanent like this. If I have to run again-"

"No!" Alec interrupted firmly as he held her to him so close his breath was on her lips. "You will not run. Never again. We do this together. The Brethren will protect you—I will protect you—and soon you'll be free. Tell me you believe that."

They both seemed to stare breathlessly at each other for a long moment before she offered him a smile. "I do. I do believe that," she murmured. "I love you, Alec Lambert. My answer is yes. Of course, it's yes! If you can give me a little more time on the no condom—child part . . ."

Alec smiled. "You can have as much time as you need." She pressed her lips against his responding smile as he drew her in for a hard kiss. He pulled her from the sofa onto his lap, molding her body to his so she could feel the hard erection that had formed, proof that he needed her and he needed her soon. "I love you, Poppy."

Caressing his hands along her unfolding legs, Alec was pushing the dress up on her thighs. She looked like a bronzed figure of perfection as she swung her body upward and straddled him in that dress. He reached around her and slipped off her high heels and let them fall soundlessly to the thick carpet below. Alec let his body sink fully into the sofa cushions as he drew her forward against him, causing both of them to breathe faster and harder in their excitement.

Poppy slid Alec's cummerbund upward until the top of his trousers revealed itself, then she reached her small hand between them and worked at unbuttoning and unzipping his tuxedo trousers. When she managed to get that chore done, she impatiently slipped her hand inside, stroking and massaging over the long length of his cock with the delicate firmness. His gasp turned to an audible growl as he stilled her hand for a moment. "Poppy," he breathed heavily, "before this goes any further—because God knows in about ten seconds I won't be able to stop—tell me clearly what you want tonight." He hoped he was seeing the answer there in her eyes. That she wanted to mate with him. "Tell me," he repeated roughly.

"I want to be connected with you," she said.

Alec's gaze was now blurred with a mix of emotions—from love to lust and back. The tears still welled in her eyes, a single drop slipping down her cheek to meet her lips just as she kissed him. No kiss in his life had ever felt so essential or so raw. He swore to himself that he would spend the rest of the night loving and savoring every inch of her amazing body . . . but later. Right now there was something much more basic, more primal, happening between them. He wanted—no, he *needed* her to mate them. He wildly reached his hand to the console table behind the sofa. From inside a small decorative box he pulled a condom and rolled it on expertly with one hand. *Oh, my God,* he was about to burst if he didn't get inside her soon. "Lift up for me, sweetheart."

Poppy pushed upward onto her knees; his hands reached under her dress and tore the strap to her thong. He pushed what was left of the lacy fabric out of his way and began to direct her down on him. Alec held his breath as she eased herself down on him slowly. He thought he might die from that extreme pleasure alone. "Come here," he said as he pulled one of her thin dress sleeves down on her shoulder until her right breast was bared to him. Taking her hardened nipple into his mouth like a ripe fruit, Alec felt as if he was being overwhelmed with sensations. "*Oh, damn*," he gasped, dropping his head back and away from her breast, focusing his gaze now on her incredible eyes as he felt her hot flesh, every inner muscle, clench around him and pull him in deeper.

Lord, have mercy on his soul, feeling her around him just then was the most perfect sensation he could ever have imagined. She was warm and lush, drawing him in deep and stripping him of every bit of his control. At that point, it was just a matter of holding on to his sanity as he stared into her eyes and watched her fangs emerge above his lips and her eyes tinge with a brilliant blue. She was the most beautiful woman he had ever seen as her nails bit into his shoulders and she began to move on him until he thought he wouldn't be able to breathe. He groaned as his head lolled back and he took in the viscerally sharp pleasure, repeated her name like a prayer on his lips as his hands slid under her dress and gripped the firm swells of her bottom.

"Alec, help me," she pleaded softly and his hands gripped her soft flesh so he could move her on him faster, directing her body and plunging her down on him at the perfect angle. The moment he felt her begin to release and squeeze around in what was already a fiercely tight fit, he flipped her onto her back against the sofa cushions and held her hips high as he shoved his pants down and plunged into her several more times, dragging out the anguished fire of her release.

She came so beautifully for him and then gripped around him so hard he felt as if he couldn't move, but he forced himself to. He thrust into her several more times as he watched her eyes turn completely blue and she released again, this time squeezing over him till he exploded inside the condom with the gentleness of a cannon. As he came, his body shuttered and he thought his head might pop from his shoulders. He was groaning right above her fangs, and seeing her Dhampir side beneath him with such raw need that matched his own was an indescribable pleasure.

Moments later he fell exhausted against her and there was a long silence where they just breathed in unison with each other. "That was amazing," he said before remembering he was probably crushing her against the back of the sofa. He lifted his weight onto his elbows for a few seconds to gather himself before using what strength he had left to pull her back into a straddling position over him on the sofa. "Just stay on me right like that," he instructed. "I'll need you again, soon."

***

Poppy smiled as her head lay against Alec's chest. "After that round I'm not sure I can handle '*again, soon*' just quite yet."

"Ah, but I have great faith in both of us," he purred in reply. They lay like that for a long while, letting the silence of the moment do all the talking. She loved this man. She loved him more every moment she spent with him. Yet there was still a part of her that wondered if she would ever truly be free enough from Irina to love him the way he deserved to be loved. He was an Elder, a great leader, a great man whose significant qualities included honesty, passion and unwavering strength of character. *Not to mention one rockin' hard body.*

"You've gone quiet on me," he broke into her thoughts. "Are you changing your mind?"

She shook her head against his chest and sighed blissfully. "No."

He tipped her chin up to him so he could kiss her, and when he pulled back there was such caring and gentleness in his eyes, Poppy no longer doubted that he loved her, even with all her clumsiness and the fact that she was being hunted by a madwoman. "Are you ready?"

Poppy straightened herself up a bit on his lap. "I want to make sure you're—"

He silenced her with a gentle hand over her mouth. "I'm sure, little flower."

Slowly, Poppy opened several buttons on his shirt and pulled his collar back on his neck, once again seeing all the old scars on the right side of his neck. She then pulled the collar back on the opposite side where there were no scars. She had a momentary twinge of guilt, but it didn't last. She wanted this more than anything she had ever wanted in her life—she wanted him to be hers forever. Poppy massaged her hands over his chest and shoulders, feeling every line, every ridge as she called to the surface the Dhampir within her. Within seconds she could feel her fangs pressing against her lips.

Alec watched her with such anticipation and heat in his eyes it made her burn for him again. His breathing grew heavier the more his excitement increased, until it seemed it was impossible for him to look away from her.

Bringing her wrist up to her mouth, she sank her bite into her skin and collected her own blood onto her tongue. As much as she had tried to deny her Dhampir side in the past, she loved the taste of blood, vampire or human. Her Dhampir side required that she feed on blood once in a while. But drinking now, knowing what she was about to do, excited her more than she ever remembered in the past. She moaned as she felt Alec's cock swell inside her once again, filling her to the brink in an instant as he relaxed his head back against the sofa and prepared himself for what was to come next. This was something he had wanted from her since the first night they had been together. "Come, sweetheart," he murmured. "Feed your thirst."

With the quickness of a whip, she pulled his head back and heard his breath catch as she sank her teeth into his throat, his body tensing against hers almost instantly. Her blood was now mixing with his, and the combination of the two was shocking in its power to turn her on. It was like that perfect mix of salty and sweet, warm, exactly like the sunny heat and scent of his body. She could feel the blood racing through her system as this uncontrollable need for him seemed to shoot up inside her, lifting her higher—like a rocket.

Poppy pulled him closer to her as she continued to drink, and the thought of soon being able to give him their mixed blood from her mouth—to transfer to him the same rush of incredible energy she was feeling now—excited her beyond all measure. From then on, every time they made love, she would know that he was truly hers. He would be connected to her in every way that mattered.

Her blissful thoughts were interrupted when she felt the long length of him suddenly soften inside her, and he was strangely stiff in her arms. She forced herself back, realizing she had not been gentle with him at all, and that's when her whole world change in an instant. Alec lay there unmoving against the back of the sofa, his eyes opened wide, stiff and unblinking. "Alec?"

CHAPTER TWENTY-FOUR

"Alec?" Poppy whispered again, breathless in her fear. "Alec, please!" Her hands moved over his chest, feeling for a critical beat from his heart. Instead, he lay there, stiff and motionless. The realization struck her that she had just done something unforgiveable.

Poppy wasn't sure how much time had passed before her stunned mind started reacting. She needed to get Alec help as soon as possible, and she feared she needed to do that without alerting the four guards standing outside their door, all of whom had the ability to hear a pin drop inside the room. Poppy gently pushed from Alec's lap, then rushed to the bathroom to run several cloths under warm water. She returned to Alec to clean him as gently as she could before lifting his body in her arms and moving him to his bed.

After pulling his bedroom sliding doors open just enough for someone to see Alec from his chest down if he peaked in, Poppy next ran to Alec's closet. Slipping off her dress and tossing it in the middle of the room, she grabbed one of his pressed shirts off a hanger, closed a few buttons then rushed to the suite door. Inhaling a deep breath, she ran her fingers through her hair to mess it up around her shoulders then swung the door wide, relieved to see that the guards had remained about twenty yards down hall, as Alec had ordered. "Do you need something, Miss Honeywell?" Sampson asked politely as he walked towards her, taking in her half-dressed state.

"No! No! I don't need anything," she began with a little more cheer than was appropriate. "We're having a very exciting night." Sampson stared back at her with an expression that seemed to say 'OK'. Poppy was beyond anxious and totally embarrassed by this point to be standing in front of

Sampson in so little clothing as though it was perfectly normal. But thankfully, he didn't appear suspicious of her. "Actually," she began, clearing her throat, "there is something Alec has requested. A very specific request."

"Of course," Sampson replied. "What is it?"

"He has expressed his desire to try something new this evening. I was wondering if, while he's taking a quick rest, if you would mind tracking down Maya for us . . . and bringing her up here."

Once Sampson caught her meaning—an implied threesome between Alec, Poppy and Maya—the guard's brows lifted in total surprise. "Maya Brunetti . . .?" he said, slowly and carefully. Obviously, Sampson assumed—just as everyone else at The Oracle would probably correctly assumed—that innocent Maya was not into threesomes.

"Is there another Maya?"

Sampson brought his hands up. "No. No. We'll go get her."

"Yes, right now," Poppy encouraged, hoping to get him to move a little faster. "He'll be awake any time."

About ten minutes later, Poppy was brushing her hand gently over Alec's cold cheek and fearing she was about to break down and cry at any moment. She had hurt him. She had hurt the man she loved deeply beyond any measure she thought herself capable of hurting anyone. Was this why her mother had warned her not to be with men? Did she know Poppy could do this to someone?

Poppy was saved from trying to come to terms with that possibility by a knock at the door. She rushed across the room and opened the door so fast it surprised both Maya and Sampson on the other side. "You asked to see me?" Maya said as Sampson cleared his throat a couple of steps behind her.

"Yes!" Poppy replied vociferously as she grabbed Maya's wrist and yanked her into the room. Before shutting the door on Sampson she gave him the calmest smile she could manage, given the situation, and asked, "Would you guys mind hanging back a bit? I know Alec's used to this sort of thing . . . all of you listening . . . but I'm still getting used to it."

Sampson's brows lifted high, but she gave him credit for maintaining his even expression. "Of course, Miss Honeywell. We'll be down the hall—way down—if you need anything."

"Great," she replied, quickly shutting the door in his face.

"Poppy, I really don't think I need to be here for this," Maya said with a crimson blush to her cheeks as she looked around and saw the obvious signs of an intimate night between her and Alec all around them. Poppy then silenced her with a quick hand over her mouth, handing her a prewritten note on a small notepad she grabbed from the console table next to the door.

I need your help.
Alec's in his bedroom. He's not moving.
I know your first thought is to get the doctor, but it's more serious than that.
I'm so sorry. I didn't know who else to turn to.

Maya's eyes widened as she read the note. She then rushed toward Alec's room. When she reached his bed she touched his cold skin and then ran her fingers across the fresh blood marks on his neck. Poppy could see the concern in her expression mounting as she continued to examine him. She grabbed the notepad from Poppy and quickly scribbled:

How long has he been like this?

Poppy signaled fifteen with her fingers, representing fifteen minutes.

Do you understand what is happening to him . . . That he is turning?

Poppy nodded miserably. Though she had prayed otherwise, in her heart she had known Alec was somehow turning into a vampire from her bite. She didn't want to think about it too much because she was trying to keep herself from crumbling into a million pieces. Thankfully, Maya seemed to understand, going into immediate response mode on behalf of both of them.

We need to get him off sacred ground before it becomes too painful for him to be here.
The only viable exit is the roof.
Go over there and make whatever sounds you have to in order to distract the guards . . . then meet me on the roof.

Poppy nodded and turned some loud music on while Maya whispered as low as she could in her ear, "He will have cash stored in here somewhere. Lots of it. Find it. We're going to need it."

After a few minutes of humiliating pants, moans, and words that were extremely embarrassing out of context, Poppy escaped through the bedroom window, which she knew would not have periodic eyes on it from the guards at the ground like Alec's private balcony would, and headed up to meet Maya on the roof. Maya was already down at the south end of the building with Alec's long body swung fireman-style over her small shoulders. Poppy started toward them but suddenly stopped when a familiar feeling flooded her every instinct. It was there again—that sense that someone was watching her from outside sacred ground. No, this time two people. The feeling was so incredibly overwhelming that she had no doubt it was real. She scanned across the night but could see nothing. She knew they were there somewhere, but Maya was waving her hand for Poppy to get her butt moving, so she was forced to let the nagging feeling go.

Helping Alec was more important.

As Poppy made her way across the roofline she reminded herself that once she stepped outside of sacred ground she would make herself an easy target for Irina. But right now she had to stay focused on what Alec needed. She had to find a way to make right the unforgiveable thing she had done.

The threat posed by Irina could wait.

***

Maya was driving as fast as she could across the snowy landscape away from The Oracle, hearing Poppy's tears in the back seat as she hovered over Alec's still body. "What have I done?" she said miserably. "I'm sorry. Please forgive me . . . please forgive me."

The poor woman was a wreck, and Maya wasn't sure what to say to give her any kind of solace because she was still just trying to process everything herself. They hijacked an SUV after basically kidnapping their Brethren leader who was currently turning into a vampire from the bite of a Dhampir, which technically shouldn't be happening. This was some serious shit they had gotten themselves into! "Poppy," Maya began as calmly as she could while keeping her eyes peeled for any vehicles that might be following them. "I know you're upset, but I need you to tell me everything that happened tonight."

Poppy stared up at Maya through the rearview mirror, her eyes red and her cheeks still wet with tears. "We were celebrating," she began quietly. "He told me he loved me and he wanted me to connect us."

"Connect you by mixing your blood through a bite?" Maya asked, trying to clarify things for herself.

Poppy nodded. "Yes. But as I drank from him I could tell something was wrong. He became stiff and I think he stopped breathing then, and his skin turned cold all of a sudden. When I realized what was happening, the only thing I could think to do was send for you. I'm so sorry I brought you into this. I just didn't know what else to do."

"It's OK, Poppy," Maya said as reassuringly as she could. "You did the right thing. We're gonna find a way to help him, I promise. But I need you to answer one question for me. It's very important. Did Alec ever have Dr. Li test your Dhampir bite venom after he brought you to The Oracle?"

"No," Poppy replied as she propped herself up on the seat.

"I supposed Alec didn't think about having you tested because he assumed you would have been tested at The Hallow."

"I was not tested at The Hallow, either. Joseph kept me a secret from everyone there."

"Yeah, I'm kind of realizing that." Then without warning, Maya jerked forward in her seat on a breathless gasp. She felt a sudden, sharp pain shoot through her entire body like fire and struggled to maintain control of the SUV. Her foot slammed on the brakes and the vehicle slid out of control across the icy highway until it stopped in a ditch at the side of the road.

"Maya, what's wrong?!"

"Pain," she replied. "I just felt an incredible amount of pain there for a moment. It's gone now, though." Maya worked the vehicle through the snow and back out onto the dark, deserted highway. "We have to keep going. Alec's guards will know Alec's missing by now. They'll be on our tail."

"Where are we going?"

"I'm not sure yet," Maya replied as she watched Poppy drop her head to rest on Alec's chest again. "Did you know that your bite was venomous enough to turn a human into a vampire?"

Poppy shook her head fiercely. "No! My mother warned me that I could hurt someone because of Irina's curse, but I never thought . . . I don't know if she knew . . . *Oh, God*, how is this possible?"

"That's a good question. Only a vampire should have powerful enough venom to turn someone into another vampire. But it's going to be all right, Poppy," Maya said, trying to keep her focused. "We just need to think this through. We've done the best thing by getting Alec off Oracle lands. As the transition happens and he gets closer to becoming a vampire, the pain would have become unbearable for him if he'd remained on sacred ground. Removing him from sacred ground would have been the first thing Dr. Li would've done if we'd taken Alec to him."

"So he's in a great deal of pain right now?"

"He's in some pain," Maya fibbed, knowing that Alec was right now in more pain than he'd ever known in his life; also, that there wasn't a damn thing any of them could do to ease it. Poppy folded herself over Alec and squeezed him, as if hoping to absorb any pain he might be feeling. "Let's start at the beginning. You said your mother was Dhampir, so she was half human. Is that right?"

"Yes," Poppy replied. "My father was a witch."

"Well that would make you only one quarter Dhampir. Your venom level should be nowhere near high enough to turn a human."

"It's the curse!" Poppy cried into Alec's chest, completely miserable now. "My mother warned me, over and over, and I didn't listen. I didn't listen . . ."

Just then Maya felt anther hard jerk to her chest and a sense of pain that was so overwhelming she had to slam the car to a stop again, this time sending the vehicle off the side of the road into a larger ditch that would be even more difficult to get out of. Maya sucked in another hard breath as she wheezed hard over the steering wheel. "Give me his hand," she instructed Poppy. Poppy looked at her strangely. "Give me his hand!"

Poppy did as she asked and Maya gripped his stiff fingers until she could clearly feel the unbearable pain Alec was suffering, and it broke Maya's heart because she didn't know what to do to help him. Poppy must have seen the fear and anguish in Maya's eyes, because she grabbed Alec and held him even tighter than before. The second she did, the pain coming through his hand eased to a bearable level. Maya blinked at Poppy, who was huddled there over Alec's body, in astonishment. Something Poppy was doing was causing his pain to ease in that moment.

"Poppy, whatever you're doing you need to keep-" Maya's next words were cut off by a sharp howl in the not so far off distance. The piercing sound was the same loud and angry howl of a Lycan Maya recognized, from weeks ago, on her balcony. "Stay here," Maya ordered Poppy. *"And don't let go of him.* Not for any reason. Understand?"

Poppy nodded and squeezed Alec harder as Maya shoved open the door and rushed toward the back of the vehicle. Scanning through the dark night, Maya determined that they were about forty minutes from the American border into Idaho, still in a relatively remote area with no road lights. *Why on earth was the howl of a Lycan this far south?* That was almost unheard of. A strange, yet familiar, feeling came over Maya as she stared at her hands. Then it came to her. She was starting to *feel* again. Her Empathic abilities were coming back to her, and the strongest feeling was pounding at her head repeatedly like a drum. "Phinneas?" she whispered out into the night. "Is that you?"

The howl sounded again, only closer this time.

Maya shouldn't allow herself to think the howl of the Lycan was *him.* That Phinneas was somehow still alive. But she wanted to believe; she needed to feel his strength right then, when she was feeling so lost as to what to do next. "I have to leave," she said sadly. "I have to help Alec. I don't know how to help him."

Another howl. This time louder. Then another. And another. Except, the howls were now on several sides of her. Maya's breath came in sharply as she realized she wasn't hearing the howls of a single Lycan, but of an entire clan of Lycans. The sounds were growing closer, coming fast through the trees on three sides of her. She breathed in roughly as she started to process that she and Poppy and Alec were nearly surrounded by strong, powerful creatures that could kill more easily than any other species in the supernatural world. And yet she found herself not moving, fascinated at how the howls sounded like unified calls, calls among a pack that were there for their own survival.

Was Phinneas there, running with this pack? If he wasn't, then it made no sense why an entire clan of Lycans would be following them this far south—or rather, chasing after them this far south. What if her senses were wrong? They had, after all, just come back on line, so to speak. "*Oh, shit*," Maya said with a rush of breath as she heard the howls come closer and she realized how much danger they were all in.

Seconds later, Maya jumped back into the front seat of the SUV, revved up the engine as high as it would go and ground their way out of the snow pile to pull back out onto the highway. "What's happening?" Poppy asked, with worry tinging her voice as she lifted herself once again from Alec. "The howls are getting closer?"

Instantly, Maya felt another wave of pain hit her chest and she slammed her hand over her heart to try to calm it. "Poppy, you need to keep holding onto him. Something that you're doing is easing his pain. Do you understand?"

Poppy didn't question Maya any further and simply wrapped herself around Alec's body again, holding onto him as if she were holding onto his very life. "Please, Alec," she whispered. "Please don't feel any pain. I would give my life for you to not feel any more pain."

Maya inhaled a couple of deep breaths as her own pain began to fade away. "That's it, Poppy. You're doing it. You're lessening his pain. Just keep holding on to him while I figure out our next move. We've got a couple of different balls we're juggling here," she continued to talk it through to herself—but out loud so Poppy could hear, too, and maybe even Alec. "The good news is, my Empathic gift is back . . . and just in time, I would say. The bad news is, we still need to find a way to help Alec. We probably have half The Brethren on our tail by now. And it seems we've picked up a pack of angry Lycans along the way. Have I missed anything?"

"Yes," Poppy replied. "I felt someone watching us as we left The Oracle. Someone already knows we have Alec. I've felt the same presence a couple times while I've been staying there. It could be someone watching for Irina."

"That's right," Maya replied worriedly. "Irina will be able to sense you now that you've left sacred ground. I'm sorry. I didn't even think to grab one of the necklaces."

"That's not important," Poppy replied with surprising calmness. "Helping Alec is the most important thing right now. Not Irina."

Maya gasped and she double clutched the steering wheel again as she came forward and a giant surge of angry pain hit her chest as powerfully as a cannon. Somehow she managed to keep the vehicle from veering off on the road this time. The more familiar she was becoming with these Empathic feelings hitting her now that her gift was back, the better she was able to read them. The anger was coming from Alec. "I don't think Alec agrees with you on that. He still wants you protected from Irina."

"How do you know that?" Poppy asked her.

"Trust me, I can *feel* it." She sighed. "We're going to need some help here. Maybe if we were only dealing with one of these problems . . . but not all of them at once."

"Thank you," Poppy said, quietly, seeming to be somewhat relieved by Maya's deep understanding, her empathy for Alec. Maya glanced back in the rearview mirror to see Poppy still wrapped around the young Elder. "If I haven't said it already, thank you for helping me—for helping Alec. He doesn't deserve this."

"We're doing the right thing, Poppy. What we need now is to get him somewhere he can safely finish his transition. And maybe get some help from people with a little more experience dealing with this sort of thing than us. I think I know where that is. Did you find the cash?"

"Yes, in his bedroom. There's at least ten thousand dollars here."

"Oh, good," Maya sighed. "Now we can add felony burglary to our list of problems."

"Sorry," Poppy offered. "I thought we might need it all"

"Don't apologize. We will need it. We've got a long trip ahead of us, and that's going to require gas, a Dhampir high jump over the border, a new vehicle—or rather a crap vehicle without a GPS device—and a couple of raincoats."

"Raincoats?" Poppy questioned.

"Yep," Maya answered. "Where we're going there's undoubtedly going to be a lot of rain."

CHAPTER TWENTY-FIVE

Maya found temporary escaped from the typical late January torrential downpour of rain inside the Walker Foundation Blood Clinic, in the heart of downtown Seattle. The threatening, gray skies and virtually incessant rain made it a very affable city for a coven of Daywalkers—vampires who didn't kill humans for blood, so they were more tolerant of light (overcast light being especially workable)—and one very specially gifted Dhampir. "Good morning," the bright-eyed, blond receptionist greeted as Maya entered the clinic. "Would you like to donate blood today?"

"Heavens, no," Maya replied quickly, remembering a previous experience she had here which had brought her very close to experiencing a needle in her arm. "I'm here to see Olivia Greyson. Actually, I believe she goes by Olivia Greyson-Wolfe now."

"She's not been in yet this morning. Was she expecting you?"

"Not exactly. I'm an old friend visiting from Alberta who's sort of dropping in on her unannounced. Can you perhaps tell me if she's upstairs at the condo?"

The woman's eyes went wide, as if she were terrified she was about to do something really wrong. "I'm sorry, I can't give out that information."

"That's all right," Maya replied. "I have a feeling she's going to know I'm here."

The receptionist raised a doubtful eyebrow at her, but no more than a minute later, Maya heard a tunefully sweet voice coming from the hall leading to the treatment areas. "Maya . . .?"

She swung around to see a graceful brunette coming down the long hall, her long wavy hair swinging well past her shoulders as her lips blossomed into a most effortless smile. "Maya!" the woman chirped gleefully and rushed up to wrap her arms around Maya in an enthusiastic embrace. "Oh, my gosh, I thought I sensed you," Olivia whispered in her ear before pulling Maya along to the privacy of her back office. "Why didn't you tell me you were coming?"

"To be honest, I didn't know I was headed here until about," Maya glanced at the clock on the wall, "ten-and-a-half hours ago."

"You drove through the night?"

Maya nodded. "I need your help, Olivia. And I'm afraid I come with some bad news."

"What is it?" Olivia asked, her voice and features showing immediate concern. Olivia, of all people, was used to being concerned because she was the only known *Charmer* in existence—a Dhampir with the ability to draw any supernatural being to her quite unwillingly, especially vampires and Lycans. Her unique gifts made her a valuable 'weapon' of sorts in the supernatural world, but vulnerable to the dangers that inherently came along with attracting the world's most dangerous creatures. Her loving mate and husband, Daywalker Caleb Wolfe, made sure Olivia was protected from those many dangers. *Very* protected. Smart supernatural beings didn't mess with him.

"Is Caleb here?" Maya asked her. "I don't sense him."

"He went to meet Jax this morning. Why? What's going on?"

Maya reached over and squeezed Olivia's hands briefly, then pulled back, remembering that if a Dhampir touched Olivia's skin for too long they, too, would become more and more unnaturally drawn to her. "I have Alec with me. He's not well, and I was hoping Caleb might be able to help him."

"Help him . . .?" Olivia asked with alarm. "What's wrong with Alec?"

Maya paused, questioning whether to tell Olivia at that moment was really the right thing to do. At one time, Alec had been Olivia's Brethren-assigned Guardian and the two had bonded and become very close friends. This news was bound to upset her, but Maya didn't believe she had any choice at the moment. Alec needed help now! "He was bitten . . . about twelve hours ago. He's turning, and I didn't know where else to take him that would be safe."

Olivia's shocked expression clearly revealed the depth of her worry. "Where is he?" she demanded. "Take me to him."

Within steps of the back alley door of the clinic Maya opened the doors of the SUV, and there was Poppy, still curled alongside Alec's motionless body on the back seat, her arms wrapped around him as she rested her head on his neck. Maya could feel that his pain was still in control but beginning to well up inside him again, probably because a physically and emotionally exhausted Poppy had allowed herself to drift into sleep after Maya entered the clinic. She couldn't have been out for more than ten minutes, but it was long enough for Alec's pain to return.

"Alec!" Olivia gasped, waking Poppy as she jumped into the back seat beside him and ran her hands over his face. His cheeks were cold and his body solidly stiff, and if someone didn't know he was turning, they would assume Alec Lambert was dead. "Oh, Maya . . . How did this happen? Who did this to him?"

Maya stopped in the middle of an in-breath, trying to figure out a delicate way to explain the situation to a distraught Olivia. The last thing they needed right now was to get distracted from the main objective—helping Alec. He had been turning for twelve hours already. A typical vampire turning usually happened within twenty-four hours, so they were quickly running out of time. "I did," Poppy replied in a tired, scratchy voice before Maya could respond.

Olivia turned to Poppy with a startled glare. Poppy didn't even try to defend herself, and Maya recognized that she needed to say something fast. "Olivia, this was an accident! Poppy would never want to hurt Alec intentionally. I promise . . . I'll explain everything later, but right now we need to get him somewhere he can finish his transition safely. Right now, it all needs to be about Alec. Right?"

After a moment, Olivia turned back to look at Alec and her expression faltered. "You're right," she agreed, but she pulled Alec into her arms and away from Poppy, the message was clear; she did not want Poppy touching him. "Help me get him upstairs to the condo," Olivia said to Maya. "We can take the private elevator."

When Poppy's arms let go of Alec completely, Maya sensed an increase in his pain, but it was tolerable. Although not clear just how it was happening, something Poppy was doing was helping to ease Alec, but an alley in the heart of downtown Seattle was no place to figure that out. "It's all right, Poppy," Maya tried to reassure the woman whose gold eyes were red from crying, her skin paler than normal. "Grab our things and follow us up."

Once the trio had reached the thirtieth-floor penthouse with Alec, Olivia focused solely on getting him moved into a specially designed, chilled room within the center of the spectacular space. The room was the size of a standard bedroom, but all of the surrounding walls and door were clad in steel, and the furniture consisted of two single-person sized aluminum tables with cushioned tops. Olivia carefully placed Alec on one of the tables and then reached for several bags of donated blood from a small refrigerator that was tucked into a corner. She set the bags on the table beside Alec. "I don't want to leave him alone," she said, "but it's too dangerous for us to stay with him. He may wake at any time."

"Is there nothing else we can do for him?" Maya asked.

Olivia shook her head. "At this point, we just need to let the process happen. He'll need to feed as soon as he wakes, and he may reject the donated blood. If he does, he won't care what he has to do to get the blood he needs, including trying to feed from one of us."

"What're we going to do if he won't drink the donated blood?"

"Caleb," Olivia sighed. "He's already connected to Alec because of having given him his blood to save Alec's life. Caleb could let Alec drink from him long enough to get control of his thirst."

"Would Caleb do that?"

That was a good question. Alec Lambert and Caleb Wolfe had never seen eye-to-eye on much of anything. At one point, Caleb believed Alec was challenging him for Olivia's affection, but he soon came to realize the truth—that Olivia's heart only belonged to him.

Poppy, who had been standing quietly behind them, finally said, "Let me stay with him. I don't care if it's dangerous. I want to help him however I can." Up to this point, Poppy had been relegated to watching from the door, as Olivia was hesitant to allow her anywhere near Alec. Maya understood why Olivia was so protective; she and Alec had been very close for a long time. But she also felt for Poppy—literally *felt* Poppy—because her Empathic gift was taking in the overwhelming pain and sadness rolling through the woman who she could *feel* loved Alec so much.

"I don't think that's a good idea," Olivia answered her, coolly, then turned to Maya. "If she did this to him, why did you bring her here? How could you let her anywhere near him after what she's done?"

"Because he loves her," Maya replied, simply, as she took Alec's hand. "I can feel his love for her now. He wants her to be with him, and you need to let her honor his love and his wishes."

"Are you crazy? We can't let her near him. Soon, no one will be able to be near him, except for maybe Caleb and Jax. He'll be much stronger and controlled only by his thirst."

"I know you're upset, Olivia," Maya continued. "But there's something Poppy's doing—I'm not sure just what it is—that eases his pain."

"There's no easing of any pain when you're being turned," Olivia argued. "You know this. He probably feels like he's burning in the fires of hell right now."

"I can feel his pain," Maya assured her, "and it's bearable. And that's *also* because of Poppy. I know it is!"

"It's all right, Maya. You don't have to defend me," Poppy began in an even voice before facing Olivia directly. "I know what I've done is unforgiveable, and because you're so close with him I'd never ask you to forgive *me*. But I swear I would *never* do anything intentionally to hurt *him*. I didn't know I could do this. I mean . . . I was warned, but-"

"You were warned?"

"Olivia!" A cheerful female voice was coming from the elevator in the living room. Recognizing the voice, Olivia gasped, and her whole expression faltered for a second time, but for a very different reason.

"Gemma," she mouthed to Maya before pushing both Maya and Poppy out the door to the chilled room, closing it tightly behind her and rushing away to greet her friend in the open living area. "Gemma, what're you doing here?"

Gemma May Walker typically swept into a room like a summer storm. She was boisterous, impulsive, and completely unruly. She could blow a person over with her opinions before they ever knew what hit them. But Maya didn't know a single person who didn't just adore her, including her mate, Jax Walker. "Oh, don't give me that wide-eyed innocent look, Olivia Greyson-Wolfe," she said, tossing her hand through the air. "I know Alec's here. I sensed him while thumbing through the half price racks at Nordi's—where I got this really cute slip skirt on sale, by the way," she added as she wiggled her behind at the group. "What do you think?"

"It's a little cold and wet outside for a slip skirt," Olivia pointed out.

Maya was just confused. Gemma had been born and raised a Dhampir until only recently, when she was turned into a vampire by Jax. Maya thought it fairly certain that Gemma, with her vampire powers, could sense that something was very wrong with Alec, but at the moment she didn't seem to have a clue. "He wasn't just going to slip into town and not tell me, was he?" she continued with a smile. "The coward. I thought we were both fine with how we left things. I mean, I realize I'm a hard woman to forget . . ."

Olivia cleared her throat loudly as Maya shot a quick glance over to Poppy. She was simply standing there, not showing an ounce of emotion on her face. "So you're downtown today, Gemma?" Olivia asked, trying to shift the conversation.

"Well, of course. I'm always in town for the half-yearly sale. Andie's watching Sophie today, and Jax was going to meet me later so we could come by for a brief visit." She rolled her eyes. "Evidently, he and Caleb are still worried that I might eat you—or something—now that I'm a vampire. Of all the ridiculous things!"

"Gemma's a newer vampire," Maya explained gently to Poppy, who still said nothing as she stood there behind Olivia and Maya. "It will take some practice before she can control the draw of Olivia's gift for any length of time."

"Newer *Daywalker*," Gemma clarified. "It's been six months, and I feel perfectly like my old self—except that every once in a while my senses can go a little haywire. It's the damndest thing. But as I explained to both of those overbearing sods, I'm getting my senses, and this Charmer thing with Olivia completely under control."

"Uh, that's good," Olivia answered, rather unconvincingly.

"Now, where is he? I gave the man three of the finest months of my life. The least he can do is say hello."

Maya glanced over to observe Poppy reaching to brace a hand against the back of the sofa beside her. Gemma Walker had at one time been in a very serious relationship with Alec, and Maya just wanted to kick herself that she he hadn't thought this through better before bringing Poppy here. Alec needed help, and Maya didn't know where else to go—but she hadn't thought about how much it might hurt Poppy to be surprised by the woman Alec first believed he was in love with. And although the two women looked nothing alike, the similarity of their somewhat differing shades of red hair was hard to miss.

"Gemma," Olivia began carefully. "I think your senses might really be a little off today. There's something I need to tell you about Alec . . ."

***

Poppy stood there, listening to Olivia and Maya explain to an increasingly shocked and upset Gemma what had happened and feeling as though all of the dreams she had for her and Alec were slipping away. Just twelve hours ago she had been happier than she ever thought possible, and now it all appeared to be nothing more than a mirage. She felt so stunned by everything that it was as though she had lost her capacity to speak. What could she possibly say to defend herself, to make up for what she'd done to Alec? She could hardly believe it! All she wanted was to go into the other room and lie down next to him, be with him. If he was in pain, she wanted to share in that pain. She didn't care how dangerous it might be.

Gemma stared at Poppy now with an angry spark in her eyes, but it seemed somehow to Poppy that she was becoming immune to it. Neither Gemma nor Olivia couldn't hate her any more than she already hated herself. "I need to see him," Gemma said. "I know the pain he's going through right now."

Poppy wanted to shout, "*No!*"—that *she* needed to be with him—but she knew she'd lost that right when she'd done this to him. Still, she had to try. "Please," she cried. "I understand that you both hate me for what I've done, but I need to see him."

Olivia and Gemma stared at Poppy for the longest time before Olivia finally turned back to Gemma. "He's dangerous right now, Gemma."

"I'm not a Dhampir anymore, Olivia," Gemma reminded her, some frustration clearly rising to the surface. "I'm a vampire; I can handle myself."

As Poppy watched Gemma head towards the room where Alec was being kept, the room where she wanted most to be, Poppy felt as if she couldn't breathe. She saw a reprieve in the form of a large outdoor balcony and so made her escape. As soon as she stepped into the cool winter air she took several deep breaths, hoping just to feel *something* again, but it wasn't working. There was no way to fix this, no way to make things right.

"I'm so sorry, Poppy," Maya said, quietly approaching from behind her. "I should've thought to tell you about Gemma when I suggested we come here. Things have been over between Alec and Gemma for a while. She chose Jax. And Alec didn't fight that choice. He wants to be with you now."

Poppy blurted out an awkward, little laugh, as if Maya had just said something absolutely ridiculous. She stood there perfectly erect, holding her arms close to her sides. "Maya, can they help him?"

"Yes, they can help him better than just about anyone else right now," she answered honestly. "They are good vampires, so they can help Alec from falling to the dark side when he wakes. Gemma's mate, Jax, knows a lot about this sort of thing, and Caleb is linked to Alec by blood. At the very least, this is a safe place for him to make the transition—with people who understand exactly what he's facing."

"Then it was right to come here," Poppy admitted, but she was still unable to turn around and face her friend. If she faced Maya right now, she feared she would break down and cry again, and she had already cried for most of the trip here.

"I believe you can help him, too. We just have to figure out what you're doing—"

"I wasn't helping him, Maya!" Poppy said, raising her voice and swinging around. "I did this *to* him! I refused to listen to all the warnings my mother gave me about being cursed, and now I've taken away his human life. He'll no longer be an Elder—and he'll probably never be able to return to The Oracle. *His home.* He will have to live on blood and stay in the shadows. I've done this to him . . . and you think he still wants to be with me? If I were him, I would *hate* me!"

"Listen to me," Maya said, louder and more forceful than Poppy had ever heard from her. "You *were* helping him. I felt it! I feel his relief when you were with him. And I feel his worry now that you are off sacred ground and exposed to Irina. He loves you! He still loves you! And he needs you to fight with him."

Olivia and Gemma had returned and were standing just inside the patio doors, quietly, behind the two women on the patio. "You've gotten your gift back, Maya?" Olivia asked.

Maya nodded without turning around. "Just after this happened . . ."

Olivia sighed deeply. "Is what you say true . . . That Alec loves her? That she can ease his pain?"

"Yes," Maya answered emphatically. "We just have to figure out how she's doing it."

Olivia walked up to Poppy, the soft set of her face exuding resolution and concern, almost bewitching in the effortlessness of her beauty. "Then we need your help, Poppy," she said. "Let's try this again. My name is Olivia. This is Gemma. It's nice to meet you. Now, let's get to work."

CHAPTER TWENTY-SIX

"I still don't think it's a good idea to leave Poppy in there alone," Olivia said, the concern in her voice intense now as she and Maya both paced the open living room. Gemma was noticeably distant—at the far end of the condo, which was leading both women to believe that Olivia's Charmer gifts might increasingly be affecting her. "It's been nearly eighteen hours since Alec was bitten. He could wake anytime now, and it will be too dangerous for her. Maya, can you feel any difference in his pain?"

"Still the same, and definitely still controlled. That has to mean something, right? I would've expected him to be feeling an unbearable amount of pain by this time, and I would've had to tune it out because it would be just too hard to take in."

Olivia plopped down onto the sofa with a heavy sigh. "Maybe we just want to believe it means something because we don't want to face the fact, this is happening to *him*—of all people. He would never want to be a vampire."

"You're right. He wouldn't. But didn't you tell me that the pain Caleb felt during his transition was beyond anything he could describe?"

Olivia nodded sadly. "Something must be making Alec's suffering more tolerable." She then silently looked at Maya with a sincere expression. And after a moment or two, she said, slowly, "Who is she?"

Maya knew Olivia was referring to Poppy. "Her mother was a Dhampir and her father a witch. She's been on the run from a female warlock her entire life. Joseph asked Alec if he would protect her for a little while."

Olivia's lips widened into a soft smile. "Sounds like something he'd volunteer for. He's always been a Guardian at heart." She then seemed to ponder something for a long moment. "So Alec's in love with her?"

Maya nodded, noticing that Gemma had come back across the room but was remaining quiet. "Poppy told me he'd admitted his love for her last night, and I can feel that love in him now. This happened because he had asked her to connect them." Maya glanced between both women as she continued. "I know you're angry at her for hurting him like this . . . and you've a right to those feelings. He's been an important part of both of your lives. But just try to put yourself in Poppy's position for a moment. In the span of a just few seconds she went from the happiest moment in her life to what must seem to her the worst. She's in just as much pain as he is . . . it's just a different kind of pain."

"I can appreciate her pain," Olivia offered sincerely. "We all can. We've all had our love tested by unfair circumstances. Every day, I am so grateful Caleb didn't turn away from me once he discovered I was a Charmer. He's never stopped fighting for me, and on some days I don't know how it's possible to love him more." She glanced at Gemma, who was now standing a few feet behind her. Turning her head, Olivia said, "And you feared Jax would never love you as much as he did his first wife, yet every day he calls you his angel. You can hear in his voice how much he loves you—every time he says the word."

"You can, can't you?" Gemma smiled with the recognition of the truth of Olivia's words, though she still seemed a bit off as she turned around and walked out to the patio without another word.

"Is she all right?" Maya asked. "I've never seen her like this before."

Olivia shook her head. "She's been trying very hard to deny that my Charmer energy affects her since she's become a vampire. It's taking its toll on her."

"Mmm," Maya sounded softly.

Olivia was quiet for a long while as she watched Maya. "You've had the cruelest test of all of us, haven't you?" she said. "I know you still miss Phin terribly."

Maya nodded, her emotions for Phin still revealing itself in her eyes. "You know, I've tried to move on. I met a man, Simon Kendrick. He's a talented witch and a good man. He treats me well, and there are days I feel happy. It's just . . ."

"Not Phin," Olivia finished for her.

"Not Phinneas," Maya agreed softly. "The frustrating part is, I didn't figure that out until after I gave my virginity to Simon."

"Oh, Maya," Olivia murmured as she wrapped her arms around her. "I'm sorry your first time wasn't everything you wanted it to be. I know you had been saving yourself for Phin. But I'll tell you something. My first time wasn't great, either. But that was OK. You know why?"

Maya shook her head. "Why?"

"Because when I found something really great—a man who wasn't just having sex with me, but loved me—it was all the more special, and I recognized that right away. You will, too. I know it. Simon may or may not be Mr. Right, but he has already helped you. Look, you've gotten your gift of *feelings* back. That must mean he's helped you move on in some small way."

"Yeah, I guess you're right."

"And when Mr. Right does come along you will know it. And you'll be just as happy and in love as I—"

"Olivia Greyson-Wolfe!" The patio doors swung wide, nearly breaking off their hinges as a tall man—*as in very tall*—with lots of wavy dark hair and a shadowed beard on his face stormed into the room. "What in the *hell* do you think you're doing?"

Maya broke into a big smile as she cast a welcoming glance at her old friend. Olivia had a perplexed look on her face, as if deciding how best to answer the man's open-ended question. Caleb Wolfe was obviously not happy at the moment, but he would never harm a hair on Olivia's head. He just like to bluster his displeasure every once in a while.

Maya just kept smiling. "You were saying . . .?"

Olivia frowned at her.

***

Poppy was lying beside Alec, curled up on the narrow table as she held his hand and kissed him gently on each cheek. She had no idea if she was helping him. Maya said his pain level felt the same . . . tolerable. Poppy was grateful for that—and to be able to be there at his side. He still felt deathly cold and hadn't moved or shown any signs that he was aware of anything that was happening to him, but Poppy wanted to believe he was both awake and aware. Somehow, believing he was there with her, the two of them together in the quiet as they had been many times for the last few weeks, was helping to ease her mind in some small way as she prepared herself to do what she knew she had to do.

"I don't know if you can hear me, but I need to say this to you," she began, but her determined expression soon crumbled as new tears started to fall from her eyes. "*Damnit* . . . I promised myself I wasn't going to cry anymore. I know you need me to be strong right now, but seeing you like this hurts. Knowing that I did this to you hurts so much!"

Poppy wished Alec could just *say* something, give her *any* kind of signal that he could hear her, even if it was the smallest lift of a finger, but there was still nothing.

"What I wanted to say is that I can't regret any moment I've spent loving you. As I said before, you're an easy man to love, Alec Lambert . . . But I was absolutely wrong in doing so. I should've listened to my mother's warnings. If I had, you wouldn't be in such pain now, facing what you're about to face. I'm truly sorry for that."

She stroked her hand repeatedly along the side of his face, somehow wishing that this simple gesture would be enough to make everything right again. But she fully realized that it wasn't. "I know you can't forgive me. I've taken away your human life. I've taken away the chance for you to help your people—to be a truly great Elder. There's nothing I can ever do to make up for that." Poppy's tears started to fall in streams, and it became nearly impossible for her to see through her blurry eyes. Instead, she let her lips brush his skin, feeling her way along the lines of his rough jaw and cheek, allowing the tears, her sadness, to just come. "But I want you to know that I love you," she murmured. "And that love has made me strong. I promise to keep learning the craft and increasing my strength, and maybe, someday, I won't have to run anymore. I'll protect myself so you and Joseph don't have to do it anymore. I'll find a way to be strong enough to beat Irina."

Just as she finished speaking these words Poppy heard a loud commotion and a deep male voice coming from the other end of the penthouse. She realized Olivia's mate must have returned—Caleb, the vampire Maya believed could help Alec. The tears began falling so hard now that she began to shake uncontrollably. "I love that you wanted us to be connected," she said miserably. "I love that you cared about me enough to want that. But fate stopped us, and I'm glad it did. It spared you from feeling connected for the rest of your life to a woman who could do this to you."

Poppy understood the inevitable truth that because she had mixed Alec's blood with her own, *she* would feel the blood connection to him for the rest of her life. But Alec would be spared any such feelings because he had not been able to take the mixed blood from her. She would take that pain and own it as punishment for her recklessness. She turned her hand over to brush her knuckles over his cheek. "I will miss you," she said, with such feeling that it felt like her heart was cracking open right that moment. Then she voiced a solemn oath, knowing fully the significance of it. "I free you of all responsibility for me! You owe me nothing from this day forward! You owe Joseph nothing! And I owe you everything for how much you've given me, for letting me know what it was like to be loved and to feel as though I had a home for the first time in my life."

Poppy kissed him one last time just as the door burst open. She sat up on the table, quickly clearing the tears from her eyes. She hopped to her feet as the tall man she assumed must be Caleb Wolfe seemed to fill the whole room the moment he crossed the threshold of the door, closely followed by Olivia and Maya. "Everyone stay outside that door," he ordered, but he left the door open so all of them could still see what was going on.

His shoulders were broad, his legs long and lean, and his grey eyes seemed to sparkle with a little blue underneath. Poppy stepped out of his rather large way as he moved straight to the bed to examine Alec. "Do you have any idea the danger you've all put yourselves in by bringing Alec here?" Caleb asked—to no one in particular. "I sensed what had happened to him this morning, but Jax and I weren't able to get back here right away. I didn't think you would be careless enough to bring him into our home."

"Don't be ridiculous," Olivia said right back to him, interpreting his shouted remark as being meant for her. "Of course, I'd bring him here. He's my friend and needs our help. Where else would I take him?"

Caleb turned his head toward his wife and scowled, but it was the scowl of a man who knew he couldn't win an argument by challenging Olivia's long standing friendship with Alec. The importance of her relationship with her former Guardian was understood between them. That didn't mean Caleb had to like it, however. Around each other, Alec and Caleb were more like chest-thumping boys when either one of them got it in his head that the other was wrong . . . which was pretty often. "When he wakes from this, his thirst will be uncontrollable. *He* will be uncontrollable. That steel door will not stop him. Did you give any thought to that—to your safety?"

"It's my fault, Caleb," Maya interjected before Olivia could respond. "I'm the one who brought him here. It was never my intention to put Olivia in danger. I just didn't know where else to take him."

"You did the right thing," Olivia insisted, shooting a meaningful glance at Caleb before turning her attention back to Alec. "Caleb, we have to do everything we can to help him. It breaks my heart to think about the pain he's suffering. You of all people should understand that."

"I do," Caleb answered sincerely. "But that does not come at your expense . . . understand?" Olivia nodded, and Caleb seemed to appreciate that small concession on her part. "What I can tell you is that he's not suffering a great deal of pain. In fact, right now," he added with a pulled brow, "his pain seems very manageable. I actually feel more frustration and stress inside him than I do pain."

"It's probably boredom at hearing us all argue like this," Olivia said with a small but wicked smile.

Caleb turned back as he sensed his wife standing right behind him now. "What did I say about staying outside the door? I swear to God, Olivia, if you endanger yourself any more I'll take you over my knee later."

Olivia's brows simply lifted as if she were considering that thought for a moment.

Maya rolled her eyes and peeked her head around Olivia's shoulder. "I want to *feel*! It's not fair; I have to be much closer for my gift to work. She stepped in behind Caleb and reached her hand around him to touch Alec's arm. "He's definitely stressed about something. Isn't that strange?" she remarked to Caleb. "Shouldn't he be in too much pain to bother with being stressed?"

Maya then made a funny little sound before sweeping her eyes up to Caleb. "Can you feel that?"

His brows furrowed as he turned back to Alec. "Yes. He's-"

"Better!" Maya finished for him. "He's much better."

Olivia did a little jump as she clasped her hands together. "Caleb?"

"Yes. He's definitely better," he agreed. "That doesn't make any sense. He should be feeling the utmost pain right now, just before the transition is completed."

Just then, Gemma pushed her way into the room with her mate, Jax Walker, right behind her. It was obvious by the way Jax's eyes followed her that he was concerned about her. "Did it work?" she demanded. "Did she help him?"

"Did who help him?" Caleb questioned.

"Poppy. The woman who was just-"

They all turned around at once. "She's gone!"

Jax joined Caleb at Alec's bedside. "Something is different here. This is not a typical turning."

Caleb nodded in agreement as his grey eyes returned a meaningful look. "Something is healing him, especially in the last few minutes. That shouldn't be possible."

"Poppy was somehow helping his pain," Maya interjected. "I felt it on the drive here. That's why we had her in here with him. We just couldn't figure out how she was doing it."

"Well, whatever she was doing," Jax added, "she did so in the last few minutes . . . because . . . I can feel his rapid improvement."

Caleb brushed his fingertips across Alec's cheeks and mouth and then rubbed the damp drops he collected between his fingers. "Tears," he said . . . *her tears* are *healing him*."

CHAPTER TWENTY-SEVEN

Alec wanted to yell at the top of his lungs! He wanted to howl! But he couldn't move a single muscle in his goddamn body. Not even his eyelashes. Never had he felt so helpless, or ever had something frustrate him so much. *Thank God*, the pain he had been feeling for what seemed like days had lessened to where he could begin to think somewhat clearly again. He understood what was happening to him; that he was in the process of turning. His body had been feeling as though it were being manually stretched into something that was not natural, and now somehow it was relaxing again . . . back to something more like normal.

Whether she realized it or not, Alec realized that Poppy was responsible for his pain slowly fading away. He could feel the effect every time one of her tears rolled into his mouth. This woman was not cursed, she was gifted *extraordinarily* gifted. But the sound of her misery had broken his heart and incited his frustration all at the same time. He wanted nothing more than to wrap his arms around her and promise that everything was going to be fine, but he couldn't even so much as form spittle in order to keep her butt planted right there beside him.

He was furious when she had put herself in such danger by going off the security of sacred ground and making herself visible to Irina. She wasn't prepared to defend herself on her own, yet. She needed him, and *he* needed her. What the devil did she think she was doing, running off on him? Did his telling her that he loved her—that he wanted to spend the rest of his life with her—mean nothing?

Now it was just about twenty-four hours since he'd been incapacitated by the bite, and about seven hours since Poppy had left the penthouse on her own. All Alec could do was lie there and wait for this damn venom to finish with him so he could get off his butt and go after her. Every hour that went by was one more hour of distance she would be able to put between them, and it would make it that much more difficult to track her.

"Has there been any change?" Jax Walker asked as he came into the room, addressing Caleb, who was standing above Alec. Alec, for his part, was thinking about the one man he detested most of the time but was connected to nonetheless—Caleb! Would he never get Caleb Wolfe out of his life?

"He's improving," Caleb replied, lifting his hand away from Alec's heart. "His heartbeat has returned, which means he still has a soul."

"That is a miracle," Jax replied. "In two centuries, I have never heard of a heartbeat returning once a turning began. The gift this woman possesses is truly remarkable."

"It is," Caleb agreed. "His pain is continuing to improve, and I would guess he's going to be coming out of this any time. He's plenty pissed, though. It's like he's shooting darts through his mind."

"That has to be about the woman who left," Jax answered. "I should have gone after her."

"We needed you here," Caleb pointed out. "We still do not know exactly what we are dealing with." Caleb then peered back over his shoulder towards the door as if he were able to see right through the thick metal. "I don't want to wake Olivia and Maya just yet. Maya looked like she hadn't slept in two days, and my wife is worn out with worry. I don't like it."

Jax patted Caleb on the shoulder. "There will be plenty of time to take care of her, just as you always do. You are a good husband, Caleb."

Caleb frowned at Jax. "Am I a good husband even when I want to take her over my knee for worrying me like this? She could be pregnant with our child, and yet she brought a man into our house who was turning."

"Alec is not just any man. He was her Guardian. You know Olivia would not let him go through this alone. The same is true for Gemma and her past connection to him. We have to accept that."

"I suppose you're right."

"I am right. But that does not change the fact that my granddaughter needs you to rein her in once in a while or she could fall victim to her own mischief."

A smile curled Caleb's lips. "You realize it's still weird to think of Olivia as your granddaughter when you look only a few years older than me."

"That is all part of the fun of being immortal," Jax replied. "Now, if you will excuse me, I would like to check on my own mate."

Alec could only lie there and listen as the vampires talked above him. The bastards were truly in love with two of the three most special women in this world. Olivia Greyson had been his charge to protect, and as with any man, it was impossible to be around The Charmer and not fall in love with her on some level. But it was not real. He'd learned that the hard way.

And Gemma May . . . at first it was a hot fling, but then he'd come to care for her so deeply that he had asked her live with him at The Oracle. For a time he fancied himself in love with her. Looking back on it now, he could see that the idea of a strong woman at his side, loving him as he took on his new role as Elder, was more about him than her . . . more about his feeling supported at the time than it had been about love. He had been unsure if he would make a good Elder. Now he knew he was a good Elder. He knew who he was. And Poppy was the right woman for him. He had no doubt about that.

There was no special gift tugging at his emotions, as was the case with Olivia, and no need for a strong woman like Gemma to reassure him as he found his way. He had already established that on his own. Poppy could simply be looking at him as if she was curious about something, and that, in turn, would make him curious. She could innocently trip while walking down a hallway, and that would make him smile. Together they could be making love for the third time when they were both exhausted, and still it would be the most amazing sex he had ever known. So knowing that Poppy was now out there in the world on her own, trying to survive, separated from him, cut him in a way that was more painful than the hell he had experienced over the last twenty-four hours.

He had to come out of this soon, because he had to find her.

This was about more than just keeping her safe from Irina. This was about how much he wanted and needed her in his life.

CHAPTER TWENTY-EIGHT

Alec awakened with a single desperate gasp for air and in a single, swift motion swung upward to a seated position on the table. His mind seemed to be moving ten times faster than his body because all her could think about was getting out of this metal box of a room so he could go after Poppy. But his lungs burned with the frigid air they now took in, which he hadn't expected. His body, flexed and stiff, ached all over. And his eyes watered with tears as he started to blink for the first time in he wasn't sure how long. Somewhere he seemed to have lost track of time. "Shit," he cursed. "I feel like I've been run over by a truck. And why am I in this freezing room in nothing but my underwear?" he demanded through harsh breaths as he stared back at Caleb and Jax.

Together, the undeniably large Caleb/Jax duo formed quite the wall standing before him in such a small room. And right now they were blocking his escape through the only door. Caleb's dark brows squeezed together, curiosity showing as his grey eyes studied Alec intently. "Vampires like the cold. That and the darkness help them to adjust when they first wake."

"Well, good for them," Alec replied rather grumpily. "But what the hell does that have to do with me?"

The two men gave each other a meaningful look before Jax, clad in his typical head-to-toe black clothing, took a step forward. "You *do* realize what has been happening to you, do you not?"

"Yes," Alec replied, but he offered no more, to the further puzzlement of the other two. He swung his legs over the edge of the table but found it much more difficult than it should have been, which didn't make much sense to him. "Can I at least have my damn clothes back?"

"Over there," Caleb nodded towards a corner chair.

As Alec slid off the table and onto his feet, moving around a bit more, his muscles began to respond better—almost like his body, which had been motionless for so long, was starting to wake up. He shuffled into his pants and shirt and noticed that neither Jax nor Caleb was moving to clear his path to the door. He sighed inwardly. As usual, the damn vampires would never make anything easy. "Look," he began, shaking his head, "I get that you guys think I'm going to go all '*vampy*' on your ass, but I'm not. I have more important things to deal with right now—like the fact that you guys let the woman I was protecting walk right out the door without so much as a '*where are you going*'."

"*You* are not going *anywhere*," Caleb warned. "You were bitten by a Dhampir whose venom was powerful enough to turn you. For whatever reason, your body might not be recognizing what has happened, but I assure you, you've changed. I *feel* it in you."

"Enough with the '*feeling*' shit. Christ, you guys are over sensitive." Alec was pissed. They were wasting time! Time he needed to search for Poppy because he had no idea where to actually start looking. "Now get out of my way!"

Caleb pushed Alec back with one hand when he tried to force his way between them. But with no success. The two vampires restrained him with almost no effort, which was slightly deflating to his Guardian ego. He had just enough time to recover his momentum when Jax whipped something across the room at him with the speed of a bullet. Alec blinked with amazement that his reflexes were able to focus in and catch something traveling at that speed. The object molded in his grip as he turned his hand over and could see it was a donation bag of Type O blood. He simply stared at the ice cold bag for a moment and felt his heart begin to beat in his ears, sounding like a very loud kettle drum. His blood began accelerating through his arteries. There was something powerful and demanding in the need he had for it as he swirled the red liquid within the bag and swore there was a distinct scent coming from it, salty and a little bitter, like a very dark red wine.

The heart-rhythm in his ears became so insistent that it drowned out all but one thought his head. *He had to taste it.* A sharp pinch rolled across his gums as he fixated on the bag. Then, before he could stop himself, he pushed the bag to his lips and bit into it, sucking down its contents with very little control. The blood was just something his body had to have, and as he took it in he could feel the strength returning and his body responded. When he was finished, Alec raised his head to focus on Caleb and Jax. "What the hell?" he said roughly, reaching his fingers to his mouth and feeling the sharp fangs that cut into his skin with the lightest touch. Shocked by what was happening, he dropped the bag to the cold, metal floor.

"Congratulations," Caleb said with a dry smile. "You're definitely not a vampire. If you were, that bag would've just whet the pallet."

"Then what the hell am I?" Alec demanded.

"Hybrid," Jax answered as he stepped closer to examine him, the older vampire having absolutely no fear that Alec would hurt him in any way. *The cocky son of a bitch.* "Or Dhampir . . . However you prefer to look at it, though, Dhampirs typically are born into it. Either way, this is something I have never seen before—reversing a turning to a hybrid. From everything I know about the venom, that should not be possible . . . unless—"

"—Unless what?" Alec pressed.

"Unless the Dhampir you came here with carries both the venom and the anti-venom in her system. Which is rather startling, considering that none of us have ever heard of a vampire anti-venom."

Alec blinked at both men, clearly not taking in what they were telling him. While he had been paralyzed under the venoms effects he understood that Poppy was easing his pain through her tears, but he hadn't been clear-headed enough to realize she was actually saving him from being doomed to a life as a vampire. Suddenly it occurred to him that being Dhampir, he could live with that, because there was a part of him that would still be human. Trying hard to put the pieces together, Alec asked, "What're you suggesting? That she has the power to reverse the venom? Has either of you ever heard of someone being able to do such a thing?"

"Never," Jax answered simply. "And if someone knew she had the power to do something like that, she would be—"

"Hunted for the rest of her life . . .," Alec finished for him in a quiet voice as full awareness started to settle in on him. He now had a very bad feeling that this '*curse*' Poppy believed she had wasn't a curse at all, but a very powerful gift—one that she didn't understand how to use. But he'd bet that Irina did . . . and she planned to steal it. "I've got to find her!" Alec blurted out. "Poppy is also a witch, and if the warlock who's chasing her gets to her . . . she'll kill Poppy to steal her gifts, and that would put enormous power on the wrong side of the supernatural world."

Caleb blew out a hard breath in disbelief. "Alec, I realize that you think you have this whole thing figured out in just the two minutes since you've discovered you're a hybrid, but let me assure you, you don't. Your body needs time to adjust. What you just went through was not a normal turning, not even close. You're going to have to give your body a chance to catch up, then learn how to use your new senses, or else you'll have no hope of tracking her."

"I don't have time to let my new senses sink in like some kind of day at the spa!" he snapped back. "Didn't you hear what I just said? She's being hunted by a warlock—a warlock who can sense her now that she's out in the open. You just said yourself how dangerous it could be if someone evil were to find out what she could can do. Well, I believe this warlock already knows, and that's why she's been hunting Poppy."

Alec lunged towards Caleb, determined to push the vampire out of his way, but Caleb, with his well-developed vampire strength held him in place without exerting much effort at all. "This will do her no good right now," Caleb asserted, firmly. "You *must* give your body time to adjust. It will catch up in a few days. In the meantime, we will teach you how to track her."

Jax touched Caleb's arm, a simple gesture to remind him to ease up his all-too-strong hold on Alec. It seemed as though Jax, at least, understood the panic Alec was feeling in that moment, the absolute need to do something. "Are you connected with her?" Jax asked, and Alec was caught off guard by the question but wasn't sure why. He and Poppy were supposed to be connected, but they never finished. "I can feel how much you love her."

Alec shook his head and suddenly felt the need to exhale deeply, as if it were just hitting him how much he would lose if Irina got her hands on Poppy. "We didn't finish. That's how this happened. She's connected to me, though."

"Then that may be your best option at this point," Caleb suggested. "If you're not connected to her, it will be difficult for you to track her with this much time having gone by and you with no experience, *but Poppy can find you.* You'll need to use that skill of hers to draw her out." With an arrogant smile, Caleb raised one of his brows and added, "Not bad for a dumb vampire, huh?"

Alec just returned an ugly expression, refusing to give the vampire any credit for actually coming up with a decent plan, considering the constraints of the situation he was working against. "Why are you such a pain in the ass?"

Caleb just chuckled softly in return.

"Will you two knock it off, already," Gemma said loudly through the door. "You're behaving like sparring children."

"Caleb, let us in so we can see him," Olivia pleaded in a much nicer voice.

"Sorry, my sweet," Caleb replied gently, obviously realizing he was walking a fine line with his wife. "We need to make sure he has full control before I let him anywhere near you."

"Do I look out of control to either one of you?" Alec frowned.

"Caleb Wolfe!" *So much for the sweet wife.* "Open this door right now or you can find another place to sleep tonight."

Caleb turned back to the door with a hard scowl. "I'm not sleeping anywhere but in our bed."

"Christ," Alec cursed. "I don't have time for this! There's an innocent woman out there all alone and defenseless. What if this was Olivia? Would you be standing here listening to someone else argue about where they were sleeping tonight?"

"No," he replied darkly. "I'd already be gone."

"Exactly my point!"

"With one big difference," Jax pointed out. "He has been a vampire for a while. He has his full strength and knows how to track. All things you do not have at the moment."

"Caleb!" The door suddenly pushed open into the room, smacking Caleb on the back. Gemma created a path for Olivia as she ran though the small opening and straight over to Alec, wrapping her arms around him in a tight hug. "You scared me to death," she mumbled into his shoulder.

"I'm all right, little Charmer."

Gemma smiled up at Caleb and Jax. "Don't mess with the bull, I always say." Then she sidled up to Alec with a small sway of her hips. "Nice of you to come back to the living, Brethren boy."

"It always worries me when you're nice," He replied dryly. She smiled, and Alec could see she was much more affected by what had happened to him than she was letting on. Gemma and Alec were in love with other people, but they had shared a small window of time together when they both really needed each other, and because of that they would always hold a place in each other's hearts.

Alec's attention then became aware of Maya, who was standing quietly in a corner of the room. He could see by her expression that he had really scared her. As soon as they made eye contact, Maya quickly went to him and curled her small arms around his waist as he pulled her head to rest against his chest. "Thank you for helping her," he said, and she nodded her understanding that he meant Poppy. "It took a lot of courage for you to do what you did . . . and it probably saved my life. We may never have known she had the power to help me if you'd taken me to Dr. Li."

"Alec . . .," she replied worriedly. "She's out there by herself and has now been exposed to Irina for ten days."

"*What?*" he said stumbling backwards. "Ten days! You're telling me I've been out of it for ten days!"

"I told you, what you experienced was not a normal turning," Caleb interjected. "She was able to lessen the venom's effects, reverse the process. But it took your body a lot of time to begin to recover, and you're not finished yet."

"Ten days!" Alec felt completely stunned and lost, not knowing if Irina already had Poppy in her clutches. "Shit! I have to find her, now!"

"Don't worry, Alec. Caleb will help you," Olivia offered and then turned to the husband frowning behind her. "He understands there is no time to lose and that this is our best option until you gain your full strength and senses," she offered, logically, knowing full-well how much Caleb would disagree with that sentiment—but also knowing he wouldn't say no to her. "Right, Caleb?"

"Right, my sweet," Caleb replied with a sigh.

CHAPTER TWENTY-NINE

Poppy entered the dimly lit hole-in-the-wall bar uniquely called *'Willy's'* shortly after five o'clock. The bar was on the outskirts of a very small town somewhere in British Columbia, one she couldn't even remember by name because she had been in a new place every day for the past two weeks. There was a lone bartender working the room who certainly had downed a few too many beers over the years, evidenced by the bulging belly hanging over his cinched jeans. The tables were all full. Some customers were ordering just drinks, but there was also a run on food orders in progress, which was keeping the bartender busy, especially considering that he was also the cook.

"Sorry about the wait," he said as he lumbered over to her booth. He had a bit of a limp and was definitely not in physical shape to be hustling this many tables at once. "What can I get you?"

Poppy realized then that she had stumbled on a good opportunity for herself. She could use a good opportunity—and some food and rest after having traveled, mostly on foot and completely on her own for two weeks. Dhampirs were fast and strong, but their human side still got tired. "Cheeseburger," she replied. "Extra rare . . . and a soda. Whatever you have."

"I've got Coke, Sprite, and I think there's some lemonade left. You're gonna' have to be a little more specific."

Poppy debated for a second. "Actually, lemonade would be great. Is it pink?"

The bartender frowned at her. "Just the regular stuff."

"OK, that'll work." Poppy then quickly scanned the room as he wrote down her order. "It's crowded in here tonight," she observed. "Are you working this place all by yourself?"

He shrugged his shoulders in resignation. "Biker rally. They ride into town every year at this time for a couple weeks. Nice enough folk . . . and they like the cheeseburgers."

"Ahh, so you have a specialty. Glad I'm trying one."

He smiled politely, his rounded cheeks red with exertion. "I haven't seen you in here before. Passing through Elk's Cove?"

That was the name of the little town, Elk's Cove. "I was, but now I'm seeing an opportunity to stay a little while. I've got a lot of waitressing experience and I'm quick on my feet. I could use the money. Perhaps for the length of a biker rally; then I could be on my way?"

The bartender raised an eyebrow, intrigued. When Poppy left Seattle, she had regrettably pocketed about a thousand dollars of the cash that she and Maya had taken from Alec's room when they left The Oracle. Even with her exceptional thriftiness, it was already running low.

Poppy crossed her legs under the table and brushed her long, cherry hair behind one shoulder as she smiled up at him. She might be a klutz, but she knew the game. Poppy had been on the run with her mother for a very long time. Most of the time, they would stay out of sight and keep to themselves as they moved from place to place, but they had to pay the bills somehow. Being Dhampir, she understood she was attractive to humans and that she was aging slowly. She could still easily pass for a woman in her late teens, early twenties. Her mother taught her how to use that advantage with some social skills for engaging humans in conversation to quickly gain their trust. Often, it provided a place to sleep for the night or an offer of temporary employment. That was just their reality of surviving life on the run. She may have set it aside temporarily while staying under the protection of Joseph and Alec, but she would always remember how to fall back on the skills that had allowed her to survive to this point.

"The name's Willy," the bartender replied, offering a beefy hand.

"To go with the sign," she teased lightly. "My name is Poppy."

"I' tell you what, Poppy, while I'm cooking up your burger and about three other orders, why don't you take this order pad, hit those tables in the corner, and show me what you got? Grill closes at ten. If you make it 'til then, you can come back tomorrow."

"Can you pay me cash under the table?"

"Seventy bucks a night plus a free meal . . . and you can keep all your tips."

"Deal," she said, bouncing to her feet with a renewed sense of energy. She left her jacket in the booth and pulled on the sweater she'd been carrying over her jeans and tee shirt. It wasn't the sexiest outfit for attracting tips, but at the moment it was all she had to work with. As she walked toward one of the tables where three men who had already been watching her exchange with Willy were seated, Poppy wondered if she should have mentioned that she might have to pay for a few broken dishes over the week.

Probably not. *Don't think about it, Poppy.*

By the end of the night, Willy seemed to be impressed with her energy, smile and enthusiasm, especially considering how many people had rolled through the bar in a few short hours. There were a couple of broken glasses—unfortunate miss-steps—and one or two mixed up plates at tables, but, overall, things went fairly smoothly. "So, do I get to come back tomorrow?"

"Yeah," he chuckled. "You caught on pretty quick, and you seem nice enough. I' tell you what. If you can stay the next couple of weeks, through the biker rally, you've got yourself a job."

"Sounds good."

He nodded his approval. "Gotta' a place to stay?"

She shook her head. "I thought I'd just head into town and stay in one of the motels."

Willy waved that idea off and pointed a finger out the window to the main road. "Follow the road east; there's a nice little bed and breakfast about a quarter mile up—The Comfy Cove. Stella runs the place, and if you tell her I sent you, you'll get the special Willy discount. It's quite a deal."

"Thanks," she smiled, pocketing the cash Willy gave her for the night and the sixty-plus dollars in tips she received, most of which came from the one table of men who seemed to enjoy watching her run around. It felt good to pocket her own money, cash she had earned. She hadn't liked taking Alec's money, even though she believed he would understand how much she needed it to survive on those first couple weeks.

When she got to The Comfy Cove she got settled quickly. Willy had been right about Stella. The bed and breakfast owner was very friendly and gave her a corner room that was small, but clean and bright. And when Poppy explained she was just passing through town and would be leaving after helping Willy at the bar for a couple weeks, Stella offered to let her have the room for free if she helped her clean up in the kitchen after the other lodgers finished breakfast and lunch. That worked well for Poppy, since as a Dhampir she needed very little sleep and was full of energy. She would be able to do both jobs and have a place to sleep, pocketing a fair amount of cash before moving on, giving herself a bit of a stipend each day.

Her room had all the basics she needed—a shower, full size bed, and a small writing desk where she could work. She pulled out her map of British Columbia, locating Elk's Cove, and made a plan for where to go from here. She made notes of how many days she would stay in between and where she would pass larger cities where there would be churches built on sacred ground. Those would become key areas for her to be safe if she sensed Irina was getting too close.

Poppy stared out her window into the night, trying to clear her mind of everything and see if she could sense whether Irina was closing in on her. Knowing it was just a matter of time before the warlock located her, she tried to be as prepared as possible. Poppy still couldn't sense Irina at all, which meant she would be able to get some sleep for at least one more night.

When Poppy crawled underneath the warm blankets she tried to get her mind to stop racing. She had completed her checklist for the day, but now that she had slowed down and was relaxing, memories seemed to assail her. Sensations of a single whisper, a single touch, a single kiss. As isolated, individual memories they didn't have the power to break her, but when added together they felt hauntingly real, and they pulled at her heart with exceptionally cruelty.

Alec.

Frequently, in her dreams, she could feel his familiar arms wrapped around her as they had been every night for weeks. He would whisper promises in her ear that everything would be all right. That he'd keep her safe. That they'd be together forever. That was the funny thing about dreams . . . they would lie to you.

Poppy stared at the ceiling with the same thought in her head she'd had every night for the past two weeks; that she wanted to go back to Seattle. No matter how little sense the idea made, she found herself wanting to return to face Alec, to face what she had done to him. To ask him to forgive her. To just pick somewhere in the world and make a stand against Irina, as Alec said . . . together.

Poppy was tired of running.

She had tasted glimpses of a normal life with an amazing man who wanted to have a child with her, a family. Before she met Alec, Poppy had never allowed herself to want for those things, but now—all she seemed to think about were *those things*. She wanted them. She wanted to somehow fight for them. But she always came back to the same question. How could Alec ever forgive her?

Frequently, she would reach out to *feel* him, now that she had connected with him on the last night they were together. She would promise herself it would be for the last time. That she would get over him. But it never was the last time. When

Alec had finally awakened from his transition, Poppy felt the chill in his bones, the confusion in his head, and the blood thirst on his tongue. He was short tempered and frustrated, which was not like him. In fact, she could feel the frustration in him at that very moment, even though it was the middle of the night, and that made her sad. He was struggling with something, and there was nothing she could do to help him with it.

Poppy tried to not let herself tap into her connection for too long because it only made the separation from him that much harder. But in some small way that very connection let her pretend he was there with her, even if it was just for a few minutes. "I'm sorry," she murmured.

They were the same words she said to him every night.

Within a few miles of The Oracle, Irina Danchev moved in and out of the moonlight filtering through the trees, walking purposefully with a slow sway of her hips. Her long, flowing dress was nearly as black as the night around her, as black and perfect in color as her flawless hair. Even in her later years, Irina was still a beauty, with all the confidence of a woman who accepted the extremes pulling on her life. On the one hand, she desired to kill. As quick and unmercifully as a serpent, and as brutally as a lion, until she could feel on her tongue the power she reaped from that kill. On the other hand, she was a mother who believed in teaching her sons to take pride in the enormous gifts they inherited from her. To be commanding and strong.

At least when they weren't pissing her off, that is.

"Why didn't you warn me, *eldest* son," she hissed angrily, "they had a Natural Shifter at Bodmin Moor? They nearly killed me!"

"Oh, don't be so dramatic, mother," Simon Kendrick answered, adding emphasis with a roll of his eyes. "They were never truly any threat to your life. Besides, you know your games of revenge with this woman don't interest me."

Irina's expression grew cold. "*Don't interest you?* You can stand there and tell me that your rightful inheritance of power—power that was *stolen* from you—doesn't interest you?"

"I *have* power," Simon answered, in a commanding tone, exactly as Irina had taught him his entire life. "After all, I am *Charles's* son. Isn't that what you've always told me? And I believe you got a small sampling of that power at Bodmin Moor."

Irina lifted her head and raised her brows, as if she was, at least, vaguely interested. "Yes . . . The jumping force field was an impressive trick."

"It was not a trick!" Simon answered angrily. "*My gifts, my witchcraft,* will be revered even by you, someday."

"Witchcraft, you say . . .?" Irina was purring now. "Son, you can't dance with the devil and still expect to be praised by the Gods. You're already on the dark path. You just can't see it through that very thick cloud of vanity surrounding you."

Simon's face grew tight with anger as he listened to Irina implying he was evil like she was. He would never be as twisted and soulless as his mother. That he knew. Maya kept him on the side of good—a side that was worthy. She was the greatest thing that had ever happened in his life. A true blessing. As long as Simon had Maya Brunetti in his life, he would remain on the side of good. "I have a good life here at The Oracle, mother. I don't need you fucking that up for me."

"Are you forgetting who sent you here in the first place? Who offered this life to you? Your apathy makes me sick. Why am I the only one fighting for something you're not even smart enough to want?"

"Let's not pretend you ever did any of this for me. To you, all this has ever been about is power. I've seen glimpses of Poppy's power. Fuck, she doesn't even *realize* . . .," he said with a shake of his head. "Are you going to stand there and tell me that if I'd been the one to inherit that power I wouldn't already be dead because you would have cut my chest open and eaten my heart for it?"

Irina smiled at him wickedly, and there on her twisted lips was the answer to his question. "Of course, I would not kill my firstborn son—Charles's son. I love you just as much as I loved him."

Simon's gaze narrowed on her. "You are at your most dangerous when you believe 'love' is your martyr."

Irina laughed at that. "Yes, I suppose you're right . . .," she said as she began to walk around him. "But I don't need your help anymore. You've been almost useless to me from the start of this. I swear, you and your brothers act as if I sent you to these Brethren strongholds on vacation or something."

"I told you she was here."

"And yet you failed to deliver her to me for a whole month," Irina pointed out.

"She was being kept on The Elder's floor, protected by all of his guards. Exactly what did you want me to do?"

"*Oh*, I don't know . . . perhaps use just a hint of that impressive magic of yours." She turned back around to him, her eyes gleaming in the low light. "It's of no consequence now. I know where Poppy is . . ."

"Well, it's about time. I really thought you were starting to slip in your old age." Irina gave Simon a truly ugly look in return for that comment. Her son just ignored her and appeared almost bored as he asked, "So, I assume you already know that she's alone? That The Elder's no longer protecting her?"

"Did that dim-witted little Empath who has you locked by the balls give you that information? Honestly, I should just kill her and put you both out of your misery."

Without warning, Simon extended his arm and clasped his strong hand around Irina's throat. "You so much as come near her and I'll show you exactly how much power your firstborn son has," he seethed. "She's mine! And no one—not you, not anyone—will touch what's mine."

Slowly Simon released Irina, the warning in his eyes burning long after Irina felt his fingers release from her throat. Then her expression seemed to morph into one of respect. "Perhaps I've underestimated you all these years. I feel the darkness growing inside you, Simon. It's only a matter of time . . . Don't ever be fooled into believing a woman of such goodness and virtue could ever appreciate what you're becoming? But I do."

"I said, stay away," he repeated in a dark voice.

"Of course, my son. I'm just your mother, imparting my pearls of wisdom to you. What do I know?"

Irina moved around Simon, carefully, appreciating the raw fury she could see and feel coiling through his body just then. But she still meant what she had said. She may have chalked him up too soon as a miserable failure of a son. There had always been something about Simon—something remote—as if he truly didn't care about anything or anyone other than himself, at least until this Empath of his came into his life. Irina could deal with that . . . as long as he showed proper respect to his mother.

"Now, if you'll excuse me," she said as she turned to leave through the same darkness she had entered from, "I need to pay a visit to your half-sister. While you, my son, have a dance you need to finish."

CHAPTER THIRTY

"Why are we wasting time?" Alec impatiently shot the question at Caleb, while the Daywalker calmly surveyed the mountainous landscape around them from atop the steep trail. Caleb had been nothing but *calm* during the four strenuous days of training Alec received from him and Jax, and then through ten additional days while the two of them searched for Poppy. Alec, though, was starting to go out of his mind with worry, and that worry came out as sharp criticisms. "Is there any particular direction you're heading, or have you just decided to let the wind direct you through Canada?"

Caleb simply offered a sardonic grin while still managing to convey complete ease with his two current obstacles: the deep-snow wilderness surroundings and Alec's worsening temper. Alec knew he was being ill-tempered, but, in his defense, there was the fact that it was nearly freezing outside and Caleb Wolfe stuck out like a *goddamn* 'Immortal-sore-thumb' hiking for days in nothing more than jeans and a long sleeve tee shirt. Caleb did, however, purchase an insulated jacket at a camping supply store they passed just after they crossed the border into Canada. Evidently *this*, he decided, wouldn't look suspicious to hikers who might encounter them on the snowy trail. "Would you prefer we head back to Seattle?"

"No," Alec scowled. "No, I wouldn't prefer we head back to Seattle." *Poppy* wasn't in Seattle. She was out here somewhere, trying to survive on her own. And besides, Alec was tired of being attended to by the kind, well-intentioned women in Seattle who were driving him crazy (and now, fortunately, were Jax's responsibility). "But I'd like to know we at least have a direction, that we're not just randomly changing directions with changes in the wind."

"That, I'm afraid, is up to you," Caleb replied, as if he possessed some great wisdom the rest of the world was lacking.

Alec wanted to yell. He wanted to holler. That just sounded like a bunch of crap to him! Or a bad line out of a martial arts film. "Really? That's the best you've got Mr. Miyagi? What's with all the cryptic bullshit?" He pulled at his jacket, at least grateful that he was much less affected by the cold weather now that he was a hybrid. But after spending the past few days traveling on foot over the border into Canada with Caleb, he was tired of getting in touch with his *sensitive side.* It seemed to spin him in all sorts of directions because it was like he was walking around *on sensory overload* all the time. He was adapting to his hybrid changes as fast as he could, especially considering his constant worry over Poppy, but in Alec's opinion, Jax and Caleb wasted too much time *feeling* the world around them. It drove him nuts! Alec was a Guardian long before he was an Elder. Guardians acted, they trusted their instincts. And now, when Poppy needed him the most, he was stuck somewhere in the wilds of British Columbia because Caleb Wolfe had a feeling.

"It's too soon," Caleb replied, calmly and evenly. "You don't yet have the patience or the objectivity for this."

"I have plenty of patience! I'm known for my patience, for thinking before . . ." Alec really didn't want to finish that sentence because it very easily bordered on a lie, ". . . and I'm objective. Tons of objectivity. But that all goes out the window when . . ."

Alec wanted to say '*when the woman you love is out there alone and running for her life*'. But because he felt those words so deeply, so personally, the absolute last person he wanted to admit them to was the one Daywalker he'd failed in front of before.

A couple of years before, The Brethren had assigned Alec to be Olivia's Guardian, responsible for her safety. In order to get her away from the vampire, whom Alec saw as a threat, he pretty much bullied Olivia away from Caleb by telling him the truth about exactly who she was—a Charmer, the only known one known in existence. Alec had made sure Caleb was aware of her power to draw and allure vampires and that her power might also be influencing all of the feeling Caleb believed he had for Olivia, and so, obviously, there could never be any shared future between them.

And boy, had he been wrong!

After being under Alec's protection for not even two hours, Olivia was taken captive by the vampire coven that was hunting her. So Caleb Wolfe, more than anyone, understood what it felt like to be terrified that the woman you loved more than your own life might not be coming back to you. Alec had witnessed Caleb fight for Olivia with senses and strength that were more than superhuman, sharp senses that were sustained solely because of the true and constant love he felt for Olivia.

Now *Alec* was fighting for someone. He had strength, at least—strength much greater than before—and he had powerful senses he could use to his advantage. But he was afraid of failing because *this woman* was *his* entire future this time. *Everything to him.*

"It's not your fault," Caleb broke into his thoughts as if he could read them exactly.

Alec stared up at the tall vampire, whose upper body was much longer than Alec's, making him taller even if Alec were to match the vampire's current haunched position on his heels. "Are you talking about Poppy . . . or Olivia?"

Caleb stared back at him with a pulled brow, as if he didn't like that question very much.

Alec shook it off. "I was just thinking about the time when Davin captured Olivia. It had been my job to protect her—"

"No," Caleb interjected firmly. "It was *my* job. I should've never let her leave with you that day. I failed her. I failed her many times before I held on for good." Caleb lifted from his haunches to his full six-foot-plus height and turned directly toward Alec displaying an unquestionably sincere expression. "Poppy's yours to protect. And you're doing all right with that."

Alec just stared at the man, completely baffled. "How can you say that? We're standing out here in the middle of nowhere, with no clue where we're going. I don't even know how to find her."

"Yes, you do," he replied in a deep and confident voice. "You just don't realize it. We're here in this spot right now because you've been leading us here—not me. If you weren't so foul-tempered and stressed out, you would've realized it by now." Alec could only stare back, blankly, at Caleb. He just didn't know what to say to the man because he didn't understand how that could even make sense. "You said the two of you were in the process of connecting when this happened," Caleb continued.

Alec nodded. "Yes, but I also said, she was not able to finish. We're not fully connected."

"Somehow you're connected . . . or a door has been opened on your side that you are not aware of. You may not yet know how to step through it, but she definitely does. Because I'm connected to you, I can feel it when she connects."

Alec slapped his hands angrily against his sides. "Why didn't you just tell me you were feeling her though me? We could have sped this process along."

"I'm not feeling her through you. I'm following you. You are leading us."

"And I'm telling you, it's not possible for me to lead us because Poppy and I are not connected. I never drank from her. I would know if I drank her blood," Alec said irritably. "*I wish* I was connected to her. And I'm *sick to death* of this stupid connection *we* have," he said gesturing back and forth between Caleb and himself. "It's been on overload ever since I woke up!"

"Now you know what I've had to live with for years," Caleb grumbled.

"Then why did you do it?" Alec challenged him. "Why give your blood to save a man you don't like? When you knew it would connect us for the rest of your life?"

Caleb stared out to the mountains beyond them. "I did it for Olivia. She'd lost so many people in her life, I feared it would have broken her if she had lost you that day. That would've broken me." Caleb leaned a bit closer to Alec and, still wearing that sincere expression, said, "That is what you do when you've been given the gift of a successful mating. You honor them. You never stop fighting for them."

Alec sighed with exhaustion. "I'm not mated to Poppy."

"Perhaps not. But you are somehow connected to her. Each time she reaches out to you, you start heading off in a direction, almost as though you don't even realize what's carrying you there."

"So what do I do? How do I target this . . . this connection, if I don't even know how to feel it?"

"You must be open, but you can't force it. You'll be opening the door for her, and that, in turn, will influence you."

Alec stared back at him, looking miserable and totally confused. "Will I be able to *feel* her—*feel* that she's all right?"

Caleb shook his head. "Not yet. But the fact she is reaching out for you tells us she is alive. She is checking in on you, a few times a day. That is good."

Alec looked away for a moment, disappointed with Caleb's answer, but he didn't have a choice, did he. "Whatever it takes to find her. I'll do whatever it takes."

***

Poppy had just finished unloading four platters of burgers and refreshed a table full of drinks when she suddenly felt a familiar pull in her chest. That was followed with a little queasiness in her stomach, but it was a good kind of queasiness. Her heart began to beat a little faster as she took a couple of deep breaths. "Alec . . .," she whispered. She glanced back to Willy, who was standing behind the bar. "Everyone's taken care of for the moment. Is it all right if I step outside for a minute and get some fresh air?"

"Heck, yeah," Willy chuckled, throwing his bar towel over his shoulder. "This place has never been so organized. I'm not quite sure how you've done it. May have to keep you around another few days."

"We'll see," she smiled before stepping out the back door, unable to avoid the small, uncontrolled sigh that escaped her in spite of herself. Despite the fact that she was liking it here, it was time for Poppy to move on. She'd already been in Elk's Cove longer than she had planned. She had managed to save up nearly fifteen hundred dollars, which would help her get to the next town, find a place to lie low, and buy some supplies. But the risk of staying so long in one place had been worthwhile, mostly because her connection to Alec felt stronger here, and it seemed to be growing in strength by the day.

Poppy could feel him now. He was open and more relaxed than she had felt him since he had regained consciousness from his transition. And she could feel his strength returning, his determination. That made her happy. "Thank God, you're all right," she whispered, wrapping her arms around herself, trying to wrap around the happy feeling so she could hold on for as long as she could.

She inhaled a deep breath and tried to sense how close Alec was to her. Definitely closer than the last time she had reached for a connection to him—much closer. Was it possible he was making his way back towards The Oracle? She just then realized the sleepy little town of Elk's Cove was near the border to Alberta. Had *she* absently been making her way back to The Oracle, as well? The Brethren site wasn't her home, but in her time there it had begun to feel like a home, or the closest thing to a home she had ever known.

A regretful smile crossed her lips as she heard the entry door bells tinkle inside the bar. She would have to let go of her connection to Alec to attend to a new customer. These little moments were all she had left with Alec, and she promised herself that when they happened she would stop whatever she was doing and treat them as a lifesaving breath, because that's what they were to her. Every day Alec lived, survived, thrived, felt as if he was also somehow saving her.

"Table six," Willy said to her as she came back inside. She decided then that she would complete her shift and move on from Elk's Cove that night. Her instincts were telling her it was time to go. A part of her was going to miss this place. The small community with an 'everybody knows everybody' sort of feel felt comfortable now. She imagined what it would've been like to grow up in such a town. Of course, she had done that in just about every town where she had ever stayed for any length of time. "I closed out the tab on table three and cleaned up table four for you," Willy added.

"Thanks," she smiled and headed over toward the corner booth where the new customer waited. "Can I help—?"

Poppy's breath cut off with a harsh gasp as she stared back at the lone woman in the booth.

"Why yes, I believe you can help me," Irina said with a wicked smile.

CHAPTER THIRTY-ONE

Poppy was trapped for sure, so she quickly shifted her focus from Irina to the innocent humans seated throughout in the bar. They were all enjoying their food and drink, and none of them had any clue how much danger they were actually in because of her. Poppy mentally mapped how many people there were and where each was located.

"Oh, no," Irina warned her. "Don't get fidgety on me, Poppy. You and I both know your Dhampir quickness may be able to save one or two of them, but I can kill the rest without even exerting myself." An almost playful smile came over Irina's lips as she tapped her finger against the worn bar table. "I'm actually surprised you would leave yourself out in the open like this. Did you think you could hide among the humans? That I would not come for you here in their world?"

"They are innocents, Irina. It's me you want. Leave them out of it."

"You brought them into this, so it's only fair I use them to teach you a lesson." Poppy inhaled a steadying breath. What had she done by exposing these innocent people? She should have moved on after a few days. Her mother taught her they always had to be moving. Poppy had let herself feel too settled at The Oracle, and now that feeling had betrayed her by affecting her judgment. "Are you going to asks me what I want?" Irina questioned. "Or shall we just reminisce about the last time I saw you—the night I killed and fed on your whore of a mother."

Poppy shut her eyes against the shocking image that flashed through her mind. Her mother had been in such horrible pain, just as Alec had been during his turning, and Poppy had been helpless to stop either. She fought to keep control of all of the emotions rolling through her, but her stomach rolled with queasiness and she could sense the eyes on her back. "Poppy, you all right?" Willy asked from behind the bar.

Irina responded by rising to her feet, slowly, her eyes locked on the bar owner. Poppy got the message loud and clear, '*deal with him or he's dead*'. "Fine," she answered as she turned and walked closer to Willy so she could speak quietly. "Willy, I'm afraid I'm suddenly not feeling well. I need to leave. Now."

With a hard glare past Poppy's shoulder, Willy eyed Irina. "You sure you're gonna be all right?"

"Of course. I'll be back at my regular time tomorrow," Poppy replied calmly, even managing a smile on her lips. "It's probably just something I ate. Somewhere else," she added quickly. "Not here. Your burgers are truly the best."

For a moment, Poppy thought Willy was going to stare right through her to Irina. He was a perceptive man, and he didn't appear to be buying her sudden illness, which she thought had an authentic ring of truth about it. "Girl, if you need help, you just need to ask. There're a dozen men in here. That slip of a woman would have no choice in the matter."

Well, actually, the dozen men would have no choice.

If poor Willy had any idea what he was up against, he'd have the sense not to get involved. "Thank you," Poppy answered softly, "for everything. But I promise, I'm going to be fine. This is my aunt. She will take care of me."

He groused at that a bit as he shifted his ill-fitting pants beneath his rounded belly. "Your aunt, huh. Well, at least let me get you the money I owe you for today." Poppy was already shaking her head at him when Irina walked over to her, took her arm, and pulled her toward the door. They were already outside in the cold, moonlit night when she heard Willy say from inside, "Something's not right. Come on!"

Poppy could hear people getting to their feet and heading for the door. "Idiots," she heard Irina laugh under her breath as the warlock released Poppy's hand and swung around to face the door through which the men were about to charge any second.

"No!" Poppy cried. "Don't hurt them!"

Irina swiped her hand across the night and began to chant. Men's voices could be heard yelling as fists began to pound at the old, wooden door, but it didn't budge. Then Poppy could hear the footsteps heading to the back of the bar, but Poppy knew they would be unable to escape through the back entrance, as well. Irina had barricaded the entire bar and everyone inside by putting a spell around the building. Even if they tried to break through either door or a window, it would not give. "You can't just leave them trapped in there like that!"

Irina turned to Poppy, smiled, and then started moving into the trees. "That is up to you," she replied. "Are you coming? Or shall I light the building on fire?"

Poppy had to follow Irina quite a distance uphill in the darkness, but as she rushed along she began to make a plan for escape. She would wait to make her move until Irina released Willy and the other patrons from the bar, but until then, she needed information. "Why are you doing this? I have never been a threat to you. Has your entire life . . . all of this . . . been about nothing more than revenge against my father because he loved my mother?"

Irina stopped abruptly. They had just reached the crest of the hill. The warlock wheeled around to face Poppy and spat out, sharply, "Charles loved me! Oh, he claimed to love your mother, but she did not understand him. Not like I did. *I saw* how Charles craved to explore his craft—to prefect it. I supported him in it. Your mother distracted him. She seduced him to steal him away from me."

"That's not true," Poppy insisted. "My mother loved my father. She would have supported anything he desired."

Irina's eyes began to illuminate, eerily casting from them a bright white light—a cold light of pure hatred—into the night. "Your mother was a whore. She stole Charles away from me when I was pregnant with his son!" Poppy blinked back, stunned by what Irina had just confessed. Poppy had no idea that Charles had left Irina when she was pregnant. "A beautiful son . . .," Irina continued. "His father's son . . . a powerful witch in his own right. But his power should be even greater." Irina's lifted her head to stare right at Poppy, her eyes truly full of hatred. "You stole that from him."

"I don't know what you're talking about? I've never stolen anyone's power. I wouldn't know how. I didn't even know I had a half-brother!"

Irina continued talking, as if she hadn't even heard Poppy. "I wanted my son. I wanted the child created from the love shared between Charles and me. And I wanted that love to be immortalized through him, forever. He was to be the most powerful witch this world has ever seen. Everything I've sacrificed was done for him, but because of *you* that sacrifice was all wasted."

"You're crazy," Poppy whispered. "I've nothing to do with your son."

Irina just continued to talk, more to herself than Poppy it seemed. "I studied Theban texts for months, translated every symbol, until I got the words just perfect. It was the perfect spell!" She stopped for a moment, her expression appearing lost as she faced Poppy. "Our son—Charles's first born—was to be blessed with more power than this world has ever seen. A witch to be feared and respected as the most powerful creature in the supernatural world. Oh, it was going to be so perfect! But after our son was born, that kind of power never developed in him. I thought my spells, all the gifts I had so painstakingly cultivated, had failed me."

A look of madness had been creeping into Irina's eyes as she spoke, and its intensity increased as she continued speaking. "Then, two months ago, the night I killed Mary and discovered your existence, everything suddenly made sense. Even before he left me, Charles had betrayed me with your mother, impregnated her while he was still with me—while I was already pregnant with our son." Irina's eyes then came directly back to Poppy. "Are you going to ask me how I know that?"

"Oh, my God," Poppy whispered; she could see where Irina was going with this. "I was born first."

"Yes!" Irina hissed. "Because you were Dhampir you were born in only five months. *You* became Charles's first-born child. And the joke was on me—because for his entire life I believed my spell had failed—that I had failed our boy." Irina's eyes then focused directly on Poppy's. "Until the night I watched you cast my Dhampirs to the fires of Hell as easily as you could set a piece of paper on fire with a match. *You* have my boy's power. And it's shared between your Dhampir and witch abilities. That's why you can send someone to the fires of Hell with a single thought, why you have the venom of the most potent vampire."

Poppy shook her head. "I don't want that kind of power! I never wanted it!"

Irina drew her hands into fists as she gritted her teeth and then hissed, "All these years the power was *wasted* on *you!* You aren't even *worthy* of it! All you could manage to do with it was to turn an Elder!"

Poppy's mouth went dry. "How did you know . . .?"

"Your half-brother told me," Irina said as she turned and walked straight to the edge of the sharp bluff. "He's closer to you than you think."

"Who is he?" Poppy questioned, looking back down from the bluff they were standing on and seeing Willy's several hundred feet below them. Her Dhampir senses allowed her to still hear the voices of the people trapped inside, who were now panicking because they could not escape through any door or window. A couple of cars had since stopped, and their occupants were scattered around the building trying to help those trapped.

"It doesn't matter now," Irina smiled in response. "All that matters is that I don't intend to let you keep that power." Irina circled her hands into the air in front of her and chanted more words in a language Poppy guessed was Bulgarian. Suddenly, a blinding, bright light wrapped around Poppy and she realized she was trapped inside a shield. "It's time for you to feed me."

Poppy fought to free herself from the force field, but her Dhampir gifts were not strong enough. Then Irina's expression relaxed, just watching while Poppy continued to attempt to fight her way through the invisible shield. "The Elder . . . you could've healed him, you know."

Poppy stopped her pounding and sucked in a very hard breath, surprised at what her captor had said. "*Healed?*"

Irina smiled, wistfully. "That's really the most ironic part. You turned him, but you also possessed the power to heal him. Instead, you left him to his fate because the only thing you truly know how to do is *run*. Your mother would be so proud."

Irina's voice was grating on Poppy ears. She wished she could block the sound altogether but she felt Irina's words sinking to the pit of her stomach. The realization that she could have helped Alec—but had once again chosen to run—made her physically ill. The self-awareness was almost too much. Irina was right! Poppy always ran. She never planted her feet and faced anything. She saw herself as this cursed, disaster-prone woman who was, at times, deeply lonely. But all that changed on the day she met Alec. He healed her soul in so many ways. But the *one time* she could have healed him in some way, she had failed him miserably. What kind of a person did that to someone they claimed to love? "How can I heal him?!" she demanded. "How?!"

"The time for healing is long gone," Irina said, with obvious pleasure, and Poppy felt as though her stomach had completely dropped out of her body. Irina then turned back to the edge of the bluff. "You thought to hide from me among the humans? That I wouldn't come for you if there were witnesses from the other side? You were wrong!" She lifted her hands, her nails perfectly tipped in bright red polish as she circled them in front of her. "Build me a house of fire!"

A wall of fire, with flames surging about twenty feet high, shot up from the ground in front of the bar far below them. The people outside who were trying to help those trapped inside turned in shock to see the wall of flames behind them. They yelled for those inside to run to the back of the bar and then rushed along the side of the building to get to them, but Irina was relentless. She circled her hands, drawing a wall of flames around the sides until it surrounded the bar. Everyone was now trapped by the deadly heat. "No! Stop!" Poppy cried out as the flames started to grow so high they cast an orange glow throughout the entire night sky above them. "They're innocents!"

Irina ignored Poppy's pleas and drew her hands together as if she were directing the final note of an orchestra. As she did, the flames started to move toward the building. The victims below were no longer screaming in terror because they were being choked by the flames. Irina then turned back to Poppy and, using her very long, red-tipped fingernail, pointed to Poppy's collarbone and began to draw a line downward. As she did, Poppy gasped harshly as a crippling pain in her chest felt as though a sharp knife was carving into it, and, looking down, she saw a trail of blood erupting from her chest and cascading downward to her stomach. Poppy knew what was happening. Only a short while ago she had watched helplessly while Irina had done this to her mother. She was going to open Poppy's chest, then reach in to pull out her heart.

In that very moment, something changed. Poppy Honeywell realized there was nowhere to run. It was time for her to take a stand against Irina, whether she was ready or not. Poppy raised her head and hands to the orange sky and remembered what Simon had told her. "*You must channel all of your energy and focus on that one result you most want.*" With a voice as strong as she had ever used, Poppy loudly bellowed, "No!"

With that one word, the force field around Poppy blew outward and smashed into Irina like an invisible wall, knocking the powerful warlock flat onto her back. Poppy then focused every ounce of energy in her head on one, single thought. The scattered clouds above her began to move and close in on one another other, swirling together into one giant mass directly over the bar. They became an ominous gray force in the night sky. "You can't save them!" Irina shouted angrily from her prone position on the ground, unable to rise because of the force of Poppy's counter-attack.

The force in Poppy's hands, the pull in her heart, and the focus in her mind became nearly overwhelming as she pulled her hands down and exhaled loudly, almost grunting with the effort. "Drown the fire!" she cried and then repeated, louder each time, "Drown the fire . . . Drown the fire . . . Drown the fire . . ."

The sky opened up and rain—rain so hard it nearly knocked Poppy off her own feet—poured from the clouds overhead to the bar below. In seconds, the water had suffocated the fire, just before the flames reached the people outside. Those inside broke through the back door and rushed away from the building, choking and sputtered, lifting their faces and taking the rainwater into their mouths while at the same time trying to get much needed fresh oxygen back in their lungs. But they were alive!

Poppy was trying to calm her breathing, trying to ease the viscerally sharp pain coming from the deep cut inside her chest as she stared at her hands and felt an overwhelming combination of emotions—relief, strength and amazement— unlike anything she had ever experienced. For once in her life she had not run. She had stood her ground and saved herself and others. And it felt really good.

"Don't be too proud of yourself," Irina seethed as she returned to her feet. "You think you can conjure up that kind of power yourself? You had help there."

"What're you talking about?"

"I'm talking about that baby in your belly—the Elder's child. Are you going to stand there and pretend you didn't know? You think that's going to save the child's life?"

Poppy blinked and brought her hand to her stomach. Alec's baby! Could it be true? Was she carrying their baby?

"Now I'll not only be able to consume your power," Irina said with evil malice, "but destroy a future Elder as well."

***

Alec was beyond frustration with how long it was taking to find Poppy, and he just wanted to punch something. He had decided that Caleb Wolfe would make the perfect punching bag when a huge jolt sent him to his knees right there on the trail. It felt like someone had just hit the sidewall of his stomach from the inside. "Shit!" Alec cursed as he sucked in a huge breath.

"I felt that," Caleb responded.

"Yeah, well, so did I," Alec growled before he lowered his head and tried to get a grip on the pain that wasn't yet easing. "Will you stop being so damn tuned into me?"

Caleb simply scowled at him. "It's kind of hard to ignore when you go to your knees in pain in front of me. I tend to notice these things."

"Well stop—" Alec didn't get out anything further because a second punch ripped through his stomach even harder than the first one. *Oh, fuck!* He wasn't sure whether he and Poppy had some kind of connection, but that punch felt like a warning or a call for help coming from her. "Shit!" he cursed a second time, aloud but under his breath. "Please, don't tell me something's happening to her. *Please, God!* Let her be all right."

"We've got to keep moving," Caleb pressed.

"I don't know where the *fuck* I'm going! Can't you get that through your thick *hair*?"

Caleb yanked Alec back up to his feet as if he weighed nothing more than a tissue, which certainly wasn't the case.

Alec weighed in at a muscle-filled two hundred and five pounds. "So you're giving up on her, then," he growled. "The woman you claim to love. You're just giving up."

All of that was said in statements, not as questions, and that infuriated Alec. He shoved the vampire back with all the strength and anger he felt at that moment. "I'm not giving up on her!" he yelled, and for the first time he could really feel the hybrid within him coming forcefully to the surface. There was immense strength in his body now, power that he wasn't used to, and it astounded him sometimes. "I don't want to be wrong!" Alec pushed Caleb hard a second time his hands connecting with Caleb's chest, but this time the vampire didn't move an inch. "I don't want to lose her because I guessed wrong!"

Caleb simply watched Alec for a moment while Alec fought to regain control over his anger. "You're not guessing," he finally replied. As emphasis to Caleb's point, Alec suddenly felt a third jolt hit his stomach, and a sense of dread came over him the likes of which he had never experienced in his life. Caleb nodded as he sensed the impact of it on Alec. "You're being sent a message. Concentrate and focus on what is being communicated to you."

"I'm trying," Alec growled, frustrated that his new senses were telling him that Poppy was in mortal danger and he was fumbling around the woods like a blind-assed squirrel?

"You're fighting them," Caleb declared firmly. "You're a hybrid now. You have to start learning how to see the details of what your senses are trying to tell you. Trust them! Think of your senses now as an array of instincts that, when combined, will enable you to act decisively. You just have to trusts them—trust yourself!"

Alec slowly nodded, letting the man know, despite his current anger, that the words he was saying were getting through to him. He had to listen. Poppy's life could be at stake.

"Someone's reaching out to you," Caleb continued. "Someone who has a connection with you somehow."

"Yes, it's Poppy."

"I'm not so sure about that. But to feel it that strongly means we're close, so I don't believe you've guessed wrong. You just need to focus so we can take this last step."

Alec rubbed his hand back and forth over his stomach as he tried to focus on what he had felt. "It was like I was being yanked by a rope." He then lifted his hand and pointed northeast. "From that direction."

"OK, then," Caleb replied evenly. "That's where we head. Let's narrow down the towns?"

Alec pulled out his map of British Columbia, the one useful purchase made at the outdoor store where Caleb got his jacket. "In that direction we've got Goat River and Legrand, both with populations of 700 people or less."

"Sounds like good places for a woman on the run with very little money to blend in." Alec grimaced at the thought. He hated thinking about Poppy being out there, trying to survive with no money. Maya told Alec she had taken a little from the ten thousand they brought with them from The Oracle, but it wouldn't last her for long. He wished she had taken all of it because he had access to more money easily. Poppy didn't. "Which town's first?" Caleb asked.

Alec looked closer at his map. "Actually, it looks like we pass through a tiny town first, population just a few hundred." Alec folded the map back up and shoved in his vest pocket. "Elk's Cove."

CHAPTER THIRTY-TWO

Poppy stepped back from Irina and placed her hands protectively over her stomach. She could now feel the slight roundness to her belly, remembered her bouts of queasiness at the bar, and realized that Irina was right. It was true. She was pregnant. She couldn't believe that after all her worry about having a baby, all she could think of now was how much she wanted the precious, little life inside her. This was Alec's baby—their baby—and this little he or she needed to be protected at all costs. And it was all up to her. "You will not touch my baby," she warned Irina.

Irina just laughed, and Poppy could feel anger—a fury like she had never experienced before—rolling through her. Her hands squeezed tight with the urge to do something. "Uh, uh, little witch. You may have been able to pull one trick out of your very inexperienced hat, but I'm not some simple Dhampir you can just wish into the fires of Hell."

Irina stepped towards Poppy, circled her hands and once again a shield of bright light surrounded her. "Now where were we? Oh, yes . . . I was about to kill you." Irina pulled her hand forward and Poppy could feel her body being pulled toward Irina as though she was on a rope. She tried to dig her feet into the ground, but it was no use. Then she felt the sharp blade-like pain carve once more into her chest. She could barely breathe for how crippling the sensation felt. She wanted to cry out!

Irina just laughed and continued to draw her lethal cut lower, toward Poppy's stomach, threatening the new life inside her. If Poppy didn't do something now, she and her baby, *Alec's baby*, would be just another one of Irina's nameless, faceless victims.

She couldn't let that happen!

Poppy yelled, "*No!*" as she threw her hands out in front of her. Just as before, when she could feel a powerful force pushing from inside her, she could feel it now, but it was even more charged. The lighted shield around her seemed to fracture into hundreds of jagged pieces and blast away from her in all directions like shrapnel. Irina suddenly found herself in its direct path. Her eyes widened with shock just as hundreds of pieces of shard glass sliced into her body. The force of it threw her back off her feet and sent her stumbling over the edge of the cliff.

Poppy gasped a couple of hard breaths and ran to the edge to look down. The rain had stopped and the moonlight had escaped the clouds and was shining down on the bar and the hillside below her. People were still hustling frantically about the bar, and she could see that although he was a little flustered, Willy was safe and sound as they all waited for police and medical help to arrive. A short distance up the hillside, she could make out the moonlit outline of Irina' body against a rock below. Blood seeped everywhere as she lay there with her eyes wide open and unblinking. Poppy had just killed a warlock . . . her worst nightmare, the woman she had been running from her entire life. She almost couldn't process it, but she *could* process that her baby was safe.

"You're all right, little one," she breathed hard as she covered her hand over her belly. "It's going to be OK now." Poppy repeated several times, pausing each time to fully comprehend what this all meant. She was still in tremendous pain from the open wound in her chest, but the bleeding had stopped and she had saved her baby. She didn't have to run any longer. Poppy could walk to the next town and settle down for good—if she wanted to. She and her baby could have a home of their own—if she wanted that. She could give herself and Alec's baby the safe life she had never known.

But then, in the midst of this reverie, she stopped herself with a single thought, one that erased every other thought, idea or notion—"Alec!" she said aloud.

She looked down at her stomach, stroking her palm over her belly and feeling the cut in her chests starting to heal itself quickly. She could breathe easier. Another benefit she guessed she could attribute to Irina's supposed 'curse'. "We can do the same for him! We have to find him. We have to heal him. If there's any chance, we have to give him his life back—to return to The Oracle and rule as Elder, like he's supposed to."

Without another word she inhaled a final, deep breath, held it, and focused on his energy. She felt that he was very close, so she turned and ran in an all-out sprint in the direction she sensed him to be. For the first time in her life Poppy Honeywell wasn't running away from something, but to something. To someone. And it felt really good. She would deal with his anger at what she did to him when she found him. Right now, all she could think about was doing the right thing—finding a way to heal him and to let him know he was going to be a father.

That was the least she could do.

***

Caleb suddenly stopped on the trail, his head coming up alertly as he put his hand out in warning for Alec to stop. Alec sensed something, as well. Ever since he had stop letting his fear get in the way of his senses, he was becoming alert to every little detail around him. Someone was coming, moving at a speed much faster than a human could run and cutting through the air as quietly as the wind, which meant only one thing—whoever was coming was more than human.

Alec's heart started to beat faster and harder in his chest. Caleb turned back to him with an '*I told you so*' smirk on his lips. "It's a Dhampir. A female Dhampir."

"I know," Alec responded as he pushed past Caleb and ran across the high terrain so fast his feet barely hit the ground. It didn't matter that it was the middle of the night and the only light was what was left of the moon falling toward the horizon. He could feel his way over the terrain without having to focus on it. His body, powered by his new senses, knew where to take him.

Alec realized he was setting himself up for a major disappointment here. *What if it wasn't Poppy?* But, somewhere deep inside him, he knew it was. He crested the top of a forested hill and raced right along the edge. Even through the darkness, Alec's improved Hybrid vision could see the woman running towards him, the significant blood on the front of her clothing that scared him to death, but still he shouted his thanks to the heavens in that very second. *She was alive!* "Poppy!"

They ran straight into each other's arms and collided with a force that would knock normal people off their feet. "Careful, sweetheart! You're bleeding!"

But Poppy ignored him and wrapped herself around him. "I'm, OK! I'm, OK!"

Alec then threw his arms around her equally as hard and pulled her tight against his body. "Thank God, you're safe," he rejoiced. "You had me so damn worried."

Poppy was breathing hard—not from over-exertion, but almost as if she was in shock. "I can heal you," she said, but Alec didn't register what she was saying. He continued to be more concerned with her condition and the fact that her clothes were soaked to the bone and her skin felt as if she'd been shoved into an ice bath.

"You're freezing," he replied, unwilling to let her move an inch in his arms even though she was now getting him just as wet. He wanted the warmth from his body, which wasn't nearly as much as it used to be when he was human, to soak into her.

"I can heal you," she repeated into his shoulder.

"What?" he questioned as he pulled her head up to face him. But he took one look at that beautiful face and was a goner. His lips were on hers before he even let her answer his question. Alec Lambert wasn't asking. He was taking. He kissed her as if it would be their last kiss on this earth together—with passion, love and possession, and his body felt more alive than he could remember in any single moment of his life. Poppy still seemed stunned in his arms. He figured he had to knock some sense into her with a deeper, longer kiss before he'd feel her gradually melt in his arms and into his kiss. He nipped at her bottom lip and then explored her mouth with his tongue like a man starved. If it was possible to complete a mating with just one kiss, this would've been the one to do the job quite thoroughly. "Oh, God," he breathed roughly at her ear. "Don't you ever run from me like that again. Do you understand? No more running."

Poppy pulled her head back and looked up at him with such loving confusion it made his breath catch. *Why was she so surprised?* "I—I don't understand. You're not angry at me?"

"Yes, I'm angry," he said, but his voice was slightly hoarse, letting her know there was more emotion at play here than any real anger. "I'm angry you left me!"

"I didn't know how to stay," she defended, shaking her head away from him. "Not after what I'd done. But I know now I can heal you. Please let me try. Let me try to do this for you."

He kissed her again, and then brought her head to his chest. "Listen," he said. Warmth radiated from his chest, his heart beating strongly as she huddled there against him. She felt so perfect he didn't want her to move, but her gaze soon shot up to him with surprise.

"You have a heartbeat?!"

He nodded at her with an empathetic smile. "You were already healing me, sweetheart. I never fully turned." He gave her quick flash of his fangs as he added, "I'm a hybrid now. Think you can learn to love a hybrid?"

Her eyes welled up and spilled over with tears as she looked at him with a question still behind her tears. "But how? I don't even know—"

"With these," he answered as he kissed the tears that were falling from her eye.

When he pulled back from her, he thought he would see that she was relieved, but instead she looked more upset. "If I'd stayed, I could've healed you fully?"

Alec's expression filled with worry as he stroked her wet hair. He would never lie to her, but he also refused to let her feel guilty about 'mostly' healing him. To him, there was a big difference between being a hybrid and being a vampire completely dependent on blood for food and unable to ever walk in the sun again. In *his* mind, she *had* saved him. "We're never going to know that," he answered gently as he kissed her again, softly this time. "But I am strong—stronger than I've ever been, and more capable of protecting you and the family I hope you'll consider having with me someday."

She smiled at him. "Does that mean you want me to stay with you?"

"Poppy," he said with feeling. "I never wanted you to leave. I meant every word I said to you that last night. I want to be mated to you. That doesn't change because we faced our first supernatural challenge. We're going to face a lot of them. But I need to know you're going to fight for us as hard as I am."

Poppy nodded quickly. "I'm not running anymore."

Caleb discreetly cleared his throat behind them, reminding them that he was still there. "I hate to break up this romantic reunion, but we need to get her someplace safe for the night."

"Yes," Alec agreed as he stared into her eyes. "And we need to get you warmed up."

Poppy nodded and squeezed her hands over Alec's arms. "There's something you need to know. Irina's dead!"

"What?" Alec questioned anxiously, pulling her face back up to him.

"I . . . I killed her. It's a long story. And there are many things I need to explain."

Alec rubbed her cold arms vigorously once again. "There will be time for that once we get you settled." He turned back to Caleb and nodded at the insulated jacket he knew the vampire didn't really need. Caleb handed it to him without delay. "Thank you."

"I believe this is where we go our separate ways," Caleb said, realizing that since Irina was dead, the threat to them was now gone. "I've a wife to return home to. She and Gem have probably driven Jax close to worried insanity by now." He then seemed to consider something else. "Unless, that is, you plan to bring Poppy back with you to Seattle."

Alec stroked his hand along her precious face. "No. I'm taking her home—back to The Oracle." The smile that lit up Poppy's face at that moment gave Alec all the assurances he would ever need about their future life together. She would be the strong, supportive force at his side that he had always hoped for as he ruled as Elder. And when they were alone together, she would be his to cherish and protect, his to provide for, to earn and deserve her love every day. He couldn't wait to start his new life. He let go of Poppy and faced Caleb eye-to-eye. "I want to thank you for everything you've done to help me—even when I perhaps didn't deserve it. You and I haven't always agreed on things . . ."

"We've never *agreed* on things," Caleb replied dryly.

"Well, yes that's true . . . but you taught me a lot out here. More than you know. I'd like to consider us amicable friends, at least."

Caleb cocked one brow. "That's a big step for one so arrogant."

Alec frowned at him. He was trying to extend a bridge here, and, as usual, the vampire was making it difficult. "Look who's talking."

"Well, I did save your life."

Alec's frown transformed into a knowing smile. "So you did."

Caleb replied with the closest thing to a smile Alec had ever seen on the man, but his expression changed, morphing into something much more serious as he looked at Poppy but continued to address Alec. "You'll have to keep the knowledge of her gifts to strictly those you trust with her life. "If the wrong people find out what she can do, she'll become a weapon either side could use to get the upper hand in this never ending supernatural war . . . just like Olivia."

Alec's expression was quiet as Poppy watched him. "I realize that."

"Do you?" Caleb questioned. His raised eyebrow kept the question on the agenda "Because it occurs to me that The Brethren would find great use for a Dhampir who has the power to reverse a turning."

Alec couldn't pretend that wasn't possible, or even more likely. Of course, a Dhampir who could save a human from being turned would be invaluable to The Brethren. But he'd seen firsthand the lengths both The Brethren and the supernatural forces against Olivia would go to if they thought they could capture and use her when they believed she could tip the scales in their favor. *Hell*, at one time he had been a part of that on behalf of The Brethren. He saw what had been done to her in the pursuit by both sides for power and control—to use Olivia as a weapon for their side. He would not allow the same thing to happen to the woman who would be his wife. He turned to Poppy. "Caleb's right. I don't want to see you hurt by what others deem more valuable than your own wellbeing."

"I want Joseph to know," she answered without hesitation. "He's my family, and he would never agree to anything that would harm me. You and I can figure out the rest of it together."

Alec smiled at her with approval.

"Well, then, until our paths cross again," Caleb said before he turned and vanished through the darkness, as silently as the vampire always entered it.

CHAPTER THIRTY-THREE

Alec and Poppy walked until they found a very *rustic* but clean roadside motel. After getting settled in a room, Alec made sure Poppy immediately got out of her wet, bloody clothes and steered her straight towards the bathroom to enjoy a long, hot shower. Poppy released a deep sigh of pleasure as the hot water sluiced over her body. She carefully washed and inspected the wound on her chests that was healing nicely, and then caressed her hands over her slightly swollen belly, a smile radiating over her face at the thought of telling Alec he was going to be a father. Poppy was surprised how excited she was about her pregnancy now that she no longer had to worry about Irina. Her life could settle into something "normal," but she wasn't quite sure what to think about that. She had never known a normal life.

When she finished, she wrapped a dry towel around her and flopped down on the big, king-size bed, luxuriating in the feeling as every muscle in her body sank into the overly soft but still supportive mattress beneath her—and she didn't care; it just felt good to stop for a while.

A few minutes later she felt the mattress depress behind her from Alec's weight as he came to lie with her. He pulled her back into him and wrapped his arms around her, curling his head into her neck. To Poppy, he smelled amazing even though he had help only from cheap motel soap and his natural scent. Even better, his voice had that husky, relaxed quality to it as he spoke. "Feeling better?"

"Yes," Poppy sighed as she turned around and curled into him more fully.

Alec seemed to really like that. He stroked her neck and then pulled back so he could inspect the Irina-inflicted wound that was still healing on her chest. "I know this wound pattern, Poppy," he said, his expression grimacing with worry. "Irina did this to you, didn't she? She tried to–?"

Poppy stopped him with a gentle hand to his mouth. "I'm fine. It's healing quickly."

"Sweetheart, I need to know what happened."

"And I'll tell you," she replied. "But for now, can you just keep holding me? When I left Seattle I didn't think I would ever feel your arms around me like this again."

"I can do better than that," he said, rolling Poppy back until she was flat against the mattress. Slowly, he pulled the towel open in front of her and began to smooth kisses all along the scar that was healing; her neck, her stomach, each breast. He was so gentle; Poppy couldn't seemed to stop sighing. "I can finish what we started the last time we were together," he said, and then he rolled Poppy onto her stomach and pulled the towel away from her completely. Her nude backside was open to him, and he took his time appreciating every curve, every line, with kisses—just as he had the front. "I've missed you," he murmured while nuzzling her shoulder. "I've missed making love to you."

Shivers ran just beneath Poppy's skin as Alec's hand slowly caressed the slope of her back and moved downward to the swells of her bottom. She sighed and he responded with a smile she could feel on her skin. His gentleness made Poppy question how she could have ever walked away from this man. "I'm sorry," she murmured. "I'm sorry I left you. I was just so shocked by what I had done—by what I was capable of doing . . ."

"You can't hurt me anymore, sweetheart." Alec's breath was warm on her skin as his teeth scraped against her low back and his hands began to massage her hips and thighs. Poppy was so relaxed but her breath was growing deeper and more erratic. She wasn't sure how she was supposed to concentrate for any serious conversation when he was making her shudder like this. "My body has accepted your venom and been healed by your tears. You don't have to be afraid." His teeth bit, just briefly, into the fleshy part of her hip and she squealed as he said, "We have something to finish."

"Are you sure?" she asked him as she tried to turn to face him. But he kept her in place and returned his kisses once more upward along her back. His weight increased against her back as he rose above her, held her down—and she felt his warm breath on her neck.

"Yes," he whispered, almost hissed. She shivered at the dark tone and tremor in his gravelly voice. Poppy found their position on the mattress as he pinned her down to be an incredible turn-on. His voice at her ear sounded hungry, fierce, like a man who knew what he wanted and would stop at nothing to have it. The excitement was building in her body, her breathing, as she clenched the sheets tightly between her fingers. "And this is mine to finish," he said, bringing his wrist up to his own mouth and sinking his teeth into it. Poppy could instantly smell the scent of his fresh blood.

Alec brushed Poppy's cherry hair back from her shoulder, exposing the slender curve of her neck, and a moment later, his fangs sank into her throat. Her whole body jerked with a moan of both pain and absolute pleasure. She arched her back as he held her firmly but supportively, her body softening beneath him as she allowed him complete control. His hand moved to her hip and slipped inside to her thigh, where he pulled her legs apart and began circling two fingers around her clit, causing her hips to undulate against him in response. "That feels perfect," she breathed as he continued to swirl her body higher.

Poppy's vision began to blur in front of her and her whole body heated. Her blood surged faster through her veins, and she heard Alec groaning as he drank behind her. She understood what he was experiencing then. She had felt that rush herself when she had first drank their combined blood. The mix was like an erotic charge that shot through the blood stream and demanded that the mating be completed. The powerful drive was why she'd such a hard time stopping once she had begun to sense something was wrong that first time. And since then, her body had felt such an ache, such a deep longing for him, that at times she thought it would break her. "More," she pleaded. "Please . . . more."

***

As he drank, Alec's body was suffused with a scorching pleasure the likes of which he had never experienced in his sexual life. His woman was pleading him for more—and she was going to get it. Did she understand the power she had over him? Did she understand that the energy he was currently receiving from her blood was taking him over in a way that was no longer possible for him to rein in? He didn't want to hurt her, but as a hybrid he was now much stronger. His sexual hunger was stronger. He would not be able to hold back and he desired the same from her.

Alec's fingers circled faster, causing her soft moans to deepen. He knew she was on a very sharp edge and ready to fly off, and that's exactly where he wanted her—ready to fly. He lifted his fingers from her flesh—to her loud protests—and then lifted his head, pulling his fangs from her tender throat. The next couple of breaths were the hardest and the sweetest he had ever inhaled in his life. He and Poppy were now joined, mated. He could feel in his mind the pathway that had opened completely between them. His body felt fused to an almost unbearable moment in time when everything about her was somehow branded upon his brain, singed into his soul. Poppy Honeywell was now his to take care of, to watch over and protect. She was no longer an assignment given to him by Joseph; she was his partner, the reason for his existence. And no one would ever be able to separate them again.

"Alec," she pleaded, just before he pushed forward inside her. The moment he felt her surround him, felt her inner muscles reach for him and take hold, he groaned into her shoulder and lost all control. In just one, powerful thrust from him, she gasped out her release, coming all around him. Her walls gripped him like the tightest fist as her back arched and her nails dug into the sheets. No preliminaries, no continued thrusting, just one hard entry and she was lost. And so was he.

Alec's body jerked forward as he followed her into a mind blowing orgasm that was too powerful to hold back. After a few gasping breaths that cut off his ability to speak, he was about to apologize for going off as fast as a teenage boy when he realized he was still rock hard inside her. Their connection was causing an erotic high the likes of which he had never experienced before. He slid briefly from her body, flipped her over on the sheets and plunged into her again. She cried out this time as his hand clasped around her upper thigh as he pulled her to him, somehow finding the strength to start rocking into her.

Poppy's eyes blinked open and she found him right there above her, his fangs over hers as he breathed hard against her lips. He could see now he was suffusing her in sensations that worked like a drug to prepare her for what was to come. With each hard thrust into her, a little more blue filtered into her eyes until they were glazed over, leaving her in an erotic haze. The closer she got to her next orgasm, the farther her head tipped back and the wider her mouth opened, her fangs punching out. Alec could see on Poppy's face that she wanted to drink, needed to drink. And far be it from Alec to ever deny this woman anything.

His hands slid under the curves of her bottom and he lifted her to him. He was not being gentle, but she met him thrust for thrust—and it drove him insane. She started to choke back a scream as she tightened around him. "No!" he rasped; all the blood in his body feeling as if it were surging to one exact, perfect moment. "Let me hear you."

With that, Poppy cried out, then dragged her nails over his back. His second release was so monstrous his flesh burned. He dropped his neck to cover her mouth, soon feeling the sharp punch of her fangs. *Holy shit*, the moment was hotter than anything he could ever describe. He was exploding inside her as she drank from him—and involuntarily, his back arched deeply. For a few moments it seemed like his release was never going to end, that he would stay lost in a permanent erotic high. But then he collapsed against her in total exhaustion and couldn't move a muscle.

When he finally regained some of his senses he heard her murmuring beneath him, and from out of his post-coital haze he realized he had his full weight on her. He rolled to his side and was surprised to hear a gasp as she covered her mouth with her hands. Her hands were shaking, and he worried she thought something was wrong with him after what had happened the first time they tried to connect. "Hey," he assured her. "I'm fine. I'm better than fine. I'm perfect."

She wrapped her arms around him and held him for a long while. After a few minutes he could still feel her shaking. He was really worried she was starting to lose it, but then he realized she was laughing. "It happened didn't it?" she asked. "We're mated. The connection was right."

"It damn well better've been after that," he teased.

Poppy smiled and lay back, reached for his hand, and placed it, palm flat, over her belly. She had always had a soft, lush stomach, but this time her belly was even more appealing to him, with a roundness that seemed to mold perfectly to his palm. "I've something to tell you," she said softly as she threaded her other hand through his hair. And somehow he knew. He knew before she even said a word, and he could feel the joy spreading through him like the sun. "You're going to be a daddy."

"A daddy," he said, the words catching in his throat. "A dad! And you're all right with that?"

Poppy's smile broadened and she nodded eagerly. "More than all right. Since the moment I found out, I've wanted nothing more."

He hugged her and then placed several kisses her over her rounded belly. "I love you," he said, "and I will love this baby."

"Will you be disappointed of it's a girl?" she asked. "'cause I think it might be a girl. I can just somehow feel it." She looked at him now with such hesitancy it caught him off guard. "I know you need a boy to take your seat as Elder someday."

"Damn, Poppy," he said gently, placing his hand over her mouth to stop her words. "Even if we eventually have a boy, I would be proud to have my first daughter take my seat as Elder—if that was her wish. These old rules about men only inheriting the Elder's seat were created by men two hundred years ago. I think it's time for a female Lambert to cause a little chaos, don't you?"

Poppy sighed contently and snuggled up against him. "Do you really mean it? You would let our little girl become Elder?"

"In a second," he answered as he kissed her. "Now you and the little one get some rest, sweetheart. The sun will be up soon and we need to get an early start back to The Oracle."

Poppy nodded and fell asleep almost instantly in his arms. She had been tired. Alec smiled as he watched her sleep. She was all his now. And *damn*, he was going to be a dad.

What more in life could he possibly want?

CHAPTER THIRTY-FOUR

As soon as the sun rose the next morning, Alec was up, hating the thought of having to wake a still-sleeping Poppy. She had slept peacefully in his arms, probably more soundly than she had since this whole ordeal started. All he wanted to do was get her back to The Oracle so they could settle into their new life together and he could spoil her and their new baby on the way. He smiled as he kissed her cheek. Alec Lambert was going to be a dad, and he'd be a good dad, too. He knew it! Especially if it was a little girl, as Poppy believed. The little tike would probably have him so wrapped around her little finger that she would be ordering *him* around in no time. "Hey, sleepy girl."

Poppy squirmed in his arms, "I'm awake," she murmured, departing sleep with a lazy smile but then proceeding to fall back asleep once again.

"You don't look awake," his teased her softly in her ear with a kiss. How could he blame her? After everything she'd been through, she needed rest, and Alec decided that he should just let her have a little more time to sleep, but he realized he would feel a lot better when he had her back where she belonged at The Oracle instead of holed up in some 1970s era roadside motel. He gently stroked her back until her eyes opened and blinked up at him again.

"No, I'm awake," she said a second time with a sleepy voice.

"Sorry, I know you're still tired, but we need to get going. I've arranged for a team to meet us just across the border. Are you up for a little more walking today?"

She nodded and rolled herself onto her feet. Alec came around the bed quickly and wrapped his arms around her as he pulled her against him and rubbed his hand over her stomach. "Slow down," he said. "We don't have to race out of here. How is your wound feeling this morning?" he asked as his fingers brushed her collarbone. He could feel her cut was completely healed and he felt relieved."

"All better," Poppy said then blinked a few times toward the muted television that was tuned into the local news. "Has there been any word about the bar?"

Alec nodded. "Everyone's all right," he said, stroking his hand through her hair. "That was a very brave thing you did, saving those people. You're going to have to tell me sometime how you did it. On television they're explaining it as some sort of freak weather phenomenon. They will be talking about it for a while around here, I'm sure, but there was no mention of you or Irina."

"That's good," Poppy replied, kissing his jaw and then making her way towards the bathroom.

It wasn't long before Alec and Poppy had taken to the road, walking together on the chilly morning, sometimes laughing sometimes quiet, just enjoying each other's company. They stayed to the shade of the forest because it was such a bright day. About a quarter mile from the clearing where they were to be picked up, Poppy suddenly stopped on the trail and glanced back over her shoulder. Alec could tell that something was bothering her. "What is it?" he asked her. "You've been distracted since you woke up this morning."

She glanced away from him for a moment, as if she were debating whether or not to tell him, which he didn't like. He wanted to know if ever something bothered her. "Do you sense that?" she finally asked him.

Alec frowned, disturbed by the fact he hadn't be paying closer attention. "I'm afraid I'm still getting used to all these new senses." He dropped back to be beside her and tried to focus in on whatever it was she was picking up on. "I don't sense anything."

"No, it's gone now," she said quietly. "But I sensed it before . . . the night I went off the property with Gideon, then again when I dove into the lake. And the night Maya and I left

The Oracle with you. Somebody's been watching me, and I know it's not Irina."

Alec blinked, confused. "Why've you not said anything to me before now? It could be one of Irina's Dhampirs who doesn't yet know that she's dead."

Poppy nodded her head. "I don't think so. I don't sense they are Dhampir."

"What do you sense?"

She shrugged her shoulder. "There's something about it . . . like they're watching . . . just watching. I don't necessarily sense they want to harm me."

Alec continued to walk forward but as he did, he tried focusing his new senses. Since they were still so new to him, he couldn't pick up on what Poppy was sensing as clearly as she could, but he could definitely now tell that someone was there, and that made him uneasy. He wrapped his arm around her to pull her along. "Let's head this way," he whispered, nodding to the right. "It's a little more direct way to the other side where we're meeting the team."

They reached the other end of the clearing in just a few minutes but had made such good time they were nearly a half hour early. Alec pointed to a grouping of trees about three hundred yards ahead. "There," he said. "The end of that gravel road is where they're going to meet us. Let's get situated in the shade there and have some water while we wait."

Alec and Poppy started for the trees but hadn't made it more than a few steps when Alec felt something large bulldoze him across his back, sending him crashing to his knees. Poppy fell forward beside him, trying to catch her breath after being struck by a large boulder. "What the fuck?" Alec charged as he snapped his head around to see they were under attack from everything from boulders to logs coming straight at them through the air. There were so many things coming all at once that he didn't get a chance to seek out the person or the force that was attacking.

He could respond only by shielding Poppy with his body and pushing both of them behind a small grouping of rocks in the middle of the field, but not before Alec was hit with bruising force by several more objects. If he were still human, he would most likely already be dead. The grouping of rocks they used as protection didn't offer much cover, but at least Poppy and the baby were no longer a wide-open target. His hands quickly searched her for injury. "Are you all right?"

She nodded. "Who's attacking us?"

Alec snuck a peek over the rocks just as a giant log smashed into the cluster they were behind, blowing several fragments loose. "I can't see anyone," he said as he turned back to Poppy and saw that her forehead was bleeding from being struck by one of the rock fragments. He cursed himself for not picking a more public place to meet the team. They were sitting ducks out in the open field like this. He ripped his shirtsleeve and dabbed at her wound before quickly scanning the field to calculate their limited options. "I'm going to try to get their attention by going for that cluster of boulders over there. While they're busy dealing with me, I want you to go for the trees over there, where the team is supposed to meet us, and find cover. If you can, keep running down that access road so you can meet up with them sooner as they're coming in."

"But Alec, what about you? There's no cover out there!"

Alec simply soothed her worried protest with a kiss and placed his hand protectively over her stomach. "You and the baby come first, all right? Do as I ask. I know you have the speed to get you both to better cover quickly. I love you." That was the last thing he said to her before darting out into the clearing. His new Hybrid legs moved swiftly toward the direction the objects appeared to be coming from, and he was able to dodge and leap over most of them. Then, suddenly, he saw who their attacker was.

Irina Danchev morphed into view from out of nowhere, and Alec immediately recognized Sienna's cloaking gift at work. Irina appeared half mad as she marched out into the clearing, her head and clothing soiled and bloodied, refusing to shift her focus away from Poppy, who was still huddled behind the small pile behind Alec. Irina's hands lifted into the air, raising a dozen objects on every side of her simply with the energy in her mind, suspending them in the air for just a moment before hurling them with the force of a cannon toward Poppy. "Poppy! Come to me now and I won't kill him. That's the only warning you're going to get to save his life. Do you really want someone else's blood on your hands?"

"No! Don't hurt him," Poppy shouted back.

"Shit!" Alec cursed. His plan had backfired on him because Irina was fixated on Poppy. She couldn't give a crap about him! Now he had left Poppy to defend herself alone. Alec raced back towards her, cutting a path between her and Irina. "Irina!" he bellowed, letting her know she would not be able to continue to ignore him. The warlock swung to him as he used his new speed and a lot of old training to dodge objects that came at him from all sides. He managed to avoid most of them, but he ran out of luck just before he could reach Poppy. An enormous log hurled across on his blind side and flipped him onto his back.

"Oh, Damn, that was painful!"

Alec gasped out a couple of tough breaths and then, his equilibrium restored, rolled to his side to see Poppy heading back towards him. "Alec!" she cried. He was about to go damn near ballistic when he saw her running out into the open field like that, completely exposed. She dove on top of him with a grunt and he rolled them both over until she was underneath him, just as another rock hit his back.

"Are you fucking crazy?" he chastized her harshly. "Stay down!"

"How is Irina here?" Poppy questioned. "I cannot even sense her."

"She's using Sienna's cloaking gift she stole from her the night of Bodmin Moor. That's probably why you didn't sense her before she confronted you at Willy's." Alec glanced back and his eyes widened as he saw another log seconds away from flattening them both. He pulled Poppy beneath him as much as possible while waiting for the back-breaking collision that was just about on top of him. But it never came . . .

Alec looked up to see objects crashing against an invisible wall on all sides of them. "What the hell?" he whispered. He looked down at Poppy and saw she was concentrating with her eyes closed, murmuring words under her breath in a repeated chant.

"You can't keep me out!" Irina yelled as more and more objects pounded against the force field around them. Alec could see the toll it was taking on Poppy to hold the spell by repeating the incantation without ever losing focus. Irina was growing more infuriated, her face twisted with her need for revenge and she began swiping her hands through the air as fast as she could, speeding up the onslaught until there were so many things crashing around them it was as if Alec and Poppy were in the funnel of a tornado.

Poppy opened her eyes and looked directly at Alec. "It isn't just me," she said as she brought his hand over her stomach. Alec could feel the heat on her skin under his palm and blinked back, unable to believe that their baby was somehow also helping his mother protect them. "I'm not sure how much longer we can keep this up."

"I'm tired of playing games with you!" Irina screamed, and at the same moment Alec heard Poppy gasp underneath him.

"What's wrong?!" But Alec saw what was wrong almost right away. Blood started to come through her shirt over her chest. He pulled her collar back and could see her chest was being cut into as if someone had an invisible knife. "No!" he cried out the same moment the shield collapsed around them and the cut went deeper into her chest.

"You're mine now, Poppy! You and that baby you're carrying!"

Alec shot up to his feet with a dangerous warning. "You're dead!" he issued in a voice that was not his own. This warlock was not taking his family from him. He would die before he let that happen.

"You can't stop me," she hissed. "And you can't save her, Elder. She's dying!"

Just then Alec heard Poppy cry out again and he cursed himself that Irina was so far away from them. He would never be able to get to the bitch in time to save Poppy. She would have her chest carved open in seconds! "Damn you!" Alec shouted just as he heard an arrow flash past his right ear and go several more yards, striking dead center into Irina's forehead, right between her eyes. All the chaos stopped in an instant, and Alec found himself breathing harder than he ever remembered breathing in his life as he watched Irina's body fall back, stiff as a board, to the ground.

She was dead!

He glanced briefly at the arrow that had killed her and recognized the intricate tri-blade head design, red carbon shaft and white-feathered tip. Even as Alec's mind was saying to him, "No, it couldn't be," he raced back towards Poppy. When he reached her, he pulled her hand away from her wound so he could see the damage. "How bad is it?" he demanded.

"I'm all right," she said, tearing at some of her own clothing to make a ball of fabric to soak up the blood.

"Let me see," he insisted, and breathed a sigh of relief once he saw that the cut was bad but had not yet reached too deep. "Are you sure you're all right? Is the baby all right?"

She nodded at him quickly, looking a bit stunned. "What just happened?"

Alec turned toward the direction from which the arrow had come and thought he was seeing a ghost. A hundred yards in the distance, a man with blond hair was just lowering his split-limb, compound bow to his side and slowly rose to his feet. He was dressed in a structured leather vest, tunic, pants and boots, staring straight back at him. The friend, *the brother* Alec Lambert believed lost to him forever, was staring back at him, appearing very much alive even though Alec had watched him die months earlier at Brahm Hill—Lucas Rayner.

"How is this possible?" Alec said in a stunned voice.

The Red Diamond Dagger Alec had witnessed Reese plunging into Lucas's chest that night was strapped to a utility belt at his friend's waist. Lucas was alive and still protecting Alec with fierce loyalty in life even when Alec believed he was resting in death. And in that precise moment some deep part of Alec seemed to let go of the bitterness and anger he had carried around for months, the grief of believing Lucas had paid the ultimate price because he wouldn't listen.

"Alec, are you all right?" Poppy asked him breathlessly as she came to stand beside him, following his glance over to where the man with the bow was standing. "That's him!" Poppy cried. "That's the person I've been sensing watching me. Do you know him?"

Alec stroked her hair and kissed the top of her head, grateful beyond all words as he pulled her into his arms that Lucas had once again protected what he loved most. "Yes . . ," Alec replied. "He's an old friend."

Lucas simply offered Alec one of his knowing smiles and tapped his closed fist three times over his heart and then extended it to him. The sign of loyalty Lucas had always given Alec to pledge his allegiance to him. Alec then watched Lucas turn and race off the other direction, disappearing right in front of them in a swirl of wind. "Stay safe, my friend," Alec said under his breath, feeling his eyes welling with tears from the sweet relief of knowing Lucas was alive.

"Your friend just saved our lives—our baby's life," Poppy said to him.

"Yes," Alec replied with a smile. "He has a habit of doing that."

Alec kissed Poppy gently on the lips as he eased his hand over her rounded stomach, still needing that bit of reassurance to allow him to believe that everything was OK with both of them. "I love you," he said, just as both of them became aware of the sounds of vehicles approaching in the distance. "Come. I'll tell you all about him on our way home."

EPILOGUE

Alec burst into his office with only one thought in his head
. . . *he was going to kill Kane!* He'd been back at The Oracle
for only a couple of hours, and after a few preliminaries with
the staff that greeted him upon arrival and having made sure
that Poppy was settled into his penthouse for some time to heal
and to get some much-needed rest, he'd headed straight for his
office, with Sampson and Matthias on his heels—as if he had
never left.

Alec had already processed what had happened the
moments before Irina's death and was past the point of being
grateful that Lucas had shown up—still alive! Now he wanted
to know why the hell Kane had kept this information from him!
Kane had known how much he had been grieving his friend's
death, yet he still had said nothing to reassure Alec that his best
friend was alive. Why?

"Matthias?" Alec called as swung around on his feet.
"Poppy is currently resting, but when she wakes I would like
you to see that her things are moved into my room. She'll be
staying there indefinitely. Both guards gave each other a
knowing smile, which Alec decided to let slide, knowing that
the smiles were at his expense. "And Sampson, I'll need you to
set up a satellite feed to Joseph within the hour. The sooner the
better. I've a lot I need to update him on. And have Gideon-"

"Right here," the English Guide said simultaneously as he
entered the office. The man just had an uncanny knack for
knowing when he was needed.

"Thank you, gentlemen," Alec offered as both guards
turned to leave.

"It's good to see you back and well . . . and seeming more like your old self," Gideon hedged with a raised brow.

"I am," Alec replied. "And I'm sure there's a lot you need to catch me up on since I've been away. But first I just wanted to thank you for covering for me in my absence. I know it must have been a terrible burden to have to hide so much from the other Elders, but I will explain everything to them. I just needed the time to find her."

"No explanations needed, Alec."

Alec blinked up at Gideon and saw a welcoming, warm smile on his face. "That's the first time I've heard you use my given name since I became Elder. It's a refreshing change . . . and just in time because I was about to have you deported back to England."

Gideon laughed in spite of himself. "I don't believe you can have me deported. But what's important becomes a lot clearer when you fear you've lost someone, wouldn't you agree?"

Alec smiled back, knowing that before Maya would've had a chance to get back to The Oracle to find Gideon and tell him everything that was happening with him, he would have given the old man quite a scare. "I would. And . . . thank you Gideon, I missed you, too."

Gideon cleared his throat—a bit uncomfortably, Alec thought, and continued. "So I guess the first thing we should discuss is how you plan to handle the fact that you're a hybrid now. There are those within The Elder Council who will ask for your removal when they find out."

Alec looked up from his desk as if he were curious. "Funny, isn't it . . .? I'm now stronger—will live longer than any of them—and can identify first hand with what our people are going through on a daily basis . . . and yet, if given the chance, certain Elders would bounce me for no longer being just human. There's some serious irony in that."

Gideon arched a brow. "You wish to keep the information from them, then?"

"Come on, Gideon. You know me better than that. I'll be nothing but completely honest about what I am now. It would be impossible to hide it. Let them just try to remove me. I'm quite sure I'll have Joseph's support once he hears Poppy will be giving birth in a few months to our child, who will one day hold the Lambert seat on The Council."

Gideon's whole expression turned to beaming joy at this news, and why shouldn't he? He'd been like a father to Alec for many years, so now, he thought, he'd soon be a kind of grandfather. "Congratulations. That is brilliant news."

"Thank you. I really don't think I could be any happier—except for the fact that I'm going to kill Kane."

"Oh, dear . . . What has he done now?"

Alec walked over to his favorite window and shoved his hands into his pockets as he stared out. "Lucas is alive."

"Alive . . .?" Gideon echoed in a quiet voice. "Are you sure?"

"Damn sure. I just watched him disappear right in front of me in a gust of wind that exactly matches the description of our Wraith. The same Wraith whom I sent Kane and Aiden to Yellowknife to find."

Gideon's brows furrowed. "But if Lucas is our Wraith, how would Kane not know—?"

"Exactly!" Alec charged. "That *shifty* Shifter has known all the time that Lucas was alive and he didn't tell me. I'm going to kill him!"

"Perhaps it would be best to hold off on killing him until we understand why he didn't tell you," Gideon suggested.

Although Gideon's remark was reasonable, Alec replied, "I disagree." Pausing a moment to let the shock settle in, he continued, "So my first order of business is to have Kane brought up here so that I might kick his ass and get the answers he's been refusing to give me for months."

Gideon just gave Alec one of those 'oh, dear' looks the English were famous for. "I'm afraid Kane's not here at The Oracle. He and Aiden took a leave of absence yesterday."

Alec's expression morphed into a scowl. "Who in the world authorized a leave of absence for them?"

"Well, no one, really. Kane sort of authorized it for the both of them."

"Of course he did," Alec said as he returned to his desk. "Did he take one of the SUVs?"

"No, they went up into the mountains on foot. There is quite a lot of stuff I need to update you on."

"Well, at least they're not far away," Alec replied. "First, tell me how Maya's doing since she's returned? Poppy and I both gave her quite a scare."

Gideon cocked his head strangely. "Maya . . .?"

Alec frowned. "Yes, Maya . . . Small brunette, big blue eyes. Remember, I sent her back from Seattle to update you on what was going on."

"Alec," Gideon began rather uncomfortably. "We thought Maya was still with you. She has not returned to The Oracle."

Alec's eyes went momentarily blank. Then he blinked a couple of times and asked, "What do you mean? You thought she was with me? I haven't seen her since I left Seattle. If you haven't talked to her, then how did you even know where I was?"

"Kane told me—which now I'm assuming he knew because he was in contact with Lucas."

Alec raked his hands through his hair. "You're telling me no one's seen Maya in three weeks? *Where the hell is she?*"

A Note from Christine Wenrick

As an author, I have fallen in love with many of my characters . . . even some of the worst antagonists (Hello, Celeste!). That is why, when given the chance, I love to revisit my favorite characters to give fans of the series a chance to circle back around to their lives.

Jax and Gemma Walker are two of those most cherished characters for me. I wrote the following scene in *Guarding Poppy* initially because I wanted to give insight into this wonderful couple's relationship that readers' did not necessarily have in The Charmed Trilogy because the series was told solely from Olivia's point of view.

Unfortunately, sometimes in the editing process scenes must be deleted to eliminate what may be perceived as unnecessary secondary character development for brand new readers to the series. That was the case with this next scene.

But I wanted to include it for you here, the Jax and Gemma fans, as a sort of 'bonus excerpt'.

I hope you enjoy!

Christine Wenrick

***

Jax Walker moved without making a sound through the penthouse condo and out onto the sky view patio, where Gemma was sitting quietly on a bench with her back to him. He could sense that she was so lost in her worry for Alec and the pain of trying to control the effect of Olivia's gift on her that he wasn't sure she was even aware he was behind her.

"Jax," she finally said in a soft voice, which answered that question. "Please tell me you understand that my being upset about what's happening to Alec right now has nothing to do with us."

She sounded almost desperate in her plea, and Jax found himself taken aback by it. People rarely had the capacity to surprise him any more, not after two centuries of living as a vampire. Yet this small powerhouse of a woman seemed to do it on a regular basis. Had she been out here this whole time worried that her concern over Alec would threaten what they had?

No damn way!

Underneath his calm, life-educated exterior, Jax Walker was a cocky bastard. He knew it. Confidence was just something that happened to a man when he'd lived two-hundred-and-twenty-eight years but looked like a thirty-five-year-*young* man. And Jax was just as confident that Gemma loved him—even more now than the day she agreed to mate him. They were connected, each a healthy half of one whole unit. They could feel each other's moods and thoughts at any given moment. They shared a deeply intimate sexual connection. They shared a daughter, the most beautiful Dhampir child in the word, in his opinion—Sophie. Alec Lambert could never threaten that, even if he wanted to. Which, of course, he didn't, because the man was obviously in love with another woman.

"I just can't stand what's happening to him," she continued. "He wouldn't want this for his life. But that doesn't mean that I have any doubts about us. I don't. I never have."

Oh boy, the poor woman sounded miserable. He was going to have to put a stop to this. "Gemma, are you forgetting that I know you? That I can *feel* you? I have felt every day how much you love me. I feel it when we make love. *I* am the man your body desires. *I* am the man you want to be with, not Alec Lambert. He does not have the power to come between us."

She nodded in agreement and let out a relieved breath, but she still faced away from him, and he knew why. He sat down on the bench seat behind her and wrapped his big arms around her—gently, because he was a vampire built like a heavyweight boxer and, though she was also a vampire, she was still a small woman. She let her head fall back on his shoulder as he pulled her close, and he could feel a deep trembling coursing through her entire body. "You are weak from trying to fight against Olivia's gift. It is all right to admit that this is hard for you. It is all right for you to ask for help. Let me help you?"

Gemma shook her head, her short, ginger-colored locks brushing against his cheek as she kept her face turned away from him. "I need to learn how to fight this on my own. I'm a vampire now. I'm stronger than I was as a Dhampir. I can't have you fighting all of my battles for me, as you did before."

"First of all," Jax responded, "you have never let me fight a battle for you a day in your life. You have always been stubbornly independent like that." Gemma was about to object vehemently as she turned her head toward him, which made him smile because he was well aware he had been just a touch overprotective of her ever since he found her as an abandoned teenager so long ago. But he would never admit that. Instead, he silenced her with a finger over her mouth. "And secondly, *this battle,*" he began firmly, "that you want to take on yourself, is one that even vampires who have lived for centuries would lose. My Granddaughter has a gift that is that powerful. And you need to start acknowledging and respecting that."

"But Jax-"

He turned her head more fully to him and stopped her next words with a kiss. Then he lifted her as easily as a piece of paper, turning her around on his lap and in his arms to face him. He could now see the vulnerability in her eyes and it damn near brought him to his knees. She was his angel, his salvation in this life, and he would do anything in or out of his power to stop her from hurting like this. "I have always loved you for your strength and your stubbornness . . . but in this case, it could end up hurting you and Olivia. That is not acceptable to me. Do not put her in a position to have to defend herself against you. She would never hurt you. You know that. And that could end up costing her."

Gemma tipped her head down to Jax's neck and kissed him there lightly. "I don't want to hurt her. I love her. And I want us to be a coven family again, like we used to be. Not living two hours apart from each other. She's your granddaughter. I don't want to be the reason you miss more time getting to truly know her."

Jax tipped her head back in his hands until she was again looking directly into his eyes. "That will come in time. You just need to be patient. Right now, you must put me and Sophie first. And all we care about is a healthy, happy mate and mother."

Gemma nodded her head agreeably. "You're right. I do need help with this. It's exhausting trying to fight it. But I want to stay here until I know Alec will be all right."

Jax pulled his woman into a deep embrace in his arms. "If you want to stay until Alec comes awake, then you will drink from me now. I carry the same blood as Olivia in my veins. The more you take it into your system the better you will be able to fight the effects of her gift."

"Jax . . ."

"Take it," he commanded, lifting her higher onto his lap and wrapping her legs around his waist. Gemma didn't challenge him anymore because she knew he was right. She was weak, and Jax couldn't stand seeing that any more. She sank her fangs into his throat with so much force that he should have at least growled in protest, but he barely even flinched. He loved when his angel drank from him like this, holding onto him so fiercely; it was as if he were her life's blood. The surge of energy his body felt as his blood rushed faster through his veins made him feel impenetrable. He simply felt more a part of her when they shared like this.

As she tightened her hips against him, he tipped his head back as his hands stroked her arms, helping to relax her until he could feel her deep, inner trembling begin to recede. *Holy hell*, there was no doubt he would have to have her soon. He needed to feel her small body grasping him tightly, inside and out as she cried out his name. But he would wait until she was stronger and not under the effects of Olivia's gift. Until then he would just take care of her.

"I love you, angel."

ACKNOWLEDGMENTS

I *love* writing, but if not for the contributions and efforts of numerous other people these books would just not be possible.

First, I would like to thank my editor Paul. We have worked together through five manuscripts and have practically become one voice in the editing process. I swear sometimes I almost know what he is going to markup or comment on before I even send him the manuscript. You would think if that were the case I could avoid the red ink all together . . . but I prefer to look at it as keeping him on his toes.

I would also like to thank my amazing cover designer, Whitney. We have had a few challenges along the way with these dark, moody covers, but I love them! Each cover makes me wish I could see more of these sexy, male heroes . . . and that is exactly what I want the reader to feel.

For my Dad, for simply always being there to support me no matter what. I love you.

Lastly, I want to thank my fabulous book club, Felice, Susan, Toni, Becky and Rachel. Our Book Summits are a blast and I have been challenged more than once by these wonderful friends. The finished product is all the better for it. Thank you!

ABOUT THE AUTHOR

Christine is a graduate of Washington State University, where she received a BA in Interior Design. And true to form of using mostly her 'right brain', she splits her time between her commercial design career and her imaginary world of writing. She lives in the scenic Pacific Northwest where she enjoys hiking, camping and photographing many of the wonderful places that served as inspiration for her three-volume Charmed Trilogy. Her biggest reward in life comes on any given day when one of her books connects with a reader because she herself is such a lover of reading. Some of her favorite authors include Lisa Kleypas, Julia Quinn, and Kimberly Derting.

Sovereign Elder Joseph Davin stepped forward to embrace Poppy. "You're not safe here, little flower." Now Alec really felt like he was intruding on a private conversation. "I must protect you the best way I know how. I promised your mother." He then motioned back to Alec. "I trust Alec. He's a former Guardian—and a very good one. You yourself said that you can feel Irina getting closer. Let Alec take you someplace where he can protect you. In the meantime, I will find a way to deal with Irina."

Poppy dropped her head quietly, and for a moment it seemed she wasn't going to answer him. "I feel safer here with you than I will with a stranger."

"He's right," Alec finally said as he came slowly to his feet, realizing he needed to do something to gain this woman's trust. "I may be a stranger to you, but I *can* protect you. And more importantly, I can give you all the tools at my disposal so you can protect yourself. If you have a sense for recognizing the warlock who's threatening you, your Dhampir instincts are telling you that you're in danger. You need to start trusting those instincts."

Those huge gold eyes of hers locked on him fully with a look of utter determination as she walked right up to him. "I don't want any part of witchcraft, Dhampirs or vampires. That's not who I am."

"Yes, it is," he challenged her. "That's exactly who you are."

Her eyes narrowed as if she were preparing to blast him with a thousand different reasons why that was not true, but instead she replied, "I will agree to go with you on two conditions. One, you'll agree to never disagree with me again." Alec's brows arched high at that rather impossible request. "And two, I will only go with you if it doesn't require us crossing an ocean in an air-"

Poppy's words were cut off by her small squeal when Alec caught sight of Joseph sticking a needle into her arm. Her limbs gave out from under her almost immediately and he reached out and caught her when she would have otherwise collapsed to the floor. "What in the world did you do that for?"

"No worries," Joseph assured him. "It's just a little something to help her relax for the trip."

Alec blinked at him. "Relax? She doesn't like flying?"

"Terrified of it, actually. Unfortunately, Poppy lacks an appreciation for the severity of her current situation. We need to get her out of London tonight—hence, something to relax her. But once she's someplace safe she'll be no trouble at all."

Alec's gaze narrowed shrewdly. By what he had already witnessed in the few scant minutes he had been in this woman's presence, she was the very definition of the term *high maintenance*. So he doubted that very much.

ALSO AVAILABLE FROM CHRISTINE WENRICK

AND RED TREE HOUSE PUBLSHING

THE CHARMED TRILOGY

MEN OF BRAHM HILL